MW01136474

The Darcy Legacy

Joana Starnes

BY THE SAME AUTHOR:

FROM THIS DAY FORWARD
~ *The Darcys of Pemberley* ~

THE SUBSEQUENT PROPOSAL
~ *A Tale of Pride, Prejudice & Persuasion* ~

THE SECOND CHANCE
~ *A 'Pride & Prejudice' ~ 'Sense & Sensibility' Variation* ~

THE FALMOUTH CONNECTION
~ *A 'Pride & Prejudice' Variation* ~

THE UNTHINKABLE TRIANGLE
~ *A 'Pride & Prejudice' Variation* ~

MISS DARCY'S COMPANION
~ *A 'Pride & Prejudice' Variation* ~

MR BENNET'S DUTIFUL DAUGHTER
~ *A 'Pride & Prejudice' Variation* ~

ISBN: 978-1720471554
ISBN-10: 172047155X

ొల ల

To Pat Kellar, Jami Dragan and Jennifer Ray – with huge thanks, lovely ladies, for your time, attention and constant encouragement, and for helping me see the hair-raising errors. This novel would not have been the same without you!

My warmest thanks to you and all the wonderful friends I've made over the years – for all the laughter and the happy times, for the heart-warming support when I needed it most, for believing in me and keeping me writing.

My deepest appreciation for my readers – for losing themselves with me in green and pleasant Regency England, to find Mr Darcy falling in love with Elizabeth Bennet over and over and over again.

ొల ల

"Let me not to the marriage of true minds
Admit impediments. Love is not love
Which alters when it alteration finds,
Or bends with the remover to remove:
O no; it is an ever-fixed mark,
That looks on tempests, and is never shaken;
It is the star to every wandering bark,
Whose worth's unknown, although his height be taken.
Love's not Time's fool, though rosy lips and cheeks
Within his bending sickle's compass come;
Love alters not with his brief hours and weeks,
But bears it out even to the edge of doom.
If this be error, and upon me prov'd,
I never writ, nor no man ever lov'd."

William Shakespeare, 'Sonnet CXVI'

New Characters

*In addition to well-known and much-loved characters, there are a few others.
Most of them are incidental to the story and are listed below only as a memory aid.*

Lord Malvern, Lady Malvern: *Colonel Fitzwilliam's parents*

Lord Metcalfe: *Lady Catherine's neighbour and Justice of the Peace for the parish*

Captain Hayes: *Lady Metcalfe's brother; a naval captain*

Dr Beaumont: *Miss Anne de Bourgh's physician*

Mr Henry Beaumont: *his son, a curate in Surrey*

Mr Whittaker: *curate at Hunsford*

Mr Weston: *Mr Darcy's valet*

Mrs Evans: *Miss Anne de Bourgh's lady's maid*

Sarah: *housemaid at Longbourn, later Jane and Elizabeth's lady's maid*

Simon: *footman at Pemberley*

Thomas: *footman at Rosings*

Molly, Hannah: *maids at Pemberley*

Betsy, Jenny: *maids at Rosings*

Martha Gibbs: *Dr Beaumont's maid*

❦

Prologue

Pemberley, St Stephen's Day 1811

A dream. Just a dream. It must be. Flashes, too bright and in much too quick succession. Flashes of times that had been – that might have been – glimpses of times that could never be. Recollections, aching wishes… Impossible to tell apart. Had happened – had not – no matter. The flashes are dizzying, either way. Dark-brown eyes, full of questions – full of promise and laughter. Her lithe and graceful form, circling around him in a dance, at a country-town assembly. Her hand in his, skin on skin. Her touch. Lingering touches. Lingering caresses, setting him on fire. Lips curled into a smile. Soft lips under his. A slender form under a russet cloak, in a blue haze. A slender form on a carpet of blue flowers. Enticing. Warm. His? Nay, not his. Not to be. Her form slipping from his clasp – empty arms – warmth slipping away… Elizabeth… Soft lips parting. A whisper. A voice, shockingly familiar. Not hers. Oh, no, not hers. Yet it speaks of her. It speaks to his very soul:

"Marry her. Go to it! You have my blessing."

Fitzwilliam Darcy sat bolt upright with a violent start. His hand shot to the matted forelocks falling over his brow to push them aside, and his eyes darted over the moonlit room. He was alone. Well, what the deuce did he expect? He exhaled and rubbed his temples. A dream. Again. Of course.

"Blasted brandy," he muttered. "And that confounded thing."

He cast the counterpane aside and reached to open the drawer of the bedside table. The miniature was within, just where he had left it. Out of sight, but in no way out of mind. Not even in his sleep, apparently, Darcy sneered, then his lips tightened.

Lord above, this was insupportable!

He gripped the small piece of ivory in his fist as though he was of a mind to break it.

He could not have. But it was not for lack of strength that the artefact was spared. He sighed, and his grip slackened.

"Bless her heart," he whispered. "I cannot hurt her feelings so. She thought it would please me. Georgy, darling girl, if only you knew…" He gave a strange sound, half sigh and half snort. "Not her fault. Mine, for dwelling on it and drinking myself into a stupor. And Richard's goading. All that talk about giving me his blessing. Wretched imaginings," he scoffed.

But the sardonic twist of his mouth slowly fell. His countenance turned pensive, troubled, and his gaze drifted beyond the miniature he was holding, and became a faraway stare.

He scowled and shook his head to force himself out of his trance.

"This is madness," he muttered. "It cannot be. I know it cannot. Yet… 'tis too much of a coincidence. Same as last time… And there was truth in it then…"

The whispers grew barely audible, then faded into silence. Oppressive silence. There was no sound, no movement in the cold and empty chamber, just the steady murmur of his breaths. Until the eerie stillness was broken by one word – quiet, hesitant, and almost childlike:

"Father?"

Chapter 1

Pemberley, 6 February 1806, nigh on six years earlier

'*I must be dead, then,*' Mr Darcy concluded with shocking clarity – and shocking it was indeed, for he would have imagined that such clarity of thought, and indeed the very capacity to think, would have left him when the last spark of life had.

That was not the case. It was plain to see that his glassy eyes were fixed somewhere on the ceiling, yet instead of distinguishing the hazy contours of the familiar plaster ornaments, what he saw was his own ashen countenance, his mouth agape, an ugly streak of dried blood snaking from the corner of his lips towards his chin.

George Darcy had little time to ponder over the eerie and well-nigh terrifying experience of staring at his own earthly shell. A sudden movement caught his notice. Mrs Reynolds stirred in her seat and gasped, then rushed to the bed. With an expert hand, she sought his pulse under the immobile jaw, then bent forward to check for signs of breathing.

There would be none. George Darcy knew that long before she did. When the housekeeper ascertained as much, she straightened up with a sigh that was half sob, and slowly approached the chair by the bedside, where his son lay slumped, overcome with fatigue.

Mrs Reynolds shook his arm, lightly at first, then with increasing vigour, and softly called, "Master Fitzwilliam? Master Fitzwilliam, sir?"

That appellation – the old housekeeper had used it for as long as she had known him, and she had known him ever since he was four years of age. She would require some time to break the habit and not address him thus any longer, George Darcy dispassionately thought. Fitzwilliam was Mr Darcy now.

The king is dead.

Long live the king.

The lad jumped, disrupting his ruminations.

"What is it? Any change?" he muttered, his voice thick with sleep.

"I fear so," came Mrs Reynolds' sombre and subdued reply. "Your father… he is gone."

The lad winced. Mrs Reynolds briefly clasped his arm.

"My deepest sympathy, sir. A dark day, this," she whispered, then moved away to retrieve a piece of cloth and a bowl of water from the washstand nearby. She returned to the bed with quiet footsteps and dampened the scrap of cloth, then squeezed it free of dripping water. She did not make use of it. Her young master stayed her hand and reached for the cloth.

"Allow me."

The housekeeper complied. She relinquished the cloth and the bowl without a word, and the lad came to sit on the edge of the bed, then leaned forward to wipe the streak of blood with slow, diligent strokes. He dropped the cloth in the bowl when the deed was done, and remained motionless for the longest time. At last, his hand came up to close the eyelids over the lifeless eyes, and his fingertips stroked the gaunt features covered in grey stubble. He pressed his lips together. A muscle twitched at the corner of his jaw, as he clenched it tightly. There was no other movement in the frozen countenance, except a tear sliding over his cheek with surreal slowness, leaving a trail that glistened in the light of the solitary candle.

If he had the capacity to gasp, George Darcy would have. How long was it since he had seen his son crying? The lad had not shed a tear since his boyhood. Not even when his mother passed away.

"Oh, he did. But not when you could see him," an alien thought suddenly embedded itself into George Darcy's mind, and along with it came a heartrending picture: the clearest image of Fitzwilliam, his anguished face awash with tears. A younger Fitzwilliam, a vast deal younger, his features those of a child striving to be a man. Yet the lost look in his eyes was harrowingly childlike, and his shoulders, the bony shoulders of a boy, shook with silent sobs.

A wave of pain – his son's pain – rose, swelled and engulfed him.

They said there was no pain in the afterlife. Good God, they lied!

"What is this?" George Darcy asked in a tortured whisper.

Yet whatever was left of his celebrated sense warned him to expect no answer. They could not hear him. He was dead.

His agonised question had remained unuttered. It was nothing but a thought. And so was he – nothing but thought in a roiling sea of confusion that blurred the edges of perception; blurred the image of the grief-stricken boy, that of the man Fitzwilliam had become, along with everything else around them: the bedchamber, the housekeeper, the bed, the corpse. *His* corpse, George Darcy emphasised, and at that particular reminder the indistinct surroundings began to spin, faster and faster, until the bewildering pain was replaced with acute nausea, akin to that brought by severe inebriation. George Darcy groaned, wishing he could at least hold his head in his hands and be sick. Violently sick.

"Forgive me," another alien thought entered his consciousness, but this time its tenor was far from bitter and reproachful. It was mellow, soothing, and George Darcy clung to it with all his might – it was something he could fix his mind upon, to ward off the nausea – and he gave thanks when the whirling vortex seemed to lose momentum. To his surprise, the mellow thought was followed by a more detailed expression of contrition:

"I should not have forced that upon you just now. I forgot. The adjustment is confusing."

Adjustment? What adjustment?

George Darcy sought to rally whatever mental powers he still possessed. The vortex slowed further. The bedchamber and its occupants came back into focus. And that was when he became aware that, in a manner of speaking, their number had increased by one; also, that his latest questions would not remain unanswered. The ethereal form of his late wife stood between him and the lifeless shell on the bed. She dipped her head and curtsied.

"Your adjustment to your current state, sir. To mine. Welcome, Mr Darcy. I was wondering if you would linger too. I am relieved to see that is the case. It will be good to have your company."

⁂

"'Struth," George Darcy muttered. "That, I did not expect."

"What would that be, sir? Our encounter?"

"No. Well, yes, that too. But I meant… this," he added with a wide gesture encompassing himself and his surroundings. "I thought that when we go, we…go."

"Seemingly not."

George Darcy shook his insubstantial head to clear it. It made no difference, and he sighed.

"I never gave credence to such tales. Ghosts. Spirits. This is it, then? No billowing clouds and choirs of angels, nor the fires of the damned? Are we to haunt Pemberley for all eternity?"

"I cannot say. I have not found the answer to this question in all the years since my passing."

"Oh? So… have you been here the entire time?"

His lady shrugged. "Where else?"

"And you do not know why?"

"No. But I imagine the old tales must be true, at least in part. They say that some of us remain tethered to what we love."

George Darcy raised a brow.

"I had not thought you so attached to Pemberley."

"Not to Pemberley as such," she countered. "The children, rather. The dear girl especially."

George Darcy heaved a deep sigh.

"Aye. God bless her and keep her."

Behind them, the door opened, and Northcott, Mr Darcy's man, came in along with Fitzwilliam's valet and the first footman. The lad or Mrs Reynolds must have summoned them, George Darcy surmised. Northcott's impassive mien was gone, he noted. Grief darkened the old valet's lined countenance as he bowed his head to the remains of his master of upwards of three decades. Then, with a heavy sigh, Northcott made his way into the dressing room to gather what was needed in order to perform his duty for one last time and prepare his master for his final journey.

Mrs Reynolds quietly proceeded to light more candles, then went to draw the curtains and reveal the greying skies of dawn. The other two, the first footman and Fitzwilliam's valet, Weston, took up positions on either side of the four-poster bed and, moving in perfect synchrony, they began to fold back the counterpane to expose the body.

Fitzwilliam took a deep breath and stepped out of their way, but kept his eyes on the bed – or rather on the form lying upon it. He only glanced up when Mrs Reynolds came to press his arm.

"I think we should leave the master with Mr Northcott now, sir," she softly suggested.

4

The lad seemed about to protest. But then he patted the housekeeper's gnarled hand, still resting comfortingly on his sleeve, and nodded. He stepped closer to the bed and bent down to press his lips on the now smooth brow, oddly devoid of wrinkles, then straightened up. Pulling his shoulders back, he gave another nod, to no one in particular. To his own thoughts, George Darcy surmised.

His son must have understood that everyone should see to their respective duties, and that there were other preparations, which only he could undertake. Letters. Arrangements for the interment. And the reins of Pemberley, in his hands now. His, and his alone.

"Aye. There are matters to attend to," the lad said, his voice subdued but firm, and George Darcy felt the old surge of pride as he watched his son and heir leave the bedchamber with his back straight and his head high. Fitzwilliam was well-trained, and he would do his duty, just as he always had. Pemberley would not flounder in the hands of a weak helmsman. There was a vast deal of comfort to be found in that.

"We should go as well," Lady Anne's shade mildly observed, drawing him from his gratifying reflections, then elaborated, "There is more than enough for you to contend with on the day of your demise without witnessing your own laying-out."

With warm appreciation for her thoughtfulness – throughout their marriage, she had been nothing if not thoughtful – George Darcy bowed to his late wife's wisdom. As soon as the door was opened again, this time by Mrs Reynolds, he slid past the housekeeper, careful not to touch her and seeking not to dwell on how odd it felt to leave his earthly form behind.

Lady Anne cast him an encouraging smile.

"You need not be so cautious. Reynolds will not sense you."

"Will she not? What of the chill they speak of?"

"Which creeps upon one when a spirit walks by?"

"Just so."

Lady Anne laughed softly.

"A myth, my dear sir."

"What makes you so certain?"

His lady shrugged.

"The benefit of experience. In all these years, I have not sent anyone's teeth clattering at my approach. And if it were true, whenever he was at home Fitzwilliam would have been shivering constantly and our little Georgiana would have spent her days wrapped up in shawls. I was always beside them."

"Tethered by those you love," George Darcy said softly.

"Indeed."

"What of me?"

"I imagine you were likewise held back by affection for your children and concern for your heritage—"

"That was not what I was asking. But no matter. So, come to think of it, am I the only one of my line with a strong attachment to my offspring and heritage, or are there a host of my ancestors about the place, whom I shall have the privilege of meeting in due course?"

Lady Anne shook her head.

"We are alone, to the best of my knowledge. I have not come across any of your forebears."

"I see. So, there is nothing for it but waiting to learn why they are gone and we are not?"

"I believe so."

George Darcy tilted his head in a rueful indication of acceptance.

"I can think of worse fates than spending eternity, or whatever part of it, in the dear old place, close to the children. But speaking of eternity, must I resign myself to afterlife in a nightshirt? Had I known as much, I would have taken the trouble of dying in more decorous garb."

His wife's lips twitched.

"We never need wonder from whom Fitzwilliam gets his penchant for sardonic wit. But nay, sir, in answer to your question, you can see from my own apparel that it is not so."

"Indeed, you are most fashionably attired."

"You call this fashionable? Ever the gentleman, my dear. This dress, or I should say this representation of it, is over a decade old. Still, I daresay 'tis preferable to a nightgown. As to your own conundrum, you only need think of your choice of garments and will them on. With some degree of practice, you will be successful."

"As easy as that?" George Darcy asked and, as instructed, he proceeded to mentally review the contents of his wardrobe.

A few moments later, Lady Anne's pale lips twitched again.

"Not so easy, strictly speaking. You do require a fair amount of practice, and above all, concentration," she airily observed as she assessed her husband from head to foot.

He was now sporting some additions to his crumpled nightshirt: the hat he used to wear when riding out on the estate, a neckcloth, a tight-fitting dress-coat with embroidered lapels and a pair of buckled shoes. She could not suppress a giggle.

"You wore this coat at St James's in '91, if I am not mistaken. A fashionable choice, in a different combination."

The frown in her husband's countenance dissolved into a smile.

"'Tis good to hear your laugh again, madam. It has been many years. Although I would certainly prefer it were not at my expense."

His brow creased with a renewed effort at concentration, but the result was still very far from pleasing. The night-time garb was gone, replaced with a plain lawn shirt, but he had also lost the shoes and, so far, he had failed to conjure breeches. His bare legs stretched, long and pale, all the way down from the hem of his garment to the floor. His lady had the grace to glance away and share her amusement with the oak panelling. George Darcy's eyes narrowed as he thought harder, but to no avail.

"Confound it," he muttered. "Madam, would you be so kind as to inform me how the deuce am I to come by breeches?"

"I have no better answer than patience and concentration. But fear not, you are perfectly safe. No one else is likely to perceive the late master of Pemberley in a less than dignified moment, and you need not be concerned on my behalf—"

"There is that. I daresay 'tis nothing you have not seen before."

A deeper shade of grey rose to Lady Anne's translucent cheeks, giving her husband to understand that ghosts had the ability to blush. He made no further comment. Indeed, he half-wondered whatever had possessed him to utter the last one. Teasing and laughter had not formed a part of their marriage. As for hints at their times of intimacy, they had been unheard of. It had not been a bad marriage, far from it. Although not openly affectionate, theirs had been a cordial union. But never a passionate one.

Perhaps he should apologise for the remark, he pondered. Yet she suddenly seemed distracted. Her chin came up, and she stared fixedly somewhere above his head, as though she was listening intently to something that he could not hear.

"What is it?" he asked.

"I beg you would excuse me. I have a matter to attend to. Pray continue to practise," Lady Anne said swiftly, and with that, her ethereal form vanished from George Darcy's sight, which caused him no small measure of concern.

"Madam?" he called, only to be vaguely reassured when her reply entered his consciousness, in a manner that was growing increasingly familiar.

"Rest easy, I shall return directly."

"Very well," he muttered, and proceeded to do as bid – namely, endeavour to remember garments more fitting to the purpose.

He was moderately successful in conjuring up a waistcoat, a neckcloth, a plain dark coat and, thankfully, a pair of buckskin breeches. But when, true to her word, Lady Anne returned reasonably promptly, it was still in George Darcy's power to make her smile when she beheld him for, although appropriate raiment was now in place, from the knees down he was just as she had left him. George Darcy followed her glance, only to espy his bare calves, as well as his pale feet shuffling on the carpet.

"Your hessians would serve," she mildly suggested, and at her prompting George Darcy found he could picture his feet encased in the said articles with no effort whatsoever.

He added a pair of worsted stockings for good measure, then glanced up, quite satisfied with the achievement.

"Well. That is done. What next?"

"Whatever you wish," Lady Anne replied, visibly at a loss for something else to say.

"I wish I were alive and hale, but that is patently out of the question," George Darcy retorted, quick to ill-humouredly point out the obvious, only to regret taking out his frustrations on his blameless wife. He sighed. "I beg your pardon, madam. Pray tell me, what had you rushing away in such a haste?"

"Do not trouble yourself. It has been dealt with."

Her evasive answer made him frown.

"Is the lad well?" he asked.

"As well as can be expected."

"Where is he?"

"In your study. Or rather, his study now."

George Darcy thought better of bristling at the reminder. He merely glanced her way when she added, "Should we join him?"

"Might as well," he agreed, and civilly bowed and gestured that she should lead the way.

Lady Anne smiled.

"One of the few advantages of our present state is that we are no longer bound by the laws of physics."

"Meaning?"

"You will soon discover that moving about the house is very different from the manner to which you were accustomed. In due course, I will undertake to help you master new skills, such as walking through walls or dashing from one end of the house to another in the blink of an eye. But for now, if you would allow me…?"

She offered him her hand in a gesture of invitation, and George Darcy reached out in his turn. He did not feel the touch when their hands were joined, but he could most certainly sense the connection. He did not have sufficient time to explore the puzzling sensation, for in the blink of an eye, just as she had told him, they were no longer on the upper floor of the family wing, but below-stairs, in his study. Fitzwilliam's study, as Lady Anne had just pointed out.

The lad was there. She was in the right about that, too. Predictably, his own expectations were likewise confirmed: his son knew his duty. Fitzwilliam had already extracted the relevant stacks of paper from their allotted place in the third desk-drawer on the right. The papers had been waiting in that locked drawer for quite some time now. They had been painstakingly drawn. He and his son had put them together, in preparation for this very day, ever since George Darcy had received his physician's confirmation of what he had already begun to suspect: that his days were numbered.

It had been one devil of a task, starkly contemplating his upcoming demise and leaving instructions for funeral arrangements and the like, as well as setting all his affairs in order. A devil of a task not only for himself, but also for Fitzwilliam, who had been involved in the process every step of the way. Still, it had to be done. Grim as it had been to have advanced warning that the thread of his life had already been measured and severed, and all he could do was wait for it to unravel to its end, at least he had found comfort in knowing that nothing would be left to chance, and he would have the opportunity to settle his accounts, in every sense of the word.

Fitzwilliam was well-prepared. He knew what must be done now, and he would set to it. He had already begun. The papers covered in detailed instructions were neatly arrayed before him, and the lad was going through them. Standing – on the wrong side of the desk, George Darcy finally registered, when his son's gaze shifted from the sheet he was holding and came to be fixed upon the empty chair from which four generations of Darcy men had transacted their business.

"You should sit, my boy. 'Tis yours now," George Darcy whispered. Or did he merely think it? It mattered not, either way. In truth, in his present state, the distinction between the two was well-nigh non-existent, but such fine points escaped George Darcy's notice at the moment, as he watched his son stare at the empty seat, his countenance set in deep lines of sadness.

The light tap on the door made them both jump.

"Come," the father and the son called at the same time, then George Darcy caught himself and gave a rueful snort, followed by a sigh.

It was Mrs Reynolds. She advanced into the room, to quietly deliver, "My apologies for the intrusion, sir. I was told that Miss Georgiana is awake. Would you like me to speak to her about...?" Her voice trailed off, and she clasped her hands before her, the mournfully inquiring look softening with sympathy.

Her young master shook his head and drew an uneasy breath.

"I thank you, but no. She should hear it from me."

The old housekeeper nodded and followed him out of the sombre room, closing the door noiselessly behind her.

"Well?" Lady Anne asked, and her husband fully understood her meaning.

"I can scarce bear it," he dejectedly owned, "but yes, I will come with you. I must. If you would be so kind as to convey us yet again..."

With a touch of his wife's hand and her superior skill in transferring them instantly from one place to another, they were in Georgiana's bedchamber several minutes before Fitzwilliam could arrive there by the established means.

They found their dear girl sitting on a stool in her dressing gown, patiently allowing her maid to comb her hair.

Nary a word passed between the maid and her diminutive mistress, and nothing was said when they heard the knock. An exchange of glances and Georgiana's nod were all that was needed before the maid went to open the door and admit her young master.

Eyes lowered, the maid bobbed a curtsy, stepped out of the way to let him pass, then left the room without being asked, quick to grasp she should allow the brother and sister the privacy that the sad moment required.

Georgiana stood and walked into her brother's embrace. He had lowered himself on one knee, so that their eyes were level, which made it easier for her to search his gaze a few moments later, when she drew back a little, her sweet visage unbearably solemn.

"So 'tis true, then. Papa is gone," she said at length.

Darcy's voice caught.

"I fear so, my darling girl."

"I am glad," she evenly replied, thus shocking everybody present. Of them all, it was only her brother who could put his shock into an audible reply.

"You are?"

Georgiana shrugged as tears welled in her eyes.

"Not for myself," she said, her words and mien belying her young years. "I will miss him dreadfully. But I *am* glad he is no longer in pain, and that he is with Mamma now. She will take good care of him. She promised."

George Darcy darted a glance towards his wife. It held a thousand questions. The first one was on his lips as well:

"Did you?"

She nodded.

"*How?*"

"I speak to her. Sometimes, when she is deep in sleep, she hears me."

"Lord almighty!"

"You may doubt the wisdom of my seeking to reach her," Lady Anne began to justify herself with an injured look, "but you need not harbour fears for her sanity. I only tried to reach out to her when she was in desperate need of comfort. Such was the case this morning, at dawn. I left you in the corridor outside your bedchamber because she was dreaming of bad things – awful things. The churchyard in the dead of night. Your grave, dark and gaping.

She was crying pitifully in her sleep. I had to find a way to reassure her that there was more to her dear papa's fate than being abandoned into the bowels of the earth."

"You mistake my meaning," George Darcy shakily replied. "It was shock, not censure. I am staggered to hear there are ways to communicate with them."

But his wife wistfully shook her head.

"Do not stake your hopes on it. I had little success. Only with Georgiana, very rarely, when she was dreadfully distressed. Never with Fitzwilliam."

"Why is that?"

"Goodness knows. But not for want of trying. Perhaps because he is over a decade older, and the years of schooling into rational thought have led him to instinctively reject the possibility. Georgiana is still young enough to believe in fairies and sprites. From there on, believing in a world of spirits does not require quite so great a leap of imagination."

The parents' gaze returned to their beloved daughter, to find her ensconced in her brother's embrace. He had moved to sit on the small sofa at the foot of Georgiana's bed, with the dear girl on his lap, tenderly enfolded into his arms. They sat thus, motionless but for the slight movements of his hand, as he ran his fingers through her hair. He bent his head after a while, to press his lips into her flaxen ringlets, then whispered:

"Yes. We must find comfort in the thought that they are together."

Georgiana smiled through her tears.

"I do. I feel much better, ever since Mamma came to tell me so herself, and promise that Papa would be safe with her."

The hand that was stroking her hair stilled, and Fitzwilliam's eyes grew wary and clouded with concern.

"Mother came?" he asked, his voice dreadfully guarded.

Georgiana gave an earnest nod, then drew back a little, so that she could have enough room to gesticulate as she elaborated matter-of-factly:

"Not as you do, of course. Or Moore, or Mrs Reynolds, or everybody else. I know she cannot. But she came to me in my dream. I woke up crying, but I think they were good tears. It certainly felt good to learn that Papa is safe and free of pain."

Fitzwilliam brought her closer yet again, and she willingly complied. She nestled into his embrace with a faint sigh as he resumed stroking her hair.

"Do you dream of her often?" he eventually asked.

"Not as often as I would wish. Every time I do, it makes me happy, or at least at peace, and my heart is lighter. Forgive me, I am not explaining it well," she added, seeking to draw away, perhaps to meet his eyes and make her meaning clearer, but this time he did not allow it, but held her close and dropped another kiss into her hair.

"Yes, you are. I understand," he whispered, and for a long time nothing more was said as they remained there, his head resting on hers, dark wavy locks mingling with blonde ones.

"Can we go riding this morning, Brother? I would like to be out of doors," Georgiana said after a while, only to shake her head and answer her own question. "No, I imagine we cannot. You must have a vast deal to do today."

But Fitzwilliam was of a different mind – the right one. He lightly stroked her cheek and replied gently but firmly, "That is as may be, my dear love, but I will always have time for you. Always."

When one did not strictly speaking possess eyes, how could they be stinging, George Darcy wondered, and when one's heart was no longer beating, how could it still flood with tenderness and relief? He could not tell. Doubtlessly in the course of time he would find himself perplexed by countless other matters. But as he stood beside his wife watching their son comforting their daughter, he could not find it in him to spare another thought for the conundrums of his new plane of existence. Nothing could dim the warm glow of love.

Chapter 2

Pemberley, Spring 1806

The funeral had come and gone, and the bustle of activity that had unavoidably descended upon Pemberley at that trying time had long given way to the customary quiet. Days of it – weeks – months. How many? George Darcy could not settle upon a number, and it mattered not. He idly wondered if the household and its new master were finding the never-ending quiet as tedious as he did. He scoffed. He would do well to grow accustomed to the tedium, for decades of it were looming before him. Or centuries, perish the thought.

He scowled. The dark shapes of the billowing clouds rolled off the face of the moon and came to rest just underneath the pale, glistening orb in a sombre mass, lightly tinged with silver. The familiar surroundings, moonlit now, took sharper contrast around him, but George Darcy paid them no heed and continued to stare unseeing out of the window. The voice behind him, softly uttering his name, was a surprise. Yet he did not start, but slowly turned towards the translucent shape framed in the doorway.

"Madam? Is anything the matter?"

"No, nothing. I merely came in search of you. I am surprised to find you here. Not your usual choice, is it?"

The gentleman shrugged.

"The moon unsettles me. Besides, I have no wish to intrude upon the lad. Perhaps I should make it my habit to linger here instead. I have always liked this room," he said, casting a glance around him at the small chamber, its walls adorned with a collection of old prints.

"I know. I have always wondered why you did not make this your study."

"I saw no reason for it. Perhaps it was because the adjoining chamber had been the master's study in my father's time, and his father's and grandfather's before him. Besides, the study was the master's domain, whereas this little room here was my own, and I could simply open the door and come in, if fancy took me, for a few moments of tranquillity, and leave the troubles behind, on my father's desk."

"Not unwise," Lady Anne acknowledged, then came to join her husband at the window. She looked down and sniffed. "Reynolds is becoming complacent in her old age. She should take the girls to task more often. Look, there is dust on this windowsill."

Her husband chortled.

"My dear, this is hardly an issue," he chided, and his lady sighed.

"Perhaps. But this unsettles me about as much as the moon unsettles you," she added with a self-deprecating smile. "Where is he now, do you know?" she soberly asked a moment later, raising troubled eyes to his face, the lightness gone from her tone and mien.

"I heard him say he was for bed, but I am prepared to wager he is still pacing in the long gallery."

Lady Anne sighed.

"He is too young for this. Not yet three-and-twenty, yet with such a burden of responsibility thrust upon him."

"You speak as if it was within my power to prevent it," George Darcy snapped, his air no longer rueful, but belligerent. "I did not choose the timing of my exit. With all my heart I wish I could come to his aid. Do you not think it weighs on me to see his troubled countenance from morning till night?"

He was a little mollified when his lady had the grace to look abashed. "Of course. I know you would assist him if you could. This must be hard for you, the powerlessness—"

"Hard, you call it? 'Tis galling, madam. Maddening!"

"I know the sentiment. Especially when one is forced to sit by and watch them struggle. Or worse still, watch them suffer."

He flinched.

"Indeed. Sometimes I cannot help thinking that powerlessly watching loved ones suffer misery and hardship is the punishment they speak of. The living, they do not know better, so they call it hellfire, or the chains that shackle the spirits of the damned. I fancy this is worse. And for the life of me I cannot fathom what sins we have committed, you and I, to warrant it."

"No one is free of sin. I had my share. And you, can you not in all honesty think of any?"

George Darcy bristled.

"What do you reproach me of?"

A brow arched, Lady Anne eyed him squarely.

"You know very well that I am thinking of your coldness towards our son."

George Darcy gave a disbelieving snort.

"*My* coldness? Madam, that is beyond the pale. Do you imagine I did not wish to openly show him affection?"

"What held you back?"

"His distance. His reserve," the gentleman retorted. "Had he been more open himself, had he been less—"

"Less like me, perchance?"

He grimaced.

"I would not have put it quite so bluntly."

"You might as well speak your mind, sir. Eternity is too long for dissembling."

"Eternity…" he echoed. "Is this what we are facing? Eternity – here – as we are?"

"You have asked me that before. I told you, I know not," Lady Anne replied with some impatience.

"Aye. You said," George Darcy ill-temperedly conceded. "Well, never mind that now. We were speaking of other matters."

"So we were."

"You think I failed our son," he observed sternly.

It was not a question.

"Not failed him, as such. You raised him well. But you did leave him to struggle alone after my passing – as I have already shown you," Lady Anne pointedly added, and no sooner had she done so than the harrowing image of Fitzwilliam in his boyhood, grieving in anguished silence, materialised once more before George Darcy, to break his heart anew.

He squeezed his eyes shut, but to no avail.

"Have mercy, madam," he groaned, and at his entreaty his wife must have relented, for the tormenting vision vanished into thin air.

Old mannerisms resurfaced, from the time when he inhabited a body endowed with a pair of lungs, and George Darcy's chest expanded as though with a deep breath.

16

"So, this has— ? This is— ?" he began, but could not continue.

"This is what happened. 'Tis a memory. My memory. I thought it only fair that I should share it with you," Lady Anne said, the words heavy with resentment.

George Darcy winced.

"He never said… He never—"

"Never showed weakness? Had he ever been allowed to?"

George Darcy did not answer the rhetorical question.

"Poor lad," he whispered instead. "I never knew he took it so hard. I thought—"

"You thought unexpressed feelings must be weak or non-existent," she said, each word emphatically distinct. "You were one for demonstrativeness. Why did you not take the first step? At least on the day of my passing, if not sooner, could you not have given him a fatherly embrace? Offer kind words perhaps, instead of reminders that he must be strong and do his duty?"

"I—"

"You know very well that duty is ingrained into his very soul. We raised him so," Lady Anne resolutely continued. "Could you not have told him how proud you were of him, how well he was doing? All he had ever wanted was your approval."

"He always had it!"

"And yet you never said as much. Instead, you lavished time and affection upon the steward's son," she said with unprecedented bitterness.

Her husband's eyes narrowed, and he shook his head in mild exasperation.

"You never liked George, did you?"

"No," Lady Anne replied bluntly, with more than a touch of spite.

"I thought as much. But I never knew why. Was it because of his mother?"

"Not at all," she retorted, supremely disdainful. "Whatever Mrs Wickham was—"

"You do know there was nothing of consequence between us," he forcefully cut her off. "The mildest of flirtations perhaps – ill-judged, I grant you – but nothing more than that. I trust you never thought George was mine."

"Of course not," Lady Anne snapped. "I never did you the indignity of believing you so lost to decency and duty.

But that is not to say I was reconciled to your willingness to give her and her son the time of day."

"Well, madam, if eternity is a time for uncomfortable truths, then perhaps I might say that had I found the same cheerfulness and warmth in my own wife, my own son—"

"Empty cheerfulness. Feigned warmth," she replied with energy. "We are what we are, sir. All of us. Who can escape their nature? I lack cheerfulness and open manners, and so does Fitzwilliam, the dear boy. Whereas you lacked the good sense to look beneath the surface. Have you heard talk in the servants' hall about your cherished *protégé?*"

"I do not frequent the servants' hall," George Darcy loftily replied. "I am shocked to hear that you do."

"You will be surprised to see what you are driven to by boredom. There is only so much time that one can spend haunting the elegant side of the house."

"Is it thus, then? We cannot fade out, not even for a while?"

"No. We cannot. We do not have the luxury of fading in and out of consciousness, nor the comfort of sleep. There is nothing but tedium, hour upon hour upon hour, and heartache alternating with vexation when we see the living suffer, or commit follies which we cannot prevent. Which brings us back to my earlier point. Since you have not heard what your dear George Wickham is up to, then pray let me enlighten you. He is a scoundrel and a rake of vicious propensities, which he oh-so-carefully kept from your knowledge, but not from everybody else's. He trifles with the maids. Drinks with the lowest sort and gambles heavily whenever he is away from Pemberley and Lambton—"

"How would you know that? Have you followed him, perchance?"

"Do not speak such nonsense. You know I cannot leave this house any more than you can. But word travels. And last I heard, he took himself from Derbyshire barely a fortnight after burying his father. Took himself to town, doubtlessly to indulge in worse excesses, and left vast debts behind him, which our son honoured in his stead. This is the man you would desire Fitzwilliam to provide for by means of a valuable living. Worse still, this is the man you laughed, hunted and played at cards with, while our son was left to his own devices."

"If you are seeking to make me feel guilt-ridden and dejected, madam, you are supremely successful in your purpose," her husband replied darkly, and at that Lady Anne pursed her lips with lingering resentment and gave a resigned sigh.

"I daresay 'tis fruitless to speak of it now. You cannot go back and alter the past. But you must see that I have amassed a fair amount of bitterness and anger. I could not share my views with you in all the years since my passing. Now I can."

"Praise be," he replied with heavy irony. "So, this is how you envisage us spending eternity together? Revisiting old grievances and errors?"

Lady Anne visibly cringed at the prospect.

"I should hope not. It would be unbearable. But I trust you will agree I deserved a fair hearing."

George Darcy bowed his head, silently acknowledging the truth of it. With a restrained curtsy, Lady Anne chose to make her exit, seemingly of the opinion that after the much-needed clearing of the air, some distance was in order. She did not inform him where she was going, and George Darcy did not ask. He knew full well that in due course he would go in search of her, and he would find her. If more reproaches were to be his portion, then so be it. His inherent fairness compelled him to reluctantly see some justice in them. Besides, he would sooner have reproaches rather than the wretched quiet. Why he was tethered to his ancestral home, he could not tell, but for the sake of his enduring sanity, he was humbly grateful he had not been condemned to never-ending solitude and silence.

⚬❦ ❦⚬

The days slipped seamlessly by. They blended into months, then into years, with but a handful of memorable happenings marking their passage.

Georgiana found a friend in the neighbouring Vernons' second daughter, and then she lost her when Miss Laetitia left her home for a fashionable seminary in town.

Lady Anne was vindicated in her husband's eyes as regards her opinions on George Wickham when a housemaid had to relinquish her place in the household, once her delicate condition became so advanced that it could not be kept a secret for much longer.

Arrangements were made for her in a distant village of her choice, the matter handled quietly by her master and Mrs Reynolds, with no assistance whatsoever from the father, whom no one had seen in Derbyshire for quite some time.

Lady Anne's nephew, Major Richard Fitzwilliam, came to stay whenever he could be spared from his duties, and brought much-needed company and good cheer to both his cousins, which greatly pleased their parents.

Although occasionally some surface or another still seemed in need of more careful dusting, Mrs Reynolds markedly grew in her late mistress's estimation when the old housekeeper was quick to dismiss the forward little baggage employed to replace the unfortunate housemaid George Wickham had trifled with.

The impudent creature seemed to labour under the misconception that her young master was cut from the same cloth as the son of the late steward, and that she stood to gain if she offered him all manner of improper comforts. Lady Anne could tell that her son, bless his heart, was too fair-minded to jump to conclusions, but she seethed with impotent vexation when she saw the saucy thing pinching her cheeks and pushing up her bosom to display it to advantage just before bustling into his study – and one evening, his bedchamber – and then proceeding to give a consummate performance. She blushed, stammered, batted her lashes in the most provoking manner, and humbly begged the kind master's pardon for disturbing him – the very picture of the flustered and inexperienced new maid who had misapprehended the timing of her chores and the housekeeper's instructions. Thankfully, Mrs Reynolds was not born yesterday, and took matters into her own hands, sparing her master the inconvenience of requesting a dismissal.

Sadly, it was not Mrs Reynolds' place to deflect attentions from more exalted quarters when, with less forwardness of manner, but the same self-serving intent, Miss Powell – and later on, the youngest Miss Wallace – took to accompanying their respective brothers and calling at Pemberley with the flimsiest of excuses, to display their own sets of batting lashes and sundry personal attributes. Neither one prevailed. Discouraged by Darcy's patent disinclination for the married state, they eventually ceased calling, and metaphorically speaking, Lady Anne could draw an easy breath.

Relief also came from another source, along with a good measure of smug satisfaction, when a certain letter was delivered to Pemberley. It was addressed to the new master in George Wickham's hand, and both Lady Anne and her husband had the opportunity to read it over their son's shoulder.

Judging by the turn of his countenance, George Darcy must have experienced different sentiments, but for her part Lady Anne could only feel a surge of angry pleasure when she read that the simpering scoundrel had resolved against taking orders and relinquished every claim to the family living destined for him.

The pleasure vanished, leaving only the anger, when she came to the paragraph where young Wickham impudently suggested he deserved some immediate pecuniary advantage in lieu of the preferment.

Her anger only grew when her son saw fit to pen a reply conveying his compliance with the request. But at least they were blessedly free of George Wickham at long last, and the parishioners of Kympton would not have a wolf in sheep's clothing for a vicar.

A fair while later, Major Richard Fitzwilliam returned to Pemberley, and this time Lady Anne and George Darcy had mixed feelings about his arrival, for their nephew took great pains to persuade their son that he and Georgiana should remove to town.

There was wisdom in the scheme; the doting parents could not dispute it. Their son and daughter had secluded themselves at Pemberley for too long. Darcy would benefit from leaving the country neighbourhood and its confined and unvarying society, otherwise he would fall prey to the marriage schemes of someone of Miss Powell's or Miss Wallace's ilk. As for Georgiana, it was high time she was placed at one of the best finishing schools; high time she left the cosy cocoon that was Pemberley and opened her eyes into the world in which she would be expected to move when she grew older.

Major Fitzwilliam was finally successful in his endeavours. One fine spring morning, the Darcy carriage left Pemberley, and Lady Anne and her husband followed it with their eyes from one of the windows of the long gallery until it vanished from sight, taking their son and daughter with it.

The house was unbearably quiet in their absence, and Lady Anne was more aggrieved than ever that she could not find the means to relocate to the townhouse in Berkeley Square.

"I could never follow Fitzwilliam to Cambridge, nor on his other travels," she told her husband, "but I reconciled myself to that, because it would have been heartbreaking to leave the sweet babe behind. You travelled from Pemberley but rarely, and the times you took Georgiana with you were fewer still. I felt my rightful place was here, with her, should she need me. How I wish there was a way of joining them! They will return in the summer, I know. But for now…"

For now, everything was still, and nothing happened. One another's company was their sole succour and amusement as the days slipped seamlessly by, blending into months, with no memorable happenings marking their passage.

In truth, the passage of time had little to no meaning for the immaterial guardians of the empty house. They had no one to watch over, and nothing to witness but the comings and goings of the handful of servants left to care for the place.

Days – weeks – months of sameness. How many? George Darcy and Lady Anne had ceased counting them. Their son and daughter would return, eventually. When, they could not tell.

Nor could they know that, far to the south, in an inconsequential manor-house deep in the mellow country of Hertfordshire, events would transpire, and be far from inconsequential to their line.

Chapter 3

Longbourn, 10 August 1809

Mr Bennet steepled his fingers under his chin and kept his hooded eyes on the visitor, although he had long closed his ears to the man's monologue.

Mr Collins cut an ungainly figure, and he was tiresome to boot. In different circumstances, Mr Bennet might have found passing amusement in his folly and presumption, but as Collins had already sinned one time too many in his eyes, Mr Bennet's patience was running unsurprisingly thin.

With some degree of benevolence, Collins' first sin could be forgiven. After all, it was not his fault that, from birth, he had been Mr Bennet's heir presumptive, and the beneficiary of the Longbourn entail. Not his fault either that he had become the heir apparent, ever since Mrs Bennet's untimely demise two years ago.

Struck down without warning, the poor soul, Mr Bennet mournfully mused. Carried off by a severe bleeding caused by a miscarriage, the apothecary had solemnly speculated at the time. And they would never know if she had been carrying their sixth daughter or the long-awaited son that would have blasted Collins' hopes of inheriting Longbourn. Thus, Mr Bennet had been left with five girls in his sole care – the eldest eighteen, the youngest eleven – and with precious little knowledge on how to go about raising them.

The details had fallen within his wife's remit: the scolding, coaxing and cajoling, the day-to-day, the meals, the social engagements, the purchase of ribbons and the ordering of dresses. All he had ever done prior to Mrs Bennet's passing had been to engage masters for those ones of his daughters who would not waste their time, their tutors' patience and his money.

He should have taken their education in hand from the beginning, Mr Bennet reproached himself, not for the first time. The only one whom he had lovingly taught, without seeming to, was his second daughter. Lizzy, darling Lizzy, the one offspring who took after him in every way, and with whom he could communicate without a word. Teaching Lizzy had always been its own reward.

Not so with his three youngest, and he knew it all too well by now. Over the last couple of years, ever since he had been left in charge of everything, he had unavoidably seen the need to exert himself and correct old errors. Take steps to guide them, or at least take an interest. Masters were engaged for all the girls, to teach them the rudiments of music, drawing and singing, and moreover keep them out of mischief with sensible employment.

Perhaps he ought to have remarried. Then his daughters would have had female guidance, and he – a chance to break the reviled entail. But there were no unattached ladies of the right age in the environs, bar the widowed Mrs Long, who frankly was too far past her prime to give him reasonable hope of an heir, and he would be damned if he could endure the woman's prattle. At least Mrs Bennet, God rest her soul, had been mildly diverting with her chatter. Nothing of the sort could be said of the senseless Mrs Long.

As a second marriage was both unlikely and unpalatable, perhaps he should have engaged a governess for the girls. But the housekeeper's mothering skills – good old Hill, she was the very soul of efficiency and kindness – Jane's angelic influence, Lizzy's good sense and the employment provided by the masters seemed to jointly keep his three youngest under good regulation.

His brother by marriage, Edward Gardiner, and the man's kind and softly-spoken wife had done their part in providing comfort and assistance. They visited often, and the older girls were regularly asked to go to town and stay with them. Mary was never keen. She was happy to lend a hand in caring for her much younger cousins – babes, really – but London held no attraction for her. Jane, bless her, could find joy wherever she went, and as for Lizzy, she took the greatest pleasure in her sojourns in town. Of course, being deprived of Lizzy's company was a hardship, but he would not be selfish. He always allowed her to go.

"Do you remember, sir? Mr Bennet? I hope you do remember," Mr Collins said loudly, having presumably grown aware of his inattention.

Plain civility obliged Mr Bennet to offer a perfunctory apology.

"I beg your pardon. Remember what, exactly?"

"That I have long wished to heal the breach between my sire and yourself, and I wrote to you to that effect when the unfortunate circumstance of Mrs Bennet's passing provided me with the opportunity to re-establish a correspondence between the two branches of our family. You do remember, surely."

"I do," came Mr Bennet's grim and curt retort.

In truth, he did not. He had been too caught in the distressing events to register that the loss he and his daughters had suffered was, to Mr Collins, an *'opportunity.'* Since, in his supreme self-centredness, the man had just seen fit to remind him of the one sin that Mr Bennet had forgotten, the host returned with fresh impetus to mentally cataloguing all the other ones. He was saved the trouble. Mr Collins proceeded to exemplify them yet again.

"Then you may remember that I wrote at the time about my concern at being the means of injuring your daughters' prospects. Had you been the first to go, circumstances would have been sufficiently dire for my amiable cousins. But as Mrs Bennet had predeceased you, upon your own demise their situation would be pitiful indeed."

Mr Bennet folded his hands, his fingers entwined tightly, as he found himself caught between repentance and vexation. The repentance was for the flippant manner in which he had often teased his wife whenever she had chosen to mention the entail. It had always been an uncomfortable subject for him, so he had addressed it in the only way he knew to tackle uncomfortable subjects: with sarcasm. How many times had he cut Mrs Bennet's laments short with some quip or another? Once, if memory served, he had asked her not to dwell on such gloomy notions, and instead think of better things – that he might be the survivor. Now it had come to pass. He *was* the survivor, the poor woman mouldered in her grave, and his sense of guilt was not in the least diminished by the fact that, even as he had heartlessly teased her, he had never doubted he would be the first to go.

It was a fair assumption, after all, since he was twelve years her senior. But one should never disregard childbed and its perils.

Guilt did not sit well with him. It never did. So, between guilt and vexation, Mr Bennet chose the latter. Vexation at the pompous and unfeeling fool who sat before him and carelessly spoke of his daughters' plight, should they be orphaned.

Yet Collins was in the right. No man of common decency would word it as he did, but he was in the right: the girls would lose their protector and their home, should anything befall him. He *had* sought to improve their fortunes since he had lost his wife; had made a number of sensible investments under Gardiner's guidance, as well as several improvements to the estate, and had put an end to purchases of fripperies and nonsense. But more had to be done, and he dearly hoped he would be granted sufficient time to fulfil his wishes. If not, the Gardiners and Phillipses would of course join forces and look after the girls, but with any luck it would not come to that. With any luck, he would be around to see all his girls settled.

All of a sudden, Mr Bennet had the strangest urge to chortle. He never thought he would see the day when he would agree with Mrs Bennet, yet the poor soul was in the right about this at least: good marriages were the girls' best safeguard against the uncertainty at Longbourn. The fact that his definition of a good marriage was at variance with his late wife's was beside the point. The crux of the matter was that he, as the sole living parent, would have to launch the girls upon the marriage mart and guide them in their choices.

Heaven be praised, he would not be forced to attend every wretched ball and assembly. Mrs Phillips, his late wife's younger sister, had already undertaken the role of chaperone, and was often escorting Jane and Lizzy, the only ones old enough to be out.

He occasionally joined them to please the girls, but otherwise there was no real need for him to keep a watchful eye at such events. He was well acquainted with those likely to attend. There were no surprises in their little market town, no dashing young bucks coming out of nowhere to make designs upon his daughters – and besides, his two eldest were astute and sensible. Now, heaven help him with the next contingent. Mary would not say a word above those that common civility required, but as for the last two, he would have to keep a tight rein on them, if their persistent wilfulness was any indication.

"Ahem! Most pitiful," Mr Collins reiterated with a loud cough, breaking his host's chain of thought.

Admittedly, it was a too long chain, Mr Bennet inwardly owned. His propensity to drift was fabled. Nevertheless, he scowled.

"Yes, well. I thank you for stating it so plainly. Now, sir, is there a purpose to this conversation?"

"Naturally, Cousin," Mr Collins replied, looking rather offended. "There is a purpose in everything I say and do."

"I am glad to hear it. Well then, what is your purpose?"

Mr Collins made himself more comfortable in his chair, then took a sip from the cup of tea that Mrs Hill had placed before him, cast a glance at Mr Bennet's fingers, by now drumming on the back of his other hand, and finally began.

"It strikes me that your fears for your daughters' future and my discomfort at eventually inheriting their home can be resolved in one stroke. The solution is simple: I must marry one of them."

"Must you?" Mr Bennet retorted crisply, and the tapping on the back of his hand grew faster.

Oblivious to its implications, Mr Collins proceeded to elaborate:

"Why, yes. Then, when you are taken from us, it would be only natural that my wife's sisters should live with us, help around the house and assist Mrs Collins with the children. In due course, some of them might marry and have their own establishment. Modest as it might be, it would be an advantage to living on their more fortunate sister's charity. Should some of them remain unattached, once they reach a certain age that lends them respectability, they could become ladies' companions, or some such."

Mr Bennet's stare turned flinty.

"You have it all planned in great detail, I see."

"Aye, sir, as one should."

"Yet you forgot a few crucial points."

Mr Collins' brows arched in an almost comical expression of surprise.

"Did I? What points would they be?"

"To begin with, you have not inherited Longbourn yet, and I flatter myself it may not happen for some time. What are your plans for the interim? You are at the beginning of your clerical studies. You are neither ordained, nor in possession of a living. Not even the promise of a living. So, to my mind, you are in no position to take a wife as yet."

The objections were dismissed with a casual gesture.

"Of course, of course. But all that will come. For now, I thought it sensible and proper to apprise you and my cousin Elizabeth of my honourable intentions, so that we have an understanding and her eyes do not stray, once she is betrothed."

Mr Bennet leaned forward, placing his folded hands on the desk and his feet firmly tucked under his chair, as he endeavoured to suppress the overwhelming inclination to use both hands and feet for more violent purposes than were generally in his nature. Such as grabbing Collins by the scruff of his neck and acquainting him with the tip of his boot for having the gall to raise his eyes to Lizzy.

"Engaged to Elizabeth," was all he could mutter through gritted teeth.

Some effort was required on his part in order to find socially acceptable words that would convey his sentiments. In the ensuing silence, Mr Collins spoke again, only to demonstrate that while lavishly endowed with confidence – Mr Bennet had no qualms in calling it brazen audacity – he was woefully lacking in perception and self-preservation instincts. The older gentleman readily concluded that his cousin must be thus affected. Otherwise why would he recklessly persist in prodding the Longbourn bear in his lair?

"Aye, sir. There you have it," was what Mr Collins blithely said with a flourish of his hand. "My cousin Elizabeth is my choice of bride. She has great vivacity of spirit, and I think she will suit admirably as a vicar's wife and the future mistress of Longbourn."

"Do you now!" Mr Bennet snapped.

"I do," the other most incautiously confirmed with an emphatic nod. "Granted, my cousin Jane has greater beauty to recommend her, but Miss Elizabeth appears to have more drive and energy, which will stand her in good stead in her future life, for her duties will be many and varied. And if her vivacious temper is subdued under proper guidance—"

The notion of his Lizzy's temper subdued under that man's guidance put steel into Mr Bennet's tones.

"Should you not choose a wife whose temper is already subdued, sir?"

Mr Collins' countenance grew pensive.

"I see your meaning. To be frank, 'tis only Cousin Mary who seems already inclined towards piety and reflection. She was the only one to pay due attention when I was reading from Fordyce's sermons yesterday. Why, she hung on my every word. But she is not very comely, is she? I was hoping for a more handsome bride."

Mr Bennet pursed his lips. The strong urge to acquaint the man's posterior with the tip of his boot continued to plague him, and the last remark was not helping matters. Nonetheless, as he had succeeded in keeping himself in check so far, the impudent dunce was probably safe from him as regards violent action. It was not his way to resort to tempestuous outbursts. His weapon of choice was not the boot, but the lash of his tongue. So Mr Bennet leaned back in his seat and drawled:

"Were you? But is that wise?"

"I fail to catch your meaning, sir."

"To put it bluntly, Mr Collins, do you want your future parishioners to heed the voice from the pulpit or endanger their souls by coveting the vicar's comely wife?"

"Oh! I have not thought of that," the other muttered, his eyes wide.

"Clearly. So, I fear Jane and Lizzy will not do."

"I see. Hm… Yes, you have a point, Cousin, and your thoughtfulness does you credit, seeing as it works to your two eldest daughters' disadvantage," Mr Collins mused. "Well, then, what is to be done? You are in the right, it would not do to bring the fruit of temptation into my future parish. Besides, a handsome woman might be too self-absorbed to make a good wife, particularly for a clergyman. Plainer ones strive to please and are more likely to devote themselves to hard work rather than the looking-glass. Hm… Maybe Miss Mary will fit the bill better than I thought."

"She is full young, sir," Mr Bennet intervened, eager to interrupt the repulsive monologue.

"Indeed. Perhaps we should wait a year or so before we revisit this topic."

"Longer, I should say," Mr Bennet promptly retorted. To his way of thinking, the discussion should be postponed until hell froze over, but that, he did not say.

For his daughters' sake, he had already given himself the trouble to make his peace with the heir of Longbourn, had tolerated Collins in his home for over a fortnight, and his boot and the fool's backside had remained unacquainted. A wise man would not undo all that hard work now.

"Hm… Perhaps you are in the right," Collins tentatively agreed. "It will be at least two years until I take holy orders. As I have already mentioned, I am resolved to make your daughters reasonable amends, so I am willing to return to this subject once I am ordained. Perchance Miss Mary's looks will improve in the interim. There is no telling, she is at the trying age. Or perhaps one of the younger girls might be considered when they grow up. Not now, they are but unruly children. Which reminds me: I would be sterner with them if I were you. Mark my words, you are sowing the seeds of trouble if you permit them to continue thus. Too wild for my taste by far."

"Then 'tis fortunate that I am responsible for raising them, rather than you," Mr Bennet observed tersely.

Mr Collins shrugged.

"Yes, well, who knows what the future holds? If it falls on me to find them husbands, I should not wish to see them grown into ungovernable hoydens, but genteel and biddable. With their meagre portions, they can scarce hope to receive offers if their conduct remains wild."

"Pray, do not let my daughters' prospects trouble you," Mr Bennet retorted, not of a mind to disclose that their portions had been substantially increased with careful management, ever since his wife's sudden demise had forced him to consider his own mortality. "You will be pleased to hear that I am hale and hearty. God willing, I might remain above the grass for a fair while yet."

ೂಲ ಅಎ

"Will you not join us, Papa? Hill has brought us a plentiful supply of teacakes and did not forget your cherry scones. The sun will do you good. Come, everyone else is there."

Mr Bennet glanced out of the window, in the direction his favourite daughter had indicated with a slight gesture of her hand. He could espy the summer pavilion festooned with trailing roses and honeysuckle, as well as the company gathered there. Jane, helping Lydia to some sweet concoction; Kitty, pondering over her choices;

Mary, pouring their cousin's tea, and his heir apparent frantically waving off a buzzing insect and scowling at Lydia for some reason her father could not fathom as, for once, she seemed reasonably well-behaved. At least from a distance.

"I thank you, my dear. Go ahead, I shall join you presently."

Instead of diligently following his instructions, Elizabeth came closer and ran her fingers through his hair. Mr Bennet glanced up with a smile, gathered her hand and brought it to his lips, then kept it in his.

"If you have already had your fill of Mr Collins for the day, I could bring you a cup of tea and some cherry scones here," she offered, and her father chortled.

"Tempting. But it would not be fair on you and your sisters."

"Was it so very bad then, your half-hour with him?"

Mr Bennet shrugged.

"Who should bear it but myself? After all, he is from my side of the family," he retorted lightly.

"What did he wish to speak of? Anything in particular, or was it just the customary rambling?"

Mr Bennet could not suppress a snort.

"Would you not care to hazard a guess?"

"He came to ask for Jane's hand in marriage," Elizabeth replied with mock solemnity, but her eyes were dancing, full of mischief – a clear sign that she was merely jesting. But they grew wide when she heard her father's clipped answer.

"Close enough. He came to ask for yours."

Mr Bennet could not fail to register her acute surprise. But then she gave a little laugh.

"Goodness. How flattering. I daresay this is the first time in my life that I am favoured over Jane. And undoubtedly the last."

"You seem strangely devoid of curiosity," he teased her. "Do you not wish to hear my reply?"

"Naturally. It must be excessively diverting. I imagine the phrase *When hell freezes over* featured prominently in that conversation."

This time her father laughed outright and patted her hand.

"You know me well. But yet again, your guess is slightly off the mark. I merely advised him he should seek a more biddable wife, whose good looks would not endanger his parishioners' immortal souls."

She cast him a wide smile.

"Why, thank you, Papa." Then her countenance grew solemn as she earnestly added, "And thank you for not even considering I should marry my cousin for our family's security."

Her father's eyes flashed with a steely glint when he retorted with unprecedented sternness, "Never!" Then they softened, and he pressed her hand to his lips again, before reverting to his customary approach to moments of great unease or great emotion: he teased.

"You did mention, after all, that only the deepest love would ever induce you into matrimony, and I could not bring myself to believe you had taken leave of your senses quite so grievously as to fall in love with Mr Collins."

There were tears glistening in her eyes when she put her arms around his neck and kissed his cheek, so Mr Bennet cleared his voice and added:

"I only hope you fall in love with a man with an extensive classical education. Failing that, at the very least you might wish to acquaint him with the epic tale of the twelve labours of Hercules. For your sake, I intend to give the young man a sporting chance, so you must ensure he knows what is in store for him, and is reasonably well prepared when he comes to face me. And you might as well warn the poor soul that I shall watch him like a hawk."

Chapter 4

Pemberley, 13 May 1811

"Mr Darcy? Mr Darcy, can you hear me?" Lady Anne called with no little urgency, and to her relief, she soon registered her husband's grumbling reply.

"Distinctly, madam. You need not raise your voice, or whatever it is that you are doing. How can I be of service?"

"Pray join me in the study."

"May I ask why?"

"I would appreciate your presence. Where are you?"

"In the library, making a mental note of the books I failed to read in my lifetime."

"A worthy endeavour, but this is not the time for peaceable pursuits. Pray come," she insisted, and in short order she had the pleasure of seeing his form emerging through the left wall of the study.

He had long mastered that skill, and had also acquired the ability to conjure suitable attire. His current choice was the ensemble shown in the small likeness facing the master's desk, the last one he had commissioned in his lifetime. But at the moment such details were of no interest to his wife.

"Going through masonry is still damnably uncomfortable," he muttered. "How soon should I be expected to—?" But the question died on his lips, to be replaced by another: "What the devil is *he* doing here?" he snapped.

"That is why I have summoned you. A tryst, would you say?" Lady Anne replied with a disdainful tilt of her chin in the direction of the amorous couple – young George, the reviled scoundrel, busily making advances to a housemaid, who should have known better.

"A tryst!" her husband growled. "On *my* desk?"

"Fitzwilliam's desk," his wife observed.

"Fitzwilliam's, aye," George Darcy conceded with a frown. "Not that it makes the indignity of it a shade more acceptable. When the cat's away, young Molly will play, it seems. I knew she was a worthless chit when Reynolds engaged her."

"You did not. You have never concerned yourself with the housemaids, praise be. The question is, what are we to do on the occasion?"

"Damnation! I have not missed the strength of my right arm quite so much since I passed away. Am I to sit here and witness him defiling my study? Fitzwilliam's study, blast it!" he bellowed, correcting himself when he saw his wife opening her lips to prompt the very same amendment. "Why did you summon me here, madam?" he burst out, venting his ire on the only person who could hear him. "To rejoice in my humiliation? Very well. You may have your wish, and hear me admit I was wrong to befriend him. I – was – *wrong*. There. Will that do?"

"I thank you, aye. And it bears frequent repetition. But I am not so vengeful as to bring you here for the purpose of humiliating you. I merely wished to alert you to the intrusion."

"So, what am I to do?" George Darcy bellowed yet again. "He cannot hear me – see me – I cannot deter him. And I will be damned if I am willing to sit here and watch him debauching wenches on my— on the desk! When you have tired of gloating, you can find me in the library," he growled and strode towards the wall, only to find that instead of passing through it, he forcefully rebounded back into the room, almost to the middle of it. "What devilish scheme is this?" he thundered, but his lady remained supremely unruffled by his ill-humour.

"Strong emotions affect your abilities," she casually informed him. "It has happened to me once or twice. You must regain your temper and focus solely on the task at hand, if you wish to go through."

"Regain my temper? How am I to achieve that feat, pray tell, while witnessing *this?* " he fulminated with a fierce scowl, one hand shooting in the direction of the two offenders.

But, to his enduring sanity – if ghosts were blessed with such – young Wickham saw fit to desist from his advances and released the wench from his embrace.

"You must leave now, poppet," he entreated her between kisses, "before old Reynolds finds you gone, or you will get the devil of a scolding. The old biddy can be mighty harsh."

"As I know too well. Oh, George, how I've missed you!"

"And I you, flower. Missed you something rotten."

"To think I lost so much sleep thinking you favoured Gemma."

"Who?"

"Gemma Dobbs. She was second housemaid here."

"Ah, her. Was? Oh, I see. Given the sack, was she?"

"No. She left of her own accord, a year back or more. Said she found a better place up north. Good riddance, I say. But why do you ask? George, you didn't favour her, did you?"

"Silly Molly. Of course not. I can barely remember her. Why would I look at her or anyone else, when I have you? But you must go now," he urged again, disentangling her arms from around his neck. "I have no wish to get you into trouble."

"I don't give a fig. Kiss me, George."

"Later, my sweet. Now go."

"But what of you?"

"I will wait for you in here. Lock me in till your drudgery is done."

"But what if someone comes in and finds you?"

"No one will. The young lord and master is in town, and there he will stay for the foreseeable future. As for the other servants, you said no one comes in here to clean but you. I will be safe. And if anyone should come, I can always hide behind the curtains."

"Won't you be safer in my room? Hannah's away in Lambton to care for her ailing mother, and she won't be back till Monday. Old Reynolds told her she could go. So I'm not sharing my room with anyone. Anyone but you," she added with a coquettish giggle.

"What if someone should come looking for you? Not much room under your bed, sweet-pea, and nowhere else to hide. I am better off here. Safe as houses. Go, go, I will be just fine."

At last, the young maid was persuaded to let him have his wish. She opened the door a crack, took a quick peek to assure herself that no one was around, then sneaked out, closed the door behind her and locked it as instructed. Thus, Lady Anne and her husband were left with just one unwelcome presence in the study. By then, George Darcy's translucent countenance had acquired a stony hue, and his temper was not likely to improve. Least of all when he saw his former *protégé* producing a set of keys from a safely buttoned pocket and proceeding to unlock the uppermost drawer of the desk.

"He has stolen Fitzwilliam's keys!" his wife observed with justifiable outrage.

"Or copied them while they were in my keeping," he grimly speculated.

"What is he after?"

"I know not," George Darcy growled, striding towards the wretch.

Lady Anne sighed in exasperation mingled with compassion at the sight of her husband vainly seeking to interact with the living. Swipes and well-aimed punches had no effect whatever, and Wickham's progress with the rest of the desk drawers remained unhindered, despite his former patron's efforts. One thing was certain: George Darcy's full concentration was focussed on the task at hand, for his fists and forearms kept passing through the scoundrel's body rather than rebounding off it, as had been the case a short while earlier, when he had attempted to storm out of the study through the wall.

"Is he not supposed to feel *something* when I swipe through him?" George Darcy burst out at last, in profound vexation.

But Lady Anne calmly shook her head.

"I think not, my dear, I am sorry to say. Over the years, before you joined me, I grew sufficiently weary of the lack of communication and employment that I was driven to occasional experiments. The results were always disappointing. They cannot see us, hear us, feel us. They can only frustrate us with their incomprehension."

"This goes beyond frustration!" her husband grunted as he pointlessly swung his right fist again, but to no avail. As countless times before, the fist and forearm passed through Wickham's torso, eliciting no reaction. "This is—"

"Maddening. I know," his wife finished his sentence for him, with a sympathetic nod. But suddenly her eyes darted away from her beleaguered husband to pierce the intruder with another glare. "He knows about the secret compartments!" she exclaimed in horror.

George Darcy's countenance turned a solid, eerie white.

"Aye. My fault – again. I opened them in his presence once."

"Oh, Mr Darcy!"

"I know, madam. If I could turn back time and redress my errors… But I cannot!" he burst out, fiercely pounding his palm with his fist. He grunted in shock at the force of the impact. Seemingly, the living remained unaffected by meeting with ghostly fists, but the same could not be said of his left palm. "How is this possible?" he wondered, momentarily distracted, as he stared in bemusement at his palm, then his fist.

Lady Anne, however, had no time for this.

"Look," she called, pointing towards Wickham. He has the keys to the strongbox too. What is he after? Oh, if I could have my body back for just one hour!"

"If I had mine, ten minutes would suffice," her husband retorted darkly, but once again he was interrupted.

"My wedding ring! He has found my wedding ring. Mr Darcy, do something!"

Her husband's stare grew harder than ever, and his countenance contorted with rage when he saw his former *protégé* bringing the Darcy heirloom into the path of a bright ray of sunshine, for a meticulous examination. His mother's wedding ring – his wife's – the ring that should go to the woman his son would marry – in the blackguard's hands! Why had he not placed it securely, with the other pieces? *Why* had he trusted this vile snake in the first place, old fool that he was? He had allowed Wickham to deceive him, wheedle and coax his way into his affection, usurp a place that by rights was his son's, and now the vermin sought to defraud Fitzwilliam even further. Abscond with Lady Anne's wedding ring! That was *not* to be borne!

George Darcy was momentarily distracted from his mounting rage when, without warning, from the top of the stack at the corner of the desk, a large tome fell to the floor with a loud thud. It was Markham's *Country Contentments*, the gentleman-farmer's bible, as often consulted by Fitzwilliam as it had always been by him, he noted in passing, just as Wickham hissed the crudest oath, dropped the heirloom he was not fit to touch and reached to steady the remaining pile, lest the other books follow.

For some unfathomable reason, Lady Anne cheered:

"Nicely done, sir! Although you should have aimed it at his head," she vengefully added.

George Darcy turned to her, wide-eyed.

"You think *I* did that?"

"I should imagine so. I know I did not. Unless the wretch and that foolish chit had nudged the stack too close to the edge with their antics. But given your wrathful thoughts a few moments ago, I would say it was you."

"How?" her husband gasped.

"Anger has that effect, I found. With more gratifying results if channelled," his wife said, her eyes still on Wickham.

He had just eased the stack of books towards him, safely away from the edge, and now stood stock-still, staring at the door and doubtlessly listening for signs that someone in the house might have heard the crashing noise and was driven to investigate its causes.

"*How* am I to channel it?" George Darcy spluttered. "Pray do not mention patience and concentration. At this point I can summon neither."

"I am distraught to disappoint, but for me intense concentration was always the key. Even so, I achieved but little. I could rarely move objects, and just by a few inches, so the feats remained largely unnoticed. Unless moving things by an inch or two was enough to make them fall – as you have just demonstrated."

"Hm. Now you mention it, I do remember objects having a strange propensity to fall all around us whenever I was with him," George Darcy said with a tilt of his head in Wickham's direction. "Snuff boxes, billiards cues, ornaments. Was that your doing?"

"Most likely. Playing cards, too. The chess set scattering on the floor when you turned down Fitzwilliam's offer of a game on grounds that he was a reasonably proficient player, and it was the other who would benefit from additional instruction. Or the decanter slipping from your grasp one night when Fitzwilliam was finding companionship in books, while you and your *protégé* were having a merry old laugh over brandy."

"There was I thinking I was three sheets to the wind that night."

"Perhaps you were. But I claim the credit for breaking the decanter. And some glasses, over the course of time."

"And for pinecones thrown at my head in the shrubbery?"

"No. You can blame that on squirrels. I could never make it to the shrubbery. Nor throw anything, more was the pity. Many a time I would have dearly loved to throw things at your dear George…"

"And at me, I'd wager."

"Aye. But enough said of that."

"No, we should speak further. Later though. Now 'tis distracting."

"Forgive me. Yes, of course."

By then, Wickham must have reassured himself that all was well, for he abandoned his cautious pose and returned to his despicable employment. He retrieved the wedding ring from where it had rolled away when he had dropped it, but his invisible companions were exceedingly relieved to see it placed back where the rogue had found it. Still, that was not the end of it. For whatever wicked reasons of his own, the scoundrel was not altogether finished.

"What the devil is he seeking?" George Darcy fumed, as Wickham continued to rifle through the strongbox.

The answer was made known to him soon enough, when Wickham straightened up, his countenance aglow with an infuriating look of satisfaction. In his hands there were several sheets of paper covered in an elaborate script.

Even before they were laid out on the desk, George Darcy recognised the document for what it was, and his eyes narrowed.

"My—"

"Your last will and testament," Lady Anne exclaimed. "What does he want with it?"

Nonplussed, her husband made a gesture conveying his lack of comprehension, and his stare remained fixed on the intruder, who was now scanning the pages, scornfully muttering to himself.

"Oh, aye. Everything went to the young lordling, naturally. Pemberley. The Scottish estates. Lands in Cheshire… Staffordshire. Sundry investments. Shipping interests. Mining. La-di-dah… La-di-dah… Of course, the young lord and master must have everything. Obscene wealth laid at his door, more than any decent man needs in a lifetime, and devil take the steward's son. He can have a pittance and a cramped old parsonage. Scraps from the rich man's table. Aye, let the fool's efforts to please be thoroughly wasted. Let him bow and scrape, and be grateful for a living that puts him on the par with the proverbial church-mouse. A-ha! There we have it," he suddenly burst out, and his countenance split into a grin. "Oh-ho-ho! Better than I thought. Thirty thousand pounds, and no mistake. Good. Very good. Aye, that will do me. It will balance the books nicely."

"Thirty thousand pounds? What is he speaking of?" Lady Anne asked, and a fraction of a second later her eyes grew impossibly wide, with all the horror of belated understanding.

Her husband reeled back, overpowered by the enormity of what he was witnessing, of what he dreaded, and to Lady Anne's further shock, he began to shake uncontrollably. The violent maelstrom of dark thoughts whirling through his mind was projected into hers with frightening intensity. His only coherent thought she could register was this:

"Georgiana's dowry."

It fed her darkest fears.

The vile beast had designs upon their daughter!

Murderous anger surged in her, and Lady Anne could sense it flowing in an overpowering tide from her husband as well. Two almighty tides that rose, clashed into each other and broke over them and over the foundations of their inner world with all the devastating fury of a tempest.

There was no hope of channelling the tumult of emotion – of seeking to govern it, even – and there was a great deal more than anger, livid anger, at its core. The core, or what they could perceive of it, was a turbulent mix of anguish, reproach, self-loathing, paralysing fear, and a host of sentiments that defied classification. And from it shot conflicting currents that spun out of control, imprisoning them both into a dark whirlpool of despair.

The whirlpool kept spinning, contained within the impenetrable walls that separated one world from the other. Devoid of order and unfocussed, it could not break through. Mere plumes escaped from the periphery of the wide vortex, lashing as they went. They whipped the edges of the Darcys' world and found a way without, but the disruption caused in the quiet library was a pitifully weak manifestation of the wild force still trapped in the eye of the storm. Papers fluttered on the desk. The inkwell and the sandbox shook, as did the few maps and paintings adorning the walls, and the books on the shelves. The curtains billowed out, and the windows rattled.

Wickham briefly glanced up from his employment, then shrugged. With swift and precise motions, he resumed tidying away the papers and everything else he had removed from the strongbox. The receptacle was then restored to its place, and in due course so were the fallen tome and the contents of all the drawers, until every trace of his felonious search was gone.

"Draughty old pile," he muttered when currents of air came out of nowhere to brush over him and the curtains billowed yet again, although all the casements were shut. He found the decanter, poured himself a generous measure of brandy and raised the glass in mock salute towards George Darcy's likeness. "Here's to our future connection, my dear sir," he said with a wide grin. "It shan't be long until I can call you Father."

George Darcy verily shook with the strain of focusing his rage, his crippling guilt and his fear, but his best efforts were for naught. The bust of Socrates remained firmly in place atop the bookcase, instead of toppling forward, meeting Wickham's skull and splitting it open with a resounding *'crack.'*

⁓✺ ✺⁓

"What is to be done? What in God's name are we to do now?" George Darcy repeated, as he continued to pace back and forth in the long gallery. "Fitzwilliam must be warned," he said with fierce determination. "We must find a way to reach him."

"How?" his wife brokenly whispered. "I tried. Oh, how I tried! He never heard me. And he is not even here. How can we reach him from hundreds of miles, when I could not communicate even when I was beside him?"

"By other means, then. A sign. A message. A letter."

"You cannot write it. Neither can I. If we could not so much as drop a bust on that beast's head, how do you imagine either of us could guide a pen?"

"With practice. And intense concentration. Did you not say so?"

"Aye, but…"

"We must find a way. And there is no time to lose!"

Without another word, George Darcy vanished from her sight. Quick to guess where she should seek him, Lady Anne found him in the study. No one else was there now but themselves. The blackguard had long since left, sadly unharmed despite their best efforts. His vile purpose achieved, he did not tarry waiting for the foolish maid's return, but let himself out with a key he must have copied along with the others, and quitted Pemberley at once. Eager to embark upon his abominable quest, no doubt. Lady Anne shuddered. Her husband was in the right; they had no time to lose.

Pemberley, late May 1811

George Darcy's relentless efforts were for naught. He could *not* attain his purpose. After hours upon hours and days upon days of seeking to achieve intense concentration, at long last he had learned to focus his mind upon lifting a pen and dipping it in the inkwell. Yet he had nothing better to show for it than ink-stains all over the desk and on countless sheets of paper. Lady Anne was woefully correct in her estimation: he could not finely guide the pen so as to form words.

His inadequate handiwork merely served to scare the wits out of Molly, the maid who had unwittingly aided Wickham in his nefarious schemes. For, every morning, when she came into the study to dust and clean, she found pens scattered on the desk, ink-stains on its surface, and sheets of paper covered in blots. She also found books and trinkets on the floor, overturned candlesticks and, once, a broken glass – the result of George Darcy practising on objects that were less awkward to handle than a pen, as well as the abandoned testimonies of his frustration.

At first, Molly thought someone was playing tricks on her. Or worse still, that she had been seen admitting her lover into the house, into the study, and whomever had discovered that now sought to frighten her into submission, or make her betray herself to Mrs Reynolds. Gemma Dobbs, her old rival for George Wickham's favour, would have gladly done her all manner of mischief. Or told on her. Now Gemma was gone, thank goodness, but that was not to say that someone else could not do the devilry on her behalf, or carry tales to Mrs Reynolds.

Fearfully, Molly waited for the mischief-makers to raise their heads. She wished she could speak to her lover of her fears, and that he would reassure her. Dear George was so clever; he always read everything rightly and knew exactly what to say to make her feel a vast deal better. But he had gone from Lambton, and she longed for him. He had gone to town – he said that very urgent business called him there.

There was naught Molly could do but hold her tongue and wait, and that was what she did. Yet there were no malicious hints dropped in the servants' hall about her and her dear George, and no one came to plague her about her secret.

Instead, there were different whispers. The other housemaid began to speak of strange goings-on around the house. Doors slamming shut with no good reason. Vases falling off shelves when no one touched them. Curtains billowing when the windows were shut.

When Mrs Reynolds was not around to hear her, Hannah said it was the spirit of the Grim Knight that was causing all the mischief.

"Summat must've troubled his rest. He wears the darkest frown these days. Haven't you seen his likeness in the gallery? Scowling more fiercely than ever. Never used to glare like that. I daren't go past him before dawn or at dusk. I fancy he's lookin' right at me. An' the other day, a bright an' sunny day it were, you'd think it were summer, but as I hurried past that frame – in the middle of the day, mind – a fearsome chill burst out of it an' went right through me chest. Thought 'twould freeze me into a block of ice, I did. Freeze me then an' there!"

Simon, the only footman to remain at Pemberley when the family was from home, laughed at that particular account and told Hannah she was being silly. But a few days later, as he was going about his business, he discovered that a miniature was missing from the display above the mantelpiece. The one depicting the son of the late steward, as it happened. He eventually found it smashed to pieces on the floor, at the eastern end of the gallery – right beneath the Grim Knight's likeness.

Simon wisely chose to keep the details to himself. He merely took the miniature to Mrs Reynolds, expressed the hope that it could be mended, told her he had found it by the fireplace, and ventured the opinion that the nail must have given way. But as of that day he ceased making fun of Hannah, and took to darting quick glances over his shoulder whenever the doors creaked and the windows rattled.

Lady Anne silently took note of the unplanned consequences of her husband's loss of temper, and wished she had resumed her visits into the servants' hall. Then she might have heard the rumours about the Grim Knight sooner, and encouraged Mr Darcy to smash George Wickham's miniature someplace else, beneath some other likeness. Preferably beneath his own, come to think of it. Then the household might have begun to understand that it was not the Grim Knight's spirit that was severely troubled.

Chapter 5

Pemberley, 4 June 1811

Fitzwilliam Darcy rolled his shoulders back to ease the stiffness that had inevitably come from the many hours on the road, however comfortable the carriage, and handed his hat and gloves to one of the footmen who had returned with him from town. Hands folded before her on her pristine apron, Mrs Reynolds beamed.

"'Tis grand to have you back, sir. A sight for sore eyes, this, if I may say so. And Miss Georgiana? I hope our dear miss is well."

She received one of her young master's rare smiles in response to the warm welcome, and he replied with the lack of formality he reserved for faithful retainers of many years' standing.

"I thank you, yes. She is still in Ramsgate with Mrs Younge, but they are due to travel north at the end of the month. Speaking of which, is everything in readiness for her arrival?"

"Aye, sir. The new harp you ordered came last month, and the lads have been at work in the rose garden to fashion the bower just as you instructed."

"Good. Very good. She will be pleased to sit and read there in the summer, I think."

"Oh, I do not doubt it. Now, shall I have something brought up for you on a tray, or would you rather I hastened dinner? It should be sent up in a couple of hours, but—"

"That will be fine. Pray do not trouble yourself with altering the arrangements, and there is no need to send anything up. I can wait for dinner. The innkeeper at *The Angel* in Grantham does not hold with frugal breakfasts. Either that, or he mistook my meaning and brought fare for three, rather than one."

Mrs Reynolds chuckled.

"Just some tea in the morning room, then?"

"That would be most welcome. But pray send it into the study."

"Very good, sir."

With an exchange of smiles, the housekeeper and her master parted. She hastened below-stairs to brew fresh tea and explore the pantry – for, whatever he might have had to say about lavish breakfasts, a few slices of buttered fruit-bread would not go amiss – while Mr Darcy made his way towards the study.

He casually strode in, only to be met with a cry of horrified dismay. A young maid swiftly drew back from her employment, which appeared to involve the frantic scrubbing of the desk. She wrung her hands over the cloth she was holding and, eyes lowered, she bobbed a clumsy curtsy.

"Oh. Do not fret," Mr Darcy felt compelled to encouragingly say when she darted him a fearful glance. "You spilled some ink. It happens."

"Yes, sir. I mean, no, sir," the girl stammered. "'Tweren't me that spilled it. Honest. But I'll get on with it, if it pleases you, Mr Darcy, sir."

She bobbed another curtsy and dropped her gaze back towards the desk. As he advanced into the room, her master could see the damage to its full extent. He assessed it in silence for the best part of a minute. Three sheets of paper covered in blots and shaky lines lay scattered among ink-stains, along with two pens, one broken. The untidy mess had the general air of a child's handiwork. An unruly and very energetic child, not yet trained in the art of writing.

Darcy could not forbear a frown. He had never objected to his people's relations visiting them at Pemberley and bringing children with them, but he drew the line at the youngsters having the run of the house and free access into his study. Especially when that was the result.

He squared his shoulders, clasped his hands behind his back and cleared his voice to draw the girl's notice. But before he could begin, she breathlessly burst out:

"I've already cleaned it, sir, first thing in the mornin'. I did, honest to goodness! I just thought I'd check all's well when I heard you were returned, but found it messed up all over again. Beg pardon, sir. I'll tidy it all up in a trice."

"So, this has happened more than once?" Darcy asked, displeased in no small measure. When the flustered maid bit her lip and nodded, he resumed, his voice reasonable but very firm: "Now, Molly, you may rest easy. Whoever is to blame for this will not be punished. As long as I am assured it will not happen again."

He would have imagined the girl would be reassured by his collected manner and grateful to hear he was willing to pardon the transgression and let the matter rest – a generous offer, to Darcy's mind, even if he said so himself. Yet, instead of looking relieved, the girl burst into tears. Nonplussed, Darcy exhaled in some impatience.

"Do not distress yourself," he told her. "As I just said, the matter is forgiven and forgotten, this once."

"But it'll happen again," the maid brokenly replied. "It does, sir, every night. The door stays locked, but I find the desk in a right mess every mornin', an' every mornin' I do me best to clean it. I'll always do me best, sir, but it'll happen again!"

Darcy frowned. Before he could ask the wench to explain herself, a tap on the door came to distract him. He raised his voice by a fraction and bade the newcomer enter. It was the youngest footman, with his tea. The delicate china rattled, in severe danger of sliding off the tray when he came in and saw the desk. He gasped and darted a glance towards Molly. Drawing manifest strength from the footman's presence, the maid spoke again.

"He'll tell you, sir, Simon will. An' Hannah. Hannah an' Simon know 't ain't me. 'Tis his doing, sir! The Grim Knight is to blame."

"What is this nonsense?" Darcy asked, long past the limits of his patience, his stern glance moving from one servant to the other. "Set that tray down before you drop it," he instructed Simon. "Good. Now speak up."

Although the instruction was clearly for Simon, they both hastily began at once, speaking over each other.

"The Cavalier, sir—"

"The likeness in the gallery—"

Darcy grimaced.

"One at a time, pray. Molly, you might as well finish what you have to say."

Nervously wiping her hands on her apron, Molly complied.

"I— *We* think the Grim Knight is troubled, sir..."

"What grim knight?" Darcy snapped.

"You know, the armoured gent in the third likeness, if you count from the eastern door into the gallery..."

Darcy could now grasp of which one they were speaking: the portrait of Edward Darcy, who had steered the family fortunes through the murky waters of the Civil War, until King Charles II had been restored to his martyred father's throne.

They called him the Grim Knight? And well they might, for the countenance depicted above the battle-worn armour was indeed forbidding. But then Edward Darcy had had precious little reason to smile in his troubled lifetime.

"Yes, very well. What of him?"

"His frown has grown darker than ever, we found, an' Hannah said—"

"Beg pardon," Simon intervened, apologising to his master for the interruption when he saw Darcy involuntarily darting his eyes heavenward, in mild exasperation at tales of age-old portraits changing their expression. "The gent's frown is neither here nor there. But there's somethin' else, sir, if I might."

With a silent nod, Darcy indicated that the young man should proceed.

"I haven't said a word of it afore. Didn't wish to frighten the lasses, they are jittery enough already. But there's odd things going on in the gallery, Mr Darcy, sir. Very odd indeed. 'Tis the display above the mantelpiece. The miniatures. I found one of them smashed to pieces under the knight's likeness, eleven yards or more from where it should have been if it had simply fallen off the wall. And now there's another one that keeps wandering off."

"Wandering off," Darcy echoed crisply, crossing his arms over his chest.

But the young footman was undeterred by the sarcastic tone.

"Aye, sir," he said with nary a moment's hesitation. "I found it moved from its place six times now. Nay, seven. The first time was on Wednesday, right after Mrs Reynolds summoned us into the servants' hall to say there was a letter from you, and the house must be readied for your arrival. At first, I thought nothing of it. But then it kept happening. Every morning, regular as clockwork, when I went into the gallery and walked past the dresser underneath your likeness, there was Miss Darcy's miniature, in the same—"

"Enough!" Darcy cut him off. "Fetch Mrs Reynolds. I wish to speak to her at once."

"Yes, sir. Right away, sir," the footman stammered, greatly perturbed by the unprecedented sternness, and hastened to obey. But no sooner had he opened the door than he saw Mrs Reynolds approaching along the corridor.

"You forgot the buttered fruit-bread," she mildly scolded Simon. Yet when she came closer and walked into the study, a glance at her master's countenance put paid to her good-humour. "Mr Darcy? Whatever is the matter?"

She was tersely asked to come in, and the other two to leave them. Mrs Reynolds gasped when she beheld the state of the desk, but her young master promptly halted her attempt to set it to rights.

"We shall come to that later," he solemnly said. "Firstly, pray tell me, are you aware of the rumours in the house?"

"What rumours, sir?" Mrs Reynolds asked, concerned in no small measure.

"Inane talk of visitations, here and in the long gallery."

"Visitations?"

"Spirits, Mrs Reynolds. Ghosts. Edward Darcy's, to be precise."

The housekeeper discreetly rolled her eyes.

"I did notice Molly and Hannah keeping each other company whenever they had to go into the long gallery, but I left them to it. I thought it childish nonsense."

"I agree. However, someone seems to have taken it upon themselves to feed that nonsense. Apparently, every morning Molly finds my desk just as you see it."

Mrs Reynolds' eyes widened.

"My deepest apologies, Mr Darcy. I should have—"

"There is more," Darcy interrupted her. "Worse still, Simon informs me that over the last seven days Miss Georgiana's miniature was found taken from its place above the mantelpiece and placed on a dresser."

"And he did not breathe a word of it!"

Darcy shrugged.

"He claims he did not wish to frighten the maids. But whoever is responsible for this must be stopped."

"Of course, sir. I will make it my business to root them out at once," Mrs Reynolds earnestly assured him.

"Pray do. Miss Georgiana is due home soon, and I *will not* tolerate her tender heart being unsettled in this thoughtless manner.

Pray inform the household that I am prepared to regard it as a childish trick. I flatter myself that I am a reasonable master. But if this continues, I shall give no quarter. The perpetrator will desist, or I will not hesitate to dismiss every single one of the lower servants who has access to the areas concerned. Pray tell them that I hope I am rightly understood."

Mrs Reynolds nodded.

"Yes, Mr Darcy," she solemnly said, and left to do as bid.

ം ഉരു ഉരം

Pemberley, 5 June 1811

"He will not listen. He will not listen!" Lady Anne dejectedly whispered in the hours before dawn, wringing her hands as she paced up and down the gallery, alongside her husband.

George Darcy made no answer, but continued pacing – until all of a sudden, without the slightest warning, he muttered, "Pray excuse me," and vanished from her sight.

"Where are you?" Lady Anne called after him with no little impatience and just as much vexation. "Not in the study, surely! There is no purpose in continuing with that."

"I know. I am in my chambers. His chambers, rather. And if I have to run amok to wake him and then send every movable object flying, I will, by Jove! He *has* to take note!"

Quick as a flash, Lady Anne joined him. Despite the heartbreaking urgency of the situation, her lips slowly curled into the warmest smile at the sight of her son, asleep under the canopy of the large bed, his features endearingly softened in repose.

"They look so much like the children that they were when they are sleeping," she tenderly observed as she reached to stroke the ruffled hair, adorably unruly at the best of times. She could not stroke it, not as such; but in her heart, she felt as though she had.

Her dear, handsome boy, how peaceful his sleep was. And yet they had to wake him.

Lady Anne turned towards her husband.

"How do you propose to—? Oh! What are you doing?"

The latter was merely an exclamation of surprise, and she did not expect an answer. She could easily sense the overwhelming flow of thoughts and mental images that her husband was directing at their sleeping son. Georgiana in her girlhood, a halo of golden ringlets around her sweet face. Georgiana rushing pell-mell towards her brother, only to be swept up into his arms. The pair of them walking together, laughing together, riding their horses at a gallop over the meadows surrounding Pemberley. Lady Anne shuddered as she sensed the darker messages – the vile snake in the study examining the papers and the wedding ring, grinning impudently at her husband's portrait. And again, Georgiana smiling at her brother, leaning on his arm, running to greet him. Images, countless images bursting out in such quick succession that she could scarce distinguish where one scene ended and the next began. But her daughter was the bright focus of each and every one of them.

"Georgiana…" Fitzwilliam whispered in his sleep – and sent his mother reeling.

"He can hear you? Good heavens, he can hear you! Why could he never hear *me?* " she cried.

George Darcy made a gesture of vexation at the interruption.

"Hush! Does it matter?"

"No. No! Of course not. Speak to him! Tell him!"

He obeyed. Words came, entreaties, forcefully urging their son to act.

"Go to her, my boy! Go to your sister! Right my errors and do what I failed to do – watch over her, protect her. The vile beast has formed designs on her. He would ruin her life if we do not stop him – if you do not. You must leave on the morrow, do you hear me? On the morrow you must go to your sister."

Little hope as she had of being heard – after all, she had not succeeded once in a dozen years – Lady Anne pleadingly added her own entreaties to her husband's.

Thrashing in his sleep, Fitzwilliam rolled on his back and winced. He groaned and his lips moved, but they could not make out what he was saying, if anything. And then the thrashing recommenced.

"This will not do!" Lady Anne suddenly said with great energy. "How is he to understand anything from this cacophony? We need to convey a clear message – short and simple."

"What do you suggest?" her husband grumbled. She told him, and to his credit, he was swift to see the wisdom of it. "Hold my hand," George Darcy whispered.

Whether or not that would make a difference, neither of them could tell. But it was a comfort, and it made them feel stronger.

So, holding hands, they fought to clear their minds of everything but that one message, short and simple, repeated over and over. With everything they were, with everything they had, they jointly urged their son:

"Protect your sister. Go to Ramsgate!"

⁓⦿ ⦿⦿⦿

They could only pray he heard them. The first glimmer of hope came when Fitzwilliam awoke with a violent start; remained motionless for a few moments, staring blankly into space; then flung back the bedclothes and proceeded to pace across the room muttering to himself about foolish superstitions, and how the blazes was one to now draw an easy breath.

Dawn found him donning his attire without his valet's assistance. Little more than an hour later, the Darcy carriage was thundering away from Pemberley. No one knew its destination except the coachman, the two footmen in attendance and, most likely, the housekeeper and the butler. The upper servants knew better than to speak of it. The others blindly speculated in hushed whispers. Woefully unable to leave the brick and mortar residence, Lady Anne and George Darcy could only wait. In the throes of the deepest anxiety they waited, for what seemed to be an age.

It felt like an age to the pair of them, although it was a mere se'nnight to the living – fortunate souls, who did not share the burden of their knowledge. But at long last, their son returned, and brought Georgiana with him. A silent, stricken and often tearful Georgiana, nothing like her carefree, sweet self.

As they overheard her stilted and heartrending exchanges with her brother, her parents soon learned the full extent of Wickham's treachery. They heard how the despicable Mrs Younge, the companion engaged to watch over their daughter, had in fact colluded with the snake and worked towards Georgiana's ruin. Aghast, Lady Anne and George Darcy finally understood how narrowly they had escaped disaster.

Outwardly, the house was now at peace. Nary a disturbance in the long gallery and the master's study. No longer fed, the rumours of ghostly visitations died a natural death. Mrs Reynolds made it her business to ensure it, unbending steel underneath her pleasant countenance and manner.

Whether or not his son was still giving any thoughts to the surreal circumstances that had prompted his journey to Ramsgate, George Darcy could not tell, but he was convinced that the lad had not shared the details with his impressionable sister. His son had more sense than to burden her with that, even if her spirits had not been so dreadfully oppressed already.

The dear girl was dreadfully altered. Overcome with guilt and mortification, she seemed to move through a dark haze from day to day, much as her brother sought to draw her away from self-recriminations and repeatedly assure her that *she* was not at fault. Yet it was almost as if his determined efforts to reconcile her to the past merely served to keep it ever-present in her memory.

Heartbreaking as the notion was, the distraught father began to suspect that his son and daughter might benefit from some time apart. Some time spent in a different and more cheerful setting, and in the rousing company of other people who had no knowledge of their troubles. With any luck, his son might have the good sense to see it. However, there was every reason to believe that, much like himself, Fitzwilliam was so affected by the near-disaster that he would not dare let her out of his sight unless he was convinced she would be safe.

Day after day, as his children's distress crushed him, there was but one notion in which George Darcy could find a modicum of comfort: however placid their union had been, Lady Anne must have held him in her affections. For not once, in all those dreadful weeks, did he hear her say or think "This is entirely *your* fault!"

Chapter 6

"Damnation," Fitzwilliam Darcy muttered as the thicket parted, revealing three muddy tracks branching out from the crossroads, but no hint whatsoever as to which one he should choose.

He cursed the folly of accepting his friend Bingley's invitation to call upon him at the estate he had just leased. He cursed the Hertfordshire countryside, so damnably flat, with no vantage point to help him find his bearings. He cursed the Hertfordshire roads, shockingly poor ever since he had left the turnpike. It was unthinkable that they should be so bad – there, not thirty miles from town. The road from Bakewell to Haddon, far up into what was deemed to be the untamed and indisputably rural north, was a princely avenue compared to the miserable track his horse was now struggling along, mired to its fetlocks. He cursed the notion of abandoning his carriage over a mile back, when it had become hopelessly stuck, foolishly assuming he was close enough to Bingley's estate to ride there for assistance, rather than remain mired till nightfall on a stretch of seemingly deserted road. For good measure, he cursed the rain as well – a vexingly steady drizzle that was doing nothing for the state of the track, nor for his humour – and urged the black stallion towards the crossroads as he sought to ascertain on which of the three lanes he should stake his chances.

He eventually chose the one on the right. It seemed a trifle wider, although by no means well-trodden, and he could only hope it would lead him to something other than a remote farmhouse. Yet within what must have been another half a mile he found nothing to support such hopes. The thicket might have become less dense, but if anything, the track was growing narrower. Darcy began to ponder the wisdom of turning back and exploring the other two lanes, when a cheerful sound of voices drifted towards him, from somewhere to his left. He pulled the reins and squinted in that direction through the drizzle that was now blowing fully in his face, and heaved a sigh of disappointment. No villagers that might point him on the right track, but children hopping along a path that snaked through the meadow. A boy, presumably no older than ten years of age, and an even younger-looking girl tottering behind him. Whether or not they might be able to give him any reliable directions, Darcy could not tell, but his hopes rose a little when a taller figure emerged from the thicket, hand in hand with another child, the youngest of the three.

"Hallo, there!" Darcy called.

But he already had their attention, for they were heading his way. Or perhaps their path led to the road. The boy was advancing at a steady pace, although the basket he was carrying seemed quite heavy. The girl was hard upon his heels, but the other two were dallying. Or rather, to do them justice, the taller figure – who turned out to be a young woman – was adjusting her steps to her companion's. That is, until she scooped the small child up into her arms which, as expected, greatly pleased the youngster, who burst into a fit of giggles.

Under different circumstances, Darcy might have turned a mild eye upon the simple pleasures of the Hertfordshire countryfolk, but at the moment he wished they would cease capering about.

"Is this the way to Netherfield?" he asked, raising his voice so that it would carry.

The boy was the one who hastened to answer, with a shake of his head and an eagerly delivered, "Nay, sir. To Longbourn an' Meryton."

Longbourn and Meryton, be they villages, estates or whatever other landmarks, were of no interest to Darcy.

"What about Netherfield?" he insisted.

At his second prompting, the young woman saw fit to lend assistance and stretched out her free arm to point up the road. No longer held in place, the ends of the shawl she had draped over her bonnet to keep it dry blew into the face of the child she was holding, who thought it a game and found it most diverting – whereupon the young woman seemed to forget she was about to give directions, and instead peeled the faded fabric off the rosy little cheeks, then set the youngster down and straightened her back.

"There is a bridle path to Netherfield just around the bend," she finally informed him – the first welcome intelligence Darcy had received in upwards of three hours.

The young woman was momentarily distracted when a pair of chubby hands reached up towards her, but with a shake of her head and a gentle pat, she persuaded the child to think better of asking to be lifted up again and be content with hiding into the folds of her pelisse.

The garment had seen better days, as had her shawl and bonnet, but it was clearly a cut above the homespun garb of the three children. Most likely a gentlewoman's discarded article, handed down to a lady's maid or some such. Were she one of Miss Bingley's maids, he might have a reliable guide to Netherfield. But that was highly doubtful. Miss Bingley would not permit anyone in her employ to traipse around the country in mud above her ankles like a gypsy. To her material advantage, the young woman must have a far more indulgent mistress.

"You are not in service there, are you?" Darcy sought to assure himself nevertheless.

He was answered with a flash of laughing dark-brown eyes, an exceedingly pert twitch of the girl's lips, and a prompt "I am not."

Darcy shrugged. If no guide was to be had, the bridleway would have to do. Yet upon reflection, a proper road to his friend's estate would serve much better. He had no hope whatever of describing the location of his mired carriage to Bingley's men, who would have to come and assist his own people in digging it out. Leading them and their vehicle back along the same route seemed the most sensible option.

"Is there a wider road I might take?" he asked.

"You would reach Netherfield sooner along the bridleway but, aye, there is. You will have to turn back. Take the first track on your right when you reach the crossroads."

"How far is it from there?"

"Less than a mile."

Darcy thanked her with a nod and a brief touch on the brim of his hat, then gathered up the reins and urged his mount into an about-turn. Yet the faithful beast had barely broken into a steady canter when a child's voice piped up, calling after him.

Darcy drew to a halt and glanced over his shoulder to see the young lad racing his way, unencumbered by the heavy basket. The boy tugged at his cap in salute and spoke up:

"Beg pardon, sir. I am to tell ye to keep to yer left beyond the crossroads, else ye'll find yerself at Haye Park instead."

"So, a right turn at the crossroads, and then keep left?" Darcy summarised, in a louder voice than was necessary for the lad to hear him, as in truth the question was meant for the fully-grown and thus more reliable source of information.

The young woman nodded, as did the boy beside him. The chit might have said so in the first place, Darcy inwardly grumbled, not amused by the narrowly avoided prospect of becoming further lost in the alien countryside. But at least she had remembered to give him the necessary directions before it was too late, he thought, finding it in him to be thankful. The sentiment drove him to seek a more tangible expression of his gratitude, only to discover after a quick rummage in his pockets that he did not seem to be carrying anything less than silver. No matter. Then a half-crown it must be.

Darcy walked his horse back to the boy and leaned forward to hand him the token of his appreciation.

"Give this to your... er... sister? With my thanks for her kindness," he said, and nodding his adieus to the young woman from a distance, he hastened on his way, dearly hoping she had not omitted to share other pertinent details, and that with any luck the dinner hour would find him, his mired conveyance and his people at the elusive Netherfield. Dry apparel and a glass of brandy would not go amiss. He was attired for a carriage ride, not for surveying the backroads of Hertfordshire, and the miserable drizzle was well on its way to soaking him to the skin.

⊶⊙⊙⊙⊷

Meryton, 21 October 1811

"Do you think we will be quite safe here tonight, Mr Darcy?" Miss Bingley asked, the sardonic glint in her eyes matching her tone, as she neatly fitted her gloved hand into the crook of his arm.

He made no answer. She patently did not expect one, and merely sought to make a point with her facetious comment. The point being, of course, that the unremarkable surroundings were beneath her notice, and that she was about to grace the country-town assembly rooms with her presence against her better judgement, and certainly not out of choice.

As they both knew, the choice of entertainment for the evening was her brother's. Bingley had been overjoyed to receive an invitation to the *'little assembly'* when one of the local worthies had come to pay his respects to the new tenant of Netherfield.

"What better opportunity to become acquainted with my new neighbours?" Bingley had enthused, to his relations' and his friend's growing vexation at his unaccountable delight in the scheme.

As for Darcy, he was of the same mind as Hurst, Bingley's brother by marriage: attending the assembly was a damn foolish waste of an evening. He had no interest in becoming acquainted with Bingley's new neighbours. He intended to spend no longer than a fortnight in that part of the country, and he would doubtlessly survive for that length of time without the joys of pandering to strangers. Moreover, after the excitement of locating Netherfield on the previous day, as well as the long hours of supervising the rescue of his carriage, he would have preferred a quiet evening in the billiards room, or chatting with Bingley over brandy. Naturally, some interaction with his friend's less genial relations was unavoidable. But why the deuce must he attend a public ball?

Darcy snorted quietly to himself as they made their way within. For Bingley's sake, that was why. Otherwise, in his misguided kindness, Bingley would have forgone the event he eagerly anticipated. Many and varied were the man's good traits, but what he lacked was the ability to grasp that others might take less pleasure than he in social engagements. There was no persuading him that as far as Darcy was concerned, the evening would have been far better spent with a book, and in writing to Georgiana at Ashford, his uncle's estate in Nottinghamshire. So there was nothing for it – an assembly it must be.

Their outdoor accoutrements once handed to attendants, the party of five were escorted deeper into the bowels of the sprawling building. A door was opened for them – and, without warning, country-town conviviality hit them at full blast. A blast of hot, stale air, to be precise, saturated with a mix of scents, of which that of victuals, rosewater and overheated humanity held the upper hand.

Their hearing was likewise assaulted by loud chatter, rustic music, stamping feet, hands clapping more or less in time, and lusty cries too, as the dancing couples twirled in the fast tempo of an energetic reel. Miss Bingley exchanged telling glances with her sister and released a dramatic sigh.

"Oh, Lord," muttered Mr Hurst.

Darcy inwardly concurred.

Bingley was the only one who advanced into the room with a wide grin and a spring in his step.

"How utterly charming," he said, to no one in particular.

"Oh, Charles," chorused his sisters, rolling their eyes.

Their plaintive tones were drowned out by the music, as well as by the booming voice of a ruddy-faced and portly gentleman, who seemed to have taken it upon himself to act as the master of ceremonies, and approached them with a loud exclamation of, "Ah! Capital, capital. My dear Mr Bingley, 'tis a vast pleasure to welcome you and your party."

And the rigmarole unavoidably began.

༄ঙ১ৄৄ

It came as no surprise to Darcy that fewer couples chose to line up for the following set and wait for the musicians to resume playing. Had he been in a charitable frame of mind, he might have attributed that fact to the dancers' need to draw breath and seek refreshments after the taxing reel. Yet his current disposition was not conducive to indulgent thoughts. Besides, he had seen it all before: the looks of overt curiosity and interest on young faces and old, which rendered them tediously alike, despite natural differences; the discreet or not-so-discreet sidle towards their party, in the hope of an introduction. And then, within less than five minutes, the whispers reached his ears.

"…a large estate in Derbyshire…"

"…ten thousand a year, I am told…"

"What a fine figure of a man!"

"I say. Uncommonly tall, a handsome countenance, and such a noble mien…"

Unlike their counterparts in fashionable locales, they did not even have the decency to keep their voices down, Darcy thought, the corner of his lips curling in distaste.

How did they contrive to be so well informed? Doubtlessly through the servants, he concluded, wishing Bingley would keep his house in better order.

A vain man might have taken pleasure in the lavish praise; but only a fool would be ruled by vanity and fail to grasp he would not have been quite so handsome in their eyes, had he not been so rich.

In a manner that strongly brought to mind the finger-like projections sent forth by an amoeba, clusters emerged from the amorphous mass of multicoloured muslin to insidiously but steadily gain upon Bingley. Yet the man remained oblivious to the danger, or vexingly unperturbed by it. Still sporting that wide grin, he had just renewed his acquaintance with the portly gentleman's wife and daughters, and was now being introduced to some other matrons and their collection of young charges. Any moment now, the same questionable honour would be bestowed upon him too, Darcy knew full well. He grimaced, wanting no part in the charade. He turned on his heel and walked away.

So did Miss Bingley, along with her brother by marriage and her sister. They chose a quiet spot by the panelling painted in functional dark grey but, to Darcy's way of thinking, they would be well advised to amble further.

He was proven right when, from a relatively safe distance, he could see the amoeba engulfing them as well. Bowing and still grinning – how did his jaw not ache? – Bingley was busily introducing his relations to the insatiable crowd. That is, until the musicians finally saw fit to pick up their instruments again, and the next dance began. Never one to shun cavorting in a ballroom, nor shrink from his duty where social niceties were concerned, Bingley joined the set, escorting the portly gentleman's eldest.

True to form, he proceeded to bound with relish, link arms with his partner and circle this way and that, beaming all the while, for all the world as though nothing could please him better. Just as predictably, at least to those who knew him well, he lost no time in identifying the prettiest young lady in attendance – one might safely say the only handsome girl in the entire room – and, as soon as the first two dances came to an end, he unobtrusively led his erstwhile partner towards the object of his interest and, by the looks of it, asked for the honour of an introduction.

His companion obliged him with uncommonly good grace in one so plain. Nary a frown creased her brow at having to relinquish his society in favour of a young woman about ten times prettier than herself. Thus, it was not long until Bingley had his wish and was leading the flaxen-haired beauty to the forming set.

Darcy caught his friend's glance as Bingley skipped by on a jaunty tune, hand in hand with the lady. A disarming grin was also cast in his direction and Darcy returned it, rolling his eyes upwards in amused exasperation. Pleased as Punch, Bingley shrugged and continued on his way.

When the eager dancers began to gather in new pairings for yet another set, Darcy reluctantly acknowledged it was time to do his duty by his friend's sisters. He was about to give precedence to Mrs Hurst, in recognition of her seniority in both age and status, but at his approach, Miss Bingley was prompt in coming forth and intercepting him.

"How are you bearing up, sir?" she asked, casting a disdainful glance around her. "The nothingness, and yet the self-importance of these people! I despair of my brother, urging us to attend such an insipid gathering. No refinement, no fashion and no taste."

As he caught sight of a couple of young women giggling inanely, each displaying a set of most unfortunate buck teeth, Darcy felt inclined to add *'no sense and no beauty'* to the charge, but thought better of it. Encouraging Miss Bingley in venting her frustrations would do nothing for his humour, and besides, the two ladies in question presumably could not help their inborn lack of sense any more than their dentition. Disinclined to tax himself with seeking a civil way of moving past Miss Bingley to give due precedence to Mrs Hurst, he addressed his question to the younger sister.

"May I request the favour of your hand for the next set?"

An unappealing sort of satisfaction overspread the lady's countenance, vying with surprise at his readiness to dance in such a setting. Yet Miss Bingley did not remark upon the latter sentiment. She took possession of his proffered arm with a distinctly proprietary gesture, and tilted her chin upwards as they joined the end of the set.

Eventually, Bingley did likewise, the lateness of his arrival a consequence of his reluctance to remove himself from the fair-haired beauty. Yet he had at last performed that feat, and was now escorting a very slight young woman whose countenance might have been pleasant enough, were it not for the surfeit of freckles. As if they had been holding back, waiting for him – which they might well have been – once Bingley and his new partner had lined up, the musicians struck the opening notes with gusto.

Darcy was relieved to find that the first dance was a reasonably dignified quadrille. The second was in a longways set but, praise be, neither a reel nor a hornpipe. Merely a country dance with the customary assortment of figures. Nothing stately about them, but no unseemly bounding either, so he resigned himself to the slow progression towards the top of the set, while the head couples were making their way in the opposite direction. Across from him, Miss Bingley glided and twirled with studied grace. To Darcy's right, Bingley was still chatting with his partner. That he should find quite so much to say to a complete stranger was very like him, but no less mystifying. As was the fact that he could natter incessantly and not misstep, Darcy inwardly scoffed.

Yet no sooner had he so uncharitably reflected on his friend's performance than he very nearly committed the unpardonable blunder of treading on the hem of Miss Bingley's dress as she slid past him to resume her place. For, just then, his glance disinterestedly drifted towards the top of the set – only to be arrested by a familiar countenance he would not have expected to encounter in a ballroom. Not even at an assembly such as this, for one would imagine that socialising with those in one's employ was as unacceptable in remote and unfashionable market-towns as anywhere else.

He blinked. He was mistaken, surely. The lady's apparel, while plain by the standards of the *ton*, bore no resemblance to that of a lady's maid or a lady's companion, and the same could be said of her unsophisticated but flattering hairstyle. The passing glance along the line of dancers must have played tricks on him. He *must* have been mistaken.

The head couples cast off and moved down the set, while the second couples progressed upwards, and with the distance thus diminished Darcy was promptly disabused of the comfortable notion. He was *not* mistaken. Laughing dark-brown eyes met his, and he caught a fleeting glimpse of twitching lips as she curtsied – whether to her *vis-à-vis*, or in pert acknowledgement of his look of shock, he could not tell – and then, reaching for her partner's hand, she turned away.

Darcy did likewise.

Unfortunately, he turned in the wrong direction.

"The other way, Mr Darcy," Miss Bingley belatedly supplied, just before he collided with her brother.

Thus, his humiliation was complete.

Chapter 7

The end of the second dance could not come soon enough. To Darcy, it seemed an age until it did, although in truth it was but minutes, mercifully uneventful in their passing. The other small mercy was that the last notes rang before the progression along the set brought him face to face and hand in hand with the very cause of his lapse in equanimity.

For now, a direct encounter was avoided. With nary a glance in his direction, she curtsied to her companion, then took the arm of another gentleman who came to apply for her hand in the next dance, and allowed him to lead her to the top of the new set. Yet discomfort lingered in her wake, to niggle at Darcy's mind. Doubtlessly he would eventually be faced with the mortification of having to provide some sort of an apology for his misapprehension. He had thought her in service, for goodness' sake. Worse still, said as much. Not to mention the unfortunate business of the half-crown. The very recollection of it made him cringe.

A firm proponent of tackling each unpalatable task in its own time, Darcy applied himself to the first. An apology to Miss Bingley for the instance of uncharacteristic clumsiness was decidedly in order. It was duly made and promptly accepted, and with that, his duty to her was discharged. All that remained was to escort her back to her sister, and he civilly offered to do so. Yet it soon became apparent that Bingley was of a different mind. For some reason, his friend's hand grasped his arm in an almighty grip. Whatever possessed the man, Darcy could not say. The presence of the two ladies precluded him from either snatching his arm away or irritably asking what the other was about. Nevertheless, Darcy could not help scowling as he cast his friend a questioning look.

The grip slackened, but the hand remained in place. More vexingly still, Bingley ignored him. His mien as affable as ever, he addressed himself to his freckled companion.

"Miss King, may I have the pleasure of introducing my sister to you?"

Now, had Bingley just stood up with the fair-haired goddess – she of the classically perfect features, statuesque beauty and bland smiles – Darcy might have excused his eagerness in promoting an acquaintance with his sister. That Bingley should resort to bodily restraining him for Miss King's sake was unaccountable.

It was only when he caught the fleeting wince as his friend shuffled forward that Darcy understood, and his ill-humour vanished, giving way to contrition. His fault. Of course. A glance was enough to clarify the matter. A dark smudge marred Bingley's pristine sock, just below the ankle, and it was his own clumsy foot that had put it there. It was *his* fault that his friend had to grab hold of his arm to steady himself, and was now awkwardly balancing on one foot, striving to remain inconspicuous about it. Goodness knows how he had achieved the feat of hiding his discomfort and finishing the dance in his condition. With minimal movements, presumably, and by dint of will.

Bingley must have inwardly blessed the two local gentlemen who came to ask his sister and Miss King for the pleasure and honour of their company in the next set. At least he was spared the task of escorting Miss King to her friends, and had only to apply himself to reaching the side of the room without limping. The other advantage of the ladies leaving him and Darcy to themselves was the freedom to speak freely, and he promptly availed himself of it as he lumbered towards the side of the room, unobtrusively leaning on his friend's arm.

"Heavens, man," he muttered. "Of all the times you could have chosen to make a spectacle of us!"

Snapping "You think I chose it?" would have been not only ungentlemanly, but also unkind under the circumstances, so Darcy held himself in check. He merely said, "I do beg your pardon."

"Miserable curmudgeon," the other quipped, once they were standing by the panelling, safely away from the focus of attention at the centre of the assembly room, where the dancing had just recommenced. "What good is your contrition to me now, eh?

I was about to ask her to stand up with me again, and now here I am trading insults with you, and she is partnering that bumbling buffoon. If this is your revenge for my browbeating you into attending, I say 'tis badly done, Darcy, and testament to your resentful temper and black heart," he finished with a grin and a failed attempt at nudging his friend in the ribs.

"There, now. Behave yourself. We are in company," Darcy retorted in a matching tone. "I begged your pardon. I will beg it again, if you wish. What more can I say?"

"You can begin by telling me how you came to trip – here, of all places – when you have never put a foot wrong in all the years I have known you. At least not in a ballroom."

Darcy shrugged. He was not at all inclined towards confessions. Not then and not there, anyway.

"Hertfordshire does not agree with me, it seems," he casually replied, then offered, "Shall I fetch you a glass of wine, or whatever restorative can be found?"

Bingley's brow quirked.

"You might as well, since there are no other amusements to be had."

"I am aggrieved to hear you say so," Darcy teasingly replied. "How about my conversation?"

His friend rolled his eyes in mock despair.

"Heaven help me. You call that amusement? Just go and find me some brandy, will you?"

"Very well. Brandy it is. Although, if memory serves, it has a strange propensity to weaken your ankles," Darcy said by way of a parting shot, and made his way towards the tables laden with refreshments.

Hurst was there before him, as was his wont. His neckcloth askew, he tapped the rim of his empty glass, and an obliging attendant duly filled it. Nevertheless, there was reason to hope that he would not disgrace himself in the course of the evening. Either through extensive practice or thanks to his ample figure, Hurst could hold his liquor.

Darcy eventually found what he was looking for. A cautious sip of the amber liquid assured him that, however lacking in refinement Bingley's new neighbours might be, at least he could not fault them for their taste in brandy.

Effortlessly balancing two glasses in one hand, he skirted the edges of the room to avoid the dancing couples, and eventually found his friend, just as he had left him. The only difference was that Bingley was now tapping his injured foot in time to the lively music. His ankle must be getting better.

Without a word, Darcy handed him a glass. The other took it, but made no move to drink, his gaze fixed on the capering couples.

"Take heart," Darcy muttered. "This dance is almost over, and you seem fit enough to join them for the next."

"How do you know?"

"Your left foot is dancing, and you are not wincing."

Bingley glanced downwards and raised his foot off the floor, to gingerly trace a circle with the tip of his shoe and test his friend's theory. The result was most encouraging, so he grinned widely and sipped his drink in celebration.

Darcy took a draught of his.

"Am I forgiven, then?" he muttered.

Bingley smirked.

"Only if she is not already engaged for the next set."

"Who?" Darcy asked, just to be contrary.

The other shook his head.

"I see you are determined to be vexing. You must know I am speaking of Miss Bennet."

"Am I correct in assuming that would be the flaxen-haired lady?"

"Tiresome wretch," his friend pleasantly retorted. "Had you given yourself the trouble of seeking introductions rather than standing about by yourself in the stupidest manner, you would already know." Nevertheless, patently unable to refrain from speaking of the object of his most recent fascination, he added, "Aye. You have guessed aright." He took a longer draught, and earnestly said, "Upon my word, just look at her. Is she not the most entrancing creature you have ever beheld?"

"No," Darcy incautiously replied, momentarily distracted by a light and pleasing figure going down the dance, and by rekindled recollections of pert smiles and laughing dark-brown eyes.

Bingley gave a surprised and disbelieving chuckle.

"*No?* As bluntly as that? I would call you out for it, you know," he good-humouredly said, "but one must be lenient towards the afflicted. I daresay you must be blind. Or have ink running through your veins. Come, man, admit it, she is an angel!"

"Ah. There we have it. Angel. Goddess. The fairest creature that has ever walked upon God's green earth. Will you ever change your repertoire, I wonder? Does your latest angel not deserve a new set of—?"

His teasing remark ended in a grunt, and the remainder of his brandy was very nearly spilled when Bingley's elbow found his ribs with a great deal more energy and purpose than in the earlier, half-hearted attempt.

"Hush," an admonishment came as well.

Upon reflection, the sharp nudge and the admonition must have been delivered because someone was approaching them – a tall gentleman in his late middle-age, judging by his countenance and greying temples. Bingley bowed to the newcomer, and the manner of his greeting served to show they were already acquainted. As for the name he uttered, it easily explained the shushing and the nudge.

"Good evening, Mr Bennet," he said. "A pleasure to see you here tonight."

"Likewise, sir. I trust you are keeping well. And, more to the point," the older gentleman continued before Bingley could reply, "I trust you have not been incapacitated. I fear we might have a host of inconsolable ladies on our hands, should it transpire that you have sprained your ankle after a mere three dances."

At a loss for a better answer, Bingley could only stammer:

"I… thank you, sir. I am quite well."

"I am glad to hear it."

Whether or not either gentleman was disposed to say anything further was of little interest to Darcy – which was just as well, because the matter remained undecided. Their small group was joined by a fourth: a matron sporting a crimson turban bedecked with two exceedingly long feathers. A brash and voluble matron, too, Darcy soon discovered, and he silently cursed the tedious evening, the company and his luck.

"Mr Bingley," the woman exclaimed, beaming. "So good of you to come. I hope you are well-entertained. Have you sampled the sweetmeats? The best that could be had at Harrison's, I assure you.

Oh, speaking of delicacies, I hope you will do us the honour of dining with us soon. Mr Phillips and I will be thrilled to have you and your party at our table."

Darcy caught the glance she cast in his direction, clearly desirous of an introduction, and took a step back. He sipped his drink and looked the other way. He would not go as far as to turn on his heel and abandon Bingley to his fate. His conscience forbade it for, after all, were it not for his earlier blunder, Bingley would now be dancing with his angel, rather than standing there, a fixed target for the locals. Nonetheless, there would be the devil to pay, should Bingley foist that woman upon him in retaliation.

"Or better still," the loud matron seamlessly continued with growing energy, "perhaps you should give a dinner at Longbourn for our new neighbours, Brother. I will be happy to assist Jane with the arrangements, but I assure you, she does not need my guidance. Our dear girl is perfectly capable of seeing to a good table and keeping house to the best standards. Bless her, Jane takes after my poor sister. Oh, the dear soul, how she would have enjoyed this evening!"

Whatever had befallen the said poor sister, Darcy did not wish to know. He could only rejoice in her absence from the gathering, if she was anything like her relation, now standing there, bold as brass, singing the praises of the paragon who kept a good table and an exemplary house, for the benefit of the well-off, unattached new neighbour, who *must* be in want of a wife.

With a swift move from his elbow, Darcy brought the glass to his lips and drained the remainder of the brandy in one draught. A fortnight in this godforsaken place? Lord almighty, a se'nnight would suffice. The brazen tactlessness of those people! Was Hertfordshire so lacking in marriage-minded men that any newcomer must be hounded in assembly rooms with recitals of virtues and accomplishments?

"So, what say you, Brother? Mr Bingley? Dinner at Longbourn a few days hence? I think it a splendid notion. On Thursday, perhaps?" the confounded woman pertinaciously pressed them, but her untoward insistence did not seem to injure her at all in Bingley's eyes, for he grinned widely at the prospect, which strengthened Darcy's suspicion that the much-lauded Jane was none other than his goddess.

However, unlike the matron, Bingley was not lost to every notion of propriety, and did not hasten to accept an invitation that had not come from the master of the house. He waited for Mr Bennet to second Mrs Phillips, but in that he was disappointed, for the gentleman merely said:

"A splendid notion indeed, my dear, but we must be mindful of the consequences. How should we bear our neighbours' wrath if we hasten to infringe upon their right to host Mr Bingley and his party?"

Nonplussed, Bingley and the matron stared. She was the first to recover, and impatiently replied with a flourish of her hand.

"Oh, nonsense. Wrath? Surely not, there is no cause for that. They will— Oh, here come the girls," she gleefully announced, distracted from her purpose by the sight of the dancers beginning to disperse when the musical instruments fell silent.

Bingley's countenance acquired a conspicuous glow, and his wide grin was reinstated as he beheld his angel being escorted to her father. Compelled to remind himself that snorting was uncivil, Darcy sought to muffle the sound as best he could – only to find it promptly and most effectively smothered.

The second encounter with sparkling dark-brown eyes was quite as startling as the first. With a sinking feeling, he noted her approach and belatedly registered snippets of information, subconsciously gained, as they fell neatly into place. Thus, he was marginally better prepared for what followed. The sinking feeling, however, was unchanged, when Mrs Phillips spoke:

"You are already acquainted with my eldest niece, Mr Bingley, are you not? This is Lizzy – that is to say, Elizabeth. You will meet Kitty and Lydia when you come for dinner. The poor dears, they so love to dance, but my brother still thinks them too young for assemblies," she added with a dark glance at Mr Bennet. "But what of you, sir?" she resumed. "Do you like to dance yourself?"

Beaming, Bingley saw his chance and took it.

"There is nothing I love better, madam. And if Miss Bennet is not otherwise engaged, may I be so bold as to claim the next two dances?"

His angel blushed.

"I am not engaged, sir."

The matron folded her hands before her, and the smile that crept upon her lips was intolerably smug. But she was not quite finished, Darcy discovered, when he found himself suddenly addressed without the benefit of a prior introduction.

"And you, sir? Are you fond of dancing, too?"

To his credit, despite his obvious discomfort, Bingley stepped in to rectify an error that was not his.

"Oh, I do beg your pardon," he stammered. "May I present my friend, Mr Darcy? Darcy, allow me to introduce Mrs Phillips and her brother by marriage, Mr Bennet."

"Delighted, I am sure," the matron cooed.

"Delighted," the older gentleman beside her echoed, a quirk in his lips as he finally chose to forsake the joys of silent observation. "I am pleased to see you found your way to Netherfield after all, sir."

Darcy's back stiffened. Had *she* regaled the entire neighbourhood with the sorry tale of their encounter? Or was he reading more than he ought in an innocent remark? Involuntarily, his glance flashed towards Miss Elizabeth Bennet. But she was not looking his way. Her eyes were on her parent, as she shook her head in something very much like affectionate reproof. Darcy cringed – again. Whether or not she had entertained the whole of Meryton with accounts of his *faux pas* would be revealed in due course. Yet it was plain as day that she had not kept it from her father.

Across from him, the loud matron once more laid claim to his attention.

"You are very welcome to Hertfordshire, Mr Darcy. I hope you have come here eager to dance, as your friend has."

He promptly delivered the reply that came instinctively to mind.

"I thank you, madam. I rarely dance."

"I cannot imagine why," the woman impudently quipped, raising his ire with the crass hint at his earlier ineptitude. "Nevertheless, I hope you will oblige us again tonight, for I'll wager you will not easily find such lively music, nor such pretty partners," she insisted, the ends of her feathers bobbing significantly in the direction of her second niece.

Miss Elizabeth Bennet was not best pleased, Darcy noted. She might have taken umbrage at the brash manner in which she had been recommended to his attention or, just as likely, at the very notion of standing up with one who had mistaken her for a servant. Either way, there was not gratitude but censure in her glance, when it shifted from her father to her aunt. All things considered, that did not surprise him. It was his own response that did.

"I would be honoured," he heard himself say.

❧ ❦ ❧

From the frying pan into the fire. No better way to describe his situation. What the deuce was he doing there, anyway? Standing up with her – what the devil was he thinking?

He ought to say something. She clearly expected it. She would. Say what, though? An apology was mandatory, of course, and it was high time he delivered it. They had been dancing for well-nigh a quarter of an hour, and still nothing was said.

She moved with grace and ease, a maddening twinkle in her eyes, as though she was finding the circumstance diverting. Whether or not she was also deriving a great measure of amusement from his discomfort was impossible to tell, but he thought it very likely.

His jaw tightened as he cursed Bingley's Hertfordshire estate and the miserable roads that had mired his carriage. Of all the vexations in the world, what he detested most was to feel at a disadvantage, and there was no doubt that with his mortifying gaffe he had firmly placed himself in that position. Oh, the devil take it! Let the apology be made, and the entire business laid to rest.

Admirable plan, in theory, yet the words he should employ on the occasion continued to elude him. Damn the words, he would do well to watch his steps instead. If he should disgrace himself again… He frowned. It did not bear thinking.

"Might I ask, sir, do you always dance in perfect silence, or only when in a fit of pique?"

Of all the answers he could have given to her overtures, he settled on what was doubtlessly the stupidest.

"I beg your pardon?"

Across from him, his fair partner daintily shrugged.

"I imagine you think yourself defrauded of a half-crown. Let me assure you, young Tommy and his relations greatly appreciated your largesse."

What the devil was he to say to that, Darcy wondered, more than a little disconcerted to discover that a slip of a girl had more pluck than he, and valiantly sallied forth where he did not dare venture.

But of course she would. She had the upper hand. Be that as it may, at the very least he should now follow into the breach. He knew as much, yet he had long lost the habit of apologising. He could scarce remember the last instance when he had been compelled to own himself in the wrong. The words stuck in his throat. Yet he forced them out with determination.

"I beg your pardon," he said, oblivious to the fact that, the different meaning and inflexion aside, he had done nothing more than repeat his first sentence. No belated realisation dawned. When he brought himself to elaborate, it was for the sole purpose of self-justification. "In my defence, I must say it was the first time that I came across a gentlewoman so unconventionally attired."

Late in awakening, on this occasion realisation hit. No sooner had the second sentence passed his lips than he cursed his shocking propensity for blunders. There he was, compounding the original offence with the cardinal sin of remarking upon a lady's attire – and unfavourably, too. He braced himself for her displeasure. Yet, to his astonishment, she laughed.

"Pray tell me, what would you regard as conventional attire when you are visiting your tenants? This, perhaps?" she asked, a slight gesture of her hand indicating their ballroom apparel. "Or do you prefer to leave that task to your steward?"

Darcy bristled. What sort of foppish absentee landlord did she take him for? And what did she know of him and all his duties? His reply was crisp and prompt.

"I do not. And I am not a fop, Miss Bennet."

"Nor am I a housemaid. But I daresay we have already established that."

In a sullen and resentful tone, her retort might have classed as a reproach. Yet the cheerful archness of her manner could not fail to emphasise the diverting side of the impossible situation. An insistent smile tugged at the corner of his lips. He let it have its way as he conceded her the point.

"*Touché.* Yes, I believe we have."

She circled around him in a light step, then gracefully cast off.

When the pattern of the dance brought them close enough for conversation, she airily said:

"Very well. Now that we have exhausted that stimulating topic, I fear we are left with the commonplaces. I think it only fair that you should choose the next subject matter."

"I must decline that honour. I would not know where to start."

"Oh, but 'tis quite simple. What do you imagine we might have spoken of during this dance, had we met in more… shall we say, conventional circumstances?"

They would not have spoken of anything at all, for in that case they would not have stood up together, honesty compelled him to inwardly own. Yet he kept that to himself, and parried her question with another:

"Do you talk by rule then, while you are dancing?"

"I believe I do. It would look odd to be entirely silent for half an hour. Admittedly, striking up a conversation with a perfect stranger has its difficulties. Thankfully, in cases such as these, one might easily remark upon the size of the room, or the number of couples."

"Ah. The fine art of small talk," he blithely said, and she arched a brow.

"Not a proponent, I take it?"

"Not as such."

"I see. I will not deny it, the joys of small talk are nothing to the satisfaction of coining words of wisdom that would amaze the whole room and be handed down to posterity with all the *éclat* of a proverb. But this noble endeavour requires too much dedication. I am happy to leave the agora to the philosophers. There is ample reward in simple pleasures."

"Is this my cue to inquire into the sort of simple pleasures you favour? Apart from small talk, that is. And visiting tenants – on foot."

"Oh. Do I detect censure?"

"No. That would be uncivil. I merely thought that riding would serve better."

"It would. But I seldom ride."

"Why is that?"

She gave a little tinkling laugh.

"I should be sorry to discourage you in your valiant effort at small talk, sir, but I fear this will not do. You are straying from the realm of commonplaces. You might wish to observe instead that, in your experience, the exceedingly muddy lanes of Hertfordshire seem ill-suited for long country walks. Then I would concede that you saw them at their worst. The last few days have been uncommonly wet. That would provide you with the opportunity to ask about the vagaries of the weather in our little corner of the world, and I might inform you that we can expect rain every other day from late October all the way into March, but the summers are generally dry. At which point you might give a suitably brief account of the most remarkable storm you have experienced, or the warmest day or some such, and we might safely reach the end of the dance, and part in mutual satisfaction."

Darcy's lips gave an involuntary twitch.

"I thank you for your assistance. Perhaps the wisest choice would be to assure you that whatever you wish me to say will be said."

"That is the best choice by far. You are to be commended. And now we may be silent."

She must have had a better grasp than he on tailoring conversations to the duration of a dance, for the last notes rang within minutes of that singular exchange.

She was engaged for the rest of the evening.

Would he have stood up with her again otherwise? The very notion! Of course not. He had never singled out a young woman in this fashion. Why should he make an exception for Miss Elizabeth Bennet? True enough, she had a very pleasing countenance and form, remarkably expressive eyes, and her conversation was, to say the least, intriguing. She did not prattle. She did not pry. She had not even mentioned Derbyshire, Netherfield or Bingley. And she had scarcely spoken of herself. In truth, she had disclosed little to nothing. Except that she seldom chose to ride – although she did not say why – and that she favoured simple pleasures. An unsophisticated young lass, born and bred in the country.

Why was it, then, that for the remainder of the evening he could scarce keep his eyes off her?

Chapter 8

The mellow sunlight put autumn fires in the foliage of the chestnuts bordering the drive as the two gentlemen rode away from the Netherfield stables together. It was a great morning for a ride, and spending most of the day at some distance from the house and its other occupants was a welcome prospect, Darcy could not fail to own.

"So, towards the eastern boundary today?" he asked, only to find his friend casting him a rather sheepish glance.

"In fact, I was thinking…" Bingley began, then his uncertain tones grew earnest. "Would you mind awfully if we were to call at Longbourn first?"

"Again?" Darcy grimaced. Upon reflection, he might have been a trifle more observant and noted sooner that, while never foppish, his friend was dressed with uncommon care for a ride over the estate. This should have been his first clue.

The other made a face.

"Yes, well. I fear that calling with my sisters did me no favours so far."

With a tilt of his head, Darcy silently acknowledged him the point. Mrs Hurst and Miss Bingley had reluctantly accompanied them on both their other visits, and made no efforts to show themselves pleased with either the country or the company.

For the entire duration of the calls, they sat with tight smiles pasted on their faces, and opened their lips to deliver but the bare minimum that civility required.

They sought to keep the visits short, but in that they were disappointed. Bingley refused to take any hint, and during their second call in particular, their host grew particularly chatty.

The more laconic their replies, the more eagerly Mr Bennet engaged them in conversation, until Darcy had sufficient reason to suspect it was done on purpose, for the older gentleman's private amusement.

The supposition was confirmed when he chanced to catch a brief exchange of glances between Mr Bennet and his second daughter. Her eyes held a glint of affectionate reproof as she ever so discreetly shook her head, just as she had when Mr Bennet had teased him at the Meryton assembly about finding his way to Netherfield at last.

They made a singular pair, the second Miss Bennet and her father, and in different circumstances, Darcy might have felt inclined to inwardly censure the latter for thus toying with his guests in response to their lack of civility. Yet Miss Bingley's and Mrs Hurst's sour-faced impatience was more than a little entertaining, and their reluctance to assist their brother in establishing himself in the neighbourhood sufficiently blameable for Darcy to decide that, however odd the gentleman's ways, he could not wholly disapprove of Mr Bennet.

"As you wish," Darcy saw fit to go along with Bingley's morning plans, so they turned right instead of left at the end of the drive.

The ride to Longbourn took very little time, and they soon found themselves before the Bennets' abode. A small and compact place it was, set in a modest park. So compact, in fact, that there seemed to be virtually no layers separating the family's amusements from approaching callers. Darcy had yet to dismount when he heard a voice greatly resembling Miss Elizabeth Bennet's laughingly admonishing one of her sisters:

"Goodness, Lydia, no more voile trimmings. It will look like a cabbage."

"Nonsense," came the loud reply. "I followed our aunt Gardiner's pattern point by point. 'Tis all the rage in town, did she not say so in her last letter to you?"

"Well, Lizzy," a masculine voice retorted – most likely Mr Bennet's – "if your sister wishes to wear a cabbage for a bonnet, let her. 'Tis harmless enough. Just mind you do not leave it by Mrs Hill's door, child, or she might shred it and put it in our bubble and squeak, and these days my teeth are not up to the challenge."

Peals of laughter followed the quip, and much as civility compelled him to refrain from looking in the direction of the open window whence they came, Darcy caught a glimpse of the gentleman, seated in an easy chair with his paper, and of Miss Lydia coming to perch a bonnet on his head.

She must have spotted them in her turn, for she gave a little cry of "Oh, Jane, Lizzy, look!", whereupon she retrieved her bonnet and vanished from Darcy's line of vision.

In due course, the housekeeper – the aforementioned Mrs Hill? – escorted him and Bingley within, and opened a door to admit them into a very small parlour. Miss Bingley would have called it rustic. The room could barely accommodate a few chairs, a dresser and a table that was currently covered by an assortment of ribbons, feathers, voile and muslin. The bonnet in question was now atop the heap, and Darcy felt compelled to agree with Miss Elizabeth Bennet: it did look like a cabbage.

He smiled and glanced her way, to see her rising from her curtsy. Her rather fine eyes were crinkled at the corners when they met his, and her lips gave an answering twitch.

"Ah, gentlemen. Come in," Mr Bennet said as he stood to greet them. "You find us engaged in homely pursuits. But I imagine you have little interest in bonnet-trimming, so I daresay I should escort you into my book-room for some other diversions," he suggested with a casual gesture towards the door they had just come through.

Looking more than a little disappointed, Bingley did not budge. Instead, he darted a glance at the one member of the family he had come to call upon, and stammered, "I thank you, sir. Well, I— That will not be necessary. That is to say..." he floundered, and despite the prelude, he said nothing further.

Suppressing the wish to roll his eyes, Darcy felt he should assist him, but in good conscience he could claim to possess neither skill nor interest in bonnet-trimming. Fortunately for Bingley, Mr Bennet took pity on him.

"Or we could all repair to the drawing room instead, if you prefer. I daresay we might find some other topic of conversation. Ring the bell for tea, Kitty, would you? Unless our guests would care for coffee?"

"Tea would suit us admirably, sir," Bingley spoke for both, and although Darcy would have chosen to be less emphatic, he could not disagree. "And we would be happy to remain here, I assure you. There is no need to move into the drawing room."

The words tripped off Bingley's tongue this time, with nary a hesitation at having to use such a lofty name in referring to the barely larger parlour in which they had been received on the previous occasions, but Darcy let it pass with no telling glance towards his friend. Instead, he followed Bingley's example and took one of the two available seats, while the Miss Bennets busied themselves with clearing the table. In short order, the fripperies were tidied away into a couple of wicker baskets that disappeared behind one of the chairs, just as the housekeeper and a maid came to bring refreshments.

That was prompt. The household seemed competently run, for all its unremarkable scale and status, and despite the lack of a mistress. Sadly, Mrs Bennet had passed away some years back, Darcy had learned. Thus, her daughters had to seek assistance and maternal guidance from her sister, Mrs Phillips. Thankfully, they had not learned their manners from that vulgar matron, Darcy had concluded on closer acquaintance.

As to their housekeeping skills, he could not say if they were likewise owed to their departed mother – or their aunt. He could not comment on Mrs Phillips', as the dinner invitation she had threatened at the Meryton assembly had mercifully come to nothing. It must have only been a ploy to coax Mr Bennet into giving a dinner for the Netherfield party, and thus display his daughters' talents. However, out of right-mindedness or reluctance to entertain, so far the gentleman had not obliged.

Perhaps it was just as well. The two dinners given in their honour by the families at Stoke Abbey and Purvis Lodge had been a trial. Too much insipidity and noise. Given the size of Longbourn – noticeably smaller than both the aforementioned residences – the Bennets would have settled for a more intimate affair, and in view of the father and eldest daughters' deportment, there was reason to believe they would have welcomed their guests into their home with more genuine warmth. From the little Darcy had garnered on his previous visits, and this one in particular, it was a happy home, albeit unconventional. It put him in mind of his land agent's.

Many a time he had come to find Mr Parker amid some form of cheerful rumpus or another.

"So, Mr Bingley," Mr Bennet asked, once his daughters had supplied him, the visitors and themselves with refreshments. "Are you comfortably settled at Netherfield now?"

"Very much so, sir. It suits me admirably," Bingley declared, woefully unable to find his words and resorting to *'admirable'* again. "Are you familiar with the estate?"

Darcy gave a mental snort. Of all the idiotic questions! Of course Mr Bennet would be familiar with a neighbouring estate. He must have lived within a few miles of Netherfield all his life, and he was five-and-fifty if he was a day. Darcy's mental snort was followed by another, when Bingley grinned rather foolishly at the eldest Miss Bennet, thus accounting for his distraction and sudden lack of conversational skills.

"Yes, I have been occasioned to learn something of it, by and by," Mr Bennet said with a diverted look, and Darcy, who had studied the deeds and the map of the estate with some care and attention, felt compelled to rescue Bingley from his own ineptitude and his host's wit.

"From what I gathered, Netherfield and Longbourn share a three-mile boundary along the river. We rode that way yesterday, if you remember."

"Ah. So we did. And you pointed out some works to strengthen the riverbank on the Longbourn side, and advised me to mirror them on mine. That is the stretch of land you are referring to, is it not?"

"Yes, precisely."

"That was good advice, sir," Mr Bennet said. "Mr Bingley might wish to follow it. The Lea floods quite spectacularly in the spring."

"That was what Darcy suspected. Apparently, he could recognise the signs," Bingley said blithely, once more revealing his inexperience as a landowner to all and sundry.

Anyone with eyes in their head and a modicum of interest in farming would have recognised the signs, Darcy thought, and found Mr Bennet's glance settling upon him yet again.

"I take it that your estate is similarly plagued, sir," the older gentleman said, and Darcy nodded.

"Some of the low-lying pastures are."

"I could ask Darcy for advice on how to address the matter, but I would be most grateful for yours, sir, if you are amenable," Bingley said to their host. "Perhaps different methods are required in Hertfordshire."

Mr Bennet shrugged.

"Shoring up is shoring up, sir. But you are welcome to my opinion, if you care to have it."

"You are very gracious. Perhaps we might discuss this in more detail later," Bingley replied, finally grasping that his attempts to court Mr Bennet's favour by means of agricultural conversations must have made for a tedious topic for the ladies.

If they found it so, the two eldest hid it well. It was the two youngest who had ceased to attend, and were giggling inanely in their corner, once they had finished their tea.

However courteous and obliging by nature, on this occasion Bingley must have had his own purposes in mind, and not Miss Lydia and Miss Kitty's entertainment, when he glanced out of the window and spoke again:

"Your garden is admirable, Miss Bennet," he said, making Darcy roll his eyes at the third *'admirable'* in less than thirty minutes.

His mildly exasperated look encountered Miss Elizabeth's, and found it held amusement. And well it might. Heavens, could Bingley be any more conspicuous? Aye, he could apparently, for he resumed:

"The autumn colours lend it particular charm. I should be very glad to have a closer look, if I may be so bold as to ask for the pleasure of your company."

"Oh, yes, let us walk out," Miss Lydia agreed, although no one had asked her. "Shall we show Mr Bingley and Mr Darcy around the shrubbery, Papa?"

Mr Bennet gave a vague gesture of acceptance.

"By all means, if it takes your fancy. I would not be unsociable, but neither will I object to reading my paper while the rest of you admire the autumn colours," he finished with somewhat of a drawl.

There was not much to admire, truth be told. The small garden held no eye-catching specimens rendered even more attractive by the season, just some trees with yellowed leaves and a variety of shrubs. Nevertheless, Bingley did not dawdle. All eagerness, he left the room on Miss Bennet's heels, and Darcy saw no option but to follow with the others.

Miss Lydia and Miss Kitty promptly ran off towards a swing hanging from the tallest tree without stopping to excuse themselves, and proceeded to take turns in it with shrieks of delight, leaving their sisters to show the visitors around the garden.

Bingley was rather less than pleased, Darcy noted, to amble at his side rather than arm in arm with Miss Bennet, who was walking ahead with Miss Elizabeth. Nevertheless, he went forth with good grace, until he stopped to look up and exclaim:

"What a lovely treehouse!"

He might have chosen a more manly epithet, Darcy thought, but praise be, he did not call the construction admirable. Whether or not he had paused out of genuine interest or in an endeavour to manoeuvre himself into offering Miss Bennet his arm was hard to tell, but Bingley continued:

"The youngster who had the run of it strikes me as a lucky little fellow. It must have afforded hours of amusement."

"It did," Miss Elizabeth replied. "I speak with good information, as I was that lucky youngster."

Bingley's eyes widened into a ludicrous picture of disbelief.

"You?"

For his part, Darcy was rather more adept at keeping his surprise in check, but he was no less astounded to find that she would make so little effort to portray herself as demure and ladylike, but openly declared herself a tomboy. It was as if she did not know or did not care that a languid manner was *de rigueur* in her more sophisticated counterparts.

Perhaps sophistication was not within her reach. Or perhaps the tomboyish air was a different sort of affectation. But nay, that was probably unkind. The playful twitch of her lips was wholly artless when she replied:

"Just so. I have always favoured the outdoors. The treehouse also happened to be a perfect spot for reading."

"Was it? Up there?" Bingley rather ungentlemanly continued to give voice to his incredulity.

"An uncommon choice, I grant you," Miss Elizabeth conceded, then indicated her younger sisters, who were still making a considerable racket. "As you can see, our house can be rather boisterous at times. The treetops – not so much."

"Might I ask what you were reading?" Bingley asked, sidling closer to her elder sister.

"Oh, anything and everything," she said with a vague little gesture.

"Do you know, Darcy," Bingley said, taking another step towards Miss Bennet as he kept looking up – it was a mercy that he did not trip – "I think I chanced upon *your* treehouse once. But I imagine you did not need to take refuge there to read. Pemberley must have been sufficiently quiet."

Aye. Too quiet, Darcy inwardly acknowledged. His treehouse was never used as a reading room, but had served in turn as a quarterdeck, a mountaintop or a castle turret, over hours of imaginative amusement with Fitzwilliam – and with one who later chose to make designs upon his sister's happiness and fortune, a grim thought intruded, and brought a grim scowl with it.

An affectionate soul, but never one for tact, Bingley was quick to offer:

"Oh, I beg your pardon. I thought they were happy recollections."

Darcy forced them all aside, good recollections and bad, and smoothed his countenance into the expected blandness.

"They were," was all he said.

A vast deal more tactful than Bingley, seemingly, the second Miss Bennet saw fit to change the subject.

"So, where do you hail from, Mr Darcy?" she asked.

"Derbyshire. Pemberley, near Lambton," he told her, convinced she already knew. The gossips of Meryton must have gained enough information from Bingley's servants, and widely distributed it.

But the wide smile that curled the corners of her lips seemed to be artless yet again, and her surprise genuine.

"Lambton? How extraordinary."

Failing to see what was so extraordinary about it, Darcy asked, "How so?"

"One of my aunts was born and raised in Lambton. A charming and most welcoming village."

The coincidence could be regarded as remarkable, Darcy allowed, so his guarded manner softened by a fraction.

"I take it you have visited it."

"Indeed. My uncle and aunt once took me with them on a tour of pleasure to the north of England. Sadly, it was rather a long time ago, and I remember little."

"You probably remember the bookshop in Lambton," Darcy observed, given the disclosures about the uses for her treehouse.

"I know there was one, and that we visited it," she said. "But I must own that I was less of a voracious reader at the time, and I have far more vivid recollections of a different place – a lovely shop on Angel Street, with a window full of unsurpassed delights."

A warm smile stole upon Darcy's lips without his notice.

"Mrs Allen's sweetshop, was it?"

She gave a musical little laugh.

"Of course. What else? I must say, that lady's almond macaroons and cherry confits still remain the best I have ever tasted."

Darcy's smile grew wider.

"I agree. I will be sure to let Mrs Allen know when next I see her that her confectionery made such a lasting impression."

"Pray do, and convey my thanks. Oh, and my compliments for her lavender drops. I have not found their like anywhere else."

Darcy could not fail to endorse that opinion too.

"My sister missed them greatly when she left Derbyshire for town. She found some consolation at Gunter's, eventually. His lavender *cachous* were deemed a fair substitute. But she still urged me to call upon Mrs Allen with a sizeable order, every time I came to see her at Mrs Rossiter's school."

Belatedly, he came to notice that his unexpected exchange with the second Miss Bennet had also served to advance Bingley's case with the first. Seeing them thus engaged, his friend had offered Miss Bennet his arm and the pair of them were now sauntering ahead. Thus, Darcy saw no good reason why he should not offer his arm to Miss Elizabeth as they resumed their tour and their conversation, paying but little heed to garden features or autumnal colours.

"I must confess I have not sampled Mr Gunter's *cachous* as yet," she said. "Oddly enough, I have been all the way to Mrs Allen's shop in Lambton, but I have yet to visit Gunter's."

That was a surprise. Surely, Gunter's was not beyond her reach, either in pecuniary terms or otherwise.

"Oh? I thought Longbourn was within easy distance from town."

"It is. But we do not travel there often."

Darcy thought it impolitic to ask why.

"Did you visit Pemberley while you were in the north?" he asked instead.

"Unfortunately not, although we were meant to. My aunt remembered it fondly from her girlhood, along with your parents' kindness to the children in the village, and she would have dearly liked to tour the gardens again. But the weather was against us. There was a terrific storm on the day set aside for our visit. Hailstones the size of walnuts. We had to abandon our plans."

"Oh. Could you not drive up to Pemberley another time?"

She shook her head.

"It was unwise, upon reflection, but we left it too late, for our last day in Derbyshire. On the following morning we had to begin our journey home."

"A pity. I hope you will visit on your next sojourn in the area. It would be a pleasure to show you around. Or if my sister and I should be from home, my housekeeper and the head-gardener will gladly do the office in my stead."

She made no answer other than a vague smile and a nod of her head by way of thanks, which was somewhat of a disappointment after the previous affable exchange. Revisiting distant recollections of Mrs Allen's delectable treasure trove, along with all its heart-warming associations, was a far cry from the habitual tedium of trading civil nothings with a new acquaintance. Recapturing that air held some appeal, so Darcy experimented with a wry grin as he took his cue from their first conversation, at the public assembly.

"So, would you say that was the worst storm you had ever seen?"

She easily caught his game and laughed.

"Oh, definitely. What of yourself? Did any other region best Derbyshire in that regard?"

"Cambridge did, repeatedly. And Westmorland, once."

"Oh? I would have thought it would be the other way around."

"Perhaps, had I spent as much time in Westmorland as I did in Cambridge."

"At one of the colleges, I assume?"

He nodded.

"Peterhouse. That was where I made Bingley's acquaintance."

Several yards ahead, the man in question gave a sign that he heard his name mentioned, but did not turn, which was no wonder.

True to form, it pleased him to reserve all his attention for the current object of his fancy, and Darcy left him be. The second Miss Bennet was a pleasant companion, so he could not entirely regret the change of plans and the abandoned survey of Netherfield. For it would be abandoned, Darcy could not doubt it. Bingley seemed in no haste to depart.

He was right. It was well-nigh another hour before they took their leave – an almost uncivilly long visit. But their host did not seem overly inclined to take objection. He bade them adieu in reasonable good humour, and even agreed to ride with Bingley on the following day and discuss the improvements along the Longbourn riverbank.

Chapter 9

Netherfield, 25 October 1811

Despite Bingley's insistence that he join them, Darcy saw fit to leave him and Mr Bennet to it. His friend had to learn to be his own man and manage his estate without aid or interference. So he chose to ride beyond Meryton instead, and thus while away a fair number of hours.

Not enough of them, apparently, he concluded when he returned to Netherfield to find that Bingley was still out. Worse still, he found himself the target of Miss Bingley's assiduous attentions and Mrs Hurst's bland conversation.

By dinnertime, he was dearly wishing he had joined his friend after all, for Bingley abandoned him to the others' mercy for his comfort and entertainment. His friend sent word that they should not keep dinner waiting on his behalf, for he had been asked to partake of the evening repast at Longbourn.

"He will be here in time for the third remove, I imagine," Miss Bingley sniffed when one of the footmen came to deliver the message. "They are bound to keep country hours."

Her disdain for Hertfordshire and everyone in it was liberally aired over dinner with Mrs Hurst's eager contributions, which could not fail to tax Darcy's patience. Miss Bingley's determination to recommend herself to him as a desirable life companion could not be any plainer – she had given repeated proof of it. Which begged the question, was she so devoid of understanding as to imagine that endless complaints about the wilds of Hertfordshire would serve to recommend her to one whose home was in the wilds of the north?

He could not know whether or not the Bennets kept country hours. Any which way, it was ten o'clock by the time Bingley returned to Netherfield, to find him nursing his brandy in the library.

His friend procured himself a drink and chose a seat, grinning from ear to ear.

"Such a charming family," he enthused, with a long sigh of contentment as he stretched his legs towards the fire. "Mr Bennet kept me on my toes, I grant you. Quicker wits than mine are needed to keep up with him. I daresay you would not have struggled quite as much as I did. Still, for all his singular manner, he is most obliging. And his daughters are an absolute delight."

"His eldest in particular, I imagine," Darcy drawled, rolling his eyes.

"That goes without saying. Darcy, she is—"

"Pray save your breath," he forestalled his besotted friend with a raised hand. "I know. She is the most beautiful angel you have ever beheld, and with the sweetest disposition. Now, I say I leave you to your blissful recollections of the day and retire to my chambers. It would serve us both much better."

Far from offended, Bingley shrugged, his grin still in place.

"Very well, then. As you wish."

༺ஓ ஓ༻

Hertfordshire, 26 October 1811

By nature, Bingley was not an early riser. On that morning in particular, he was later than ever. He must have stayed up for a fair while with his brandy and his mental images of his most recent angel, Darcy assumed.

For his part, he had long broken his fast and had secluded himself in the library, only to be discovered there by Miss Bingley and asked to accompany her on a walk. He could not find a gentlemanly way to refuse her, so Darcy did penance in the shrubbery for the best part of an hour, until the dreary company drove him to distraction. He made his excuses then, and repaired to the stables, no longer willing to postpone his ride until Bingley deigned to leave his quarters.

It was only when he found himself on the lane towards Longbourn that Darcy reined in and drew to a halt. What the blazes was he doing? He was not about to call upon the Bennets, surely. Of course not. On his own too, the very notion!

He turned his mount about and headed right at the following crossroads, endeavouring to pay heed to his surroundings, so as not to find himself lost in the Hertfordshire countryside again. It was too much to hope *she* would come to his rescue for a second time, he thought with a twitch of his lips and a rueful shake of his head at the recollection of his mortifying blunder.

Thank goodness she had a sense of humour and had not taken offence. It would have been a shame to offend her, and no credit to either Bingley or himself. A deuced uncomfortable business too, were he to come across a wronged neighbour every day. Casual chats about Lambton and whatnot pleased him better. Darcy smiled. He really should make a point of conveying her compliments to Mrs Allen when he returned home. The dear old soul would like that.

For some reason, his frame of mind was too mellow for tearing across the country at a gallop, and he would much rather take in the pleasant surroundings at a leisurely pace.

He had not progressed another mile along the road, when he came across a prospect that was more pleasing than many. A bend in the road once negotiated, the coppice thinned, then vanished to reveal an open stretch of land covered in an expanse of blue and yellow wildflowers. The mild climate of the south must have encouraged a late-autumn flowering, he dispassionately thought, when suddenly his gaze was arrested by a slender figure draped in a russet cloak, most picturesquely outlined against the cheerful backdrop.

He might have thought he could see Georgiana on her favourite springtime walk, Darcy told himself, in a disingenuous endeavour to explain why he had been jolted to attention. Disingenuous, aye, for even before he came close enough to distinguish her features, he knew full well who the young lady was.

She had not spotted him yet, as she bent down now and then to add to the small posy she was holding, and Darcy began to wonder whether he should either retreat or attract her notice in some manner, when his obliging mount did so for him with a loud snort.

She turned around and smiled.

"Good morning," she greeted him, and it seemed unnecessarily churlish to do anything but dismount and reply in kind.

Darcy led his stallion further away from the lane, patted his neck and gave him the freedom to graze at leisure as he ambled towards the wildflower faerie, only to find himself met with a mien that held elfish mischief rather than fairy-like serenity.

"You have not lost your way again, have you?"

The teasing reminder of his earlier blunder had no power to offend him; it was too amiably delivered.

"No. But I thank you for your concern."

"What of Mr Bingley? Has he had enough of our roads after yesterday's lengthy ride?"

"I have not had the chance to ask him. I left before he came down for breakfast. He is rarely this late, so I can only imagine he had had more than his habitual share of exercise," Darcy said, deciding it would have been both improper and disloyal to voice speculations about brandy.

"Were you not inclined to join them on their ride?" she asked as she tied a long blade of grass around the stems of her wildflowers.

"The invitation was for my friend," he replied, perhaps unwisely, for the remark could be misconstrued as a sign of disappointment.

Either way, it prompted a civil protest from her.

"Oh, my father would have welcomed your company. So would Mr Bingley, I expect. Over dinner, he repeatedly bemoaned your absence. He said he would have liked your opinion on a number of matters."

"Yes, well," Darcy said, a trifle diffidently, then decided to be truthful. "I must own this was the second reason why I thought I had better stay away."

She cast him a glance from beneath raised brows.

"How so?"

Darcy gave a faint shrug.

"I have often advised him in the past. I believe 'tis time I stepped back and let him take full charge of his affairs. My friend cannot very well command his new neighbours' respect if he constantly appears escorted by a nursemaid."

She smiled.

"I see. Doubtlessly Mr Bingley will come to appreciate the sentiment. As for myself, pray let me offer my thanks now."

"*Your* thanks? Whatever for?" Darcy asked, a little baffled.

Her impish smile grew wider.

"For not provoking my father into a too violent access of mirth by coming to act as nursemaid, complete with cap and apron. That might have threatened both his equanimity and his constitution."

His own equanimity threatened, Darcy could not quite decide if he should be discomfited by her openly teasing manner, or give in to the laughter that was bubbling in his throat.

Laughter won. She chuckled too, then sobered, which was a pity, for laughter seemed to put the warmest glow in her beautiful eyes. She blinked, momentarily distracting him with the flutter of incredibly long lashes, so that he forgot to ask what was amiss, if anything. But she explained the matter herself, when she resumed:

"Perhaps that was less than civil, and I should reserve my jests and pert remarks for longstanding acquaintances."

The protest was out before Darcy could consciously will it.

It did not cross his mind to pause and wonder at such haste.

"Not at all. I am honoured to have the privileges of a longstanding acquaintance. And there is a great deal to be said for levity and pertness."

Strangely, he did not even pause to wonder what might have possessed him to advocate them, when by nature he was a proponent of neither. Such reflections would come later. For now he asked, "Is this a favourite spot of yours?"

This time, he did note that the too personal question was something he would not have considered appropriate under regular circumstances, but it was too late anyway – he had already asked it.

She did not seem to mind, and answered it regardless.

"Yes, it is. One of several. I tend to go on many rambles," she added with a little shrug, her nonchalant and unassuming manner so delightful that Darcy surprised himself with doing no better than a trite question:

"Do you go as far as Meryton?"

"Yes, often. And beyond."

"Beyond? 'Tis at least three miles from Longbourn to Meryton, I imagine."

"That is a good estimate, sir. 'Tis three miles exactly."

His countenance must have still reflected his surprise, for she laughed mildly.

"Ah, I see I have shocked you with my country ways," she said, seemingly devoid of any wish to pander to his fashionable sensibilities by resorting to untruths. A country girl, and supremely unapologetic about who and what she was.

For some unfathomable reason, his friend's words rang in his memory, as clearly as if Bingley had just shouted them from beyond the coppice:

"Country ways? I think them charming."

He had scoffed at Bingley's remark the other day, when his friend had cheerfully cast it in response to his uncompromising view that the society in and around Meryton was something savage.

Darcy shrugged. His assessment of the local populace in general had remained unchallenged. But delivering sweeping condemnations and holding fast to one's opinions in the face of contrary evidence was a sure sign of rigidity of mind.

Only fools declared their views to be inflexible. A reasonable man would stand corrected and allow that there were exceptions to the rule, and spirited young women who shunned artifice and favoured long country walks, extensive reading and Mrs Allen's lavender drops might very well be regarded as both charming and intriguing.

It was then that it occurred to him that, were it not for the inferiority of her connections, he might be in some danger. Nevertheless, he offered:

"May I escort you home?"

"That is very kind, but I am on my way to call upon my friend Charlotte. Miss Lucas, that is. Sir William's eldest daughter?" she prompted, presumably in response to his blank stare.

With some effort of memory, Darcy could finally place the lady. It must have been the very plain young woman with whom Bingley had stood up for the first set at the assembly.

"In fact, this is a small offering for her," his companion resumed, raising the small bouquet. "Hopefully it will cheer her up a little. Word came to Longbourn that she is rather poorly."

"I am sorry to hear that. Nothing serious, I hope."

"I understand she caught a cold when she walked back in the rain from Meryton."

"Pray convey my wishes for a swift recovery," Darcy felt compelled to say in recognition of her concern for her friend's health, although his own acquaintance with Miss Lucas was limited, and added, "Pray allow me to escort you to Lucas Lodge, then."

"If you wish. But there is no need. If you look that way," she indicated, "you can just about distinguish its rooftops above the coppice."

"Oh," Darcy said, once he had turned to glance in that direction. Aye, he could see the rooftops of Lucas Lodge clearly enough, plumes of smoke escaping from the chimneys.

His brow creased into a fleeting frown. Perhaps the threat Miss Elizabeth Bennet posed to his equanimity could be measured by the surge of disappointment at finding that her destination was so very close.

He sensibly reined it in with some determination – for he was nothing if not resolute and sensible. At all times, good sense *must* prevail. There were no two ways about it.

⁓ co eo ⁓

Haye Park, 27 October 1811

Dinner at Haye Park was a tedious affair, made even more so by the realisation that he would do well to keep his distance and subdue the troublesome stirrings of his heart.

He was drawn to her. He might as well own it. Acknowledged dangers were more easily addressed. More easily avoided, rather. And she was a danger, in ways he would be wiser not to count. Not to count *again*, that was to say. He had already devoted himself to the fruitless exercise of listing the sources and reasons of her appeal, and that had only served to bring them to the forefront of his thoughts and thus emphasise her subtle and irresistible allure.

Irresistible – that, too, was best avoided. A dangerous word, for he *must* resist. Resist *her*. Keep his distance.

Not an easy task.

In fact, it was well-nigh impossible, and irksome to boot.

Why should he condemn himself to standing stone-faced, listening without comment to the ramblings of self-absorbed fools – when across the room, in *her* corner, there was laughter and every chance of quick-witted repartee?

Why should he skulk around the edges of the drawing room to escape Mr Goulding *père*'s senseless effusions, when Mr Goulding *fils* was exchanging pleasantries with her?

Why should he remain aloof and silent when his treacherous footsteps brought him to her side of the overcrowded chamber, once he had noticed that Mrs Long's wearisome company had put the sheen of boredom in her expressive eyes, although she tolerated the senseless woman and her never-ending prattle with perfectly good grace and nary a grimace?

Why should he avert his glance when her eyes unerringly found his to silently share her ruefully amused exasperation at some particularly blatant display of folly or presumption – laughing eyes, that met such impositions with mildly diverted gentleness rather than anything like Miss Bingley's spiteful malice, and cheerfully extended him the comradeship of one keen mind to another?

Why should he step away when they finally found themselves in conversation, safe from the dull crowds, and her remarks lent brightness to the dreary evening, and he felt inclined to talk, and even be witty on occasion?

Foolish thoughts, all of them, reason sternly claimed. He knew why. He knew it well enough. But, truth be told, of late it was not so much a case of why he should keep his distance. Day by day, the question had insidiously changed from *why* to *how*.

⁘

Hertfordshire, early November 1811

The question remained unanswered over the several evenings when the social rigmarole in Hertfordshire brought them together. He had no answers. Only given precepts, to which he must abide. And he would. He had to.

The only answer he could find was not a solution, but a convenient excuse that came to him as he took in her graceful form twirling across from him in an impromptu dance at Lucas Lodge, at Sir William's instigation.

The fact that there were only six other people, two of them children, disporting themselves thus concerned him not one jot. Nor that, in living memory, he had only danced in ballrooms, and not many of them either.

Those considerations could not claim him now, when his every thought was on more immediate and far more enticing matters. Such as the rosy glow the lively dance put in her countenance. The warmth in her eyes. The playful little quirk in her lips. The swish of her skirts when she skipped down the set. God help him, the glimpse of her bosom when she curtsied.

Hence his convenient excuse: for the remainder of his stay in Hertfordshire, he *would* allow himself to yield to fascination. There was no harm in giving in for a fortnight – or rather for the little that was left of it. A fortnight of indulgence, without difficult questions or self-recriminations.

A fortnight, aye – and not one day more.

Chapter 10

Netherfield, 12 November 1811

The allotted fortnight had come and gone, and nine more days besides, yet Fitzwilliam Darcy was still at Netherfield. For Bingley's benefit and his relations', he had justified it with the contents of Georgiana's latest letter. She had written to ask him if she might extend her stay with the Fitzwilliams until the middle of December, when Richard had undertaken to convey her to Pemberley along with Mrs Annesley, the motherly lady chosen with the utmost care as a replacement for the infamous Mrs Younge.

Darcy had no reason to deny the dear girl's request. The letters she had sent from Nottinghamshire had grown increasingly light-hearted, leading him to believe that in their cousins' cheerful society the clouds of the past were losing their power over her. Hopefully she would not relapse into melancholy when she returned to Pemberley, into the fabric of daily life, with only himself and Mrs Annesley for company. Only time would tell.

Had Georgiana returned home on the appointed date, he would have joined her – no two ways about it. But she had not. Thus, he had been granted an unexpected period of grace to indulge his fascination with the unsophisticated lass who tethered him to Netherfield against his better judgement. That was all it was. A period of grace, and nothing more. At the end of it, he would leave and do his duty to his lineage and estate, as he had always known he would.

There was no future in his fascination. That become increasingly clearer, the more he had learned about her. She was a country squire's daughter, of modest means and unremarkable connections. Downright abominable connections, some of them. The brash and vulgar aunt, Mrs Phillips, married to a Meryton attorney, and inadequately substituting for a mother. Two younger sisters, hoydenish and wild. Another sister, now married and settled – in Kent, at Hunsford of all places, under the patronage of his own aunt, Lady Catherine de Bourgh. The girl's husband was his aunt's vicar. The subservient position in itself was bad enough. How could a Darcy of Pemberley envisage forming an alliance with the sister of Lady Catherine's parson? But, to make matters worse, he knew the man. An obsequious fool, with no redeemable traits to recommend him. No one in their right mind would welcome Collins into their family, and the fact that Mr Bennet had consented to that union cast a shadow of doubt over his motives, his good sense and his perception.

Then there were the relations he had not even met, but of whom he had learned enough so as to harbour no desire of an acquaintance. Miss Bingley had discovered and maliciously hastened to impart that the uncle Miss Elizabeth Bennet had mentioned – the one who had taken her on a tour of pleasure to the north – was in trade and lived in Cheapside, within sight of his own warehouses.

Thus, sadly, it was supremely irrelevant that, against the drab backdrop of her unfortunate connections, Miss Elizabeth Bennet shone like a gem of the first water. That she was uniformly cheerful, uncommonly bright, and more knowledgeable than any young woman of his acquaintance on all manner of subjects, from fashionable poets to distinctly unfashionable essayists and writers.

It could not matter that she could easily hold her own in a debate. That she could read Latin, for goodness' sake, and quote from Virgil at the most *apropos* point in the conversation, and sound not in the least pedantic. That she sang like an angel and played the pianoforte with vivacity and spirit. That her laughter would brighten the dullest day, and her lithe form would unerringly catch his eye and command his full attention whenever they were in company together.

When all was said and done, it could not matter that he was drawn to her like the moth to the proverbial flame. A fascination. It would run its course. Nothing more to it. The period of grace was drawing to an end…

With a sigh, Darcy picked up the pen and resumed his letter to his sister, seeking to give a light tone to his communications, and feign a cheerfulness he did not feel.

I have neglected to convey Miss Bingley's compliments in my last two letters. Let me discharge that duty before I forget again. She was profuse in her appreciation of the embroidery pattern you had the goodness to send her, and enraptured by your design for a table. She thought it infinitely superior to Miss Grantley's. I fear your Yorkshire friend would be distraught to hear that Miss Bingley thinks so little of her efforts in comparison to yours, but I trust you will be gratified by the praise and have the heart not to gloat when next you see poor Miss Grantley.

On a different note, I must thank you for the delightful account of the amateur theatricals you and our cousins have amused yourselves with, and I am justly proud of your musical accomplishments. I am particularly gratified to hear that you were willing to play for someone other than myself and Mrs Annesley. By the bye, is the dear lady growing reconciled to the grim weather of the north? Pray assure her that spring at Pemberley is well worth enduring the rigours of autumn in Nottinghamshire. 'Tis not so very long until you can acquaint her with your favourite walks, and especially with your best-loved glade carpeted with daffodils and bluebells.

That dear place was brought vividly to my mind some days ago, when I came across its like in Hertfordshire, a few miles from Bingley's estate. There were no rolling hills for a backdrop, more was the pity, and no daffodils or bluebells, not at this time of year. But the same effect was achieved by an expanse of blue wildflowers of some sort, dotted with tall, bright-yellow ones, the name of which you would doubtlessly know, but sadly it escapes me.

The silhouette that stood amid the flowers could have easily been taken for your dear self, clad in the russet cloak you often wear on your walks. The young lady was in fact Miss Elizabeth Bennet, who seems to favour the outdoors as much as you. Should you ever meet, you would find in her a tireless companion. She thinks nothing of a three-mile walk, and muddy paths find her cheerfully undaunted.

I must say that I am beginning to see both the healthful benefits and the attraction of walking in preference to riding. I would not necessarily choose it for myself, but I would dearly love to see your sweet complexion rosy and aglow, as Miss Elizabeth's is after an invigorating walk.

He stopped short and his eyes leapt to the lines he had just written. What the deuce had possessed him, to ramble thus in a letter to his sister? Rosy complexion – cheeks aglow! He must have lost his mind. He could not possibly send out such utter—

With an almighty scowl and a round oath, Darcy forcefully dipped the pen in the inkwell. Then he stopped short once more. Crossing out the last few lines would not do. It would be dreadfully conspicuous. His letters were always fastidiously neat. Not once had he sent messy letters covered in blots and crossed-out rows. If only the ramblings had been on a new sheet. But no, they were at the bottom of a long letter, painstakingly written.

He could copy out the whole of the last page. Unless…

With due care and attention, and the aid of a carefully employed pair of scissors, the bottom of the page was neatly trimmed off. The comma after the *'three-mile walk'* was turned into a full stop. The page was flipped over, a few closing lines were added, then Darcy appended his signature beneath the *'Affectionately yours'*. He sealed the letter to his sister, jotted the direction, then diligently consigned the trimmed-off strip of paper to the flames.

∘⊱⊰∘

"Whoever is calling at such an hour?" Bingley wondered aloud, as their chaise drew to a halt behind the small conveyance waiting at the foot of the stairs that led to Netherfield's main entrance. "But… I do believe 'tis the Longbourn carriage," he exclaimed and leapt out to call towards the coachman. "Higgins, is that you?"

"Aye, sorr," the man called back, tugging at his cap. "Good e'en to ye, Mr Bingley, sorr."

"What brings you here?" Bingley impatiently asked as Darcy followed him and a less than nimble Mr Hurst out of the vehicle that had just brought them back from Meryton, after an evening with Colonel Forster and his officers.

"Drivin' Miss Bennet, sorr," the Longbourn coachman replied. "Her aunt said she ought to come on Nellie, but the master wouldn't hear of it, an' sent for the other horses. He said that were daft, Miss Jane comin' on horseback on a day like this, for it looked like rain, an' he had the right of it—"

But Bingley was no longer listening. He bounded up towards the entrance, taking the steps two at a time. He must have been quite put out to hear that his sisters had slyly asked Miss Bennet to Netherfield on an evening when he would be out.

Aye, he was clearly in a temper, Darcy concluded, on hearing his uniformly complaisant and affable friend going as far as to remonstrate with his sisters in company when he came upon them in the great hall.

They were both standing there, waiting for Miss Bennet to don her wrap, held out by one of the footmen. Bingley glowered at them, and addressed the visitor first.

"Miss Bennet. What a remarkable surprise. I wish I was informed you were expected. Caroline, Louisa, *why* was I not informed?"

Mrs Hurst fidgeted. Miss Bingley shrugged.

"It was an impromptu decision, Brother. I did not see how it would affect you."

"Did you not?" came Bingley's clipped retort. "Very well. We shall address that later. Miss Bennet, can I persuade you to stay a little longer? The pleasure of your company— That is…" he faltered, then grew silent.

The young lady gave a hesitant smile.

"I should make my way home, sir. 'Tis getting late."

"Hm. I daresay it is…" Bingley reluctantly conceded. "Unless I could prevail upon you to spend the night at Netherfield?" he added with a hopeful look. "The weather… it cannot be trusted. And given the lateness of the hour…" he floundered, casting widely for any pretext that might support his senseless cause.

Far more attuned than he to the dictates of propriety, Miss Bennet shook her head.

"Oh, no, there is no cause for that. Higgins will drive me home safely."

"Then at least pray allow me to escort you," Bingley promptly offered, abandoning the losing battle and clinging instead onto any modest compensation he could find. "John, my horse. Pray have someone bring it round directly."

"Oh, surely you need not give yourself the trouble. 'Tis raining…"

"A mere drizzle," Bingley countered. "Nay, nay, I will not be dissuaded. You must allow me the pleasure of knowing you have reached your home in safety."

He would brook no opposition, neither from the blushing and mildly-spoken visitor, nor from his more vocal sisters.

Darcy had nothing to offer to the conversation. Bingley's overt and unremitting attentions to Miss Bennet were a concern, naturally. Yet at the moment that could not distract him from a far more pressing matter. Namely, from the overwhelming urge to order his own horse saddled too, and avail himself of the godsent opportunity to call at Longbourn. See her – on a day when he had entertained no hope of an encounter. Witness surprise brightening her countenance, followed doubtlessly by pleasure. Have tea and speak of commonplaces for half an hour, maybe less. Bland nothings made exciting by the sound of her voice. A dull day ending on a cheerful note because of her bewitching presence. The sight of her. The touch of her soft hand as she would bid him a good evening and send him back to Netherfield with the sense that the day had not been wasted. With her scent clinging to his palm.

His lips tightened into a severe line, Darcy said nothing. He did not order his horse saddled. He knew better than that. And a few minutes later, as he watched the Longbourn carriage vanishing into the evening gloom with Bingley riding beside it at a trot, Darcy also knew beyond the shadow of a doubt that the time had come to put an end to the indulgence. The fascination had been allowed to go too far. It had grown into yearning. And yearning had a way of making fools of men by masquerading as good judgement.

ೊಲ ಲ

Netherfield, 13 November 1811

"But, Mr Darcy, must you leave us so soon? I— My relations and I were hoping you might stay for another fortnight. My brother's foolish scheme about giving a ball— I hope he will reconsider. Without you in attendance, it would be insupportable. Pray stay until the end of the week at least, and perhaps between us we might persuade Charles to remove to town. Or he might accompany you to Pemberley, and my sister and I could collect him on our way to Scarborough? Dear Georgiana, how I long to see her…"

Miss Bingley's less than subtle attempts to extract an invitation to Pemberley fell on deaf ears. Darcy was in no humour to indulge her. Nor would he give in to her insistent pleas that he delay his departure and talk his friend out of the notion of giving a ball.

Miss Bingley would have to fight her battles without his assistance. He had enough to contend with as it was.

The deed was done. He had called at Longbourn for the requisite leave-taking visit, and had kept it as short as civility would allow. His man had been instructed to make the necessary preparations for departure, and now everything was arranged.

All that remained was to subdue the yearning. It would be done. Distance, common-sense and duty would set everything to rights.

~°~

Hertfordshire, 14 November 1811

From the morning mist the glade emerged, but the scene that lay before him bore little resemblance to the one he remembered. For one, there was no slender form clad in a russet cloak – which was just as well. Or at least that was what he told himself. The other stark difference was that the November frosts had done away with the late-autumn flowering. The glade was no longer carpeted in blue, but shrouded in the greyish-green of wilted leaves and limp stalks, with nothing but a few brave little flowers that had withstood the inclement weather.

The urge to ask his coachman to draw to a halt, or at least slow down, was promptly conquered. Lingering there was fruitless and, worse still, unforgivably maudlin. Such recollections should not be encouraged. It was irrelevant that, strictly speaking, he had not been wholly candid with Georgiana in the letter that had required some careful trimming. The tall yellow flowers that had dotted the glade some weeks ago might have been unknown to him, but the others were unsettlingly familiar. The glade had once been carpeted with wild forget-me-nots.

Scowling, Darcy dismissed the ludicrous notion of stopping the coach after all and pausing there just for long enough to secrete one of the surviving sprigs in the book he carried in his pocket. He scoffed. His people would be right in thinking he had lost his senses. Gathering flowers by the roadside – Lord above!

No. No mementoes. Least of all forget-me-nots. Fascinations were meant to be forgotten. And it was high time he applied himself to that.

Chapter 11

Berkeley Square, London, 29 November 1811

Darcy could not bear to head home to Pemberley as yet. Georgiana was still in Nottinghamshire. All that awaited at Pemberley was solitude – and he was in no fit state for that. He was in no fit state for company in town either, but that was neither here nor there. The odd morning at his club, the odd evening at the Theatre Royal would serve better than the sound of silence in his ancestral home. He would doubtlessly populate the empty halls of Pemberley with a phantasmagoria of images born out of the pernicious yearning, for which he had yet to find a cure. He did not expect the facile amusements of the *bon ton* to provide anything other than temporary distraction. But impossible dreams would be that much more difficult to conquer if he were left to his own devices and his thoughts.

Thus, he was still in town one morning at the end of the month, when Miss Bingley and her sister came to call with their tale of woe.

"You cannot imagine what a disaster the ball was, Mr Darcy," Mrs Hurst sniffed. "My sister and I did our duty and made all the arrangements for the event our brother had set his heart upon, but what a sad waste of time and effort! With the best will in the world the society can only be described as savage. Would you believe that Mrs Phillips, that appalling creature, loudly boasted throughout supper to anyone who cared to listen that my brother's union with her eldest niece would be a great marriage, and it would throw the unmarried sisters into the path of other rich men?"

Darcy was acquainted with the vulgar woman, so no fresh evidence of her crassness could surprise him. Yet he could not possibly meet the reference to the unmarried sisters thrown into the path of other rich men with the same indifference. The yearning was still far from cured, so the notion of others beating a path to *her* door was utterly repugnant. As for Elizabeth being constantly thrown into his path by his friend's marriage to her sister, his first response – the insane burst of joy that coursed through him at the mere thought – made the prospect nothing short of terrifying.

"Had Bingley made Miss Bennet an offer?" he anxiously asked.

"Not yet," Miss Bingley hastened to answer the question addressed to her sister. "But we live in fear that the unthinkable will come to pass. Frankly, we followed him to town because we suspected that his only reason for travelling hither was to retrieve Mother's engagement ring from the family vault."

The intelligence was shocking. Goodness, was it as imminent as that? Yet Darcy merely said, "Oh. So, your brother is in town?"

"He is," replied Miss Bingley. "Which brings us to the purpose of our call. Mr Darcy, you are our only hope. Would you speak to Charles – open his eyes to the evils of such a connection? We tried. We tirelessly worked to dissuade him, but he is beyond our reach. Not even the disgrace had the power to sway him."

"Disgrace? What disgrace?"

That was novel, and more than a little alarming. Not for Bingley's sake, but *hers*. What distress was she facing?

Miss Bingley sniffed with profound disdain and brought her kerchief to her lips with a dramatic gesture. Yet, to his credit, Darcy succeeded in keeping himself sufficiently in check so as not to demand she dispense with the theatricals and say what she had to say.

"It was only a matter of time, of course," Miss Bingley spoke, still trying Darcy's patience with the supercilious platitude that supplied no useful information. "After all, considering their upbringing, one could not expect much better. Four girls, or five, brought up at home without a governess and without a mother's guidance. Misconduct was unavoidable. Even so, such unmaidenly behaviour…"

She sniffed again, and this time Darcy could not quite contain himself.

"Would you kindly come to the point, Miss Bingley?" he urged.

"Oh, yes, of course. Pray forgive me, but this is not a subject of which a gently-bred person can speak with ease. Nonetheless, I must forge ahead. Our good name requires it. My brother cannot be permitted to form so unfortunate an alliance."

He must have betrayed his impatience in some way or another, Darcy concluded, for Miss Bingley finally saw fit to cease prevaricating.

"The sad truth, sir, is that the youngest sister – you know, the boldest of the two hoydenish ones – was found in a most compromising situation. Down a deserted lane with one of the officers, embracing... kissing... Something of that nature, you understand. I do not know the particulars, and even if I did, discussing them is unbefitting a person of my character and standing. Well. As you would imagine, news of the scandalous business spread like wildfire in the neighbourhood, and everyone expected an announcement. A hasty marriage would have been the only answer to the chit's loss of reputation. A patched-up affair, aye, and most irregular, but given the circumstances, they were in no position to cavil. Yet the father did cavil – would you believe it? His response to the disgraceful situation was most peculiar. One might even say eccentric. It reached me by common report. Apparently, he said that in his opinion lack of sense was enough of a penance in itself, and it need not be compounded by the lifelong sentence of an ill-judged union. And that Miss... whatever her name is... Lydia? Aye, Lydia. He said that Miss Lydia would be most adequately punished by being banished into Kent, to learn discretion from her sister and her brother by marriage, the vicar. By the bye, the man is your aunt's parson, is he not? I fear so, and I urge you to write and inform her ladyship of the girl's vicious propensities. The vicar and his wife might seek to conceal them, and it would not do for your cousin to be unknowingly exposed to such an influence."

"So, the youngest had been sent to Kent?" Darcy asked.

"Indeed. The locals were surprised that the threat was followed through so promptly. They said that Mr Bennet was famed for his tendency to procrastinate, and they expected that nothing would come of all that talk of banishment. But nay, he must have seen how injurious the false step in one daughter was to all the others, so the chit was sent away in no time at all, with Miss Elizabeth to supervise her. You can comprehend my shock when I saw that, in defiance of all decency, Mr Bennet and his eldest daughter did make an appearance at the ball. He must have been eager to promote Miss Bennet's interest with my brother as best he could. You will not be surprised to hear that I had the most wretched evening, and I hope you will pity me for having to receive them, while all the gossipmongers watched and tattled, and my brother still hung on Miss Bennet's every word, as though she were the best match he could aspire to, and not some impecunious young woman with a shameless little hussy for a sister."

But Darcy was no longer listening to her lamentations – not since he learned that *she* had not attended the Netherfield ball after all, and was instead in Kent, visiting his aunt's parson and keeping a watchful eye over her youngest sister. Miss Bingley's exhortations were dismissed out of hand. No, he would not write to Lady Catherine and inform her of Miss Lydia's misconduct. There was no way of knowing for how long Elizabeth was unfairly meant to share her sister's exile, but with Lady Catherine in the know as to its cause, the Miss Bennets' life in Kent would be unbearable. Hopefully, the vicar and his wife *would* have the good sense to conceal it.

Another thought occurred, and with a start he gave silent thanks that his yearly visit into Kent was not at Christmas, but several months hence. Otherwise all his efforts to distance himself from her would have been undone. Surely, they – *she* – would leave Kent by Easter. As for Bingley's preposterous infatuation, something should be done about it, and the sooner, the better.

His mind was quite made up by the time Miss Bingley had to prompt him for the second time in order to rouse him from his ruminations.

"Mr Darcy? Sir? Would you be so kind as to speak some sense into my brother?"

Darcy squared his shoulders and took a deep breath.

"Yes," he said firmly. "I will do my best."

◦ஓ௸ஓ◦

Berkeley Square, London, 30 November 1811

Contrary to expectations, Bingley was unbelievably mulish. The lengthy conversation in Darcy's study, over brandy, was as unsatisfying as could be. For one who had always been amenable to reason and easily persuaded, on this occasion Bingley had remained perversely impervious to sensible arguments. Such as the duty one owed to oneself and one's relations to not form an unsuitable alliance that would put one's sister at a disadvantage on the marriage mart, and cover a respectable name in ridicule and censure.

With the matter so close to home – to his own name, and his own sister – Darcy had been particularly eloquent on that subject. Yet Bingley had blithely replied that a respectable name should carry enough weight in itself and have sufficient credit in the world so as not to be threatened by something as trifling as a vociferous and plain-spoken aunt, or a kiss down a quiet lane.

"Miss Lydia was made to see the error of her ways. She should have known better, I will give you that. But she is young, only fifteen, and no harm was done. Really, Darcy, it was a minor indiscretion, which in time will be quite forgotten. As for the aunts and uncles you speak of, why should I care? Aye, Mrs Phillips could have better manners, but then so could half the *ton*. And I can see why you would think twice about marrying someone with uncles in trade, but would I not be the worst sort of hypocrite if I baulked at that?"

"No, you would not," Darcy calmly countered. "It would be perfectly natural that you should look towards advancing in society, rather than taking a step back."

Bingley's lips quirked into a wry smile.

"I do believe you prove my point: when one's name has sufficient status, it cannot be harmed. Take yours, for instance. It seems it has not suffered a vast deal from our association, however much I still need to advance in the world, by your way of thinking."

Darcy made a gesture of impatience that still contrived to be half apologetic.

"That was uncalled for. I treasure our friendship, I trust you know that. I was not aiming to suggest you need more consequence."

"No. Just that I should seek to improve my standing by marrying for advantage rather than affection."

"There is nothing to stop you from falling in love with a lady of good fortune," Darcy argued.

But the other cast him a disarming grin.

"Too late, my friend. I fear I already am head over heels in love."

"Might I point out that over the course of our acquaintance you have declared yourself thoroughly bewitched, head over heels in love and the like for no less than… Let me see. Eleven times?"

"Thirteen," Bingley corrected him. "Idiotic nonsense. I knew not what I was speaking of."

"And now you know," Darcy irritably scoffed.

His friend's voice was low and steady when he replied, "Aye. Now I do."

Just that, and nothing else. The very absence of hyperboles, so out of character, gave Darcy pause. Nonetheless, he insisted:

"What makes you so certain?"

Bingley shrugged.

"I take it you have never been in love," he parried.

"Not to the point of turning into love's fool, no."

"Then you have never been in love," Bingley declared with an infuriating grin. "Trust me, my friend. When that blessed time is upon you, you will cheerfully own you *are* love's fool, and would not wish yourself otherwise. Moreover, you will agree with me that the poor benighted souls who scoff at love's fools are grievously to be pitied."

Darcy snorted.

"Highly unlikely. But never mind that now. What I meant was that you should have enough sense not to throw yourself head-first into the abyss over a mere infatuation."

Bingley crossed his arms over his chest and gave a mild and rather condescending laugh.

"Abyss, is it? Dear, oh dear, Darcy. I fear for Pemberley's future, if this is your view of the married state."

"Whereas I fear for your happiness, and with more reasonable cause," Darcy retaliated. "You are prepared to cast everything aside over an infatuation with someone who does not even love you!"

Bingley's amiable countenance darkened into a frown.

"What the blazes do you mean by that?"

ༀ ༀ

The conversation that followed could not be too soon forgotten. Pointing out the obvious to Bingley, and watching joy and hope draining out of him was one of the hardest tasks Darcy had to face. Yet the salient truths had to be voiced. Namely, that it was remarkably easy for anyone to deceive himself into seeing what he wished to see; and he was not the first, nor would he be the last to wilfully blind himself to reality in this fashion. And the reality was that, for a variety of reasons, Miss Bennet was not the best match one could aspire to. Moreover, that her manners might have been cheerful and engaging, but to the detached observer they bore no symptom of peculiar regard. That her serene countenance and air showed her heart was not easily touched. Nevertheless, Bingley was a catch, and she must have seen it. Her natural guardians certainly had.

"I gathered from Miss Bingley that the aunt boasted of the union as if it were already certain, and revelled in the advantages it would heap upon her kin," Darcy sought to point out. "As for the father, he might dismiss some penniless officer as an ill-fitting match for his youngest daughter, but he had allowed – for all I know, encouraged – one of them to marry a pompous and sycophantic fool who just so happened to be in possession of a living. You have so much more to offer, both in yourself and in view of your station in life. So yes, I do not doubt that Mr Bennet would give his consent. Likewise, I imagine that, regardless of her sentiments, Miss Bennet would obligingly embark upon a marriage of convenience. But what joy is to be found in that, for either of you? And moreover, would you be prepared to forsake so much in exchange for so little?"

Doubtlessly, the same arguments applied to himself as well, and were even more pertinent since he had more to lose. But personal considerations paled in the face of Bingley's manifest distress. He must have grown more attached than usual, Darcy concluded.

He sighed. If, on impartial conviction, he could assure his friend that his lady loved him, he would, by Jove. Then, were Bingley to wed his angel, he would keep his distance, if he must. Yet, in good conscience, he could not sit by and witness his friend making the same sort of grievous mistake that *he* strenuously sought to avoid. Bingley would recover. So would he.

Time cured even the deepest sorrows – real sorrows – so it would surely do away with trifling fascinations. Aye, the unwarranted distractions would lose their power. Given time.

Chapter 12

Pemberley, 8 December 1811

"Whatever is the matter with him?" Lady Anne anxiously wondered.

Ever since her son's return to Pemberley, she had often pondered on that very question, and with good cause. He was morose and restless, scarcely ate and shunned sleep. He was even short-tempered with the servants on occasion, which had never been his way.

"Is it to do with Georgiana, do you think?" she fretted. "Does he know something we do not? Something that troubles him?"

"I should imagine not," her husband sought to reassure her. "No express came, and no messenger either. Just a letter from the dearest girl, and there was naught worrisome in it. Quite the opposite."

Lady Anne nodded in agreement. She had read Georgiana's letter over her son's shoulder, just as her husband had, and could not dispute Mr Darcy's views when he resumed:

"I think she wrote good-humouredly of her outings with her cousins, and with warm anticipation of her return home. Nothing between the lines, as much as I could tell, but then I am not as perceptive as you are, my dear," he gallantly bowed to her superior judgement. "Did you notice anything untoward?"

"Nay, nothing at all. She seemed reassuringly at ease and cheerful. But Fitzwilliam is nothing of the sort. Oh, sir, just look at him!" she exclaimed, her tones brimming with compassion, as her ethereal hand shot out to indicate their son.

He was sitting by the fire, seemingly engrossed in staring at the lively game of hide-and-seek that the flames were playing with the shadows, chasing each other amid white plumes of smoke. Light and shadow played over his countenance as well, yet did nothing to alter the expression of the handsome features set in deep, cheerless lines.

"Boredom?" George Darcy opined, but Lady Anne dismissed the speculation with a shrug.

"Nonsense. Not he. Fitzwilliam never yields to such an indulgence. You know as well as I do that he fills dull moments with useful tasks. He reads, he looks over his papers, writes letters and I know not what. He certainly is not one for staring idly into space."

"Perhaps loneliness got to him tonight," George Darcy proffered.

His wife did not dismiss the second speculation as readily as the first.

"It might have. 'Tis a relief that Georgiana will be back in a few days' time, and Richard will escort her. He always knows just what to say to lift everyone's spirits. Then Christmas is bound to bring animation and good cheer. I wish my brother had insisted that Fitzwilliam and Georgiana join them for the festive season. As for Catherine, she—"

Mr Darcy grimaced at that name, even before his wife could finish her sentence. As it happened, she did not. A sudden movement in the armchair by the fireplace startled her into silence. Abruptly, Fitzwilliam leaned forward. Then he stood, reached for a fire iron and applied himself to prodding at the burning logs with an oath that made Lady Anne's brows shoot up in censorious indignation. Others might condone that sort of language in a gentleman, but she would not. Neither in her lifetime, nor beyond it. Least of all in her son.

"Now, really!" she spluttered.

Yet the maternal rebuke had no effect whatever. Fitzwilliam prodded the fire once more for good measure, and darkly muttered:

"Of all the blasted fools and besotted mooncalves! Enough, now. *Enough!*"

No one would imagine that his remonstrations were meant for the half-burnt log he had plagued with his poker. Thus, with no great leap of fancy, it could safely be assumed they were directed at himself.

Lady Anne flashed a surprised glance towards her husband and saw a smile tugging at the corner of his lips.

"It seems we have our answer, my dear," George Darcy said mildly. "By his own admission, the lad is in love."

Pemberley, 14 December 1811

"So, Coz, out with it. Let me hear everything of this Miss Elizabeth Bennet."

Fortunately for Darcy, he had just filled his glass, and had yet to lift it from where it stood safely on the tray next to the decanter. Otherwise, had the staggering query caught him in the act of pouring, there was every chance that the glass or the decanter – or both – would have met with an ignominious end. But the narrowly avoided mishap was the last thing on his mind as Darcy cast a shocked glance over his shoulder towards the chair where his cousin sat, glass in hand and a twinkle in his eye.

"What?" was the most cogent reply he could make, then inwardly cursed himself for the idiocy of it.

His cousin laughed.

"You might think I should beg your pardon for ambushing you thus, but I will not. Nothing works with you better than an ambush. And you must own, I have been uncommonly patient. For hours, mind, till I had you to myself. Nary a word, nod or wink from me since my arrival. Now, perhaps I would have apologised for my unconventional approach had I made you waste a goodly portion of this delectable brandy," he smirked, raising his glass towards the fire to watch the light glinting through the amber liquid. "By the bye, my father would appreciate the name of your supplier. Remarkable quality. French, I imagine, and doubtlessly smuggled. I grant you, given its long and arduous journey, it deserves better than to be spilled over your floorboards. But since that did not come to pass, let us return to the more rewarding topic of Miss Elizabeth Bennet," he said and took a sip, his probing eyes never veering from his host.

Vexation prevailed over the latter. His hand steady now, Darcy raised his own glass for a long draught, then made his way towards the fireplace to rest a hand on the mantlepiece, look into the flames and feign placidity. He took another gulp and spoke to fill the pregnant silence. The threatening silence, rather; for Richard could be relentless, and thus insufferably provoking, when he was of a mind to pry.

"Have you nothing better to speak of than some casual acquaintance I made?"

"Casual acquaintance, is it?"

"Aye," he firmly replied.

"Pray tell me," his cousin drawled, "how many other casual acquaintances have you repeatedly referenced in your letters to your sister?"

"Repeatedly!" Darcy scoffed. "I doubt that I wrote about her more than twice."

"Eight times, to be precise. In three letters," the other countered. "Sufficiently out of character to raise Georgiana's interest, and make her mention the matter to me."

Darcy snorted.

"And you doubtlessly amused yourself by filling my sister's head with foolish speculations."

His cousin straightened up, and his countenance lost some of its unholy merriment. He shifted in his seat, either in displeasure at the accusation, or simply to ease the lingering pain from the injury that had rendered him unfit for active service.

"I thought you knew me better than that," he said, a hint of reproach in his tone. "Nevertheless, something tells me there is more that I should wish to hear."

Darcy gave a gesture of impatience and drained his glass.

"You are getting old. Your instincts are starting to fail you," he mercilessly shot back. "There is nothing to tell."

"How very disappointing," Colonel Fitzwilliam airily replied, and redirected his attention to his brandy.

Unbeknownst to him, his late aunt shared that sentiment. It was highly disappointing that Richard did not press the matter. She would have dearly liked to see him urging her son to disclose more.

"Patience, my dear," her husband said, in answer to her thoughts. "There is a very good reason why your nephew had risen so swiftly through the ranks until that wretched chest wound had come to stall a brilliant career. He is nothing if not a consummate tactician. Besides, at least we now have a name for our mystery lady: Miss Elizabeth Bennet."

"We do," she reluctantly conceded. "I wonder if she is of the Tankerville Bennets."

George Darcy shrugged, and in good conscience could not give his wife the reassurance she was seeking. He would be the first to acknowledge that his instincts were no match for young Richard's, but something told him the lady was not related to the earls of Tankerville.

⟡ ⟡ ⟡

Pemberley, 19 December 1811

The season of goodwill was drawing nearer, bringing with it the traditional preparations. In George Darcy's lifetime, the planned entertainments were on a far larger scale. Dozens of guests were asked to come and stay, partake of festive fare and fill the silent halls with glitter, bustle and good cheer for a fortnight, all the way to the Twelfth Night Ball.

Since his passing, Christmases at Pemberley had grown quiet. His son had diligently followed in his footsteps in every way but that. The seasonal duties towards the tenants and the poor of the parish had been observed, of course, and the servants had been encouraged to keep the old customs below-stairs, but the great estate had ceased to be the focal point of Yuletide celebrations in a five-mile radius. For the first three years, Darcy and his sister had chosen to join their Fitzwilliam relations over the festive season. Afterwards, they both saw merit in remaining in Derbyshire at that time of year and reviving the old ways, but only inasmuch as asking a number of neighbours to partake of a lavish Christmas dinner.

This year would be no different. Invitations had been written and sent, or handed out in person during some unavoidable morning calls. Mrs Reynolds and the people in the kitchens knew their duty. Thus, until noisy conviviality would necessarily descend upon them, Darcy, Georgiana and Colonel Fitzwilliam were left to enjoy each other's company over long rides in the snow or cosy evenings by the fire.

Messages of goodwill came from many quarters. The most notable came from Kent one morning, a few days before Christmas.

For once, their cousin Anne de Bourgh wrote, *you will find more in my letter than the habitual account of seasonal amusements at Rosings. We are expecting a large party to come into Kent and join us for the celebrations.*

This would be the time to apologise yet again for being such a poor correspondent. I have neglected to inform you that we have had some excitement in our quiet corner of the world. A minor tempest rather, in the person of one Miss Lydia Bennet, who came to stay at the vicarage, with my mother's parson and his wife.

She is Mrs Collins' youngest sister and, as I have since learned, she was sent hither for an indeterminate time on account of 'a little indiscretion.' Nothing so very bad, let me assure you. A trifle mortifying, but fairly entertaining on the whole. I have the full details from Miss Lydia's own lips, but I shall not commit them to paper, for I have been sworn to secrecy in that regard.

Apparently, Mr Collins and his wife are in ignorance of the entire business for – as Miss Lydia so eloquently put it – they would set her out on her ear. I daresay she is not wrong. Rigid notions of propriety are likely to prevail over Mrs Collins' sisterly sentiments, for she is rather too much like her husband. They seem to have been designed for each other. They are both given to sermonising and pontificating, and seem to have but one mind and one way of thinking, which must account for their felicitous union.

Forgive me. I digress.

To return to Miss Lydia, she came into Kent with another sister, a Miss Elizabeth, but the latter stayed for a mere fortnight, and then she was promptly summoned home to Hertfordshire. Unlike Mrs Collins – who, I am given to understand, is the cuckoo in the nest as regards disposition and temper – Miss Elizabeth made for an amiable companion, but on her sister's return to their father's house, Miss Lydia found herself in dire need of a confidant, and before long she chose me for that purpose.

I will not scruple to say that her conversation and manner had begun by shocking me speechless. She is a most… singular young woman, and she seems unable to stop talking. I do believe she can outdo Mamma in that regard, and few can boast that. Miss Elizabeth kept her in check while she was at Hunsford, but on the first occasion Miss Lydia came with Mr and Mrs Collins to take tea at Rosings, she would have chattered without interruption for a half-hour, I believe, had her brother by marriage not bid her hold her tongue on pain of being sent to the parsonage forthwith and not brought along a second time. 'Tis a testament to the tedium at the parsonage if tea at Rosings counts as desirable amusement, but it must be so, for Miss Lydia fidgeted uncontrollably for the remainder of the visit, but on the whole did hold her tongue.

Whatever Miss Lydia's flaws might be, she is not backward in finding ways around adversity. She learned her lesson after that, and took to chatting freely to me only when she could do so with impunity.

I came upon her alone at the parsonage once or twice, when Mr and Mrs Collins were gone into Hunsford, and I must own that before long I began to make a point of seeking her society. Any company is an improvement to spending all my time with Mamma and Mrs Jenkinson, as you would understand.

Which brings me in a very roundabout manner to the communications at the beginning of my letter. I am pleased to say that evenings at Rosings will be further enlivened by the arrival of Miss Lydia's relations. She told me the other day that her papa had written to say he was of a mind to allow Miss Elizabeth and his eldest daughter, a Miss Jane, to come to Hunsford for a se'nnight to soften her exile. However, he had eventually reconsidered, on grounds that, and I quote, 'Jane and Elizabeth had done nothing wrong, so why should they be exposed to a se'nnight of Fordyce's sermons on her account?'

In case I forgot to mention, this worthy tome is a great favourite with Mr and Mrs Collins, which would explain Mr Bennet's quip. He then informed Miss Lydia that he had decided to accept Mr Collins' invitation to spend Christmas at Hunsford, and I quote again, 'for who should deserve that more than himself, for not taking a rod to her back – that is to say, Miss Lydia's – before it was too late.'

I must have looked quite shocked when she related that, for Miss Lydia laughed and told me her papa was not in earnest, and such was his way, he dearly loved to make sport. So we are expecting this sport-loving gentleman in a few days' time, along with his three other daughters. The young ladies were to spend the festive season with their uncle and aunt in town, but apparently Mr and Mrs Collins had insistently declared – this is the last quote, you have my word for it, so pray bear it cheerfully – 'that at the time of Our Saviour's birth, close relations should not be divided, but instead ought to gather together, hail the season of goodwill and pour the balm of righteous affection into each other's bosoms.'

I wish I could supply their definition of righteous affection for your further edification. At the moment I cannot, but I shall doubtlessly be enlightened on that score in due course. When that time comes, you must depend upon my sharing that knowledge with you. Until then, I warmly wish you and Darcy all the joys of the season and I remain,

Yours sincerely,

Anne d B

As always, Miss de Bourgh's letter was addressed to Georgiana. As always, she shared it with her brother. Darcy perused it more eagerly than ever, his glance leaping over passages in quest of a certain name, in equal measure fearing that he would find it, and fretting that he might not – an admixture of conflicting sentiments that could not fail to vex him.

When the matter was settled, he folded the letter and set it aside. The urge to read it again was dismissed with a scowl. It would reveal nothing more than what he had learned on first inspection: that *she* would spend Christmas with his aunt's vicar at Hunsford, of all the parsonages in the country! Of all the deuced impositions, there she was, brought once more to his attention, as if *that* was what he needed. And doubtlessly she would be mentioned in Anne's next letter too.

With a grimace, Darcy pushed the offending pages further away from him and, with great determination, told himself it was a good thing that, just as she said herself, Anne was not a timely correspondent.

ৎ৹৻৻ ৹৻৹

Pemberley, Christmas Day 1811

Christmas Day dawned bright and jolly – and found the colonel still at Pemberley, rather than at the seat of his eldest sister's husband in Westmorland, where most of the Fitzwilliams had chosen to spend the festive season. Unbeknownst to him, his late aunt and uncle Darcy were most glad of his presence, and held great hopes that he would cajole their offspring into good cheer and employ his famed tactical skills upon the older of the two.

He was supplied with more ammunition when least expected – namely, at the sweet, heart-warming time of gift-giving. The Christmas presents his cousins had in store for him – an account of travels into the wilds of Scotland and a small and perfectly contained writing set, presumably an affectionate encouragement to write more often – were received with grateful pleasure, on the par with Georgiana's when she was presented with thoughtful gifts from both her guardians.

Her presents to them were no less thoughtful. Especially the one she handed to her brother with a bashful smile. It was the opening of it that provided the colonel with his ammunition, for Darcy's countenance was a study in manfully mastered discomposure when, from the neat folds of brown paper, a delicate miniature emerged.

It was an exquisite rendition of a glade carpeted with flowers. And in the distance, on the backdrop of misty blue dotted with yellow, a silhouette stood, bathed in hazy sunshine and hauntingly alluring – a slender young woman draped in a russet cloak.

"My dearest girl, this is so… beautiful," he faltered. "You should not have."

Georgiana's sweet countenance grew tense, and her tone hesitant.

"Should I not? I hope… I do hope it does not displease you. Does it?"

"Goodness, no, of course not!" Darcy protested with great emphasis. "'Tis a marvellous gift, Georgiana, and I will treasure it. Such artistry… Pray do not think I am anything but delighted. Indeed, overwhelmed… Besides, how could such a rendition of your dear self ever be displeasing?"

"'Tis not meant to— No matter," Georgiana broke off and swiftly turned to retrieve one of his gifts to her – a collection of music sheets – and enthuse over its contents.

Nothing further was said of the miniature. Georgiana held her peace when she espied her brother folding the brown paper over it, then secreting the small parcel into his pocket. Her cousin also showed uncommon restraint. He carefully stored his new ammunition for a fitting time in Darcy's study, over some libation or another, once the amusements of the day had run their course, and the dozen guests expected at Pemberley had ordered their carriages, ready to brave the snowy roads and make their way home.

Chapter 13

Pemberley, the early hours of St Stephen's Day 1811

Lady Anne and Mr Darcy were growing rather tired of waiting. Their brief exchange – a raised brow, answered by a shrug – showed they were in agreement: Richard was being overcautious. Unprecedently so. It was past midnight and the lads still chatted, yet nothing of consequence was mentioned as they lounged at leisure in their shirtsleeves, with their brandy.

It was not their first. Mr Darcy and his lady knew as much, but had ceased counting. When the tedium of the conversation induced him to ponder on such matters, George Darcy's educated guess was that Richard was on his fourth or fifth glass, and Fitzwilliam still on his third. If the lad had taken it into his head to keep pace with his cousin, then heaven help him. Richard would drink him under the table with no effort. Especially if they had resorted to the strong stuff.

George Darcy sighed, longing for the joy of a fine brandy, only to hear his wife's soft chuckle. Then she elaborated on the source of her amusement.

"My dear sir, did you not hear me say that afterlife can be far more rewarding if one is in possession of a good memory and some imagination?"

Her husband arched a brow.

"'Tis one of your oft-repeated teachings. So?"

Lady Anne made no answer, but a fraction of a second later the shape of a full goblet materialised in her husband's right hand. He flashed her a quick glance.

"What is this?"

"The finest brandy you have ever tasted. All you need to do now is seek to remember."

With a doubtful mien, George Darcy raised the goblet and closed his eyes. The scent of the eminently delectable Martell 1751 invaded his senses. Then the fiery taste burned all the way. His wife smiled when she met his eyes over the silver rim.

"There, my dear," she said matter-of-factly. "I shall leave the three of you to your gentlemanly pursuits. Perhaps I should endeavour to occupy my mind with other matters, lest I hear the full commentary in your thoughts. I suspect the evening will become rather too lively for my taste. Pray give me a fitting *résumé* and… watch over the boys."

George Darcy nodded. He saw her vanish gracefully through the left-hand bookcase, then ambled towards one of the high-backed chairs, but thought better of it. Memory and imagination were the answer, his wife had told him. So, rather than risk having Fitzwilliam or Richard dropping onto his lap if they chanced to take a fancy to his seat later that night, he conjured up a replica of his favourite chair there, in a corner of the study. And a dashed good replica it was, even if he said so himself.

Gingerly, George Darcy eased himself into the comfortable-looking figment of his imagination. Ha! It held his weight too, and remained in one piece, he triumphantly thought, then snorted. Weight? What weight? He was insubstantial. That aside, he mused, he *could* feel the weight of the full goblet in his hand. Were he to lift the armchair he had conjured up, would he feel its weight too?

He shrugged, dismissed the experiment from his thoughts and settled into the seat with a contented sigh. Lifting chairs indeed. Whatever possessed him to even contemplate that? It was the lads' fault, he decided. Them and their bland conversation. Idle natter about mutual acquaintances – foolish bets, pranks, fortunes lost at cards. Flooded areas up north. Lord Malvern's latest purchase from Tattersalls. Richard's boastful nonsense about his new fowling piece. Confound it, when was he going to broach the significant topics? Or had the brandy addled his senses and he no longer trusted himself with that?

George Darcy applied himself to his own brandy, and blessed his wife's teachings. The dear soul, how would he have fared without her company and the benefit of her experience in all things pertaining to the afterlife?

When the contents of his glass began to dwindle, George Darcy was pleased to see he could refill it. Hm. Armagnac this time. An appealing aroma. It would do.

At about the same time, he was compelled to own that he had done his nephew by marriage an injustice. Nay, Richard's senses were not addled. He had merely bided his time. He must have thought he had waited long enough for the circumstances to ripen to his satisfaction, for he suddenly began without preamble. Without a warning shot either. He went straight for the heavy artillery.

"So, I take it that the russet-clad lady in the miniature Georgiana gave you is no self-portrait. 'Tis your Miss Bennet, is she not?"

Darcy's head jerked up, and so did his fortunately empty glass.

"What?"

His father snorted. Goodness, could the lad do no better than that when startled by a direct question? Seemingly of the same mind, the colonel pressed on.

"Come now, no more talk of casual acquaintances. I will not have it. Why, your hand shook when you took the ivory out of its wrappings. I doubt it was an attack of sensibility brought on by Georgiana's remarkable skill, and you cannot blame it on the brandy either. You could not have been so lost to common decency as to start the day foxed. Least of all Christmas Day."

"Leave off, Richard," Darcy muttered, but his cousin chortled.

"Not a chance. So, let us start with the obvious. True, the silhouette could be anybody, but judging by your response and Georgiana's, it was not meant to be your sister, and well you know it. Yet you are still dissembling. But we will soon do away with that. Firstly, pray tell me, how came Georgiana to paint that scene, and make you a present of it for Christmas?"

For a moment, Darcy seemed about to protest, or demand he be left in peace. But he must have seen it was a losing battle, and that he was no match for his cousin's expert skill and determination. Or perhaps he could not resist the impulse to unburden himself. His father sat up in anticipation. He was not disappointed.

"There was a passage in one of my letters," Darcy owned. "Georgiana painted what I described."

"Let us speak plainly: what you described – or rather whom – was Miss Elizabeth Bennet?"

"Yes!" Darcy snapped. "Are you satisfied?"

"Nowhere near," the other cheerfully assured him.

"I wish you would desist," Darcy observed with manifest resignation, as though he already knew it would not come to pass. "Or rather," he added with a sigh, "I wish I had not betrayed myself in such a foolish manner. 'Tis damnably vexing to be so transparent that even my little sister can see through me."

"I would not be overly concerned about that if I were you. She must be reassured. To find that you are human, after all," he elaborated, in response to Darcy's look of surprise.

In a flash, the surprise melted into scorn.

"Human! Is that the measure of a man? Succumbing to infatuation?"

"Is that what you call it?" the colonel parried.

"Aye. One devil of a nuisance, but it will pass," Darcy retorted and raised his glass to his lips, only to find it empty.

He stood – and did not stagger, his father noted. Good on him. He must have learned to hold his brandy. Across the room, the colonel raised his own empty glass in a silent request for a refill, and the lad obliged him. The colonel nodded by way of thanks – and barely waited for Darcy to resume his seat before firing another salvo from his impregnable assault position.

"What makes you so certain it will pass? Here we are, the best part of two months since your intrepid ride into Hertfordshire, and your so-called infatuation has not left you."

"Nigh on ten weeks," Darcy countered, incautiously undermining his own defences.

"Pardon?"

"We met nine and a half weeks ago; on the twentieth of October."

His cousin sat up with a grin.

"Your accuracy does you credit. I'd wager you could tell me the exact number of hours since that memorable encounter, if I pressed you."

Darcy scowled. Fitzwilliam's grin grew wider.

"I knew it!" he exulted. "Ha! The thunderbolt, was it? And about time, too."

"Nonsense," Darcy spluttered.

He might have saved his breath. The shelling continued.

"Let me hazard a guess: you find yourself thinking about her several times a day."

"I do not!"

"Oh, I think you do. And several times a night besides."

"No."

"Yes. You have never been plagued in this manner before, and now that you are, it unsettles you beyond belief. You heard the affliction mentioned by others and you scorned it as nonsense, weakness or exaggeration. It vexes you to see there was truth in their accounts, and it irks you even more to find yourself as weak as those you scorned, but there is nothing you can do about it. The more you try to focus on your letters, your steward's communications, your dinner and whatnot, the more stubbornly your thoughts turn towards her. You write letters to your sister and pepper them with her name, yet you hardly notice. And then at night you are a sitting duck. You cannot control your dreams – who can? You wake up and curse them. If they are particularly vivid, you curse yourself too, not that it makes a shade of difference. You try to fall asleep again, dreams be damned, but hours later you are still awake. Tossing and turning. Staring at the canopy. Picturing her in various stages of *déshabille*."

"Hold your tongue, Richard!"

"Why? Am I too close for comfort?"

"No. You are offensively coarse."

"You call that coarse? Goodness, you have had a sheltered upbringing."

"So had you. Yet look at you now. It must be the company you keep."

"The company I kept, you mean. Poor form, Darcy, to lay the blame on His Majesty's army. But thanks to my injury, lewd jests by the bivouac fire are but a distant memory, so you are sorely off the mark. Unless you were speaking of your own corrupting influence, in which case you are probably right. Frustration and impure thoughts are positively billowing out of you. No wonder they corrupt me."

George Darcy chortled at his nephew's charming impudence. Far less amused, his son gave a loud snort and rolled his eyes. The colonel sipped his drink and pressed on.

"Still, thank goodness for an overactive imagination, eh? No better cure for your kind of insomnia than continuing from where your lustful dreams leave off. Except actually bedding her, of course. But from what I gathered, that is not an option. A pity that—"

The cushion flung at his head went woefully off-course, which showed George Darcy that his son was far from sober after all. The deuced thing went right through him instead, and landed in his corner with a soft thud, having missed the colonel by a shocking margin.

"Clumsy pup! That could have overset my glass," George Darcy grumbled, before conceding that it was a physical impossibility. Besides, he could have conjured up a full one anyway.

The colonel derisively chortled.

"That was laughable, Coz. I did not even have to dodge it. As I was saying, a pity that she is not of the lesser sort. Then a *carte blanche* might have done the trick, and cured your ills in no time at all."

"Damn you and your crudeness! That *is not* what I want."

"The devil it isn't! Unless the last spill from your horse has turned you into a eunuch."

The second cushion did not fare much better than the first, George Darcy noted. But at least this one flew closer to his nephew – and missed both him and Richard. His son was forced to resort to a tirade of abuse instead.

"What the deuce has got into you tonight? You have always been a pestering wretch, but this is beyond the pale. Were you so starved for entertainment in Nottinghamshire that you had to come and badger me? Can they not find you some employment at Horse Guards, now that you are out of the Peninsula? You could have at least gone to your sister's and vex her and her husband instead."

"Nothing vexes Lytham, and you know it. Which is presumably why he and Maria are getting on so well."

"Regardless—"

"Regardless," the other cut him off, "I had no wish to go into Westmorland and leave you to simmer and seethe until steam bursts out and you do yourself a mischief."

"I do not—"

"Oh, for God's sake, Coz, enough of your brave front," the colonel exclaimed. "I had to endure it for upwards of two decades. Ever since you have learned to take restraint and turn it into an art form. In point of fact, once we win the war – as, by the bye, we must – if they ever decide to raise a statue to English stiff-necked pride and dogged determination, I will suggest they model it on you. You take some righteous notion into your head and obdurately defend it at all costs. No form of cajoling serves to talk you out of it. Gentle methods and amiable prodding stand no chance to sway you. Nothing works with you but an almighty battering ram. That, and fuses lit under you, until something explodes and brings down your defences. I know. The pair of us have played this game more often than I care to count, and I grant you, it can be diverting, but it grows tedious after a while. So pray, do us both a favour, come out of your cursed fortress and tell me what is plaguing you."

George Darcy gave a nod of appreciation. Fine fellow, Richard. He could not have put it better himself. Seemingly, his son had the good sense to acknowledge that the colonel had the right of it. Darcy exhaled, and tiredly conceded.

"Fine. Have it your way." He took a fortifying draught and resumed, warming considerably to the subject as he went on; yet, despite being on the wrong side of fifty – and, moreover, dead – George Darcy could instantly tell that the heat had naught to do with the brandy: "Yes, I want her. More than I have ever wanted any woman. I want her in my bed. I want her in my life. Your damned *carte blanche* is no answer, even if I could sink myself and her to such depravity. Even if she were the parlour maid I first took her for—"

Most unwisely, the colonel released an immoderate guffaw.

"This is priceless," he chortled. "How did it come about?"

George Darcy shifted in his seat, grumbling at the interruption. Richard should have kept his amusement in check, along with his curiosity. Fair enough, the details might have been diverting and he would have liked to hear them himself, but they could wait. What a foolish way of undoing all that hard work in getting the lad to talk!

He need not have fretted. His son was well past the point of no return.

"No matter," Darcy said with a gesture of impatience. "Even if she were low-born and I took her for my mistress, who the blazes could leave one such as her to come home to some nondescript female from the right circles? Not because she is some classically perfect beauty. That would be her sister. Her eldest sister, Jane. Bingley was enraptured at first sight. You know how apt he is to make a fool of himself over a handsome woman."

The colonel nodded with a wry grin, but thankfully said nothing this time. Darcy resumed:

"Jane catches the eye. Elizabeth holds it. There is naught dull or commonplace about her. Which means she could not have been of the lesser sort. Too bright for that. Too genteel. Too… perfect."

He slammed the glass down on the table beside him and stood to stride towards the fireplace. The rest of the confession was made to the leaping flames.

"I should count myself fortunate that she is not a housemaid and I cannot make her my mistress. It would have cured nothing. Merely caused me to become a laughingstock. Worse than Bingley. If she came to my bed, I would want her in my home, and honoured. I would want her children brought up here, and Pemberley to go to her son, rather than to some offspring born from duty."

The colonel's eyes grew impossibly wide.

"Heavens. You are further gone than I thought. There are no two ways about it, then. You must offer for the lass."

Darcy's head whipped towards him. The flames cast moving shadows on one side of his face and glittered in the corners of his eyes.

"And do you not think I would have offered for her already, if I could?" he shot back.

"What is there to stop you?"

"Everything. Pemberley. Georgiana's prospects. Every precept that was drilled into me ever since I was out of leading strings."

"Oh, I see," Richard evenly replied. "I thought we might come to that."

"To what?" Darcy snapped.

"To whatever it is that she is lacking. What is it? A suitable dowry?"

Darcy bridled at the tone. Nevertheless, he nodded.

"Her father is a small country squire."

"And thus unable to compensate the Pemberley coffers for the eventual loss of Georgiana's thirty thousand pounds, I imagine."

"Just so. Even if he had no other daughters to provide for. He has five."

"Some would never master continence," the colonel drawled, then proceeded to prod his cousin further. "So, are Pemberley's coffers so depleted that they could not withstand the loss? Your father left his affairs in good order, to my knowledge. What have you squandered your inheritance on?"

"You know full well I did no such thing," Darcy predictably bristled. "But how would Georgiana fare on the marriage mart if I supply her with graceless connections?"

"Ah. Therein lies the rub, does it? What are we speaking of? Scandal, or the whiff of trade?"

"Both. There are two uncles in trade, one of whom resides in *Cheapside*," he harshly emphasised, "and a sister who was caught canoodling with an officer and was consequently banished to Hunsford—"

"Lord above," the colonel chortled. "Poor lass. Hunsford? Into our aunt's keeping? Why on earth?"

"Not our aunt's. Her parson's. Collins. The middle sister is wedded to him," Darcy clarified.

"Is she? How did he contrive to persuade any woman to join her fortunes with his?"

"Precisely. Would you have me as his brother?"

The colonel laughed.

"Lady Catherine would go distracted. Insult to injury, were you to cause her to become related to her parson, over and above thwarting her ambition of seeing you wedded to her daughter."

"So you see it too," Darcy said, spreading his hands out in a gesture of defeat.

"See what? The full extent of your predicament? Aye, Darcy, your misfortunes are great indeed. You fall in love with someone who is—? Wait, what was it? Aye, now I have it. Too bright, too genteel and too perfect, but poor and with connections in trade.

I commend you for treasuring your precious prejudices above all else. I hope they warm your bed, because little else will. Oh, hush," he said, raising a hand to silence Darcy's protest. "I know. You will marry. Some prim, proper and dull miss, no doubt. And pine for your Elizabeth. Suit yourself and wait for your reward in Heaven. Myself, I would rather have my joys in this life."

"So you will marry with no regard to fortune and connections, will you? You make me laugh."

"Pray do, if it gives you comfort. I assure you, I have no intention to sell myself."

"If you have such great hopes of coming across some paragon that would answer all your wishes, what makes you think I will not?"

"Because, you poor deluded dunce, you are already hooked, as you have just demonstrated. Oh, wait. We are back to where we started: you are hooked, but it will pass."

"Precisely," Darcy enunciated.

"Very well. Keep telling yourself that, and go forth with my blessing."

The other snorted.

"Why, thank you. Your blessing! I do not recollect asking for it. You are not my father."

The colonel shrugged.

"I can only thank my stars for that."

Chapter 14

Unlike his nephew by marriage, George Darcy neither could nor would thank his stars as he sat in the quiet study. His son had by then retired to his chambers in high dudgeon, and once he had finished his brandy, Richard had followed suit.

George Darcy knew he should seek his wife and acquaint her with what he had learned, yet he could not bring himself to do so yet. He was not ready to give her a full account of all their failings. Besides, he strongly suspected that, given her upbringing and exalted heritage, Lady Anne would think their son's stance was principled and just. But she had not seen the anguish in his eyes; did not know how much it cost him to uphold the principles his parents had jointly advocated.

Duty to one's family, lineage and estate. He, too, had valued them above all else, George Darcy was compelled to own. He had followed the path of duty. Had forsaken the sweet Cambridge lass that had captured his heart in his callow youth. A tradesman's daughter was no fitting match for a Darcy of Pemberley. He, too, had labelled it an untoward infatuation and forced himself to turn his back on it. Went forth to marry the well-dowered scion of a noble family. And spent his life mildly resenting his society wife for their passionless union.

In truth, he had not given Anne a chance. Would matters have been different, had he come to the marriage without another in his heart?

Aye, Anne was a quiet, undemonstrative sort. But, as she had rightly pointed out during their quarrel over Wickham, while that was not her way, it certainly was his. He *was* one for demonstrativeness.

Would it have made a difference? Would he have brought his wife out of her placid shell, had he lavished her with affection? Had he not envisaged Constance in her place at the table – in her place in his bed?

With a start, George Darcy fought to silence his self-recriminations, and dearly hoped that Anne was indeed seeking to occupy her mind with other matters, rather than listening to the goings-on in his head. Heaven forbid that she should have heard what he was thinking. The dear soul, she deserved better than that. She had made him a good wife – had given him her allegiance and two wonderful children.

George Darcy sighed as he acknowledged his duty to the three of them, his family. And above all, his duty to his son.

He stood and focused his mind upon Darcy's bedchamber, then thought better of it. He was still unskilled in the art of transporting himself from one place to another in the blink of an eye. It would require too much concentration. His thoughts would grow too intense, too... loud. Anne might hear them. What had to be done now should be done without her involvement. Thus, he resigned himself to taking the long way round.

෩෧ ෧෨෨

The lad was lying deep in sleep before him. Or at least George Darcy hoped it was deep sleep rather than intoxication, and that his son was in a fit state to hear him. Either way, it had to be done.

Just as he had all those months ago, when he had sought to avert the Ramsgate disaster, George Darcy channelled his thoughts as best he could. With everything he had, with everything he was, he urged his son:

"Fitzwilliam? You – have – your – father's – blessing. Go to it, m'boy. Marry her. Go to it!"

Just like the last time, he condensed his exhortations into a clear message, repeated over and over.

"Marry her. You have my blessing."

Unlike the last time, the lad did not thrash in his sleep, leading George Darcy to fear he was past his reach. Yet suddenly, without the least warning, his son sat bolt upright, matted forelocks falling over his brow, a wild look in his eyes as they darted over the moonlit room. He exhaled and rubbed his temples.

"Blasted brandy," he muttered. "And that confounded thing."

He cast the counterpane aside and reached to open the drawer of the bedside table. The miniature was within; George Darcy could easily spot it. The lad brought it out, to stare at it with narrowed eyes, then gripped it in his fist as though he was of a mind to break it. He could not have, of course. But it was not for lack of strength that the artefact was spared. Fitzwilliam sighed, and his grip slackened.

"Bless her heart," he whispered. "I cannot hurt her feelings so. She thought it would please me. Georgy, darling girl, if only you knew…" He gave a strange sound, half sigh and half snort. "Not her fault. Mine, for dwelling on it and drinking myself into a stupor. And Richard's goading. All that talk about giving me his blessing. Wretched imaginings," he scoffed.

But the sardonic twist of his mouth slowly fell. His countenance turned pensive, troubled, and his gaze drifted beyond the piece of ivory that he was holding, and became a faraway stare.

"This is madness," he suddenly muttered, shaking his head. "It cannot be. I know it cannot. Yet 'tis too much of a coincidence. Same as last time… And there was truth in it then. I know not how, but that dream— There was truth in it. Ramsgate. Georgiana. Protecting her…"

The whispers grew barely audible, then faded into silence. Oppressive silence. No sound, no movement, just the steady murmur of his breaths. Until the eerie stillness was broken by one word – quiet, hesitant, and almost childlike:

"Father?"

"Yes!" George Darcy called back. "I am here. I give you my blessing. Marry her and be happy. Do you hear me? Go to it!"

A cresting wave of energy and hope carried the heartfelt entreaty; carried it to the outer reaches of his world. But not beyond. With a sigh, Darcy shook his head, returned the miniature to its place and forcefully slammed the drawer shut.

"I *am* running mad. Good God, Elizabeth, what a pitiful wretch you have reduced me to!"

Determination swelled in George Darcy like never before. His every thought came to be focused on the drawer, willing it to slide open. Willing it with all his might. Until Lady Anne's sharp reprimand pierced his thoughts and broke his concentration.

"Desist! Desist at once!"

George Darcy came out of his self-imposed trance with a start, and acknowledged her presence. She verily glowered.

"Leave the drawer," she spoke with unprecedented sternness. "And leave the boy be. You *will not* taunt him with that wretched piece of ivory. He is shaken enough already."

"He is ready to believe," he eagerly countered. "Anne, he called to me! I must get through. He needs my blessing. I want him to have it."

"Your blessing? For *that* union?"

"You heard?"

"Some of it, yes. It could not be helped. Fitzwilliam was very…" She grimaced, then settled for "…forceful. I heard enough. No fitting match for him, that. To his credit, he knows it."

"Aye. He does. And 'tis making him desperately unhappy."

Lady Anne gave an unladylike snort.

"And you would have him wedded to that Hertfordshire chit of such poor stock? Heavens! Are the shades of your ancestors and mine to be thus polluted?"

George Darcy heaved a deep sigh, then reached for her hand.

"Anne, my dear, pray listen. He loves her. Our son, our upright and discerning son loves this girl, and thinks her bright, genteel and perfect. He is nearing nine-and-twenty. Not a youth with no mind of his own, but a grown man. Can we not trust his judgement and approve of her unseen? This is what holds him back: the fear of our disapproval. What saddens me the most is that in my lifetime I might not have approved. I might have valued status over sentiment. It matters not. I see it now, with the wisdom of infinity. But it seems we did our earthly job too well, and passed our prejudices on. We must strive to pass this newly-acquired wisdom, too. Status is left behind. Our sentiments come with us, a part of our very soul. And if his soul craves this girl, what can I do but give him my blessing?"

Lady Anne pursed her lips and made no answer. A rueful little smile at the corner of his lips, her husband entreated:

"Come. Pray come and assist me, as you did last time. Let him have your blessing too."

Her countenance dreadfully pinched, Lady Anne withdrew her hand as if it had been burned.

"I want no part in this," she said with energy. "Side with the tradesmen's niece, if you must. You doubtlessly have your reasons. At the very least, you must acknowledge that I have sufficient grounds to advocate for a *society wife*."

The last words shot out with unconcealed, raw bitterness.

George Darcy winced.

"You heard that as well?" he penitently whispered. "About Constance? Anne, I—"

"Oh, spare me your contrition," she vehemently cut him off. "At least now I know what my greatest flaw was: I was not *her*. Well, that answers it and puts paid to my self-reproaches. There was nothing I could have done about it. I daresay I should be grateful to Fitzwilliam's damsel for bringing about this belated reassurance."

"She is not Fitzwilliam's damsel—"

Lady Anne made a gesture of impatient vexation, but her husband pleadingly continued:

"I deserve your anger. But nobody else does. Pray do not let my sins be visited upon our son."

"Or your mistakes?" she retorted, her bitterness unabated.

"You were not a mistake," George Darcy earnestly countered.

"If I was, then it was through no fault of mine. And apparently it was through no fault of mine that we had an unhappy union."

"It was not unhappy," George Darcy was once more driven to protest. "There was—"

"If you say *'contentment,'* I will not vouch for the consequences. It was not enough, was it? And you want more than contentment for our son."

"Do you not?"

"With the tradesmen's niece?" she sneered.

"She is a gentleman's daughter." Which Constance was not, George Darcy felt obliged to inwardly own.

"*Would* you cease bringing that person into the conversation?" Lady Anne fiercely demanded.

Flustered, he shot her a contrite glance.

"I… did not mean to bring—" he floundered. Damnation! Of all the hardships of the afterlife, losing the privacy of one's thoughts was arguably the worst.

"I agree," Lady Anne snapped, thus proving his point once more.

George Darcy sighed. He was not helping his son's case one iota. Doubtlessly, his wife's inborn prejudices would have been less difficult to conquer, had he not provoked her with unwitting and certainly untimely revelations from his past.

"Pray do not make assumptions as regards my prejudices," Lady Anne answered his thoughts again. "And leave Fitzwilliam to his rest. I beg you would cease pestering him on account of your regrets. You heard him well enough. 'Tis but an infatuation. It will pass."

It would be unconscionably cruel to allow her to sense his instinctive response: that time softened the sharp pangs of regret, but could not fully vanquish them. George Darcy made every conceivable effort to smother his thoughts into bland silence. He did not succeed.

"Fitzwilliam is not you," Lady Anne shot back. "Do not presume to think and speak for him. You said yourself, you could never understand him because of his reserve. Because he is so much like me. And that girl, what do you know of her – what she is like, what she is thinking? Do you imagine she will make him happy if she does not love him? If she accepts him merely for his station in life? For heaven's sake, George, leave the boy be!"

Racked with guilt over the pain he had inflicted on his wife, George Darcy did not need to be told why she was so incensed at her son being regarded as a desirable life companion merely because of his wealth and status.

As he helplessly watched the lad donning his dressing gown and striding out of his bedchamber, he also felt compelled to own that he had no good answer to Lady Anne's charges. No, he could not vouch for that girl's sentiments. How could he?

His wife stalked out of the bedchamber too, leaving George Darcy to wonder, among other things, why she had addressed him by his Christian name, when for decades she had never veered from '*Mr Darcy.*'

∽⊙℘ ℘⊙∾

Pemberley, 27 December 1811

"What say you of calling upon Lady Catherine, Coz?" Colonel Fitzwilliam nonchalantly asked on the following morning, as he set aside the book he was leafing through and stretched his long legs before him.

Darcy cast him a glance over his paper.

"Is it Easter already? I had not noticed."

"What an undutiful wretch you are. Who is to say you cannot visit her sooner?"

The paper rustled as Darcy turned the page.

"Why should I?" he asked.

"Out of the goodness of your heart?"

"It is precisely out of the goodness of my heart that I do not. It will not do to feed false hopes and make our aunt believe that my attachment to Rosings is steadily increasing. But by all means, go without me," Darcy added smoothly and turned the page again.

"You read uncommonly fast."

"And you think I do not see your game," Darcy replied as he dropped the paper on the table at his elbow. "Georgiana told you, did she not?"

"Told me what?"

"Who do you imagine you can fool with that show of innocence? You heard about our cousin's letter."

"Which cousin?" Colonel Fitzwilliam asked with a blank face, but when his lips began to twitch beyond control he gave in to laughter and abandoned the charade. "Very well. Yes, Georgiana mentioned over breakfast that Anne wrote last week with some fascinating tidings. By the bye, you should have joined us. A bite to eat does wonders after a night of heavy drinking. How is your head?"

"Well enough. It will be all the better for some peace and quiet," Darcy muttered as he picked his paper up again.

"Cease hiding behind that, will you?"

"And I could ask you to cease being a nuisance, but I hate wasting my breath."

"So do I, Darcy."

"Praise be."

"Do not be facetious, 'tis unbecoming. Will you go into Kent if I undertake to keep you company and share my wisdom?"

"No. And you cannot share that which you do not have."

"You are a hard-headed dullard, and one day I will wash my hands of you."

"The best notion. Let that day be the morrow. Or better still, today."

Colonel Fitzwilliam shrugged.

"Suit yourself. I am going to Rosings, and I have a mind to take Georgiana with me. I am her guardian too—"

His cousin's fierce scowl instantly told him that he had carried his teasing too far.

"By all means, go. To Kent, Westmorland, or wherever you please. But do not dare involve Georgiana in this."

"You know I was not in earnest—" the other began, but he was not suffered to continue.

"But I was. You are leaving on the morrow, Cousin. Or feel free to remain at Pemberley in our absence. I *am* leaving, and Georgiana is coming with me."

"Where are you going? I hear the air at Ro—"

"For your sake, I hope you were about to recommend I take the air in Roseacre, Rotherham or Rochdale, for if you say Rosings again, you will not be able to speak for a long time," Darcy snapped.

The other leaned back in his seat and wisely forbore to arch a brow or indicate in some other manner that he doubted his cousin could physically prevail over him and carry out that threat. Instead, he begged Darcy's pardon for pushing him beyond endurance.

The apology was accepted with ill grace and tightened lips.

There was marginally more goodwill in Darcy's words and mien later that day, when they parted to go their separate ways. Colonel Fitzwilliam headed north to see the New Year in with the rest of his family. As for Darcy, he stayed true to his word and left Pemberley as well, along with Georgiana and Mrs Annesley. It came as no surprise that he would not consider accompanying his cousin into Westmorland, but set off for town instead.

ༀ

Berkeley Square, London, February 1812

Despite the many amusements town had to offer, Darcy could be naught but acutely aware that, having removed from Pemberley to his house in Berkeley Square, he was much closer now to both Kent and Hertfordshire – that he was, in fact, about halfway between Rosings and Longbourn.

Nonetheless, with the dogged determination that his cousin had accused him of, he did not budge for two months complete. Moreover, for some considerable time he would not even open either one of the two letters that Colonel Fitzwilliam had sent him. Nigh on three decades of brotherly affection had long prevailed over the momentary hot-headedness, and their disagreement was long forgiven. Yet it was far from forgotten and besides, Darcy had no wish to find his cousin's arguments reiterated in his letters. Which was why he still had not opened them by the time a short note of apology was on its way to the Fitzwilliam seat in Nottinghamshire.

His cousin's reply was brief, to the point and very much like him.

Darcy,

Do not regard it. As we have long established, you are an ungrateful wretch, but blood is thicker than water, so there is nothing for it – I am lumbered with you till my dying day. And vice versa, naturally. On this happy note, I will hopefully see you sometime in March at Pemberley on my way into town, or in Berkeley Square if you are still there.

My reason for coming, if you must know, is that unlike ungrateful wretches who shall remain unnamed, I am not above taking unsolicited advice. So I will follow yours and seek some gainful employment at Horse Guards.

If your goodwill dwindles between now and March, pray have your people hang a red banner in the window above the main entrance of either one of your residences – or both. Then I will catch your meaning and ride off until the storm is well and truly past. Otherwise I will come under a flag of truce and undertake not to pester you on certain subjects unless I am assured you are too foxed to remember. Vale et me ama*¹, as you know you must.

Yours ever,
Richard Fitzwilliam

---

*¹ Farewell and love me (Lat.)

Chapter 15

Pemberley, 19 March 1812

Colonel Fitzwilliam's peace-making visit found Darcy and his sister only just returned to Pemberley a few days earlier. No red banner was placed in the first-floor window above the main entrance, and the cousins greeted each other as warmly as ever.

Whether or not the colonel would have kept his word as regards pestering on certain subjects, Darcy would never know. The embargo was lifted on the following morning, at breakfast. When the letters were brought in, there was a particularly voluminous one for Georgiana. She opened it and gleefully announced:

"'Tis from Anne. Would you like to hear what she has to say?"

"By all means," her cousin nonchalantly said, and leaned back in his chair.

Darcy refused to glance in his direction and helped himself to a toasted muffin.

"It seems quite long. We could each look over it later," he evenly said as he sliced the muffin in two and began to meticulously butter the lower half.

"If you prefer…" Georgiana said, visibly disappointed.

"I am as impatient as you, Georgy," the colonel smoothly intervened. "So here is a good notion: let us take Anne's letter into the parlour and leave your brother to finish his breakfast in peace," he suggested, in the most innocent manner that did not fool Darcy for one second.

The prospect of silently sitting there, while they learned its contents long before he did, was as unpalatable as listening to Anne's account there and then. Nay, upon reflection, it was by far the worst option of the two.

"There is no cause for that," he said with as much unconcern as he could muster. "You can read it aloud now, Georgiana, if you wish."

She did not wait to be told a second time. She unfolded her letter, informed them that it was dated from Rosings a fortnight prior, and promptly began:

Dear Georgiana,

By now you doubtlessly think I owe you a long and rewarding description of our disports, and you would not be wrong. I should have written a good deal sooner, but I found myself distracted, every day. I hope you will forgive me.

Let me assure you, I have been exceedingly well entertained. Better than ever. The Miss Bennets are a most welcome addition to the neighbourhood. Ever since Christmas, I have spent at least two mornings of every week at the parsonage.

You wrote of theatricals at Ashford, with our cousins, but has anyone ever demonstrated to you what delights can be found in the art of bonnet-trimming? Or in parlour games, and playing a piece à quatres mains – so very badly? You must seek such amusements, they are priceless. Your brother will approve. Even my mother does – would you believe it? Let me share a brief tale, by way of example:

One day, Mamma came to fetch me from the parsonage instead of Mrs Jenkinson. I daresay she was intrigued as to what enticed me there so often. She came in unannounced. The din we were raising must have drowned out the bell. She found us in the wildest state. Miss Elizabeth was playing a jaunty tune on Mrs Collins' pianoforte, so that Miss Kitty and Miss Lydia could teach me one of their favourite dances. They had even persuaded the demure and rather despondent Miss Bennet to make up the numbers. By the time Mamma came in, I was out of breath. I had to sit, watch and clap the time, but I must have looked a fright, beet-red, with my hair in disarray, and grinning from ear to ear as I witnessed their antics.

Sadly, Mr Collins came in and witnessed them too. He and his wife had only just returned from Hunsford, moments behind Mamma, and I declare I feared for his health, for his countenance turned almost purple. He began to reprimand the Miss Bennets in the severest manner, but Mamma clasped his arm to make him desist. He was too incensed to pay heed to the gesture, however, and Mamma had to speak up to gain his notice. That did the trick. You know that no one can speak up quite like Mamma.

After that memorable occasion, she made a point of persuading the Miss Bennets to extend their stay in Kent. She took to asking them to Rosings nearly every day, to sit with me in my apartments and sometimes in the garden if the weather was fine. And they were invited to come for dinner most evenings, along with their father.

Mr Bennet is a most puzzling character. I still cannot make him out. His daughters assure me that he loves to tease, and I am beginning to see it for myself, yet at first I was taken in by his manner. He would make the drollest and often controversial of statements with a solemnity to rival Mr Collins'. They are cousins, did I mention that? Mr Collins stands to inherit Mr Bennet's estate in default of heirs male, so I daresay it was fortunate for the Miss Bennets that he married one of them. Doubly fortunate that he made his addresses to Mrs Collins – Miss Mary Bennet as was – for I daresay she was the only one who would have accepted him, or made him happy once she had. As I said before, they are remarkably alike, with the proviso that Mrs Collins seems to me the keener-witted of the two.

But never mind Mrs Collins and her domestic felicity. I was writing of her divertingly debonair father. More than once, he made Mamma's eyes nearly pop out of their sockets with his repartee. I daresay she has never been spoken to in such a manner. His second daughter, Miss Elizabeth, takes after him. You should hear them sparring. Dinners at Longbourn must be very lively indeed.

It was only when Georgiana stopped to turn the page that Darcy noticed he had been crumbling the other half of his muffin by the side of the plate. His eyes averted, lest he flash a glance across the table and see his cousin smirking, Darcy tidied the crumbs onto his plate and reached for his cup of coffee.

The timing could not have been worse. When Georgiana flipped the page over and exclaimed, "Lady Catherine *Bennet?*", the mouthful he had just taken was promptly distributed over the front of his impeccable attire by way of a loud and mortifying splutter.

"What?" the colonel exclaimed.

As wide-eyed as all the occupants of the room – ethereal and otherwise – George Darcy could not forbear a chortle. At least it was Richard's turn to resort to the uninspired utterance. Nevertheless, the years on the battlefield served him well: Richard was also the first to recover.

"Oh, dear," he drawled. "That is bound to stain. Georgy, perhaps you should stop reading and let your brother change his shirt."

"Never mind my shirt! Georgiana, may I have the letter?"

"No, no, no," the colonel protested. "You will ruin it. There is not a dry spot before you on the table. I will read the rest. Oh, fear not, I will do it justice," he added brightly as he reached and took the missive from his youngest cousin.

Loath as he was to make a scene in Georgiana's presence, over the following ten seconds learning the contents of the letter vied with strangling his cousin for the uppermost place among Darcy's dearest wishes. Yet as was generally the case with him, reason prevailed. The more he bandied words with Richard, the longer it would be until he heard what Anne had to say.

"Very well," he conceded, motioning the colonel to begin.

Georgiana dragged her chair closer to her cousin's, so that she could still decipher Anne's writing, and Darcy left his own seat to walk around the table and lean over Richard's shoulder too. Already poised in like manner, George Darcy glanced at his wife.

"Just as well they cannot sense us. We are all becoming rather crowded here."

Lady Anne smiled. The dear girl, he could not help thinking. Kind and merciful as she had been throughout her lifetime, she had yet to forgive him for inadvertently revealing the worst of his sins. But at least she smiled.

Seated in front of George Darcy and his son, the colonel covered the pages with one hand – half in jest, half in earnest – to ensure they would not be snatched from him. Darcy made a gesture of surrender and muttered:

"Just get on with it."

"Very well. Now, where were we?"

"The top of the second page," Georgiana helpfully supplied, and they all darted their eyes towards the lines dated three days ago, and written in evident agitation:

Goodness, Georgiana! I have the most momentous intelligence to impart: wedding bells at Rosings. Ringing not for me, but for my mother!

All the arrangements are in place. You know she does not dawdle when her mind is made up.

Much to his shock bordering on horror, Mr Collins learned he would soon be expected to officiate in the ceremony whereby Mamma would relinquish the name of de Bourgh and style herself as Lady Catherine Bennet!

We are only waiting for the end of Lent. The date is set for the first Monday in April.

I scarcely know how this came about. But this morning Mamma sat me down and asked if I should like to have the Miss Bennets' company every day—

Colonel Fitzwilliam stopped reading without warning, and his head whipped around towards Darcy.

"You are not still drinking your coffee, are you?" he asked with a sly grin.

Darcy narrowed his eyes and shot him a baleful glance. He had already scanned the lines and reached the end of the paragraph. Thus, long before the other saw fit to cease poking fun at him and proceeded to read it out for everyone's benefit, Darcy knew that it went as follows:

…if I should like to have the Miss Bennets' company every day at Rosings while I am still unwed, and then take one of them along to my married home. She suggested Miss Elizabeth, for she thinks her 'more energetic than her eldest sister, and less senseless than the youngest two.'

"Charming," the colonel remarked, and resumed reading aloud:

I wish I had the courage to tell Mamma that the pair of us will never see eye to eye as regards her plans for my marriage. I still lack it, today more than ever. Her famed inability to brook opposition notwithstanding, my speaking out now would be both unfeeling and undutiful. For, you see, Mamma's own wedding plans are – if not entirely, then largely – for my benefit. She told me, as I have already guessed, that she is highly gratified by the improvement in my health and demeanour following the Miss Bennets' arrival into Kent. Apparently, at first she had sought to come to an arrangement with Mr Bennet, whereby his daughters would take turns in staying at Hunsford or Rosings, in pairs, for long periods of time. But, in that droll manner of his which I have already mentioned, he said that, glad as he was to hear his daughters and I got on so well, regrettably he could not lease them to me.

Undaunted, Mamma then proceeded to pepper Mr Bennet with more questions about himself and his life in general.

With her customary frankness, she even went as far as to say that Mr Collins had described him as a bookworm who would happily devote all his time and attention to the contents of his library, and that his stewardship of Longbourn was a laissez-faire, lackadaisical affair.

Mr Bennet laughingly replied that Mr Collins had just risen meteorically in his estimation and gained a reputation for unparalleled astuteness, for the report was entirely accurate. Whereupon the astounding offer was made:

'How would you like to spend your time in the Rosings library instead, sir?' Mamma asked him. 'I assume its richness is to your taste. To put it plainly, if we come to an agreement on several matters, I am prepared to consider marriage.'

Mamma said she then made the financial aspect quite plain to Mr Bennet. She assured me too that, according to the terms of Papa's will, my inheritance is safeguarded, regardless of any connections she may form, and so is her life interest. Her attorneys, whom she had already consulted at great length, confirmed that her ample fortune is inextricably tied into assets and investments controlled by me, Lord Malvern and your brother.

Thus, should she predecease him, Mr Bennet would receive only a fraction of the dowry she had brought into her first marriage, namely ten thousand pounds. He could naturally live at Rosings until his own demise, or the dower-house if I prefer, whereupon the said ten thousand pounds would be divided evenly between his daughters.

The terms of her private agreement with Mr Bennet are as follows: over and above the aforementioned addition to their dowry, she undertook to engage the best masters for the Miss Bennets and ensure they acquire all the necessary accomplishments, not just 'the smattering they currently possess.' Then she would launch them into society and give them each a season in town.

Never one to beat about the bush, she pointed out to Mr Bennet that his daughters must 'nonetheless know their place.' As you would imagine, he did not much like that, for Mamma said he bristled, 'How should they expect to be treated? Like paid companions, on the par with the poor, beleaguered Mrs Jenkinson?'

'Beleaguered, indeed,' Mamma sniffed as she related the conversation to me — you must picture the air of regal indignation for yourself, I cannot do it justice in a letter — 'Mrs Jenkinson thinks herself most fortunate in her position, given the state of her late husband's affairs, and I left Mr Bennet in no misapprehension on that score. I also pointed out the obvious: namely that his daughters are not the heiresses of Rosings, and should not imagine they would be treated as such, in this house or elsewhere. However, a connection with the earldom of Malvern and the ancient house of de Bourgh would work

immensely in their favour, however meagre their portions. Many a gentleman with a comfortable income will seek them for their family ties alone, and separating the wheat from the chaff will be of the essence. But I shall make it my business to teach them that.'

Long story short, they came to an understanding, and every trifling detail was put in writing, including Mamma's pledges as regards the Miss Bennets, along with their father's agreement to have no involvement whatsoever in the running of the de Bourgh estates. Even the plans for Longbourn were agreed and recorded. Soon after officiating at Mamma's wedding, Mr Collins is to relinquish his duties at Hunsford, remove to Longbourn along with his wife, and for all intents and purposes act as Mr Bennet's tenant for the latter's lifetime.

So, my dear Georgiana, before long you will have a new uncle and five more cousins. Six, if we count Mr Collins. The Miss Bennets and their father will set off for Hertfordshire in a few days' time, to settle what personal belongings should be brought into their new home. We expect them to return right after Easter.

By the bye, my mother charged the pair of us to inform your brother that she expects him for Easter, as always. Moreover, that she trusts he knows better than to fear he would find her all aflutter, and Rosings in a flurry of preparations. She would like him to bear in mind that she is no scatterbrained damsel readying for her first wedding, that the event warrants no great fuss and bother, and everything of consequence has already been attended to. Mamma wishes Darcy to know that he may bring you and the dear colonel along, if you are all amenable. The three of you are of course welcome to attend the wedding, and Darcy may give her away if he wishes, but neither he nor Cousin Richard will be 'suffered to pass judgement on her choices.' She will write to your brother to that effect herself, no doubt, but there – my duty is discharged.

As to passing judgement, pray assure your brother that I am perfectly content with Mamma's choices. More than she knows, in fact, for unlike her, I expect I shall remain at Rosings for the remainder of my natural life, so I will be glad of a bevy of sisters keeping me company for as long as possible.

Doubtlessly Mamma will continue to build castles in Spain for the foreseeable future, and speak with confidence of my removal to Pemberley. That is, until I find the courage to disabuse her of that notion, or your brother obliges me by becoming engaged to some young lady or another, thus making my thorny discussion with Mamma unnecessary. Pray be so kind and nudge him in the direction of your Derbyshire beauties, will you? 'Tis most cowardly of me, I grant you, but such a denouement would be most convenient.

Until such time as Mamma abandons hope of my becoming your new sister and the chatelaine of Pemberley, perhaps I should take Miss Elizabeth into my confidence and urge her not to become too enraptured with your home on account of Mamma's fulsome praise, nor pin her hopes on following me into Derbyshire when I wed.

I trust she will not be overly disappointed to learn that it will not come to pass, and be content with the beauties of Kent instead, even if they are much tamer in comparison.

With this, I must close. My fingers have gone completely numb this half-hour. I will only add that I do hope Darcy brings you into Kent at Easter. 'Tis too long since our last meeting, and I would be delighted to introduce you to my new sisters.

Gleefully yours,
Anne d B

⁘

"And there we have it," Colonel Fitzwilliam remarked as he folded the letter. Then he turned in his chair to look at Darcy, mischief in his eyes. "So, Coz, must I still recommend you take the air in… what was it – Roseacre, Rotherham and Rochdale? Or are you willing to settle for Rosings at last? What is sauce for the goose is sauce for the gander, eh? No one can dispute that now."

No. No one could, Darcy exulted, still stunned by the about-turn in his fortunes. If Lady Catherine de Bourgh married a Bennet, there was no reason in the world why he should not. Elizabeth's portion – or rather lack thereof – had never held as much sway as her family connections, and how they would reflect upon the Darcy name and Georgiana's prospects. But now he would not be forming an alliance with the offspring of some obscure country squire. In the eyes of the world, he would be marrying his cousin – Lady Catherine's daughter, for all intents and purposes.

The irony of it did not escape him, yet it could not give him pause. His aunt's ambitions for Anne had been doomed to failure ever since the interested parties had begun to think for themselves, and it was high time her ladyship learned to accept that Anne did not desire the connection any more than he. Nonetheless, Darcy found it in him to spare a compassionate thought for his aunt who, even then, was making plans to marry in order to please her daughter, while unknowingly undermining her own schemes.

His compassion would be short-lived, and well he knew it. She would be insufferable as soon as she discovered where his affections lay. For everyone's sake, he could only hope there was truth in his suspicion that Lady Catherine was marrying to please herself as well. After all, she could have found other cheering companions for Anne, had she set her mind to it. The fact that they happened to be the daughters of a debonair gentleman with an intriguing repartee told its own story.

Darcy suppressed a chortle at the notion that he and his formidable aunt should have quite so much in common. The Fitzwilliam *sang-froid* undone by the Bennet sparkle.

In different circumstances, sharing his reflections with his cousin might have been exceedingly rewarding. Given the present ones, he kept them to himself.

"Not the best of times for your poultry metaphors," he said instead, tilting his head in his sister's direction to remind the other that he should guard his tongue, for they were not alone. But, to his vast surprise, she cast him an affectionate glance, patted Richard's arm and said matter-of-factly:

"Metaphors aside, I expect my brother is thinking of a certain childhood tale. Have you ever heard me or your sisters speaking of *Cinderilla*[*2], Cousin?"

"Not once."

"A pity. 'Tis very apropos. Fitzwilliam read it to me often when I was little. For some reason, I could not have enough of it." She stood and came to link her arm with her brother's. A warm smile was sent his way, and Darcy readily returned it. "You see, Richard," she resumed, "the tale is about a young woman who wins the heart of an illustrious personage – some charming prince," she said, stroking her brother's hand. "But throughout their courtship, they are plagued by the girl's evil stepmamma, who wishes the prince to marry her own daughter."

"Ah," said the colonel. "And is the evil stepmamma thwarted in her schemes?"

"Naturally. But 'tis a tricky business involving gourds, magic and glass slippers. Rather too much excitement for anyone's taste," she quipped, with a little shrug and a playful quirk of her lips.

[*2] 'The Stories of Cinderilla [sic] and Little Red Riding Hood' – printed by T Wilkinson, 1799, after fairy tales by Charles Perrault (1628 – 1703).

Darcy withdrew his arm from her tender clasp to wrap it around her instead, and leaned to drop a kiss into the ringlets at her temple.

"When have you grown up?" he affectionately mused.

"Hear-hear," the colonel chimed in.

"Why, thank you, 'tis very good of the pair of you to notice. But to return to Cinderilla and her suitor, I wonder how their courtship could be less fraught. For of course there must be a courtship. The hero of the tale cannot very well march in and propose at the drop of a hat. No gentleman would. Least of all a charming prince."

The heart-warming glow that stole over Darcy as his sister delivered her gentle words of wisdom was easily checked by a flare of vexation when the colonel offered his.

"So, let it be fraught," he said with a nonchalant flourish of his hand. "A good challenge never hurt anyone. Quite the opposite. What comes with great effort is more worth the earning."

Darcy rolled his eyes. It was a fair comment, but if there was any justice in the world, one fine day it would be his cousin who rallied for a good challenge and a fraught courtship, while he sat back, grinned and supplied pithy remarks. He did not get the chance to express that hope. Georgiana spoke first.

"You are quite the collection of proverbs. I hope they stand you in good stead one day. Now, I hope the pair of you will excuse me. I must settle upon a dress fit for a wedding."

She left the breakfast parlour with a spring in her step, as her brother, cousin and late parents watched her progress with matching looks of tenderness.

"She *is* grown up," George Darcy whispered. "So much like you when we were wed…"

"Bless her," was Lady Anne's sole comment.

"Aye. And the lad, too. How I wish we could go with them," her husband earnestly added.

Lady Anne sighed.

"You are not the only one."

Blessedly free to go wherever his fancy took him, her nephew rolled his shoulders back and stood.

"It seems that gainful employment at Horse Guards will have to wait. Crossing swords with Lady Catherine is by far more appealing. So, my liege, are you in need of a squire on your crusade?"

Chapter 16

Rosings, 2 April 1812

"God love you, Coz," Colonel Fitzwilliam muttered while, somewhere behind them, Lady Catherine was waxing eloquent to Georgiana about the importance of constant practice in order to achieve true excellence in music. "To your good fortune, everyone knows you have a penchant for clinging to windowsills when you are bored or vexed, otherwise you would have been dreadfully conspicuous. Come and have tea. They will not be here for at least another hour."

Darcy rolled his eyes and did not budge, although he inwardly conceded that his cousin might have been in the right about his keeping watch over the drive. Yet, mercifully, fourteen minutes later the colonel's estimation was proven wrong. The Rosings barouche landau sent to fetch the Bennet party from the turnpike inn came suddenly into view, and captured Darcy's full attention. He paid no heed to the footman who promptly came in to announce it, nor to Lady Catherine when she stood and informed them she would repair below-stairs to the drawing room to greet her guests.

Darcy made no move to follow, his gaze fixed on the carriage as it advanced, then drew up to the entrance. Footmen came to lower the step, swing the door open and bow to the emerging occupants. Mr Bennet was the first to step out, then one of his younger daughters. Darcy could not tell which, nor did he care. His unblinking scrutiny was finally rewarded with the sight of another small slipper on the carriage step – a shapely ankle, promptly covered – a slender form clad in russet and ochre – wavy locks under the brim of the bonnet – dark-brown eyes casting a brief glance at the *façade*, then darting towards her father as he handed her out – full lips forming an inaudible "Thank you," then shaping themselves into a smile.

Darcy mirrored it, as his chest expanded with a deep breath. Lord, how he had missed her! He leaned forward, closer to the windowpane, and tension eased from his whole frame as he greedily took in the welcome sight. He shook his head in silent wonder that he had borne her absence for twenty weeks complete. The end of the torment made him almost giddy with relief. Elizabeth… At last!

He spun around with a start when a hand clasped his shoulder. His cousin – by then the only other person in the room – gave him an affectionate pat on the back.

"The bugle calls. Are you ready? You had better be. Well, then, go to it. What are you waiting for?"

∾⊙ ⊙∾

Rosings, 14 April 1812

He was *not* ready. To his chagrin, Darcy discovered as much within hours – minutes. And each passing day brought further proof that he was woefully unprepared in the face of her irresistible allure. Everything about her called to him, triggering his every sense into almost unbearable alertness, acute to the point of pain. The sound of her voice drifting from another room. Her musical laughter. Her glance meeting his for a staggering flicker of a second, across a crowded parlour. The scent emanating from the folds of her dress when she walked past or sat across from him, chatting to the others. Hardly ever to him, which was little wonder, since he was mostly silent. He could not trust himself to say more than a few inconsequential words to her – for other words burned in his throat, clamouring for release. The need to declare himself was overpowering. Too many months had gone by, wasted. He had kept away for long enough, too long. It was sheer hell to wait even longer before asking for a private interview and openly avowing that in vain he had struggled, and it would not do. That he was hers within days of their acquaintance, and it was high time she knew it.

Upon reflection, it was beyond foolish to imagine he would have responded otherwise to their reunion. He had spent the last five months longing for her. Of course the old yearning would surge beyond control and play havoc with his attempts to string ten words together without turning them into a proposal.

He should have expected that.

What he had expected was that Lady Catherine would be a nuisance, and a devil of a reef to navigate around. He had anticipated the constraints that came with dwelling under a roof that was not his: gone was the freedom to pace the halls at night if it pleased him, trade quips with his cousin over brandy, or simply seek sanctuary in the library. Ever since the very quiet wedding on the first Monday of the month, the library at Rosings had become Mr Bennet's domain – and while Darcy saw merit in becoming better acquainted with Elizabeth's father, he was in no haste to become a target for that gentleman's keen eyes and famed wit.

He had also anticipated that, despite the lack of freedom that came with living in Lady Catherine's house, his cousin Richard would find ample opportunity to comment on the progress of his courtship, mercilessly tease him about it too, no doubt, yet diligently enlist the help of their natural allies – Anne and Georgiana – to deflect Lady Catherine's attention and create auspicious moments.

What he had *not* expected was that, well-nigh a fortnight after the Bennets' arrival into Kent, his exchanges with Elizabeth would still bear little resemblance to a courtship. Granted, he was sufficiently hampered by the fact that he could not talk to her without wanting to kiss her. Nevertheless, he had nurtured the hope that, somehow, their interactions would drift back towards what they had been in Hertfordshire – amiable and increasingly light-hearted – and that the openness would grow from there. More readily so, given the family connection.

It was not so, and he could not fathom why. There was a reserve about her, an aloofness that had not been there before. Almost as though she was avoiding him.

There was good reason to believe that, fully aware of Lady Catherine's ambitions for Anne, she was loath to provoke her new stepmother. Yet why should she keep her distance when Lady Catherine was not there?

The latter instances were few and far between, in any case. To Darcy's growing irritation, his aunt was almost always *there*. Very much so. Overbearing. Clamouring for his attention and interrupting his every exchange, with anyone. Not just with Elizabeth – brief and frustratingly infrequent as they were – but even when he was speaking to Anne, the colonel or his own sister. Regardless of the topic, Lady Catherine simply had to have her share in the conversation. And every conversation with her ladyship invariably became a monologue.

At the end of yet another dreadfully unrewarding day, Darcy shifted in his seat, scowling in impotent vexation. Heavens, she was still talking! Barely less uncouth than Elizabeth's Aunt Phillips, yet certainly more irksome. At least the vulgar Meryton matron had the decency to hold her tongue during a musical performance.

He leaned forward, striving to ignore his aunt's ramblings about Mrs Jenkinson's four nieces, Lady Metcalfe and her treasured Miss Pope – a gem among governesses – and instead fill his senses with the magic of *her* song. It was a challenge. They were divided by the whole length of the room, and Lady Catherine was squarely between them. Yet he had purposely chosen to sit there, far behind the cluster of sofas and chairs occupied by the others. One of his reasons was to discourage his aunt's attempts at engaging him in conversation. The other – the overriding one – was to avoid her scrutiny. Keeping an impassive mien while Elizabeth was playing was a challenge too.

Poignant notes dripped from the harp strings, under her nimble fingers, and he drew a deep breath, as if to fill the emptiness within. Whoever had devised that instrument – the one most apt to tug at every string of a brimming heart? He never knew she could play the harp. Netherfield did not boast one, and neither did Lucas Lodge, the only other places where he had been privileged to see her sit at an instrument. There must have been a harp at Longbourn. This clearly was not one of the accomplishments she had begun to learn at Rosings – there was too much skill in the exquisite fingering. There was too much bitter-sweetness in the words as well, when she joined them to the music, and yearning swelled, untamed and unconfined.

It would have been too much, perhaps, to say that he was grateful to Miss Lydia when she barely waited for the end of the song to exclaim loudly – and thus break the magic that lingered in the air along with the last fading notes. Strictly speaking, he could not be grateful for the petulant discordance. But neither could he claim it did not have its uses in tempering the yearning with a sharp dose of reality.

"Goodness, Lizzy," she cried. "Enough of that maudlin stuff. Play a jig, so that we can dance. I long for a dance. Do you not, Colonel Fitzwilliam?"

"I *beg* your pardon?" spluttered Lady Catherine, piercing her with an icy glare. "Let me be rightly understood: if I see merit in the healthful effects of exercise, that is not to say you may commandeer my music room without so much as a by your leave. And above all, young lady, I will not tolerate your flirting with my nephew."

"I was *not* flirting," Lydia retorted hotly.

"Petulant children who talk back belong in their bedchamber," Lady Catherine enunciated. "Come, now. Be off with you."

"That is grossly unfair!" Kitty exclaimed, in a determined show of loyalty. "I do not see what my sister did that was so very wrong. We just wanted to dance."

"Since you cannot see Lydia's fault, you should join her above-stairs and reflect upon the matter at your leisure," Lady Catherine decreed with a quelling stare. "Leave at once. Both of you."

Cheeks aflame with indignation and tears of acute frustration sparkling in their eyes, the youngest Miss Bennets stood, locked hands and stomped towards the door in a flurry of skirts, without another word to anyone present. Jane made to join them, but Elizabeth was already on her feet.

"Pray excuse me," she said to the assembled party, as she briefly paused to lay a comforting hand on Jane's shoulder on her way towards the door, then hastened to shepherd her beleaguered younger sisters out of the music room.

Her countenance – a mute picture of concern – was all the reason Darcy needed to leave his seat and follow her, without any regard for what his aunt might make of it.

By the time he closed the door behind him, she was already at the foot of the staircase, one arm around each of her younger sisters. For his part, Darcy remained where he was, quite at a loss as to what he might say or do in order to offer Elizabeth some form of reassurance or at least consolation. Yet she paid him no heed – might not have even registered his presence. Her sobbing sisters had her full attention.

As impulsive and unrestrained as ever, the youngest flung her arms around Elizabeth's neck. Miss Lydia's venomous hiss just about reached him across the otherwise empty entrance hall, when she viciously spat:

"I hate her, Lizzy. I *hate* her! Mary and Mr Collins' strictures were bad enough, not to mention having to be on my best behaviour whenever I came to see Anne, but I will go distracted stuck here forever with that awful woman. I want to go back to Longbourn. I shan't stay here another day!"

"I fear you must, my pet," Elizabeth affectionately replied. "Unless you are prepared to listen to more of Fordyce's sermons."

"Lord, no! Then I shan't go to Longbourn. Aunt Phillips will have me. Or Aunt Gardiner."

"What, and bid adieu to a season in town? And to hundreds of beaus hanging on your every word?"

"The old witch would scare them all away," Kitty grumbled. "Did you not hear what she said the other day, that she will not tolerate us throwing ourselves away on the first man who asks, and we must learn to separate the wheat from the chaff? And what was that nonsense about Lydia flirting with the colonel? Goodness, if that counts as flirting, we will never be allowed to even speak to gentlemen."

Elizabeth gave a quiet little laugh and leaned to press her lips on Kitty's temple.

"Fear not, dearest, I do not doubt there will be more leniency when it comes to ordinary gentlemen. 'Tis only her ladyship's revered nephews that are not to be trifled with."

"She had no right to speak to us the way she did," Lydia fumed, dropping her arms from around her older sister's neck and belligerently balling her small fists.

"I beg to differ, love. 'Tis her house, after all. And you should have asked permission, before declaring you must have a romp."

"But that was what we always did at home, and no one cared a fig about it."

"Yes. But this is our home now. And we are moving in far more fashionable circles."

"This will *never* feel like home," Lydia declared. "As for fashion, if it takes all the joy out of life, then I have no use for fashion."

"Papa would have spoken up for us if he were there," Kitty sullenly muttered. "Lord, we shall never see him, now that he has a hundred times more books to occupy him."

"More like a thousand times more books," Elizabeth smilingly replied.

"You tease, Lizzy, but really, what will become of us?" Kitty insisted, her sullenness now seasoned with pique. "Even the small collection Papa had at home could draw him away for hours on end. I ask you, what will become of us if he never comes out of that monstrously large library, and we are left day after day and hour after hour at Lady Catherine's mercy?"

"Mercy?" Lydia scoffed. "She does not know the meaning of the word!"

"You had better learn to curb your tongues, you know. Both of you," Elizabeth solemnly admonished. "Lady Catherine is our mother now, and—"

"Stepmother," Lydia sneered. "Oh, how I miss Mamma! If she were still with us, we would be at dear old Longbourn now."

"Aye. With all our dear friends. I keep waking up in the mornings and thinking, '*Today I shall call upon Maria.*' And then I remember she is fifty miles away, and I am stuck here dancing to Lady Catherine's tune."

"Or not dancing at all, as the case may be," Elizabeth said drolly, clearly seeking to cajole her sisters into better humour.

She seemed to have succeeded, for the three of them burst into giggles, promptly stifled into their fists, in the manner of unruly children.

"Come, let me see you to your room," Elizabeth eventually said, shepherding them up the great staircase – only to stop short on the half-landing with a sharp intake of breath.

That, along with her startled glance, served to indicate he had been spotted, even before she gasped, "Mr Darcy!"

All manner of things suddenly seemed intent on taking turns in nettling him. Firstly, it was the fact that his unwillingness to return to the music room and his reluctance to interrupt their moment of cathartic release could be classed under a different name: eavesdropping. Secondly, it was the displeasure in her voice – but that was to be expected, if she labelled his presence there as eavesdropping. Thirdly, it was the irksome formality of '*Mr Darcy.*'

He had not registered it before, and he briefly wondered why, before it came to him. Presumably because she generally used no appellation in addressing him – and she hardly ever addressed him anyway. Neither explanation could appease him. Quite the opposite. The number of things nettling him simply increased by two.

And then he was presented with one more reason for vexation, as soon as Elizabeth eagerly motioned her sisters to continue on their way.

Instead of complying, they anxiously chorused, "But, Lizzy, he overheard—"

"Hush," she checked them. "Run along. All will be well."

Yet when the youngest two finally obeyed and Elizabeth turned to glance towards him, the forced airiness was gone from her countenance, leaving behind a wary look that could not fail to provoke him all the more. Of course all would be well, Darcy inwardly grumbled. What did they imagine, that he was some ogre about to devour them?

She did not seem disposed to return to the bottom of the stairs. For his part, Darcy was equally disinclined to conduct any sort of conversation across the distance between the half-landing and the door into the music room. He slowly climbed up to join her, only to find her turning her back to the next flight of stairs, as if to block his path.

"I trust you will forgive my sisters for their unguarded tongues and let that pass without a reprimand," she said evenly but firmly, thus confirming that he had not misapprehended her intentions, and her shielding pose was meant as such.

Eyes flashing with something bordering on indignation, Darcy made to protest, but she would not have it. She raised her hand to indicate he should hold his peace, and added:

"As you must have heard, I delivered one already. Perhaps not as sternly as others might have, but one should make allowances for the upheaval in their lives. They are very young, and they miss their friends and the only home they had ever known."

"You cannot possibly imagine I was about to remonstrate with them," Darcy retorted hotly as soon as she stopped talking, then sought to govern his temper and soften his tone as he continued, "I merely wished to ask if you were well. Also, if you would like me to speak to my aunt about the merits of a gentler approach."

"Oh," she said, brows arched, and seemed to ponder briefly before settling upon an answer. "I… thank you, but no. My sisters *were* in the wrong, and besides I expect that her ladyship is rarely swayed by interference or advice."

Darcy's lips twitched.

"Not even from one of her revered nephews?"

A charming blush crept into her cheeks.

"I should not have said that."

Her fingers tapped nervously atop the wooden banister, and it seemed the most natural thing in the world for Darcy to reach and capture the small hand in his as he asked softly:

"Do *you* miss your home as well?"

She drew her hand back in a flash.

"Yes. But that is neither here nor there. Excuse me. I should see to my sisters," she breathlessly delivered, and turned away to hasten up the stairs.

"Elizabeth, wait," Darcy called after her and she stopped a few steps further up to cast him a questioning glance over her shoulder. "Pray allow me to thank you for your exquisite song," he whispered. "Will you play again?"

She gave a nonchalant little shrug.

"Some other time, yes, I expect I shall. But now I should be with Lydia and Kitty."

"I see," he replied, making no effort to conceal his disappointment. "Goodnight, then."

"Goodnight, Mr Darcy."

"Elizabeth?" he called a second time, making her pause on the fifth step and eye him with something bordering on impatience. Unless it was displeasure. At the free use of her name, perchance? Surely, she could not take objection to his discarding the *'Miss.'* They were cousins now. But it was not their cousinly connection that prompted him to say swiftly, without thinking, "Might I persuade you to call me by my Christian name?"

She pursed her lips.

"I should imagine not."

"Why is that?"

"No one else does, for one thing."

"What of Georgiana?"

She shrugged again.

"I am not your sister."

"Indeed not. Must I take it, then, that forsaking the *'Miss'* in addressing you was an impertinence?"

"Not necessarily. Both your cousins have forsaken it already."

"If my cousins are to be the model, might I point out that neither one of them have ever troubled themselves with the *'Mr'* when speaking to me?"

"They been related to you for a vast deal longer. Let us revisit the topic in three-and-twenty years."

"Pardon?"

"That is Anne's age, if I am not mistaken. So, unless the colonel is younger…?"

"I imagine you can tell that he is not."

"Very well. Three-and-twenty years it is. Goodnight, Mr Darcy," she airily repeated and vanished above-stairs.

Alone in the quiet hall, Darcy shook his head. She would not give an inch. Wilful, obstinate and contrary. And utterly adorable with it – hence his difficulty in ceasing to grin like a besotted fool, so that he could safely rejoin his aunt and her entourage in the music room.

He was still smiling when the sound of Elizabeth's footsteps faded into a barely audible patter along the corridor on the floor above, but by then the quirk in his lips had grown wistful rather than diverted. With a sigh, Darcy turned around and reluctantly made his way below-stairs.

Chapter 17

Rosings, 15 April 1812

The orangery was devilishly hot, and as the arms on the ornamental clock advanced with maddening slowness towards midday, the glass structure captured and trapped the heat of the sun, so that the sweltering humidity was growing more and more unbearable by the minute. The oppressive sultriness was enough of a nuisance for one swathed in the habitual layers of linen, silk and the cursed woollen cloth. The enforced immobility was making matters a vast deal worse, yet neither that nor the infernal heat were Darcy's greatest hardships at that given moment. Elizabeth's scrutiny was by far the severest threat to his composure. And he had Lady Catherine and her machinations to thank for the protracted torment.

It was yet another of her conspicuous schemes to manoeuvre him into Anne's exclusive company. She had decreed at breakfast that it would be to Anne's material advantage to bask in the morning sun as she practised her drawing. Not in the garden. A mid-April morning could not grow warm enough for her to be outdoors for such a length of time. But the orangery would do nicely, to Lady Catherine's way of thinking. Surely Darcy would not mind serving as her model. Anyone could draw a potted plant or a garden chair, but sketching human features so as to achieve a good resemblance would test her skills to better effect.

Anne had declared herself thrilled with the notion, with the proviso that Georgiana and Elizabeth should join her and sketch Darcy too. Predictably, Lady Catherine was ill-disposed to favour any scheme that did away with the *tête-à-tête*. She argued that Anne would be much better served if she did not compare herself either with Georgiana, who was far more advanced than she, or with Elizabeth, whose drawing skills still left a great deal to be desired.

Very much in the know by now as regards his wishes and matrimonial intentions, Anne insistently argued the opposite. She must have Elizabeth draw Darcy too. And Georgiana, naturally. Indeed, it would be not only enjoyable but also advantageous to have benchmarks against which she could measure her progress.

The passing decades had repeatedly demonstrated that there was but one person alive in the world who could bend Lady Catherine's rigid will, and that was her only daughter. Naturally, Anne had her wish. Thus, in all fairness – Darcy felt compelled to own – she was as much to blame for his current discomfort as her mother. Perhaps even more so, despite the far more endearing nature of her machinations.

Endearing, aye, but not in the least helpful, given the result. For there he was now, forced to sit in a garden chair in a sweltering orangery, holding a book and striving to maintain his pose. And every few seconds or so, Elizabeth's eyes would come to be fixed upon him. Her steady gaze would glide over him, up and down, burning as it went; taking in every line, angle and feature; estimating the breadth of his brow and the length of his nose; inspecting every square inch of exposed skin – and then darting back to her sketchbook, so that she could record the result of her scrutiny on paper.

Even if he could barely see her out of the corner of his eye, he could tell from the tilt of her head if her gaze was fixed upon the paper – or on him. It was marginally better when she was staring at the paper, but not much. For then he could not resist the urge to surreptitiously observe her, and take in any detail there was to be had. Such as the small crease of concentration right in the middle of her brow. Or the enticing manner in which she bit the corner of her lower lip as she worked. And then she would dart her eyes towards him yet again, causing him to glance away like some foolish schoolboy, and sit there, frozen in the cursed pose, by turns unable to tell if she had caught him staring – or fully aware that she had, because their glances had just met, and he was still reeling from the sudden jolt of the encounter.

He shifted in his seat – or rather on his bed of nails. There was every chance that his chair had disturbed a colony of ants. He could almost feel them crawling along his spine all the way to the back of his neck, under the damnably tight neckcloth, and then making their way into his hair, wandering over his scalp at leisure and emerging at the hairline, on the other side, to descend across his brow all the way to the tip of his nose. Damnation! There were no ants marching along his nose now, surely. Were there? Either way, he felt a maddening need to scratch it. If by any chance he had been in the right the first time, and there *was* a colony of ants now at work surveying him as a newly-discovered territory, they must have sent a party to explore the side of his face too, for he could feel another awfully ticklish sensation progressing slowly down his left whisker, and then along his jaw line to his chin.

Another glance darted in Elizabeth's direction when her head was lowered – a sure sign that she was concentrating on the paper – revealed that she fought to suppress a smile. Whatever had amused her? He had no way of knowing, and he abandoned every possible conjecture when the blasted ants suddenly demanded his attention. The tickling sensation had grown infernally vexing. He could not bear it any longer. Since he was not quite so lost to every notion of propriety as to sit there scratching like some flea-infested ne'er-do-well, he settled for moving the book into his other hand and casually running his fingertips over his nose, and then over his left whisker and the side of his face. Thus, he came to ascertain that he had been plagued not by a colony of ants, but by two trickling beads of sweat, which was very nearly as bad. Nay, he decided. It was worse.

"Do you need a rest, Cousin?" Anne solicitously asked.

"Or a glass of orgeat?" Elizabeth suggested – a thoughtful notion that might have inspired his gratitude, had it not given rise to the horrible suspicion that she had seen the beads of sweat trailing along his nose and the side of his face.

"I thank you, I am well," he valiantly said – one of the grossest falsehoods he had ever uttered. "Will you need me for much longer?"

"I should think not," Anne replied with casual unconcern, neglecting to inform him just how long she expected the wretched episode to last.

Darcy suppressed a snort.

Aye, it was all well and good for the three of them, in their muslin dresses, rather than baking in a woollen coat in an orangery overheated by the midday sun. Not constricting neckcloths, but light *fichus* around their necks. Not lawn and kerseymere sleeves for them, either. Which was a mercy for the wearer – and, truth be told, for the beholder, too. Nothing short of a sacrilege, hiding Elizabeth's arms under layers of lawn and kerseymere. Her creamy skin verily glowed through the delicately embroidered muslin of her sleeves. Thin, pliant fabric, allowing full freedom of movement as she earnestly worked to rub out some lines that must have displeased her. Soft fabric too, no doubt. Cool and soft, loosely draped over her long calves and graceful thighs… over shapely hips… and fashioned into a perfectly snug fit over the swell of her bosom.

The urgent stirrings of arousal made him inwardly curse himself – not with some random and cursory oath, but with lavish, creative and comprehensive curses – as he darted his eyes from the exquisite temptation, fixed them into his promptly and strategically lowered book, and racked his mind for sombre thoughts that would serve the purpose.

Assistance came from an unexpected quarter. For what must have been the first time in his life, Darcy blessed his aunt as she sallied into the orangery to assess the young ladies' progress.

"Well, let me see how you are getting on. Ah. Delightful, Anne. Anyone would recognise him. Georgiana, yours is masterfully done, but then I expected no less. You have been studying the art of charcoal-drawing from such an early age, and must have had more than enough opportunities to sketch your brother. Yours is better than I thought, Elizabeth, but good gracious, child, what have you done to his nose? My nephew takes after my sister. He has the Fitzwilliam profile. Look up at his – and then look at mine. You can easily see the resemblance. I defy you to claim that my nose is pert, so let me tell you, neither should my nephew's be in that sketch of yours. Aye, keep rubbing that out. It will not do."

Lady Catherine's expostulations against a pert nose in a Fitzwilliam, and indeed the notion in itself, were of material assistance in resolving his earlier difficulties, so Darcy lost some of his tension, raised his book and resumed his original pose. He even went as far as to allow himself another glance towards Elizabeth, and found an impish smile fluttering on her lips. He returned it, and this time did not look away when their eyes met. She did. Yet she was still smiling when she picked up her pencil, presumably to apply herself to a more accurate rendition of the Fitzwilliam profile.

Unless they finished their confounded sketches soon, the sweltering heat, the imaginary ants and every other form of mental torture would resume plaguing him, and well he knew it. But, to Darcy's good fortune, the malicious Fates must have had sufficient sport. Either that, or his cousin had decided to take pity on him and come to his rescue. The colonel swaggered in at last, an insufferably knowing smirk on his face, cast a glance at the three sketches and airily observed:

"Well, now that the head is done, I daresay I might volunteer my services for the shoulders, if the four of you are in agreement. Darcy and I are not so dissimilar in build, after all. There you have it, Coz," he added, when the ladies declared themselves satisfied with the substitution. "You are excused. Off you go before you begin to melt. Go for a ride, or amuse yourself in some other manner. In our aunt's icehouse, by way of example."

Vastly grateful for the chance to make his escape, Darcy bade his adieus, peeked at the result of their efforts – not least the formerly pert nose – although the artists chorused to ask him to wait until they were finished, and made a beeline for the orgeat, and then the stables.

The long ride through Lady Catherine's meadows at full gallop, with the wind in his face, drove out some of his devils and momentarily appeased the others. He did not stop to while away the time in his aunt's icehouse. Not in her ornamental lake, either. Too close to the house, and the wrong time of year for bathing. Which was a pity, for he had never felt in greater need of divesting himself of several layers of formal clothing, and diving into the refreshing water in the vain hope that it would cool his ardour and his head.

⁂

On his return to Rosings a couple of hours later, Darcy had good reason to hope that by now he would be safe from doing further penance in the orangery – the sketching party must have long broken up. Even from a distance, his suppositions were confirmed when he saw Anne's phaeton waiting at the entrance – a clear indication of preparations for an outing.

'*So much the better,*' Darcy thought as he urged his mount into a faster pace, glad he had not missed the opportunity to join them.

Vexingly ineffectual as his attempts at courtship seemed to have been thus far, at least on outings he would be free from Lady Catherine's scrutiny. One of her ladyship's best traits was that she did not favour the outdoors.

He drew to a halt at the foot of the stairs, handed the reins to a groom, bounded up and made his way within, to find himself impatiently greeted by the great lady herself.

"Ah. You are here at last. Better late than never, I suppose," she observed with an admixture of reproach and satisfaction. Then she turned towards the man who was assisting Anne in donning her cloak – a young and gentlemanlike fellow whom Darcy could not place, although the stranger's countenance was vaguely familiar. "It seems your services are no longer required, sir. My nephew will drive Miss de Bourgh in your stead," she announced, dismissing him with no effort at civility.

It was Anne who saw fit to mention him by name to Darcy.

"You may remember Mr Beaumont, Cousin," she said, her lips tight, and Darcy saw wisdom in bowing without a word, rather than admitting that in fact he did not remember Mr Beaumont. "As for my outing, I think we should abide by the original plan," Anne added tersely. "I should not wish to impose upon my cousin. He has only just returned."

"Nonsense. Imposition, indeed. 'Tis Darcy's place, and moreover his duty, to squire you about the country," Lady Catherine decisively countered. "Come along, and be sure to return before the air grows damp," she instructed, shepherding them all out of the door, and hence to the awaiting phaeton.

"Should we not wait for the others?" Darcy asked, in no humour to be manoeuvred like a child.

Lady Catherine gave a brief gesture of impatience.

"They chose to walk. But I did not see why Anne should tax herself."

"I think a walk would be beneficial," Darcy promptly disagreed. "What say you, Anne? You have so much more energy of late. In fact, I have never seen you look so well."

Lady Catherine beamed at the compliment. Anne did not. She positively glared at him, then tossed her head back and allowed one of the footmen to assist her into the low phaeton, whereupon she turned to the supplanted Mr Beaumont.

"I thank you, sir. I hope you will call upon us again soon. Pray convey my regards to your father," she said.

"Yes, of course. Convey mine as well, will you?" her mother intervened. "And do remind him that I wish him to call at Rosings by the end of the week. My nephew is in the right. Miss de Bourgh has never looked so well. Nevertheless, there is no reason to grow complacent. By the bye, Anne, do not neglect to cover your knees with a throw if the air grows colder. You might as well cover yourself now. Well then, I expect to see you before teatime," she said to Darcy as soon as he had taken his own seat. "You can always go for a short drive instead of joining the others. They can dally if it pleases them, but Anne should return home long before dusk."

Darcy acknowledged the fulsome instructions with a nod, gathered the reins and flicked the matching greys into a trot.

"So, where are we going?" he asked, as he negotiated the bend in the drive.

Lowering the hand she had raised towards the others in a gesture of farewell, Anne shifted in her seat to scowl at him.

"Why on *earth* should I tell you?" she snapped, then settled back, her lips twisted into a vindictive grimace. "In fact, I have a good mind not to. Take me for a short drive, and then let us return in plenty of time for tea. No gadding about with the others. A goodly while with Mamma will serve you so much better."

"Ah," Darcy remarked with a grin. "I see where the wind blows."

"Do you!"

"Well, I am beginning to. At the very least, I see now that I should have pressed Mr Beaumont to join us."

Anne gave a loud snort of vexation.

"At the very least, you should not have flattered me like a lover."

Darcy chortled.

"I did not. Did I?"

"*'You have so much more energy of late. In fact, I have never seen you look so well,'*" she scornfully mimicked, then turned on him like a little fury. "You have never said anything of the sort in living memory. Whatever possessed you to begin today?"

"In my defence, 'tis true. You have never looked better."

"Hmph! *'I think a walk would be beneficial,'*" she mimicked again. "That was all you could think of, walking after them. Well, I think tonight at dinner I should ask Mamma's opinion on the best warehouses for wedding clothes. That should start her off nicely. We shall have a very pleasant evening."

"You would not!"

"You will have to wait and see," she archly shot back, her softened manner giving Darcy some hope that her anger was abating. "Ungrateful wretch," she grumbled, nudging him with her elbow. "After everything I did to help you along."

Darcy cast her a rueful little smile.

"Forgive me, dear girl. How was I to know?" he asked, gathering the reins in his right hand and freeing the other, so that he could put an arm around her in an apologetic clasp.

Anne jumped away with a scowl.

"Have you lost your mind?" she fiercely remonstrated, and darted a glance over her shoulder to see if the affectionate gesture had been noticed and woefully misconstrued. To her relief, no one was watching from the Rosings main entrance. Mr Beaumont must have gone in search of his horse, and Lady Catherine was presumably within. She gave a little sigh and turned to face forward.

"I beg your pardon, I did not think," Darcy said, the rueful little smile still in place. He chuckled when Anne nodded forcefully in agreement. "Would you like me to drive you back?"

Anne shrugged in resignation.

"Too late. I expect he is already making his way home."

"Where might that be?"

"His home? Just outside Hunsford village. You do not remember him, do you?" she added a few moments later, fixing Darcy with a knowing and censorious stare.

"I expect I have seen him before, but..."

Anne frowned.

"The old story. Beneath everyone's notice."

"Oh. Is it so very bad, then?"

Anne tossed her head back in defiance.

"Mr Beaumont is a gentleman."

"But?" Darcy prompted, sensing that he should.

Her shoulders slumped.

"His father is my physician," she imparted, accusation in her eyes.

Darcy flicked the reins, not needing to be told in so many words that she was reproaching him for dismissing his prior acquaintance with her physician's son from his memory, just as Lady Catherine had dismissed the man from her company: as one not worth their notice – barely above a servant.

"And before you ask how I know he is not courting me with an eye to my fortune," Anne fiercely resumed, "he is *not* courting me. There was…" She sighed. "When we were much younger – children, really – there was a connection. We spoke when we chanced to meet, and… there was a connection. He had lost his mother when he was twelve years of age. Around the same time when I lost Papa. It was a comfort, speaking to someone who understood. And we had a great deal more than that in common. Similar tastes in books and music, the same quiet disposition. But then… I lost him, too. He went to school – to Oxford. He took orders. I held great hopes that Mamma would give him the Hunsford living, and he would come to live in Kent again, but she chose Mr Collins. You see, Henry – Mr Beaumont – is not the obsequious type. Servility was never in his nature, and he lacked Mr Collins' talent for currying favour. So Mamma would not consider him. She said he thought himself above his station – his station, indeed! I sought to plead his case, yet feared being too insistent, lest Mamma grasp my reasons and shun him all the more. In the end, he found himself a curacy in Surrey. He comes to see his father whenever he can, and he always calls at Rosings when he is in Kent, but you have seen for yourself what sort of a welcome he receives from Mamma. We never…" She sighed again. "We never spoke of anything of consequence. Not openly. But last summer, at the end of his visit to Hunsford, when he called with his father to take his leave and Mamma chose to be exceedingly eloquent on the subject of my eventual marriage to you, I could not help myself. While Mamma was questioning his father as to how he proposed to strengthen my constitution and prepare me for the grim weather of the north, I took the chance to quietly tell Henry that Mamma should not concern herself overmuch in that regard, for I personally had no expectations of either marrying or quitting Kent. And then he smiled the saddest smile, kissed my hand and said he did not expect to marry either. That was all. And then he left. So, there we are. He knows all too well that his station in life is far beneath mine, and purposely or not, Mamma misses no opportunity to emphasise it. He will not speak his mind. So I shall die an old maid – unless I take a leaf out of

Mamma's book, reverse the natural order of things and propose to him myself," she finished with a forceful huff.

"You might begin by granting him the Hunsford living, now that Collins has relinquished it," Darcy observed, and her eyes widened.

"Pardon?"

"You are of age now. *You* command at Rosings, not your mother," he said, mildly diverted that she should need to be reminded of it. "You can send the new curate on his way – what is his name?"

"Mr Whittaker."

"You can send Mr Whittaker on his way, and grant Mr Beaumont the living."

"Oh. Goodness, yes, I could." She tittered. "I command at Rosings. A novel notion, that. Mamma will go distracted."

"High time she learned to relinquish power."

"Heavens. There will be a battle."

"Aye. Too true. But it would be my pleasure and privilege to support you."

Anne cast him a wide smile and reached to wrap her arm around his, giving it an affectionate squeeze by way of thanks.

"You are not such a bothersome wretch after all, are you, Cousin?"

"I am thrilled to hear it."

"Ha. So, there we both shall be, you and I, courting the headstrong objects of our affections under Mamma's disapproving eyes, while they perversely persist in not assisting us at all. That should be a challenge and a half. Henry will be as infuriatingly unhelpful as your Lizzy, I imagine—"

"Aye. And more besides."

Anne gasped.

"What makes you say that?"

"He is a man. And men tend to believe they should provide a better home than the one their lady quits to follow them."

"Not to mention that, in my experience, men are maddeningly opinionated."

Darcy grinned.

"Your cousins more than most. You were dealt an awkward hand, I grant you."

"I could not agree more," Anne retorted, then exclaimed, "Oh, bother," making Darcy laugh outright.

"Be fair, at least you will go into the fray better prepared for dealing with opinionated men."

"There is that. But just now I was grumbling about an entirely different matter. You missed the turning," Anne clarified. "Or rather, I did not nudge you in time. You will have to find a way to turn around without stranding us in either one of those ditches. Then you must take the second avenue on the left, if we are to join the others. They set out to walk to the Aeolian Temple."

"Am I forgiven, then? Praise be," Darcy teased. "I knew you did not have the heart to sentence me to tea with Lady Catherine."

"You think me tender-hearted? More fool you," Anne airily said with an impudent little grin. "I am rewarding my ally, Cousin, that is all. You have your uses. Nay, you cannot turn around here. Heavens, has no one ever taught you patience? Keep going, there is a wider stretch of road ahead."

Chapter 18

Rosings, 15 April 1812

If registered at all, Anne's quip was long forgotten. Yet as the day progressed, it brought further proof that indeed, no one seemed to have taught Darcy patience. Which was a pity, for he stood in dire need of it.

The drive to the Aeolian Temple had been for nothing. They had not found the walking party at the aforementioned garden folly, nor anywhere near it. In her kindness, Anne had offered to drive herself back, so that he could return on foot along the path snaking through the grounds – the route the others must have taken – but Darcy had refused. He would have never heard the end of it from Lady Catherine, had he left Anne to her own devices.

That was doubtlessly true, but later, once he and Anne had returned to Rosings and discovered that the others had not, he dearly wished he had accepted his cousin's offer. There was every chance he might have missed them anyway, if they had chosen to take a detour and wander along some other path, but even walking aimlessly through the grounds would have been better than being cooped up in Lady Catherine's drawing room, and endeavouring to keep himself from pacing under her prying eyes, or walking too often to gaze out of the windows.

Sitting still became utterly impossible when the gathering clouds began to turn ominously dark and give stern warning of a change in the weather, so Darcy left the drawing room to pace in the hall – then outside, under the portico – then at the foot of the stairs. An exasperated heavenward roll of his eyes revealed that he was not the only one keeping watch over the drive. In one of the upper-floor windows stood Mr Bennet. They acknowledged each other with a nod, and Darcy turned away, feeling dreadfully conspicuous.

It was a full ten minutes before he realised there was no reason why he should; that he could very well be anxious only for his sister's sake, just as Mr Bennet was concerned about his daughters – and that the very same argument might have excused his pacing in Lady Catherine's drawing room as well.

A loud clash of thunder put an end to his pointless ruminations, and simmering vexation gave way to apprehension. Where *were* they? That was no time to be caught out of doors, and worse still, taking cover under the trees. And then the heavens opened. Not a drizzle, but a veritable downpour, apt to soak one to the skin in minutes. Damn Fitzwilliam! One would have thought him able to see the signs early enough, and urge the ladies to head home long before the weather turned.

Reluctantly, Darcy climbed the stairs to take shelter under the portico, and devise ways to come to the assistance of those currently devoid of shelter.

What was to be done? Ordering the carriage to go in search of them would have been a useless endeavour. They would be far from any lanes the carriage could negotiate. Looking for them on horseback would be equally pointless. What use was one horse? Besides, *she* said she rarely chose to ride. A downpour might have been sufficient inducement, but he could not fetch horses for all of them.

He had just begun to contemplate summoning servants with cloaks and umbrellas, when a babble of voices and girlish giggles coming from within made him exhale in relief mingled with the resurfacing vexation, now that there was no further cause for apprehension. They had returned, then, and must have come in by the side entrance.

Darcy strode in, only to find that his relief was but half justified. He could see Georgiana, Miss Bennet and her two youngest siblings. Yet there was still no sign of Elizabeth.

"Are you very wet? Do go up and change, regardless," Darcy instructed his sister, then hastened to ask, "Where are the others?"

"The Rotunda," Georgiana replied as a footman came forth to take her pelisse and bonnet. "They had to stop to mend Lizzy's bootlace. They will be here soon."

From somewhere above him, on the stairs, Mr Bennet chortled.

"Not the first shoe she has ever pulled. Galloping down the slopes again, was she?" he drawled, in a manner that was growing increasingly familiar to Darcy. Sometimes he could school himself into bearing it without bristling. This was not one of the occasions. To his way of thinking, drollery was both ill-timed and ill-suited when Elizabeth was still out there, in the cold rain. And there never was a good time to liken her to a poorly-shod filly.

"Thomas," he called and, as was right and proper, his aunt's footman jumped to attention. "An umbrella, if you please."

"Yes, sir," the man was quick to answer, and went to open a skilfully fashioned door that blended into the ornamented wall.

"I will have that cloak as well," Darcy indicated.

"'Tis Miss Anne's…"

"She will not mind," came the curt reply.

Moments later, Darcy was striding away from the side entrance, along the gravelled path that led to the Rotunda. He had not paused to acknowledge Mr Bennet's half-smile and arched brow. Nor had it crossed his mind that, with Georgiana safely in the house, this time he might have had reasons enough to feel conspicuous.

The domed roof came into view among the bare branches long before Elizabeth did, but Darcy could hear a peal of laughter over the drumming of the rain on the taut canopy of his umbrella. He lengthened his strides towards the circular structure Sir Lewis de Bourgh had commissioned in his youth. Old plans showed that the baronet had originally chosen a lofty name for it – the Temple of Harmony. Yet, for as long as Darcy could remember, the folly was simply known as the Rotunda, which might have been an indication that Sir Lewis' hopes for harmony had long been abandoned.

Pondering over one's late uncle was hardly a riveting pastime, so Darcy never chose to dwell on Sir Lewis' life, his choices or indeed his garden temples. Least of all now, as he followed the path around a large rhododendron and could finally command a full view of those sheltering under the dome.

The peal of laughter that had reached his ears earlier had doubtlessly been Elizabeth's. She was smiling now, as she tossed her head back and brushed wet locks of hair from her face. Her cheeks were wet as well – rosy and wet, rainwater still dripping from the ringlets at her temple and off the narrow brim of her straw bonnet. Fitzwilliam's coat was draped over her shoulders, while the colonel stood beside her grinning from ear to ear at whatever either of them might have said and manfully managing not to shiver, although his drenched shirt adhered to his skin, transparent as if painted in watercolour.

A knot formed at the corner of Darcy's jaw as he trained his gaze upon the ornamental stonework above their heads and fixed it there, lest it should slide of its own volition to her skirts – only to discover he possessed shockingly less willpower than he thought. He also discovered the merits of petticoats, along with their limitations. Translucency, they could conquer. But they did cling to the limbs when wet.

He forced himself to look away. Not to the dome, to resume the examination of the stone ornaments. Instead, he glared at his cousin – all the more fiercely when Fitzwilliam spotted him and cheerfully observed:

"Ah. Here comes the rescue party. I thought you might make an appearance. In fact, I thought you and Anne would drive up and meet us at the Aeolian Temple."

"We could not find you," Darcy replied tersely as he closed his umbrella and joined them under the shelter of the dome.

"How thoughtful of you to brave the weather," the colonel smirked. "You need not have. We got by well enough."

"So I see," Darcy muttered. "Pray allow me," he said to Elizabeth, offering her the cloak he had brought. "This might serve you better. 'Tis warmer."

And longer. But he wisely chose to keep that to himself as he assisted her with substituting one garment for the other. Nevertheless, he could not forbear a grimace as he handed the tailored coat back to his cousin.

"You may wish to make yourself presentable. Either that, or take the backstairs to your chambers. Lady Catherine would not appreciate such displays."

Fitzwilliam gave a most aggravating chortle.

"Displays, eh? Very well. But you will have to help me into the wretched thing. 'Tis too tight to don without assistance even when dry."

"Then you should change your tailor," Darcy snapped as he sought to do as bid and ill-temperedly tugged at the item, to force his cousin's arms into the sleeves.

True enough, the cotton lining refused to slide over the wet lawn shirt. He had to tug repeatedly, with growing vigour and a number of grunts, his humour worsening by the minute – no less because, rather than applying himself to the endeavour with due diligence, Fitzwilliam seemed to find inordinate amusement in the predicament and, Darcy feared, so did *she*.

"Dear me. Thank goodness you are not my valet, Coz," Fitzwilliam chuckled when the deed was finally done, or at least as close to done as it would ever be, and the coat could be buttoned.

"Amen to that," Darcy retorted with a scowl that had no effect whatsoever on the other.

"Come now," Fitzwilliam grinned. "You must own, that *was* diverting."

"Was it?"

Fitzwilliam shook his head.

"You should laugh more, you know. Or, before you know it, you will find yourself singing from the same hymn sheet as our aunt and complaining of '*displays.*' Pray tell me you are not there already."

The comment would have been enough to make Darcy press his lips together in displeasure, even if he had not noticed that Elizabeth's were twitching with ill-concealed amusement. Fitzwilliam's penchant for making sport of him was enough of a nuisance even when they were alone. That his cousin should indulge in it in Elizabeth's presence was beyond the pale.

The opportunity to acquaint the other with the full depths of his vexation was long in coming, to Darcy's way of thinking. He could not speak his mind while the pair of them were escorting Elizabeth to the house. Yet as soon as they were within and she retired above-stairs, Darcy lost no time in seeking Fitzwilliam in his chambers. Admittance was gained by way of a firm knock on the door, and Darcy found him about to change out of his drenched shirt, while his valet was endeavouring to set the wet and muddied coat to rights.

"Never mind that, Blake," Fitzwilliam told his man once he had asked the newcomer to come in – or rather once he had learned that the one seeking him out was Darcy. "Just set it in the dressing room to dry for now, and then you may leave us. My cousin can assist me to dress in your stead," he wickedly added.

Darcy rolled his eyes, and could barely wait for Blake's exit to make his feelings clear.

"Whatever possessed you to make us look like fools before her?" he snarled.

Supremely unabashed, Fitzwilliam began to loosen his neckcloth.

"There was I thinking you might thank me for letting her see you do have a sense of humour after all, despite appearances. But, by all means, continue as a sanctimonious old prig if you believe it serves you better."

"What did *not* serve me in the least," Darcy retorted, stung, "was driving around the park for no purpose whatsoever. You were supposed to be at the Aeolian Temple. Where the devil were you? Showing them every nook and cranny? You were gone for hours. And having the time of your life too, by the looks of it. Why, you were positively oozing charm and good-humour when I came upon you."

Fitzwilliam cast him an affectionate but rather condescending glance.

"Highly diverting as it might be to see you acting the part of the jealous fool, do be sensible, Darcy, I beg you. She has nothing but my brotherly affection. Or rather cousinly affection, if you will. Knowing what I know of your sentiments for her, do you truly imagine I would come between you? Frankly, I would take offence, if you had not made it perfectly clear already that love has addled your wits beyond redemption."

"Do not talk such drivel. I know you are not a cad. But you *are* a fool. She does not know what you know. What is to stop her from growing attached to you in earnest?"

"What?"

"You heard me. Women have fallen at your feet in droves for as long as I can remember. You are glib, engaging, could talk the hind legs off a donkey—"

"Let us speak plainly. *You* envy *me?* " Fitzwilliam cut him off with a disbelieving chuckle.

"Of course I do," Darcy shot back. "You can talk to her – laugh with her. You could not be a better match for her temper and disposition if you tried. How the devil am I to compete with that? Not to mention this… this…" he spluttered, with a wide gesture in his cousin's direction.

"This – what?"

"The eye-catching look of a drenched Adonis, that is what," Darcy burst out, only to send his cousin into a paroxysm of laughter.

"Adonis!" Fitzwilliam snickered as soon as he could speak. "Why, thank you, Coz. Believe you me, I would take greater pleasure in your compliment if it did not sound quite so much like lunacy. I never thought I would see the day when I would need to point out to you that, of the pair of us, you are the handsome one. Sickeningly so, I might add. Whereas the affectionate and the charitable would at best allow me to boast of chiselled features and some sort of rugged manliness. Heaven help us," he snorted. "That it should have come to this! I expected I would have to play nursemaid till you found your feet and proposed, but I draw the line at closeting ourselves in my bedchamber and comparing our charms like a pair of nervous damsels. Must I begin to list all your advantages, not least the material ones? Well, be assured I shan't. Go and pour yourself some of Lady Catherine's brandy," he sensibly suggested, indicating the decanters on the small table in the corner of the room. "'Tis nowhere near as decent as yours, but it will serve the purpose. Then go and look for the lass, for goodness' sake, and find a way to talk to her and laugh with her yourself. I grant you, there is a grain of sense in your ranting. She does not know what I know. I did not consider that. Well then, tell her. I will keep my distance till you do, if it gives you comfort. But get on with it and court her. And when you do find the right moment to propose, pray do yourself a favour and do not model your offer of marriage on our aunt's. Here endeth the lesson," Fitzwilliam concluded with a wide grin, then pulled the wet shirt over his head, cast it on a chair and began to energetically rub a drying cloth over his arms and torso.

But Darcy did not pour himself a brandy. Instead, he bade his adieus and made his exit. The rousing speech, however flippant, was welcome and he appreciated it. But he could do without a further exhibition of rugged manliness, complete with strongly defined muscles and assorted battle-scars.

Chapter 19

Rosings, 15 April 1812

Finding someone at Rosings Park was never easy. Not merely due to the sheer magnitude of the place but, as was often the case with country houses that had evolved for centuries around some ancient kernel, the layout of the main reception rooms was straightforward, but little else was. Too many corridors in the areas reserved for the family. Too many small parlours where one might choose to sit in peace and quiet with a book when the library was too cold, the music room too crowded or the drawing room too unappealing – for that was where Lady Catherine invariably held court, whether she was entertaining visitors or not.

Exploring all those small parlours was even more difficult when subtlety was of the essence, in preference to blatantly wandering about and opening every door. Not to mention that he might very well be wasting his time. Elizabeth could still be in her bedchamber – out of bounds – or in the private sitting room she shared with her eldest sister.

The only sitting room to which he had access without a special invitation – apart from his own, naturally, or Fitzwilliam's – was Georgiana's, so Darcy bent his steps thither, in the faint hope of a fortuitous encounter, or at least some information. Yet he had barely gained the upper floor when he came across Anne's lady's maid, who had a message to deliver along with a curtsy.

"Miss Anne sent me in search of you, sir," the woman said. "She is in her sitting room, and would be glad of your company."

What *he* was jolly glad of, Darcy discovered as soon as he followed his cousin's invitation, were his allies, however brazenly outspoken some of them chose to be. For Anne was not alone. On the small sofa by the fire sat Elizabeth.

"Ah. No sketchbooks, I am pleased to see," he sought to quip as he made his entrance. "For a moment, I thought you summoned me for the final touches."

He noticed his error only when Anne discreetly rolled her eyes, just as all his allies were apparently wont to do every so often; even Georgiana on occasion.

"Summon you? Whatever gave you that notion?" Anne protested as she turned away from her companion, her glance wordlessly threatening him with all the plagues of Egypt, should he be quite so much of a dullard as to bring up the lady's maid. "Do sit though, now that you are here," she seamlessly added, indicating the spare seat on the sofa.

Darcy was all too glad to do as bid. At his approach, Elizabeth gathered her skirts out of the way and shifted slightly to make room for him, but if he expected a more open sort of welcome, he was to be disappointed. It was only Anne who cast him an encouraging smile as he joined them.

"There is fresh tea, Cousin," she said, indicating the accoutrements on the small table beside her. "Would you care for a cup?"

"I thank you, yes. But do not trouble yourself. I can pour it," Darcy said, gesturing towards her to remain comfortably seated in her armchair.

He stood, prepared his cup and resumed his place on the sofa, warmed by a wisp of hope and an incipient sense of comfort. This was so much more promising than the madness below-stairs. He should have asked Anne or Georgiana to orchestrate such moments more often, away from the bustle of a whole household milling about, and above all safely away from Lady Catherine, her shrewd eyes and matchmaking schemes.

He sipped his tea as he silently pondered on an opening topic, but thankfully Anne took it upon herself to assist in that as well.

"I wonder where we might go tomorrow. Weather permitting, I think we should have another outing. Together this time, hopefully," she finished with a smile, which Elizabeth returned.

"We should have waited for you at the temple," she acknowledged. "But after a while we imagined that you were not coming, and that Lady Catherine had prevailed upon you to rest instead."

Anne gave a quiet little laugh.

"Mamma did urge me to conserve my strength, take my tonic and content myself with a walk in the shrubbery, but I was eager to drive out. As for that vile stuff, my tonic, I do wish Dr Beaumont would keep it for himself. It does deliver a short burst of energy, but 'tis awfully bitter and smells like pond-water. Looks like it, too. I imagine neither of you will go tattling to Mamma, so I will own that whenever she is not around to watch me take it, my lady's maid and I are diligently treating my washbowl and a small crack in the floor with Dr Beaumont's much-lauded tonic, and I am no worse for it. Well might it amuse you," she added with a little shrug in response to her companions' affectionate chuckles, "but it does the trick. The level of the liquid in the bottle decreases nicely, which keeps Mamma and the good doctor happy with no inconvenience to myself. But never mind that now. Tell me more about your morning rambles, Lizzy. Where did you go when you left the temple?"

"The cherry grove. Kitty had a great wish to see it. She has heard much of it from you and Georgiana. But there were barely any blossoms, so she was rather disappointed."

"Give it a day or two. The grove does look a picture in the spring, although 'tis not as striking as the cherry tree walk at Pemberley. Dozens upon dozens of them, stretching as far as the eye can see, and all in bloom. A stunning display, Darcy, and a most fortunate arrangement. Do tell Lizzy about it. I doubt I can do it justice," Anne said, skilfully and most considerately turning the conversation so as to include him.

Darcy had a warm glance of gratitude for his obliging and ever so wise cousin. She knew him well – of course she did. Asking him to speak of Pemberley was the surest way of setting him at ease. The beloved place could provide any number of topics on which he might effortlessly elaborate. At least under normal circumstances.

This time, however, not even Pemberley could work its charm and render him fluent. Anne's helpful little ploy might have stood a chance, had he taken any of the other two seats in the room.

As it was, when dark-brown eyes turned upon him in expectation, so very close, it was utterly beyond him not to lose himself in their depths again.

He had long ascertained they were not dark after all. Nay, they were specked with amber, with golden hues and hints of hazel and, even on a dull day such as that, they caught the light and shimmered. They would verily sparkle in dappled sunlight, should she stroll on a bright morning along the path Anne had asked him to describe and do full justice to its springtime glory.

Less than an arm's length away, a brow arched and rosy lips twitched. It might have been in either bemusement or amusement at his continued silence, but Darcy did not pause to ponder on the precise reason why her lower lip was curled just so. Studying its enticing fulness in minute detail was far more engrossing, as his mind's eye conjured up the picture of her standing in the maze of whitish-pink blooms, her hair dotted with a scattering of petals, her lips tantalising him from a vast deal closer, at a time when he would be at liberty to crush them under his.

Somewhere at his left, Anne gave a small sigh of exasperation, and with some effort Darcy drew himself from delectable but all too premature imaginings to finally say:

"You give me too much credit, Cousin. I cannot find the words to do it justice either. But I think the cherry tree walk at Pemberley is best seen, rather than described. I hope Miss Elizabeth will see it for herself someday," he daringly added.

The gambit did not pay off. Elizabeth glanced away and replied with a distinct lack of enthusiasm:

"I thank you, but I do not imagine any of us will leave the south for quite some time."

Anne spoke before Darcy could think of the best way to contradict that statement.

"What of your tour of pleasure with your uncle and aunt from town? Did you not say you were to go to the Lakes?"

"It was a passing thought we had a while ago, but the scheme is likely to be abandoned. My uncle now fears he cannot spare the time."

The fact that she must have been speaking of the tradesman uncle from Cheapside gave Darcy but a momentary pause, before he earnestly suggested:

"What if you were to propose a substitution, and tour Derbyshire instead? You and your relations might enjoy revisiting Lambton and Mrs Allen's shop," he said with a faint smile, in an endeavour to recreate the comfortable warmth of another conversation on that subject, all those months ago. Yet she did not seem inclined to contribute, so he insisted: "The Peaks have much beauty to recommend them, and hopefully the weather would be more accommodating and allow a trip to Pemberley. Georgiana and I would be delighted to receive you," he concluded, and this time it did not even cross his mind to be so maladroit, and indeed high-handed, as to suggest that his housekeeper or the head-gardener might show her around in his stead.

It made no difference. Elizabeth merely said:

"A very kind offer, but it would be too much of an imposition." Then, just as he began to protest, she added with a touch of archness, "Besides, their proposed trip was for July, so I would have missed the spring blooms anyway."

"Oh, fear not, the grounds of Pemberley are a joy to behold at any time of year," Anne intervened. "I do miss the pleasure of strolling through your gardens, Darcy. In fact, I would suggest we all descend upon you, were it not for my reluctance to add fresh grist to Mamma's mill. Of course," she added with a mischievous little grin, "you could explore the beauties of Pemberley at your leisure, Lizzy, if we went along with her schemes and you came to live there as my companion, but you must find it in you to forgive me. I will not marry my cousin Darcy even to please *you*."

Elizabeth gave a perfunctory smile and raised her cup to drink the remainder of her tea. For his part, Darcy busied himself with his own beverage as he wished his cousin might have found a more subtle, or at least not quite so flippant way of letting Elizabeth know that Lady Catherine's claims and schemes had no substance. Still, to his way of thinking, a flippant approach was better than none, so he sipped his tea and made no comment.

But Anne was not quite finished.

"Bless Mamma," she said, shaking her head. "She has always had my best interests at heart. In her way, she is in the right. I can scarce do better than you, Cousin. But, to her misfortune, the pair of us would much rather choose for ourselves. So she will have to console herself with marrying my new sisters off. You are safe for now, Lizzy, but from what I gathered she has already determined that Lady Metcalfe's naval brother will be a good match for your sister Jane."

"Oh," Elizabeth said with a rueful little smile. "'Tis most thoughtful of your mother, and indeed a pity that she is such a firm proponent of elder sisters marrying first. Kitty and Lydia would have been in raptures at the mere mention of a naval captain. But I fear Jane has no thoughts of matrimony at present."

"Does she not? How so?" Anne asked.

No answer came. Elizabeth merely gave a flourish of her hand.

"Well, let us hope that she reconsiders by the time Captain Hayes returns from his assignments in the Pacific. If not, I should drop a word in Mamma's ear, to save her from another disappointment. But perchance the captain might change your sister's mind. He is quite charming, you know. Come to think of it, if Jane cannot be persuaded, he might do very well for you instead," Anne said, and nodded sagely.

Darcy arched a brow over his cup of tea.

Elizabeth gave a conscious little chuckle.

"I thought you said I was safe from matchmaking schemes for now," she protested.

Anne laughed.

"Yes. From Mamma's. But I shall make no promises of the kind."

"Well, let me assure both you and Lady Catherine that, same as Jane, I am in no great haste to wed. And in any case, I would not set my sights quite as high as a naval captain."

"Very well. Let us leave Captain Hayes on his quarterdeck for now, and pray for his safety. He is not due back till September anyway. We might as well think of more immediate matters. Such as finding a way to see Darcy's cherry trees this spring."

"That would be—" Darcy began, but before he could say *'delightful'* or some other word to that effect, Elizabeth spoke as well.

"I thought we have established that would be impossible."

"Oh, let us not dismiss it out of hand," Anne said blithely with a little careless wave. "Who can tell what the future holds? Who would have thought last Christmas that, come Easter, you and I would be sisters? Or, for that matter, could the pair of you have envisaged, when you were introduced, that mere months later you would be connected by marriage?" she observed, her mien a picture of cheerful innocence.

It was the greatest effort for Darcy to keep himself from openly glaring at her as he inwardly grumbled that either Anne had spent too much time with Fitzwilliam and learned his wicked ways, or the penchant for causing mischief was passed down in their blood. Whatever game she had just played for her own amusement when she said that the charming Captain Hayes might do very well for Elizabeth was irksome enough in itself, but the last hint was utterly uncalled for. Ill-timed, and too broad by far. He suppressed a snort. Assistance in orchestrating opportunities for courtship and sidestepping Lady Catherine, he appreciated. Teasing remarks, he could well do without.

"My aunt's happy tidings were a most agreeable surprise," he evenly observed, in an endeavour to smooth over Anne's comment, "but no less astonishing, I assure you. Who could have foreseen such a denouement?" he finished with a forced chuckle.

"Precisely," Elizabeth said to Anne, a distinct edge to her voice. "When your cousin left Hertfordshire so suddenly last autumn, I did not expect our paths would ever cross again. You can imagine my surprise when I learned you were related."

She was still half-turned away from him, so – short of drawing to the very edge of his seat and peering into her face – to Darcy's growing frustration, he could not see enough of her countenance to ascertain what she had made of Anne's remark, if anything. Nor could he tell what *he* was to make of her comment about his abrupt departure from Netherfield and their paths never crossing. Was it a mere denial in response to Anne's foolish question? Or was there more to it than that?

Her tone suggested the latter, and cast a new light on her altered manner. Good Lord, had she been hurt by his desertion? Was that the reason why she was now keeping him at a distance? Why she no longer spoke to him as freely as she had five months ago?

True enough, he had not engaged his honour with an open courtship during his stay in Hertfordshire – he had made every effort not to – but he *had* singled her out. Indeed, how could he not, when she was the brightest gem the place had to offer? Of course he had sought her out whenever they had been in company together – her conversation was more stimulating than anybody else's.

Back then, he could tell that she took more pleasure in debating some topic or another with him than in exchanging bland pleasantries with her neighbours. Yet he had imagined it was but a reflection of their well-matched intellects. That she had enjoyed pitting her wits against an equal – a novelty in her confined world – but, while the attention might have gratified her, it had not engaged her heart.

The very notion that his abrupt departure might have left a void in the unvarying routine of her life, that his absence might have pained her, was beyond endurance. Whatever he had suffered was of his own infliction. But it did not bear thinking he might have injured *her* as well.

Darcy shifted in his seat, staggered by the sudden speculations. Tenderness surged, bittersweet and overwhelming, at such an explanation for her baffling reserve that had kept him in check ever since her arrival into Kent. Far from the dreaded lack of interest, it could be self-defence. By fiercely denying him any foothold, as she uniformly did these days, she might simply be protecting herself from further disappointment.

He drew a deep breath. Much as he regretted giving her ample reason to distrust him, melancholy thoughts could not carry the day. The hope that she might have already grown to care for him was exhilarating.

Would she doubt his sanity if he offered for her, then and there? His lips twitched. Very likely. Yet by the time he had filled his lungs again, his mind was already made up. Very well. Let her think him insane rather than inconstant. He would not leave her in uncertainty a moment more.

He caught Anne's glance and held it, then meaningfully looked towards the door. He bit his lip when a repetition of the same had no effect whatever. Anne must have thought he was silently chastising her for the misplaced quip, for all she did was cast him a repentant smile and discreetly mouth a word of apology – but did not budge. Darcy rolled his eyes and sought to conquer his vexation. Of all the moments Anne might have chosen to be dense! Fine. If he must openly ask her to excuse herself from her own sitting room, then so be it. He opened his lips to deliver a terse, "Anne, would you be so kind as to leave us?" when she finally grasped the unspoken message and stood.

"Goodness, is that the time? I should dress for dinner. Do wait for me here, Lizzy, would you? I shall not be long."

"I had better not," Elizabeth replied without a moment's hesitation, much to the others' disappointment. "I should change as well."

"Nonsense," Anne protested warmly. "Your attire is perfectly suited for dinner as it is. Even by Mamma's exacting standards," she sought to quip. "Do stay. 'Tis the warmest room in the house by far, as you would imagine. Mamma demands they keep the fire burning constantly in my chambers on pain of death. Stay here, to ward off the chill. You came home quite drenched," she nervously prattled.

But Elizabeth was already on her feet.

"True, this *is* the warmest room by far," Darcy hastened to have his say, as he inwardly cursed himself for causing the upheaval by prompting Anne to leave. All things considered, he should have guessed Elizabeth would reject a *tête-à-tête*. Damnation. What was the answer, then? Proposing with an audience, for goodness' sake?

He sighed, faced with the almighty task of conquering his impatience now, when the promise of happiness was so close, after all the abject months of self-denial. One step at a time, he told himself, and sensibly resumed:

"Let us all sit for a little longer. You need not change either, Anne. Lady Catherine will not upbraid you, I am certain," he said with a tight smile. "The urn must have kept the water hot. Have some more tea, Elizabeth," he urged her, the *'Miss'* be damned, as he reached to take the empty cup she was still holding.

Her fingers were ice-cold underneath the saucer, and he wished he could set the cup aside and warm her hands in his. Yet at the moment, pouring a beverage was all he was allowed to do for her comfort. At least he had guessed aright about the urn; the water *was* hot. So he made a fresh pot of tea, filled Elizabeth's cup and returned with it to the sofa, modestly pleased to see that, once Anne had settled back into the armchair, she had resumed her seat as well, however reluctantly.

He handed her the tea, then busied himself with the fire in the grate to ensure it was burning as brightly as ever. The shawl draped over the back of the sofa was a happy discovery. It gave him the opportunity to care for her in any way he could, and place it around her with a softly spoken "May I?", the feel of her slender shoulders under his fingertips, beneath layers of cashmere and muslin, tantalising him with the promise of better days. Of times when he would be free to linger for more than a casual touch – lean forward, even, to press his lips on the back of her neck, beneath the enticing ringlet that curled into a tight spiral of dark amber, a perfect foil for the glow of her skin. He leaned back, wary of dwelling incautiously long on happy days, when he would resume his seat beside her not so as they could recommence some restrained exchange of civil nothings, but at liberty to gather her up into his arms and kiss her breathless. He suppressed a sigh. One step at a time.

"I thank you," she said, flashing a brief glance towards him that somehow succeeded in not meeting his eyes. "But I am not in the least cold."

"I am happy to hear it," he replied as he took his seat and resigned himself to the exchange of civilities, if that was all that could be had. "I was concerned you might have caught a chill."

"I am quite hardy, I assure you. I have not caught a chill in the best part of two years."

"A remarkable achievement," he said, a trifle more tersely than he had intended, her stubbornly trenchant aloofness getting the better of him. Goodness, how was he to make amends, if she would not even let him try? With diligence and patience, the angel on his shoulder primly counselled. One step at a time. It did not come easy, taking advice – not even from guardian angels – but he softened his tone nevertheless, when he added: "Truly, you should beware. Your hands are very cold, and you look flushed. I hope you are not coming down with something."

His hand came up instinctively, before reason could speak up and overrule the impulse to touch her cheek and assure himself that the flush was not caused by a fever. What gave him pause was her wide-eyed look of consternation as she drew back with a start.

"Forgive me. I thought I should see if you were feverish," he ruefully whispered, the very underpinnings of his hopeful speculations shaken by her response. She had just withdrawn from him in… what? Distaste?

He got his answer a fraction of a second later, when her colour heightened into hues of scarlet, and it mercifully brought him a modicum of reassurance as to both her health and her sentiments. No, it was not the flush of fever. It was a fierce blush.

She raised one hand to explore her cheek with the back of her fingers, and must have felt the heat of the blush steadily creeping in, for she pursed her lips in an adorable grimace of frustration and blushed more fiercely still, in a manner that made him yearn afresh to ask Anne to leave them, so that he could open his heart to his stubbornly distrustful love at last.

"I am not feverish. Appearances are misleading," Elizabeth declared, letting her hand drop and turning away from him with the transparent pretext of setting her teacup on the oval table at her elbow.

"Yes. They are," Darcy replied with energy. Careless of Anne's presence, he earnestly continued, "Leaving Netherfield when I did was a mistake. I wish I had stayed."

Elizabeth shrugged.

"You may take comfort from the thought that you could not have stayed a great deal longer anyway. Mr Bingley and his relations left as suddenly as you a mere fortnight later. I daresay unpredictability must be one of the delights and privileges of your set."

"I do not belong to any *set*, Elizabeth," Darcy said, his mien solemn.

Anne's, on the other hand, was all gaiety when she chimed in:

"Unpredictable? Darcy? Goodness, no, that will never do. I assure you, Lizzy, my cousin is the very essence of predictability. Most of the time," she teased, with a little smile.

Darcy grimaced as he hoped Elizabeth would take that to mean dependable, not dull. He dismissed the matter, struggling instead to marshal his thoughts into finding the best way to plead his case. Yet, mere moments later, the fragile structure collapsed like a house of cards when the door swung open and the least welcome member of the family swept into the room.

"Ah. There you are," Lady Catherine said, then frowned. "Goodness, 'tis exceedingly warm in here. They should not overdo it. Anne, you ought to ask your maid to open the windows for a quarter of an hour or so, while you are down for dinner. Elizabeth, your sister wants you."

"Which one, ma'am?"

"Kitty, I think. Or Lydia. Something about ribbons," Lady Catherine said with a careless wave of her hand. "They were prattling on as they came up to change. Pray see that they make haste this time. Tardiness is unacceptable, and they must be cured of that dreadful habit. I cannot abide it."

With a twinkle in her eye and a warm smile towards Anne, Elizabeth stood, dropped a curtsy and left to do as bid. Her cheerful tolerance of overbearing relations was commendable, but for his part, Darcy was as far removed from like sentiments as he could be. He flashed a stern look towards his aunt and stood. But before he could voice his protest at her manner or, heedless of consequences, follow Elizabeth out of the room, Anne left her seat as well and came to wrap a quelling hand around his elbow. Eager to prevent him from saying or doing something he would live to regret, she promptly intervened:

"I decided this dress would do, Mamma. I hope you agree. Oh, but you could advise me on what jewellery I should wear with it. Would you? Do come," she urged, indicating the door into her bedchamber.

Far more attuned to her helpful little schemes than Lady Catherine, Darcy patted her hand, still ensconced in the crook of his arm. It was probably too late by now. Elizabeth must already be in her sisters' chamber; and if not, what privacy could be had on the corridor, with his aunt at large and everyone else milling about?

It was impossible to tell whether or not he might have persuaded her to hear him out, had Lady Catherine not turned up like the proverbial bad penny to hinder him in his endeavours yet again.

His eyes narrowed as he cursed his aunt and assessed his options. He could try to find a propitious moment after dinner, but success was doubtful and privacy hard to come by. He suppressed a long sigh of frustration. Waiting till the morrow was as maddening as could be, yet by the looks of things, he would have to make his peace with it. Somehow. Although goodness knows how he would endure dinner and worse still, the long hours of the night.

As for now, one good turn deserved another, he determined, and Anne had done him more than one good turn. Besides, given her galling intrusion, disobliging Lady Catherine held vast appeal at that point in time.

So he smiled pleasantly and said:

"There is still another half-hour until dinner. Shall we sit? Anne and I have spoken in some detail today, Aunt, about her plans for the running of the de Bourgh estates, now that she is of age. I think it is a splendid notion that she should take an interest. She would like to begin slowly and learn from you as she goes along, so at first she will address some minor matters. One of them is the Hunsford living."

Anne cast him a bright smile, then turned towards her mother and said matter-of-factly:

"Yes. To my mind, the parish can do no better than Mr Beaumont. I trust you will have no objections to my writing to offer him the living."

⋖⋗ ⋖⋗

As it happened, Lady Catherine had objections aplenty, and they expected no less. She firmly declared that Anne ought not trouble herself with the burdens of running an estate, and instead should devote all her energies to preserving her health. They argued that Anne must learn to run her own home in preparation for the future, and she would not ask Lady Catherine to labour at the helm forever. Which was, of course, contrary to her ladyship's wishes: that Anne removed to Pemberley, leaving her to rule at Rosings as she always had. The royal seat would not be shared, much less relinquished altogether. The Queen of Rosings was not prepared to become the Queen Mother. But Rome was not built in a day.

By the end of the stormy conversation, Anne had her wish as to the Hunsford living and Mr Beaumont's preferment. A letter would be drafted, jointly signed and sent. She could only hope that the gentleman would accept the offer, but that was a wholly different matter, and she wisely did not share too many details with her mother.

There were very few other concessions from the part of the ruling queen, but that did not trouble Anne unduly. She knew full well that a battle of wills would be unavoidable whenever her chosen course of action differed from her mother's – and invariably the battle would be lost if the disputed point was not worth the effort, but won when her heart was set on it.

Lady Catherine was irritable over dinner – which was no surprise, given the challenge to her rule – and as the evening progressed, Darcy's humour grew to be no better than his aunt's. Elizabeth was almost as far from him as the table could divide them, and afterwards she did not play, did not sing, and there was no hope whatsoever for private conversation.

All he could orchestrate was the briefest of exchanges, when he took the seat Kitty had just vacated, next to the sofa where Elizabeth sat with Jane.

"I hope you had a pleasant evening," he began with a bland civility, and received the same in return.

"I did, I thank you. Did you?"

"It could have been better," he candidly acknowledged with a rueful grimace, then opted for a straightforward question. "Might we speak on the morrow?"

She gave a dainty little shrug.

"I imagine we shall. One must have some conversation, by and by."

"That was not my meaning. Will you walk with me?"

"Anne had mentioned some plans for an outing in the afternoon."

That was not his meaning either, and presumably she knew it.

Nevertheless, he clarified:

"I was rather hoping for a walk in the morning. With you, if you would."

"Were you? The weather is notoriously unreliable at this time of year."

Darcy's mild vexation at her evasive manner promptly grew into something worse when a deep voice drawled behind him:

"You are not planning another walk in the rain, Lizzy, surely."

Although far from subdued, vexation still gave way to yearning when her countenance lost all trace of that damnable reserve and her eyes crinkled in merriment, in a fashion that was achingly familiar from months ago, in Hertfordshire.

"I would not say I planned one for today, Papa."

"Yes, well. Do have a care. There is only so much excitement that my constitution can bear at my age, you know," Mr Bennet said, taking a seat beside his daughters on the sofa.

Whatever was keeping the gentleman from his habitual pursuits in the library, tonight of all nights, Darcy could not pretend to know, but Elizabeth's father was currently vying with Lady Catherine for the title of his least favourite member of the household.

Mr Bennet easily won that contest by remaining precisely where he was for the short period of time until Elizabeth leaned to drop a kiss on his lined cheek and declared she would retire for the night.

There was truly no need for Mr Bennet to exert himself further. The title was already won, and the crown was his. Nevertheless, just as Darcy sought to excuse himself and escort her to the door in the hope of gaining a less evasive answer regarding a private conversation on the morrow, Mr Bennet made a bid for the even grander title of Darcy's least favourite person in all the southern counties by choosing that precise moment to inquire into the sort of crops that thrived in Derbyshire, and if there was any scope for implementing Lord Townsend's principles in the harsher climate of the north.

Fitzwilliam eventually came to his aid and asked Mr Bennet if he would indulge him with a game of piquet, but by then Darcy had no more goodwill to spare for tardy cousins than for overbearing aunts and their agriculturally-minded second husbands, and he retired to his quarters wishing them all at Jericho.

Hours later, his temper had eventually settled, but sleep still eluded him, just as he had predicted. A devil of a torment, that. Under the same roof, and yet at no greater liberty to speak to her – to hold her – than if they had been separated by hundreds of miles. Knowing that there were not a hundred miles, but less than a hundred footsteps between her bedchamber and his made matters marginally better, and also infinitely worse. It led unerringly to picturing her abed, and that was but a flicker of a thought from picturing her beside him.

There was not enough brandy in his sitting room to induce sleep once that mental image had taken hold, so Darcy did not trouble himself to leave his bed and go in search of it.

What left his bed a few moments later was an unyielding pillow, forcefully cast onto the floor when it perversely refused to assume a more accommodating shape, despite repeated pummelling.

Darcy shoved another one under his head and pulled the counterpane up to his chin, forced to acknowledge that the overstuffed pillow might have had a better fate, were it not for a new and most unwelcome notion; namely, that sleep would not come any easier even once she had accepted his hand in marriage – as, by God, she must! Quite the opposite, in fact. Heaven help him if it was to be a long engagement, he thought, and flung the coverlet aside to go and pour himself a brandy after all.

Chapter 20

Rosings, 16 April 1812

Finding someone in the grounds of Rosings Park was virtually impossible when one had but the scantest knowledge as to where one should look. The house posed enough challenges, as did the ornamental gardens, but given the size and full expanse of the estate, an uninformed search was woefully on the par with that of the needle in the haystack.

When he came down for an early breakfast, only to learn from one of his aunt's footmen that Elizabeth had contented herself with a toasted muffin and a cup of coffee and had left the house more than half an hour ago, the only pertinent piece of information Darcy could extract from the man was that she was seen walking with her sketchbook and a satchel in the direction of the rose garden.

Nothing of interest would lie therein, not at that time of year, so Darcy was not in the least surprised that he could not find her there. He diligently explored a larger section of the ornamental gardens, well beyond the yew hedge that bordered the rose beds, just in case, then settled upon leaving by the furthermost gate and walking in a fairly straight line for the distance one might be expected to cover at a brisk pace in half an hour. When that proved fruitless, he widened the search in an arch towards the left, then to the right.

Neither endeavour brought any satisfaction, and the best part of two hours later he was severely disappointed, felt more than a little foolish, and wished he had brought a spyglass and, better still, his horse. It had initially seemed a sensible choice to go on foot, as she had, but after the lengthy and thoroughly unrewarding time spent scouring the grounds, a search on horseback held all the belated appeal of hindsight.

He turned back when he came in sight of the park paling bordering the road that ran past the parsonage towards Hunsford village. Whatever might have made him bend his steps towards the tail of the lake, he could not tell, but it was a remarkable and much-needed stroke of luck – for there she was: a bright spot of colour in the distance. He thanked his stars and hastened on his way, far too pleased with the sudden change in his fortunes to think that, had he walked in a straight line from the shrubbery rather than the rose garden, he would have come across her in twenty minutes, not two hours.

The bright spot of colour eventually acquired its proper size and delectable shape, and he could see her clearly. Charcoal in hand, the sketchbook resting on her lap, she was sitting on a wooden bench set against the trunk of a towering oak tree just coming into leaf. She had removed her bonnet, and the sunshine put glints of copper in her chestnut-coloured locks when she turned her head to cast a glance towards him.

It was rather fortunate that she had already noticed his approach, sparing him the task of finding some other way of making his presence known, so as not to startle her. Thus, he could simply say, "Good morning," – although it was drawing closer to midday – and civilly follow it with "May I join you?"

Her full attention now back on her sketch, she briefly tightened her lips – in concentration on her task, or displeasure at his question? – before she said, as she traced a few bold lines:

"Pray do. Unless you came to find fault with my perspective and my grasp of detail."

The customary mixture of sweetness and archness in her manner made it as difficult as ever to tell if she was teasing him or she was in earnest, but Darcy availed himself of the free seat on the bench nevertheless. She paid him little heed, her eyes darting up and down between the scenery ahead and her open sketchbook. The landscape she had chosen for a model was already recognisable, slowly taking shape on the white paper. Darcy refrained from steadfastly keeping his eyes on her handiwork so as not to disconcert her and, after a brief inspection, he leaned back against the tree trunk, his gaze ahead. He remained thus when he began speaking.

"I will endeavour to comply. But 'tis somewhat of a hardship."

"What is?"

"Not commenting on your perspective."

This time she did turn to face him, a brow arched.

"I see. Very well. Have your say, if you must. What offends you? The shape of the birch? The reeds? The lake? Or the overall angle?"

"I was not speaking of your sketch. No one could find anything wanting, nor dispute your skill with the charcoal. What I had in mind was your general perspective."

"You will have to do a little better than pithy remarks, sir."

"I was hoping to. What I meant to ask is why would you assume I came to find fault? Can you not imagine I came to find you because I simply could not stay away?"

Her eyes widened. Despite himself, Darcy gave a little rueful chuckle.

"Forgive me. That was blunt," he said softly, reaching to gather her small hand in his, the charcoal still poised between her fingers. He drew it from her slacking grasp with his free hand, lest it mar the artwork, and set it on the bench between them as he stroked the back of her fingers with his thumb. "I would have liked to court you as you deserve to be courted, before blurting out that I was bewitched within days – hours – of making your acquaintance. I should have said so – long ago. I wish I had. So much time lost. Besides, courting you now, at Rosings, has its... difficulties," he felt compelled to clarify, although he was convinced that by then she knew enough of Lady Catherine and her ways to make any further clarifications needless. Still, he pensively continued, "Your change of circumstances should have made everything easier, and in the main it does, but at the moment it complicates matters too. In many ways, it would have been preferable if you had remained the second daughter of a gentleman of little consequence in Hertfordshire."

Her hand twitched in his, and her chin came up.

"I am still the daughter of a gentleman of little consequence from Hertfordshire, sir."

"I beg your pardon, that was badly put. What I meant," he said, struggling for better words, "is that I should have courted you then. There was a wealth of opportunity, and a great deal more freedom. My sole excuse – and a poor one at that – is that your connections rather served as a deterrent. Needless to say, I should have known better. Their condition in life may be far beneath my own, but they made you who you are, and you are flawless, so whatever they did must have been right. As for their want of propriety – aye, that could be mortifying, and it often was, but the same can be said of my aunt. If anything, Lady Catherine's shortcomings are far less excusable. *Noblesse oblige*, and an earl's daughter should know a vast deal more about ladylike deportment than an attorney's wife," he said with energy, glad that his words were coming with greater ease, now that his case was taking shape and he could explain his standpoint better. Yet, just as he had begun to feel less tongue-tied, the flow of his discourse was abruptly interrupted by an exclamation coming out of nowhere:

"Heaven help us, *what* is the lad about?"

Darcy started and instinctively turned to look over his shoulder for the source of the irate remark. Yet he saw no one. And the voice gave him pause. Had he not known better, he would have said it sounded like… Well, a little like his father. He glanced around again, not in the least amused by the prospect of anyone interrupting his proposal.

It was equally unamusing to suspect that he had started hearing things. Nevertheless, after all the galling interruptions – particularly on the previous day – he was glad to note that no one was there.

He straightened in his seat, and turned back towards Elizabeth, to see profound displeasure in her most expressive countenance. He suppressed a smile. So she was not fond of interruptions either.

"What I wished to say," Darcy resumed, "is that I have wasted too many opportunities already. I will not waste any more time on my aunt's account. Little as the result will please her, she *has* raised your consequence, and you will be more readily accepted in society as Lady Catherine's stepdaughter than as an unknown young lady from three miles north of Meryton."

"'Struth! Was I expected to teach him how to go about it? He is a grown man of eight-and-twenty – has lived in the world – spoken to people – read books. There are more than enough in the library. How can he make such a cursed hash of it? He pines for the lass for months on end and now he sits there, insults her and calls it a proposal!"

This time Darcy released Elizabeth's hand, sprang to his feet and looked around in earnest. Whoever said that would pay for his impertinence.

Eavesdropping was bad enough, but mocking him – in his hearing – and at a time like this! Who was it? They knew him well – too well. Well enough to know about the months of pining. Surely it was not one of Fitzwilliam's jests! That was beyond the pale, even for him. And there was naught amiss with his proposal – not that it was anyone's affair but his. He was going about it in the proper manner. As for insulting her, he had just complimented her, for goodness' sake, and declared that her eminently vulgar aunt was nowhere near as much at fault as Lady Catherine. How was that insulting? And, more to the point, how *dared* he, whoever the impudent wretch was?

"Who goes there?" he called, and looked up too, for good measure. No one in the tree, risking life and limb. And the voice was a mature one, not that of a child. And still uncannily like his father's.

"What the devil is he doing now? Who is he looking for?"

Darcy spun around towards his companion.

"Elizabeth, could you ascertain where that came from?"

She cast him a severe glance and picked up her charcoal from where he had left it, on the bench.

"There are a great many things that I fail to ascertain right now," she said crisply, "not least your reasons for this strange performance. Pray amuse yourself at leisure, if you must, but kindly step out of the way. I would like to get back to my sketch."

"And now he has vexed her. Lord help me! How difficult can it be? If he will have that lass and none other, must he antagonise her so? I will not see my line wiped out from the face of the earth, by Jove! Get your wits about you, Son! Just tell her you love her," the voice in his head forcefully commanded.

"Son? What insolence is this? Enough, I say!" Darcy exclaimed, turning on his heel to cast a fierce look around.

For a moment, there was naught but silence. He could only hear the faint rustling of the wind through the yellowed reeds. Even the twittering birds seemed to have been hushed by his outburst. And then a shocked whisper filled his head.

"Fitzwilliam? Son, you can *hear* me?"

He spun around again, his eyes darting searchingly this way and that.

"What is the meaning of this? Where are you? *Who* are you?"

The ensuing silence lasted for a mere fraction of a second.

Then a torrent of words came.

"He heard me! Aye. Truly, he *did*. Who knows? I cannot say. For the life of me I cannot fathom how I could hear him from hundreds of miles – not just his words, but whatever is going on in his head. And he heard me, too. No, of course he is not asleep. He was talking to the lass, making a hash of it. He must be wide-awake, yet he could hear me nonetheless. Fitzwilliam? Can you hear me still? By all that is holy, I swear he could hear me a moment ago, Anne!"

"Mr Darcy? Are you well?" Elizabeth added her voice to the cacophony.

Stunned by everything else that he was hearing, he could only whisper, "Anne?"

"No, sir. 'Tis Elizabeth. You should sit. You seem to be unwell," Elizabeth urged, but the voice in his head drowned out her advice. It was a great deal louder.

"Yes! You can hear me still. Thank goodness. But what wretched timing, eh? The lass will think you fit for Bedlam. She is in the right, my boy, you had much better sit. This could unhinge anybody. Sit down, Son, and listen—"

"Son?" Darcy repeated, mightily struggling for a grasp on sanity.

"It must be the sun," Elizabeth agreed. "Another bright morning, I grant you, and warmer than yesterday. Have you been walking over the fields for long? Do sit, Mr Darcy. I fear you might be suffering from sunstroke."

"Come, now, my boy," the voice in his head urged as well. "Listen to the lass, sit yourself down and let me do the talking, else she will think you have lost your mind if you keep talking to the trees. Also, I have no notion how long this will hold, the connection, and I must have my say while it does."

"How is this…? No… impossible," Darcy whispered as he took their advice and sat, clasping the hand that had somehow made its way into his, as though it were a lifeline.

"I think not," Elizabeth countered. "'Tis sunstroke, most likely."

The voice in his head, however, readily agreed with him:

"Impossible, aye. Anyone would think so."

It was too confusing for his scattered senses, and for the first time since the beginning of their acquaintance, instead of seeking to pick out Elizabeth's voice from a crowd as he was wont to do,

Darcy endeavoured to dissociate himself from it, so that it would not distract him from the other, which continued:

"Yet here we are. Goodness knows how. The only other time when I could conquer the obvious limitations of my current state was when I was beset by violent emotion. In this case, it must be anger at your bungling that proposal so. By Jove, you will not be the last Darcy of Pemberley, if I can help it. So I will tell you this: if your happiness and the future of my line rests upon this lass, then bestir yourself and make a better job of trying to secure her. Whoever courts his lady by insulting her connections, my boy? Or sits there talking about Catherine, of all people?"

"Catherine," Darcy echoed numbly.

"No, sir. Not Anne, nor Catherine, nor any of my sisters. *Elizabeth*," she slowly and distinctly said her name again, syllable by syllable and with some emphasis, but Darcy made no answer as the voice in his head chuckled.

"Can you not hold your tongue, lad? I did warn you that you should. Seemingly, you need not speak out loud for me to hear you. Now, still yourself and listen. I would rather not miss this chance to say what must be said. Lord knows I missed too many. All those years, when I should have told you— Yes, yes. You are in the right, my dear. Fitzwilliam, I should not entice you to look back. You should look ahead. So go forth, my boy, and know that you do me proud every day. You always have. I could not have left your sister in better hands, and I know Pemberley will flourish in your care. Your mother and I… er… Hm. I thank you. Aye, of course. Of course I can say it, and I shall. A pity I had to die before I learned how, but there we have it. What I wished to say, Fitzwilliam, is that your mother and I love you very, very dearly, and we both hope to remain tethered to this world for long enough to see you and Georgiana happily settled. Now, I trust you will not mind if I tell him— I must. You can see that, can you not? God bless you, my dearest. Fitzwilliam, if this lass – Elizabeth – is your choice, then hasten to secure her. I— *We* trust your judgement implicitly. And she seems a good sort of girl, bright and spirited. I would have liked to know her better. But I daresay I should be glad to be around for long enough to learn anything at all about the future mother of my grandchildren. So gather your wits together, lad, as I said, and cease rambling about her station in life and whatnot.

Just tell her you love her. If you put your mind to it, I daresay you can be trusted to strike the right note between some self-absorbed dunderhead offended by her connections and a lovestruck mooncalf who readily avows he has spent the last five months wasting away for the love of her," his father said with an affectionate chuckle, and Darcy could not help echoing it, despite the surreal experience of receiving guidance in matters of the heart from his departed father, and the equally surreal novelty of actually laughing with him. But better late than never.

His father's voice had a melancholy ring to it when he replied:

"Aye, too true, my boy. I wish… Well, too late now," he checked himself, his tones suffused with the greatest sadness. "I take comfort in knowing that you will do better than me in every regard. You will make a fine father, and if I am not mistaken, the young lass will bring joy and laughter to my grandchildren's lives, and yours. By the bye, if you prefer not to play the part of the lovestruck mooncalf when you secure her, once you are married pray do not wait for the afterlife to tell the lass she means the world to you. Believe you me, it will serve you better if you say so – and show it, too – while you are living. And it bears frequent repetition."

Mindful of his father's instructions at last, Darcy did not give his reply aloud. Instead, he earnestly thought it:

"Thank you. For your blessing, and everything else. Thank you."

"Better late than never, eh?" his father wistfully voiced his own earlier thought. "Well, what is done is done. Look into the future. Now, first things first, secure the lass. You have my unreserved blessing, my boy. Go to it, and be happy."

Thoughts burst forth in response. Unconstrained and all ajumble, they swirled in Darcy's bewildered mind, and it was with the greatest effort that the instinctive exclamation remained mute and did not pass his lips:

"You said that before! Did you not?"

"I did."

"So… that was *you?* Even then?"

"Aye. Even then."

"And… about Georgiana? Ramsgate?"

"That, too," George Darcy sighed, clearly dreading that subject and any reference to his sins – and Wickham. "But I would have had no hope of success without your mother," he added, his voice lighter.

"My… mother?" Darcy faltered.

"Yes. She is here, too. Did you not hear me speaking to her? She hears everything you say – can hear it in my thoughts – but to her great sadness she could never reach you herself, much as she had tried over the years, since her passing. Yet if I could reach you, 'tis all thanks to her. She taught me all I know about channelling every energy towards a purpose. Thank you, my dear," he fervently said.

As for his son, he sprang to his feet again. This need to keep his lips glued together and the storm of thoughts silent in his head – it would not do. Not any longer. It was imperative to have a private moment and the liberty to move, react and speak without fighting to restrain his impulses for fear that Elizabeth might think him either suffering from sunstroke or unhinged.

"Excuse me. Pray excuse me. I must— I will return shortly," he stammered, speaking directly to her for the first time since the beginning of the unearthly exchange.

He remembered to bow, then stalked away towards the woodland on the left side of the lake, where no one would mind if he spoke to the trees. It *was* imperative to have his turn in freely saying everything that must be said – ask questions – receive answers – fully grasp his father's thoughts – his mother's – before the unimaginable connection was lost. If not, it would haunt him forever. And he *had* to clear his head, before he could begin to reword his proposal and strike the right note between – what was it?

"…self-absorbed dunderhead and lovestruck mooncalf," were the last words Elizabeth thought she could hear him say, with something like a snort of laughter.

Arching a brow, she followed him with her gaze to see him striding towards the edge of the wood, some fifty yards away, and remain there, pacing back and forth, head bowed and hands on his lapels. What was he about? She could not tell. She shook her head, picked up her sketchbook and, casting glances towards him now and then to check that he had neither vanished out of sight, nor done himself a mischief, she began to absent-mindedly draw tufts of grass and shade the surface of the lake, inescapably caught in all manner of reflections on the singular events of the day.

Chapter 21

Rosings 16 April 1812

Elizabeth had no notion of the time. She could not tell how many minutes, or dozens of minutes, had elapsed since Mr Darcy had abruptly excused himself and left her, after that most disquieting episode when he had appeared to have but a tenuous grip on himself and reality. A harrowing sight, that – more so because it had been utterly unexpected. She would never have imagined him so susceptible to the effects of the April sun. A tower of strength brought down by something as trifling as the weather. Unnatural and deeply perturbing to see him thus. Deathly pale. His gaze – that had a way of being sometimes provoking, often thrilling and uniformly unnerving – suddenly turned into a glassy stare, devoid of the spark of reason. His hand cold and clammy, clinging to hers even as he had failed to recognise her, yet allowed her to lead him to the bench, as defenceless as a bewildered child.

The fear for his safety had quickly muted, and then overridden, her anger at his inconsiderate remarks on her family connections, until she could think of nothing but his welfare – and the avowal that he had come to find her because he could not stay away.

She could still see him from her place on her bench. Still pacing. She justly prided herself on her eyesight and the acuity of her hearing, but could not be sure if he was talking to himself. She could hear nothing from that distance, nor see his lips moving. She frowned. Perhaps she should have followed her first impulse to run to the house for assistance. At first, she had thought it would be advisable to remain at hand and follow him if the need arose, rather than let him vanish into the thicket, which would have left the servants faced with the difficult task of combing through the vast expanse of woodland with no inkling as to where he could be found.

It was a relief that he had not gone far, so she had kept her place, and kept an eye on him as well. It would be wise to stay close by to offer assistance, should he collapse. He seemed in no danger of that yet. But sooner or later she should decide on a more practical course of action than sitting there to watch over him.

Thankfully, the day was still young, and with any luck he might recover from his sunstroke if he kept to the shadows, as he was doing now. A drink of water would serve, if any could be had. Or a cold compress, or some such. And keeping still and quiet, if the stubborn man could be worked upon and made to listen.

To her moderate satisfaction, his pacing slowed after a while, and eventually she saw him draw to a standstill next to a tree, to lean his shoulders and a booted heel against it. Should she go to him, or leave him to settle down a little, lest the intrusion trigger further disquiet and bring back the restless pacing?

She chose the latter, at least for a while. Comfortably settled on her bench, Elizabeth resumed sketching the grove – an endeavour begun once her sketch of the tail of the lake was quite finished – and applied herself to that task for want of better employment while she kept an eye on Mr Darcy. And, since he was now standing still for a change, she took to drawing the outline of a tall figure leaning against the trunk of a well-established tree.

ༀ

He had not moved from that position for a fair while, and at last Elizabeth saw wisdom in gathering her belongings in her satchel, retrieving her bonnet and crossing the expanse of grass to join him.

She slowly approached with some misgivings, fearing she might disrupt the recovery process and he would resume uttering disjointed words that made no sense at all. But, to her relief, when she came closer and Mr Darcy noticed her approach, he pushed himself away from the tree trunk to greet her with a bow.

Seeing him reverting to customary conduct was reassuring, as it was to note that his countenance was no longer deeply troubled, nor his gaze unfocused. She bobbed a curtsy as he stepped towards her with an open smile, which she found more than a little disconcerting. There was nothing odd or unnatural about it. The oddity was that the solemn and often aggravating Mr Darcy should smile so widely, as though at a good joke.

201

"Have I not frightened you awfully, then? I half expected you to bring a small army of footmen to restrain me."

"It did cross my mind," she laughed lightly in response, "but I thought better of it. It seemed wiser to ensure you would not go far, or that at least I should be able to inform the small army where they could find you."

"A wise choice indeed."

"Thank you. I gather you are feeling a little better?"

"Much better. 'Tis kind of you to ask."

"Does your head hurt?"

"Not at all."

"Still, you had better sit. And I daresay you should have a drink of water."

"I will be sure to take your very good advice as soon as we return to the house."

"Sooner than that would be better. The brook might be an option," she said, indicating the small stream that snaked amongst trees, rocks and tufts of grass to feed the lake. "Is the water safe to drink, do you imagine?"

"Probably not."

"I was afraid you might say that. Then I would trouble you for your kerchief, if you happen to have one about you. Mine is not big enough."

"Big enough for what?"

"An effective compress."

"Pray rest easy. I assure you, I am not suffering from sunstroke."

Elizabeth rolled her eyes with the same mild exasperation she often showed her younger sisters when they were talking nonsense.

"I find that rather hard to credit," she said, making no effort to hide her scepticism. "Then can you explain the episode I have just witnessed?"

"No. Not today," he soberly said, then chuckled. "Or I will run an even greater risk of being carted off to Bedlam."

"You are not wholly safe from it. But for now I am reserving judgement. Your kerchief, sir? And do sit. That spot by the beech tree will do. You should lean back and close your eyes."

"I am deeply grateful for your concern, but I am well. Better than ever, in fact."

"Is that so? Most reassuring. But pray tell me, sir, do you ever do what you are told?"

He smiled.

"Rarely. In truth, hardly ever."

"Then let this be one of the occasions. Your kerchief, Mr Darcy."

He finally obliged with a wry quirk tugging at the corner of his lips, and Elizabeth thanked him, then went to dip the square of exceedingly fine lawn in the clear water of the brook, thinking it was a pity he did not deem it safe to drink. She squeezed out the excess and returned to find him still standing, watching her with a warm look and a smile she might have called indulgent. She creased her brow into the stern mien of a governess and pointedly indicated the patch of dry leaves and grass at the base of the beech tree with a firm nod.

"Woe betide me if I disobey," Mr Darcy said with another provoking little chuckle, and she pursed her lips.

"Indeed. I see your neckcloth is already loosened. That is very sensible," she remarked, crouching beside him once he had complied and sat. "Now pray lean back and close your eyes."

This time Elizabeth was satisfied to see him doing as bid without demur, and she folded the wet kerchief into a rectangle, then carefully placed it on his brow. Eyes still closed, his countenance grew serene under her ministrations and his lips twitched, then curled up into an impossibly wide smile.

"In good conscience," he casually observed, bending his knees up to support his forearms, "I must assure you yet again that I am perfectly safe from sunstroke. But this is no less enjoyable for that."

"I am pleased to hear it," Elizabeth replied, seasoning her tones with more than the usual archness, lest they betray her sudden and absurdly missish discomposure at the unfamiliar circumstances – and the unfamiliar sight.

For she could not fail to own, it *was* disconcerting to see him thus. Smiling. Eyes closed. And in such proximity. The discomposure grew exponentially when his eyes flashed open, and she was caught staring. She pushed herself up and stood.

"On second thought, however small, my handkerchief might be of some use too. It would be sensible to alternate them, so that the compress remains cool," she said, growing quite cross with herself when she noticed she was babbling.

She frowned and opened her satchel to rummage in it for the said item, and seek it under the sketchbook and the box of charcoals. She found it at last, so she set down the satchel and went to soak the smaller piece of lawn as well.

She retraced her steps towards his side, this time with rather more reluctance, in no great haste to feel missish and foolish yet again, when it came to replacing one compress with the other. It was particularly unnerving to feel his eyes on her as she approached, but the task was made a little easier when he closed them and waited, silent and motionless, for her to crouch back down beside him and do what she deemed needful. So she swapped the kerchiefs with sparse, business-like motions, resorting to an airy manner in the process:

"There. They should be changed a few more times, then you will presumably be safe to return to the house." Most vexingly, his eyes flashed open as she spoke, so she gave a little shaky laugh. "Sadly, I doubt that Lady Catherine keeps a sedan chair for cases such as these, but your valet's services or those of a sturdy footman will perchance suffice. If you move closer to the brook and are willing to swap the compresses yourself, I will go and get someone," she said, hurriedly making to rise from her crouch.

"No need. Pray wait," Mr Darcy entreated.

The hand that was still fiddling with the kerchief, unnecessarily repositioning it as she spoke – or rather babbled in the silliest manner, Elizabeth inwardly chastised herself in some exasperation – was suddenly clasped in his, and her retreat hindered. Not just hindered, but stopped altogether – and so abruptly too, that her already precarious balance was completely lost.

A small cry of surprise and dismay left her lips as she fell sideways, beyond hope of regaining her footing. It was but poor consolation that she had a soft landing when she found herself most mortifyingly placed between Mr Darcy's chest and his long legs, bent at the knees and hips. The impact forced the air out of him with a muted grunt, and his hands shot forward to hold her arms in a belated attempt to steady her.

"Forgive me," he said quickly. "You are not injured, are you?"

"No. Just my pride," Elizabeth quipped to make light of the profound embarrassment, but a fierce blush crept into her cheeks.

She might have turned positively scarlet, had her kerchief not chosen to entertain her at that precise moment by sliding off Mr Darcy's brow, to cover one eye and part of his nose. A rather perfectly formed nose, upon reflection, but that was neither here nor there. Laughter bubbled in her throat at the ludicrous picture, and even more so when, instead of raising a hand to push it away, he sent it flying into the grass with a vigorous shake of his head.

The bubble of laughter burst and grew into an ungovernable fit of giggles that easily vanquished the mortification. Even more so when he began to laugh as well, as unrestrainedly as she – a novelty that might have surprised her, had she been able to spare it a thought. But she could not. She gasped for breath, overcome with mirth at the absurdity of their situation, and the fact that she was bounced up and down with his hearty laughter only added to the silliness and the hilarity. It was Darcy who was able to speak first.

"You have no equal, and this is hopeless."

"What is?" she choked out, seeking to redress herself, but his hands tightened their hold around her arms, presumably to keep her from slipping onto the grass.

"My endeavour at dignified decorum. Not a chance, is there? I thought it was called for – indeed, mandatory. I was wrong."

"You are talking in riddles again. You need a fresh compress. And I need to stand and regain my dignified decorum – the little of it that is left."

"Pray wait. I thought a proper speech was in order. As you might have noticed, I do not excel at that," he whispered softly and his eyes crinkled at the corners, but the glint of self-deprecating amusement left them almost as soon as it came. There was no trace of it when his hand came up to stroke her cheek with the back of his fingers. Dark fire had completely consumed it by the time his thumb began to trace a tingling line along her jaw, to the corner of her lips. His other hand released its hold on her arm and came to rest between her shoulder blades, bringing her closer. Close enough for Elizabeth to feel his warm breath brushing her lips when he whispered her name. Close enough for his eyes to fill the world. She blinked. They still filled the world – impossibly dark; mesmerising – when his lips found hers.

"Oh," she might have gasped, but the breathless sound was lost, or perhaps it remained unuttered when the kiss deepened into the sort of hungry abandon she had found in the few romantic novels she had read, and scoffed at. Preposterous exaggeration and artistic licence, she had dismissively called that sentiment, and as divorced from reality as could be.

Surprisingly, she was mistaken. It was all too real, that rush of feeling. As real as the sudden and unconquerable flush that should have sprung from shock, or at least mortification, but it had not. It spread out from the very core of her being and was not mortification, far from it. It rather felt like feverish excitement, and a bewildering sense of both fulfilment and anticipation. Anticipating what? She hardly knew. But when his hands spread over her back to clasp her so tightly that she could barely breathe, she thrilled to the sensation and readily recognised it as something she had been unconsciously anticipating.

She closed her eyes when she felt heat rising in her cheeks, yet even then she knew it was not an outraged maidenly blush. There was no sense of outrage as his lips claimed hers with ever-growing fervour, but a positively brazen wish that he would not stop. That, and a strange urge to run her fingers through his hair and learn its texture. She gave in, and discovered it was silky, which surprised her, and very tangled, which did not. Another brazen notion came on the heels of the first: that she rather liked how his breath grew fast and shallow and his kisses positively fervid when she tangled her fingers in his hair. Unseemly to delight in that, was it? Aye, probably. And it was equally unseemly to rejoice in the thrill that coursed from her scalp to her fingertips when a low moan rumbled in his chest – a deep sound that might have signalled pain, but she sensed beyond a doubt that it did not.

Thrills were the enemies of common sense, that she knew of old, and such well-established truths remained unshaken as common sense was currently put into abeyance. Time seemed suspended too, its natural laws and indeed its very definition becoming blurred and meaningless as the rush of feeling ruled supreme.

Apparently, distance meant nothing, either. Miles and miles away, at Pemberley, George Darcy rather wished the connection, which had of late become one-sided, were fully severed now. He was as pleased as Punch that the lad was happy, but he could do without the details.

With a great deal of effort, Mr Darcy *père* sought to close his mind to the surfeit of information as he muttered softly:

"I rather thought he would tell the lass he ardently admired and loved her. But I will not quibble if this works just as well."

It might have, but for the most unfortunate interruption, coming in the form of a loud snap of a twig underfoot, and a voice full of righteous outrage:

"*Mr Darcy!* I thought you the last man in the world who would trifle with a maiden's honour in a grove."

⁓⊙ ⊙⁓

How was it possible to feel both scorched with shame and showered in ice-cold water? Elizabeth could not tell, yet ice and scorching shame left her struggling for breath as she gracelessly disentangled herself from the immodest embrace and sprang up, pushing against Mr Darcy's shoulders for the briefest moment, then drawing her hands back as though burned. She picked up her skirts to flee the curate's sight and the spot of her humiliation, but Darcy's hand caught her wrist in a vice-like grip.

"Elizabeth, wait! Pray wait!" he urged as he scrambled to his feet.

"Unhand me," she breathlessly demanded, and mortification rose again, dwarfing the sense of gratitude, when she found her request seconded by the man of the cloth.

"Unhand the lady, sir. Have you no shame, to molest her even as I stand before you? A member of your family, no less."

"Hold your peace, Reverend. You have no understanding of the matter," Darcy hissed through gritted teeth without sparing so much as a glance at the irate clergyman, whose temper was becoming more explosive by the minute.

"I will not have your insolence, sir, regardless of your station in life and your family connections," the man fulminated. "Unhand her this instant, or I will not answer for the consequences. Frankly, your transgression is all the more repugnant, given your standing. There is nothing more disgraceful than trifling with a poor relation. You will not get away with it, I solemnly assure you. You will do right by this young woman, if I have to drag you to the altar by the tails of your coat!"

The curate's admonitions sent his blood boiling, to the point that Darcy felt he could not answer for the consequences either. Had Mr Whittaker not been protected by his clerical garb, he would have been in dire straits indeed. As for the threats, it was unlikely that the rotund and florid-faced man could inflict bodily harm upon him, so it was not the stern injunctions that compelled Darcy to obey, but Elizabeth's stricken look and her fitful efforts to tug her wrist free.

"Pray wait," he whispered softly as he released his hold, but to his profound dismay she turned on her heel and made for the house, almost at a run.

Darcy ran his fingers through his hair, caught between the desperate need to chase after her and the imperative to set the meddlesome clergyman to rights before untold damage was done to Elizabeth's good name. However strongly his heart tugged him in the first direction, he knew full well that he could not follow her until he had settled the matter with the deeply aggravating individual. Expelling the contents of his lungs in a rush of anger and exasperation, Darcy turned upon the curate.

"I would not trifle with anyone's honour. Least of all *hers*—"

"Fine words," Mr Whittaker scoffed. "A pity they do not match the evidence of my own eyes."

"Your eyes misled you," Darcy icily retorted. "What you have interrupted was not an indecent assignation, but an offer of marriage."

"Is that so? Then why did the young lady not speak up in your defence, but could not wait to flee your presence?"

"It was *your* presence and your righteousness she fled, sir," Darcy exploded, at the very limits of his patience. "Not to mention that we have not had the chance to conclude our conversation – thanks to you!"

"Now see here," Mr Whittaker spluttered, then loudly cleared his voice and proceeded to puff up his cheeks and his chest in a show of mortified dismay and injured dignity. "Well, then, if that be the case, you will do well to go about it swiftly and in the proper manner, or else I—"

"*You* will do well to leave be," Darcy shot back. "I had the devil of a job finding a moment alone with her, with all the commotion at the house—"

"Aye," the curate sneered. "And you could not wait to avail yourself—"

"You have said enough," Darcy cut him off, clenching his fists. "Good day, sir. If you were on your way to Rosings, pray proceed. I would much rather not walk back with you. And above all, I trust you will have the decency to keep the matter to yourself. Pray mind your own affairs and allow me to repair the damage, rather than blundering in and ruining everything. More than you already have, that is," he resentfully added as he bent down to collect his hat, Elizabeth's forgotten satchel, her bonnet, and the two damp kerchiefs. That task accomplished, he stood, donned his hat and came to tower over the flustered churchman.

"Do I have your word, sir?" he demanded to know.

The other threw his arms up in the air.

"Oh, very well. I will keep silent. But not for long, mind," the man blustered. "If I do not receive happy tidings of a betrothal within a fortnight, her ladyship will hear of this shameful incident. And believe you me, measures will be taken."

Darcy did not doubt it, although he flattered himself that he had a much better notion as to what measures Lady Catherine would hasten to take. He nodded his adieus and stalked away, still supremely unwilling to walk back to Rosings shoulder to shoulder with the bumbling curate. If only Anne had already sent him on his way, he inwardly grumbled, and muttered an oath as he hastened along to redress the mischief the irksome fool had caused.

Chapter 22

Rosings, 16 April 1812

Elizabeth closed the door behind her and leaned against it, releasing a shaky breath. Yet, despite having walked as fast as possible all the way from the tail of the lake, she could only stand motionless for a few seconds. Still clad in her outdoor garments, she began to pace from one end of her bedchamber to the other. It was only when she absent-mindedly tried to unbutton her pelisse that she noticed how badly her hands were shaking. She stared at them, willing them to cease trembling, and when they would not obey, she brought them to her temples with a groan.

What had she done? A momentary folly, a lapse of judgement – nay, of sanity – had been enough to land her into *this*. The enormity of it defied imagination.

She let her hands drop and resumed the frantic pacing.

Mr Whittaker's horrified outburst had spelled it out so very clearly. Her good name – tarnished. A poor relation caught on an assignation. Her cheeks blazed anew, hotter than ever, at the thought that he was right on both those counts. And good Lord, the consequences! There would be consequences. The little she had registered from the man's irate bluster left her in no misapprehension of the matter. He would not keep this to himself. In the misguided notion that he was acting in her interest, he would not let it rest.

Heavens above, she would not be forced to wed now, surely! No, of course not. Papa would not insist upon it any more than he had when Lydia— Good heavens! She had been as thoughtless, as lost to every notion of propriety as Lydia. What would Papa say? She gasped. And Lady Catherine, too! Goodness, Lady Catherine would be insupportable.

At least she would have an ally of sorts in Lady Catherine. Her stepmother would never countenance her marrying Mr Darcy. But should Lady Catherine hear of this, there would be no hope of peaceful coexistence. And inevitably her conflict with her ladyship would affect everyone else. Goodness, seeking to live together had been enough of a challenge already. Trading Longbourn for Rosings had not been easy for any of them. Now it would be sheer hell. For her own sake, as well as her relations', she would have to make a life elsewhere if – *when* – all this came to light. Her uncle and aunt Gardiner would take her in, but... what of Papa? How could she leave him? And Jane, whose affectionate heart still ached for Mr Bingley, and needed tenderness and succour? And Lydia and Kitty too – who would reconcile them to the strictures that came with living under Lady Catherine's rule? How could she tear herself from them all – just because, for a few moments of insanity, she could not conquer her attraction to Mr Darcy?

Good Lord, the humiliation! Discovered in such disgraceful circumstances! In Mr Darcy's arms – nay, his lap – kissing with mindless abandon. She bit her lip. Was there a way of making Mr Whittaker hold his tongue? Of making him see that, far from assisting her, he was worsening the intolerable situation? Powerlessness. Matters taken out of her hands. Involving others, who had no reason or no business to become involved.

She verily growled, angry with herself beyond imagination, as she spun on her heel to pace the other way. Why, oh, *why* had she not returned to the house as soon as Mr Darcy had left her on the bench to take himself into the grove?

Of course she had been concerned – he seemed so dreadfully unwell. She gave a loud snort of exasperation. She should have left him in the woods to fend for himself, if her reward for seeking to ensure his safety was *this* wretched business. As for the utter folly of wondering what he might have said next...

She frowned. There, she might as well own it, at least to herself. She had been intrigued, nay, fascinated and unpardonably gratified, to learn he could not stay away from her.

'I was bewitched within days – hours – of making your acquaintance.'

The words reverberated in her memory, as if she had just heard them spoken yet again, with the same mesmerising depth of feeling.

She shivered – then hated herself for it.

Attraction. So, he felt it too – and what of it? He had not acted on it when she was but an unknown young lady from three miles north of Meryton. He had not deemed her worthy of him then. Only now, once Lady Catherine had raised her consequence. She glowered, belatedly smarting at the insult. That alone should have been enough to send her on her way. She should have seen that no good whatsoever would come from yielding to attraction. The old adage was coined precisely for cases such as those: marry in haste, repent at leisure. What was there in store for them but lifelong repentance, should this morning's indiscretion lead to an ill-judged union based on nothing more substantial than attraction?

Her eyes darted to the door when she heard the sudden knock, only to see it opening before she could even bid whoever it was to enter. The flare of anger at the intrusion died out as promptly as it came, when the newcomer was shown to be her eldest sister. Jane walked in, pressed the door shut and rushed towards her.

"Oh, Lizzy!" she exclaimed. "Thank goodness you are here at last. How I needed you! But… dearest, whatever is the matter?" Jane asked, the eagerness in her countenance giving way to anxious confusion.

Elizabeth winced. She must look a fright, if the mere sight of her had given Jane pause.

"Nothing that cannot wait," she valiantly declared. "Have your say first. You needed me? What happened?"

"This came by messenger while you were out," Jane replied, unfolding some sheets of hot-pressed paper and handing them to her.

Elizabeth took them, and found to her extreme vexation that her hands were still shaking and she could barely keep the letter still, so that she could read it. Jane could not fail to notice it as well.

"Lizzy, you are trembling! Goodness, never mind Miss Bingley. Do sit and tell me what has distressed you so."

"Miss Bingley!" Elizabeth exclaimed in her turn. "What does she have to say?"

"That she and her relations have finally read the London papers," Jane retorted tersely, her tone and the severity of her countenance wholly out of character for her. "As I said, never mind that. Tell me what troubles *you*."

"I shall," Elizabeth promised. "But what of the London papers?" she insisted.

"They carried a notice of Papa's marriage," came Jane's curt reply. Then she elaborated: "Miss Bingley wrote with profuse apologies that our happy tidings had but recently come to their attention, and sent her best wishes."

Elizabeth snorted, quick to grasp how and why the Bennets' society had suddenly become far more appealing to the Bingleys. And then, to her shock, she found herself bursting into inane, nervous laughter. What charming suitors they both had, she and Jane! How readily both gentlemen had changed their stances, now that Lady Catherine had raised the consequence of all the Bennet sisters.

Indeed, if one of Mr Darcy's lineage and standing now deemed *her* a good enough candidate for the honour of his hand, what an attractive prospect Jane must be for Mr Bingley, who could only boast of a lesser fortune made in trade. And how foolish they had been, she and Jane, to trust appearances and grow attached to cold-hearted and calculating men.

"Diverting, is it not?" Jane remarked with a tight smile, but Elizabeth could not return it as the false mirth drained away, leaving the sting of tears in her eyes.

"Not as such," she owned, then forced herself to give her full attention to Jane's plight, for now. "So, what of Mr Bingley? Did his sister convey his best wishes too?"

"Yes," Jane said in a harsh whisper, lowering her gaze. "But she also said— Oh, Lizzy, this is the worst part," she exclaimed, glancing up again and clasping Elizabeth's hands in hers. "Miss Bingley said they are coming to take the waters in Tunbridge Wells, and asked permission to call upon me. They will be here on Tuesday at the latest. In fact, she intimated that her brother might arrive a vast deal sooner!"

Elizabeth frowned.

"Did she!"

"She did. Miss Bingley said that she and the Hursts would set off for Tunbridge Wells directly. As for her brother, she wrote— But here, here. See for yourself," Jane breathlessly added, retrieving the letter from Elizabeth's hands to turn the first page and scan the even writing for a while. Then she held the sheets under her sister's eyes.

She did not press Elizabeth to take them, presumably in case her hands were still unsteady, but pointed at the relevant fragment.

"This is where it starts. This paragraph, here."

Obligingly, Elizabeth bent her head and began to read.

My brother had barely spent any time with us while we visited our relations in Scarborough. Instead, he went away for weeks on end, to stay with an acquaintance of his near Allendale. To explore the hills and the moors, he said, but Louisa and I were not so easily deceived. I trust my brother will forgive me for sharing my thoughts with you, dear friend. I do so with warm hopes of his future happiness. For you see, Louisa and I have long suspected that he vanished into the wilds of the north because he was pining over you, my dear Jane. I daresay he could not forget you.

Our speculations were confirmed a few days ago, when he came to Grosvenor Square to let us know he was determined to return to Netherfield and win your affections. Sadly, we were in no position to inform him that you were no longer residing in Hertfordshire, but in Kent. Mr Hurst's exceedingly deficient butler had omitted to forward the London papers, and we only saw the notice of your father's second marriage this morning, when Louisa and I were perusing the old papers. By the bye, my sister and I are delighted to offer our best wishes on such a happy occasion. I entreat you to pardon the unfortunate delay, and believe we would have written a great deal sooner, had we but known.

Really, my brother should have had the kindness to inform us of your happy tidings, if he had already found the notice in the paper. If not, he must have heard the news by now, from your acquaintances in Hertfordshire. He might have written to Mr Bennet to convey his regards and best wishes, but if not, I am convinced he would like me to express them on his behalf as well.

Having reached the last line, Elizabeth took the letter from her sister to turn the page and read the rest, too caught up in Miss Bingley's tidings to note that she had no difficulty in holding the sheets steady now.

We have had but one communication from him since his sudden removal to Netherfield. A note came earlier today, and we opened it with great anticipation, eagerly hoping to find that his suit had been successful, but to our distress Louisa and I learned he has yet to follow you into Kent, and is in fact at the Pulteney, awaiting a reply from Mr Darcy.

Apparently, Charles sought him at his house in town, in Berkeley Square, learned that Mr Darcy was visiting at Rosings, and sent him a message or two, which remained unanswered. That, sadly, caused a great deal of offence.

When you become engaged to my brother, dearest Jane – and with all my heart I hope that happy day will be upon us soon – you will learn something of his writing style, yet love him in spite of it. Suffice to say that his letters often puzzle their recipients, and the note he sent today was no exception. I have no notion why my brother wrote to Mr Darcy, nor what he was expecting in reply, but what I could gather to my profound unease was that he is deeply vexed with his friend. More vexed than I ever thought Charles could be.

Thus, I am forced to trespass upon your kindness, my dearest Jane. Your generous nature will hopefully induce you to pardon me for ending my letter of congratulations by asking for a favour. I dearly hope so, and I shall be forever grateful for your assistance. Long story short, my dear Jane, should my brother make a tempestuous appearance at Rosings – which might happen in a matter of days – could you find it in your heart to prevent a rupture between longstanding friends? Doubtlessly Mr Darcy was much engaged with his aunt, and had no intention of offending by not replying to messages as promptly as my brother would have wished. I will endeavour to smooth matters between them to the best of my abilities when I come into Kent to pay my respects to you and your dear family, but I would appreciate your aid in this matter more than I could say.

Until the joyful day of our reunion, I remain
Your affectionate friend,
Caroline Bingley

"I see," Elizabeth said crisply as soon as she finished reading, but her mien softened into compassion when she looked up from the sheets of paper and caught her sister's anxious glance.

"Do you, Lizzy? What *do* you see? Can you ascertain Mr Bingley's motives? For I confess I cannot."

Elizabeth sighed and put one arm around her.

"Me neither," she owned. "I cannot safely say. But there is more than enough reason to suspect that if he does come into Kent, 'tis because of our changed circumstances. Otherwise…" She sighed again. "Otherwise he would have found his way to you a great deal sooner."

Under the sheen of tears, Jane's mild grey eyes acquired glints of steel.

"Yes. He would have, would he not?" she rasped, and folded the letter with quick, nervous motions.

"And it does not speak well of either his character or his intentions that he is still in town, awaiting Mr Darcy's express instructions," Elizabeth acidly remarked, then let her arm drop from around Jane's shoulders to indicate the missive with a disdainful little gesture.

"As far as I could see, the main message – apart from Miss Bingley's sudden urge to court you herself, and you cannot misapprehend *her* motives there – is her keen wish to avoid a breach between her brother and Mr Darcy, little as their friendship had advanced her cause so far. But if she still harbours hopes of success, then she is welcome to him," she muttered under her breath, narrowing her eyes.

Yet a mere fraction of a second later, the scowl became a wince, when – always candid and hardly ever gullible – an inner voice sensibly asked, '*Is she really, Lizzy? Come now, is she?*'

A good memory was unpardonable in cases such as these, Elizabeth grumbled, shocked at how vivid her recollections were, when they ambushed her without warning in a concerted effort to speak to all her senses. It was not just the kiss itself that she remembered, but everything about it – about him. His scent. The taste of his lips. The tension in his shoulders. The tight clasp of his arms around her. His hands, stroking, claiming, splayed fingers digging into her back. His warm breath on her face. The throbbing of her lips, bruised by his kisses. The warmth spreading through her at the onslaught of far too vivid recollections. The insane wish to be held and kissed again.

'*See?*' the voice in her head snickered knowingly.

'*Oh, do be quiet!*' she snapped back.

Very well. Miss Bingley had no business to either kiss him or wish to marry him. But did *she?* What business had she to daydream about his kisses, when her consequence or lack thereof held more sway over him than her person? Attraction – she had never denied it. She never could. He was maddeningly attractive. Yet a happy union was based on love, respect, and a similarity of tastes and disposition. Attraction did not last a lifetime. Did it?

"There," Jane said, resignedly pursing her lips into a grimace. "Now you know as much as I do, and if troubles should come, they will be faced, and that is all there is to it. But what of you, Lizzy? What are your troubles?"

Elizabeth drew a steadying breath, and began.

"Uncannily similar to yours, in fact. And Lydia's."

"Oh?"

After the briefest hesitation, the confession came out in a rush:

"Mr Whittaker discovered me kissing Mr Darcy."

The wide-eyed look of surprise in Jane's countenance was almost comical. Yet Elizabeth was not in the least inclined towards laughter.

"How…?" Jane whispered.

"How could I be so shameless? I am still struggling to grasp that."

"No," Jane earnestly denied any intention of uttering such harsh words. "How did that happen? And what happens next?"

"I dread to think," Elizabeth whispered. "Mr Whittaker will not let this rest. He was… formidable – spoke of dragging Mr Darcy to the altar by the tails of his coat…"

Neither of them so much as smiled at the ludicrous picture.

"There would be no need to drag him, surely," Jane said, yet concern slowly crept into her gentle visage and her brow furrowed. "You do not think he was merely toying with you, Lizzy. Do you?"

Elizabeth sighed.

"I cannot think him so dishonourable. No, it was a proposal of sorts. But I cannot be made to marry him over an indiscretion," she anxiously exclaimed.

Jane reached for her hand to stroke it, then kept it in hers.

"Would it be so very bad if you were, dearest? You have always liked him—"

"I did. In Hertfordshire," Elizabeth bitterly retorted.

"And now you do not?"

"Now… I do not *know*," she said, troubled confusion in her eyes. "In truth, Jane, what *do* I know about him? First impressions. Handsome. Rich. More clever than most. Can make exceedingly intriguing conversation if he gives himself the trouble. Very well. I will own I was duly intrigued. You may go as far as to say I let my fancy run away with me. And what good did that do – when he left, never to return?"

"I am no stranger to that disappointment, Lizzy," Jane mildly observed, and Elizabeth pressed her hand, contrition clouding her countenance.

"I know. Forgive me," she whispered.

"At least Mr Darcy came to take his leave of you. And he is here now," Jane pointed out, but Elizabeth would have no truck with such arguments.

"Only because Lady Catherine is his aunt," she countered. "And because Papa's marriage has raised our consequence. Mr Darcy did not omit to mention *that*. And also that I would be more readily accepted in society as Lady Catherine's kin than as Papa's daughter," she added with renewed bitterness.

Jane frowned.

"That was uncivil. And hardly likely to recommend his suit."

Elizabeth gave a mirthless little laugh.

"Oh, there was more. He was just as eloquent on the subject of our connections. Their want of propriety. Their condition in life, so far beneath his own—"

Jane's eyes widened.

"He said that?"

Elizabeth pursed her lips and nodded.

"He did. Very clearly. So, what will you have me do, Jane? Gladly tie my fortunes with a man who does not scruple to say he would be marrying beneath him? If he says so now, what will he say if we do wed? And even if he did not say it – even if he did not think it – even if he made his offer in the most gentlemanlike manner – how am I to know what lies beyond fine words? Is he kind, principled, just? I do not know. Would he make a good husband? Or would he tire of me in three months, or in twenty?"

"As Papa tired of Mamma, you mean," Jane evenly observed, making Elizabeth start.

"You should not say that," she admonished, shocked in no small measure that sweet and gentle Jane, who never had an unkind word to say of anyone, would pass judgement on their father's behaviour as a husband.

"I know. And I would not have, had I not suspected you were thinking it."

They glanced at each other, exchanging uncertain smiles, then Jane put her arms around her younger sister and gathered her into a warm embrace. Elizabeth returned it, and they remained thus, finding comfort in each other, when none could be found in unsettling reflections or unrewarding speculations.

They glanced up and drew apart when the indistinct rumble of voices coming from the adjoining sitting room caught their notice, soon to be followed by a knock on the connecting door. This time the caller waited to be asked within and, straightening her shoulders, Elizabeth did just that. It was a maid who entered, dropped a curtsy and noiselessly closed the door behind her, carefully balancing a bonnet and a satchel in one hand.

"There is also this kerchief, ma'am, but 'tis wet. I'll leave it with your laundry, shall I?"

"Pray do," Elizabeth casually agreed, but rather than making her way across the bedchamber towards the dressing room, the maid gave her a flustered look.

"Yes, Betsy? Is there anything else?" Jane intervened, her tone encouraging and gentle as was her wont, but it did not seem to set the young maid at ease.

"Aye, ma'am. Mr Darcy is within," she indicated the sitting room with a tilt of her head, "an' he's hoping for a private word with Miss Lizzy."

Elizabeth gasped.

"Will you see him, ma'am?" the girl hesitantly asked her.

Of course not, common sense angrily dictated. Had he utterly lost his mind? A private word in her sitting room, one door away from her bedchamber? Adding more fuel to the already explosive situation? Was the dreadful scene with Mr Whittaker not bad enough?

What if you were not discovered in the grove? Then would you see him?' the other voice chimed in – the one that had questioned her candour as to relinquishing Mr Darcy to Miss Bingley, and then snickered at her. It did not snicker now. It whispered like a serpent, compelling her to envisage herself walking into the sitting room – into his arms. Held tight. Kissed breathless. As if nothing else mattered.

'Oh, hold your tongue!' Elizabeth lashed out, and for a moment feared she had spoken the harsh words aloud.

But Jane did not look outraged, nor did the maid seem cowed by such odious treatment, so at least Elizabeth was reassured in that regard. As to the maid's question, there was but one possible answer.

"No," she said with great determination. "Pray tell Mr Darcy I cannot."

The maid made no motion to withdraw. Instead, she fidgeted and shuffled on her feet.

"Must I, ma'am? I…" She gulped. "Beg pardon, but 'tis—" she stammered, then forced the next words out, "Truth be told, I daren't. I've never seen him thus…"

Elizabeth stared.

So, he was terrifying maids out of their wits now?

"Seen him how?" she asked.

"Agitated, ma'am," the girl squeaked. "He verily looks like thunder."

"Does he!" Elizabeth scoffed. What reason had he to be agitated? It was not his reputation that was hanging by a thread.

"I will come with you, Betsy, and deliver the message," Jane calmly offered, but with a start Elizabeth reached out to press her sister's arm and stop her.

"I thank you, dearest. You are too kind. But I will not have you fight my battles."

She gave a little sigh of vexation when she saw the maid's eyes widening at the remark. Goodness, how had she become so addlebrained as to stumble from one blunder into another?

"Are you quite certain?" Jane insisted, and Elizabeth wished she had not, for it merely served to emphasise her own unfortunate reference to fighting battles. The maid glanced from one to the other, in equal parts curious and anxious.

"Thank you, Betsy. You may leave us now. And drop that wet kerchief into the washbowl. I will dispose of it myself. Pray return to your duties," Elizabeth saw fit to dismiss her.

Yet the maid still fidgeted. Then – astoundingly – she disagreed.

"I reckon I shouldn't, ma'am."

"And why not?"

"I were at work in your sitting room, dusting the dressers and whatnot."

With a little huff, Elizabeth conceded her the point.

"I see. Then perchance you might see to Miss Kitty's and Miss Lydia's bedchamber instead," she suggested, wary of finding Betsy some employment in her own bedchamber or Jane's.

With any luck, despite his untoward agitation, Mr Darcy might have the good sense to keep his voice down. Nevertheless, she would prefer Betsy were further than one door away, on either side of the wretched sitting room.

She waited until the girl bobbed a curtsy and left, then drew a deep breath to steel herself for the encounter. Jane cast her a concerned glance as she stroked her shoulder.

"I will come with you, naturally," she said, and this time Elizabeth could not find it in her to disagree.

"Thank you, dearest. Would you? That is, if you can bear it."

"Whyever not?" Jane asked, her surprise apparent until she saw Elizabeth nodding meaningfully towards Miss Bingley's letter. Then she shrugged. "Do not trouble yourself. Of all the things Miss Bingley had to say, her references to Mr Darcy are the least of my concerns," she declared, and followed her sister towards the sitting room.

Chapter 23

Rosings, 16 April 1812

Betsy was patently in the right about his agitation, Elizabeth discovered as soon as she opened the door and saw him pacing away towards the far end of the room, and not leisurely either. He must have heard the muted click, for he spun round, only to scatter her senses with a devastating smile. She caught her breath, vexed with her ludicrous response and no less with him. What business had he to stand there and look so unaccountably pleased – and impossibly handsome to boot? And then he advanced towards her in long strides, to send her cheeks aflame with the inexcusably delectable suspicion that he meant to kiss her, and weakened her defences with the deep intensity in his voice when he fervently said, "Thank you. I feared you would not come—"

He stopped short, and the unadulterated joy in his countenance gave way to disappointment when Jane followed her into the room.

"Oh," he said, and finally remembered to give a restrained bow. "I was hoping— Elizabeth, may we have a private word?"

The blatant lack of welcome for her sister bordered on outright incivility, and while understandable, it could not fail to add to Elizabeth's ill-humour.

"No, we may not," she declared. "Frankly, I am staggered that you would even consider it, under the circumstances. You should not be here. I must ask you to leave."

He gave a pained grimace as he ran his fingers through his hair.

"You are absolutely right. I deserve the severest censure. I have already placed you in an intolerable situation. I know this is not helping matters," he added, gesturing around him as if to show he was referring to his presence in that room, "but you must see the lack of options. There is never any privacy to be had in this house," he argued, with a huff of exasperation.

"And you must see 'tis nothing short of madness to seek privacy *now*," she pointed out, incensed at his obtuseness. A man who prided himself on his understanding should have gathered as much already. And then she gasped. Perhaps he had. Surely this was not a ploy to force her hand and bring everything into the open – was it?

"No, I *do not* see that," Mr Darcy countered forcefully, and too loudly by far, which only served to fuel her misgivings and thus antagonise her all the more. "Quite the contrary. Elizabeth, we must talk."

"Lower your voice, sir," she commanded. "What is there to talk about? Let me assure you, I will not be coerced into a hasty marriage through public ignominy."

"Coerced?" he exclaimed, his mien frozen into horror.

"I asked you to lower your voice," Elizabeth hissed. "Pray leave before more damage is done."

He made no move to leave; but as to her other instruction, he obeyed it to the letter. His tones dropped to a whisper when, supremely indifferent to Jane's presence, he spoke again, his eyes boring into hers and clouded with the deepest sadness.

"You cannot imagine I would ever coerce you into anything. Is it so unreasonable to hope that you might love me?"

Remorse rose in a wave that threatened to engulf her. She had injured him with her suspicions, and she was sorry for it. Yet she had to speak her mind. And, for months on end, he had injured her too.

"Love you? I hardly even know you," she ruefully whispered back. "And what I thought I knew was shown to be a figment of my imagination."

"What are you saying?" he asked, his countenance a mask of dejected confusion.

What was there to be confused about? Very well. If he must have it spelled out, then she would oblige him, Elizabeth decided.

"I am saying that I thought you might be drawn to me for myself, and not because your aunt has raised my consequence."

A strange sort of aching tenderness softened his gaze, yet only added to the sadness.

"Elizabeth, I *am* drawn to you for yourself," he pleaded, but by then she had warmed up to the subject, and would not settle for half-truths any longer.

"Be honest," she adjured him. "Would you have sought me out, had I remained just as I was – some young woman three miles north of Meryton?"

He flinched.

"I… believe so," he said, reaching for her hand.

Elizabeth bit her lip. Well, she did ask for honesty and seemingly her request was granted. She had received no ardent protestations of regard, but a cautious admission that he might have bent his steps her way – eventually. It was not enough.

She wrenched her hand from his clasp. With a deep sigh at her withdrawal, he trailed his fingertips along her arm instead, sending her skin tingling, yet she refused to allow the caress to silence her.

"But I cannot believe anything of the sort," she rasped. "In fact, I think you would have been content to stay away."

He let his hand drop and flashed a fierce glance towards her at the accusation.

"*Content?* Elizabeth, those were five months of hell!"

"Yet you stayed away, regardless," she shot back, this time disdaining to acknowledge the injured look he cast her.

What she did acknowledge at long last, with deep contrition, was her sister's presence. The dear soul, despite what must have been acute mortification at witnessing a scene such as that, Jane had steadfastly remained beside her, doubtlessly to protect her good name from further harm, should she be discovered having yet another ill-judged *tête-à-tête* with Mr Darcy. Caught in their heated exchanges, they had both forgotten her. Yet there she still sat, on a chair by the folded worktable, seemingly absorbed in a study of its intricate marquetry.

Would it be a proper sign of gratitude for her sister's forbearance, Elizabeth wondered, were she to fight Jane's battles too? Or would Jane be further mortified, should Mr Darcy be thus involved in her troubles? Elizabeth shrugged. Judging by Miss Bingley's letter, her brother had already involved him. She *would* protect Jane from painful encounters with a self-serving suitor, if she could. Jane deserved better than another heartbreak at the hands of Mr Bingley.

His countenance a study in dismay, Mr Darcy seemed to be struggling for words.

"Elizabeth, if there was a way—" he began, but found her ill-disposed towards theorising.

"The same goes for Mr Bingley," she coldly observed. "He chose to take himself to the Pennines for months on end – to pine, if one is of a mind to credit Miss Bingley, and one seldom is. But of late he had apparently abandoned that pursuit as unrewarding and, for whatever reasons of his own, is awaiting your permission to travel into Kent—"

"Lizzy!" came Jane's quiet reproof, but her mild glance suggested it was not an indication of disagreement, but of delicacy. Which was just as well, for by then it was too late to change the subject anyway.

"Bingley is coming into Kent?" Darcy asked, startled.

Elizabeth shrugged.

"Pending your express permission, by the sound of it," she dismissively replied.

"My… permission?"

"Yes. 'Tis all in your correspondence, according to Miss Bingley. Have you not read it?"

"No. My mind was occupied with other matters," he said, his eyes never quitting hers.

"Well, I imagine you should take your mind off other matters, and see what your friend has to say. Then perhaps you will ascertain if Mr Bingley is also expecting gratitude for having the goodness to overcome his scruples about our Hertfordshire connections and their condition in life. For if that be the case, you ought to warn him he might be disappointed," she scathingly concluded.

"Good God, Elizabeth! I am not expecting your *gratitude*," Mr Darcy exclaimed, once more past caring that they were not alone, or perhaps deciding that if he must have a wider audience, then Jane was preferable to Lady Catherine and most of the others.

"Then what is it that you want?" she asked, forgetting to protest for a third time against speaking too loudly.

There was no need.

His voice was barely above a whisper when he answered, "You."

However quiet, the word reverberated into her very soul. It was that much harder to heed the dictates of reason, when reason was overpowered by the dark fire in his eyes; when every nerve tingled at a mere touch. His fingertips brushed against her wrist and slid over her palm to capture her hand and bring it to his lips. Warm lips on her skin in a featherlike caress. And warm breath too, when he whispered, "You are everything I have ever wanted."

If he was conscious of his power over her – and how could a worldly man of eight-and-twenty *not* be, when she was standing there, breathless and trembling like a simpleton? – then this insistent use of it was a form of coercion too. She withdrew her hand and took a step back from the treacherous closeness that rendered her incapable of coherent thought. Dark eyes swept over her, alert, intense and anxious, as he reached out to halt her retreat, just as he had earlier, in the grove. He thought better of it this time and let his hand drop, but the manifest intention put an altogether different sort of fire in her eyes and stiffened her shoulders.

"And you are accustomed to having everything you want," she choked out, the words catching in her throat.

"No, of course not!" he protested hotly – and disingenuously too, she did not doubt. The master of Pemberley *must* be accustomed to unquestioning compliance to his every wish, his every whim. Even then, it was patently obvious that he required a great deal of effort to settle his temper and offer some form of apology. "Forgive me," Mr Darcy said, and forcefully exhaled. "I forgot myself."

Brows arched, Elizabeth cast him a solemn look.

"Does that happen often?"

"I hope not," was all the assurance he seemed prepared to give.

Thus, she could not hold back a terse, "So do I."

Rather more wary of tempestuous outbursts now, he indicated the sofa with a hesitant gesture.

"Elizabeth... let us sit."

"Let us not," she retorted. "Mr Darcy, no gentleman should need to be told – repeatedly, I might add – that this morning has brought one disgrace too many, and you should *not* be here."

He made to speak; to argue his point, in all likelihood, or voice some other form of protest – for judging by his air, which she could only describe as one of mulish obstinacy, he was not about to comply without demur. So, raising her chin, Elizabeth determined it was time to bring the heavy artillery into action.

"I have no wish to cause further acrimony in this house. But if neither I nor your own conscience can make you see that my quarters are out of bounds, then you shall have to hear it from my father," she declared crisply, and with an urgent, "Come, Jane," she stormed away into her bedchamber – the one impregnable refuge she still had.

Darcy broke his stride along the thankfully deserted corridor to bring the heels of his hands to his temples with an almighty oath. This was a disaster! Good Lord, *how* had he bungled it so dreadfully? He spun round, casting a long glance behind, towards the door firmly closed against him, then furiously shook his head and continued on his way. Every nerve in his body urged him to go back, and every shred of reason berated him for even contemplating it. Of course he could not go back, to raise her ire more than he already had. So his steps carried him further towards his own quarters, too distraught over the hideous debacle to imagine what his father might have had to say of it, if the occult connection had endured.

It had not. Some time before Elizabeth came to find him, the unimaginable link had begun to fade and was ultimately broken, leaving him to marvel in bemused gratitude at the miracle of having basked in his parents' love more openly, more fully, than he ever had. A sense of peace had enveloped him – a profound sense of peace, such as he had never experienced before. The joy of being told in so many words that he had always had his father's love and confidence had warmed his heart and salved a great many hidden sorrows, and the unreserved exchanges that followed had gone a long way towards healing a few more. It was a great sadness that he could not hear his revered mother's voice, yet somehow the very fact that they had connected through his father had brought the three of them closer than they had ever been in his entire life.

The end of the connection was met with bittersweet regret rather than outright anguish. It could not last. Of course it could not last. He was left to hope it might happen again. He would have been grateful for more time, more chances to make up for the past, but – he sensibly argued, if sense could come into it at all – he could not and should not wish for the connection to endure indefinitely. He could not wish for the spirit of his departed father to be lodged forever in his head.

He certainly could not wish it later, when Elizabeth followed him into the grove. Nor could he wish it now, when all he could do was rack his mind for a way out of the quagmire.

It was not his own father, but Elizabeth's, who came into his thoughts and ominously loomed, threatening to add more complications to his woefully mismanaged suit.

The man seemed harmless enough, although irksomely inclined to make sport of everything, but would Mr Bennet remain harmless should Elizabeth set her parent on the warpath against him?

It was impossible to fathom what the man would do. Indeed, did Elizabeth consider what she might unleash if she involved her father? She must be confident that he would not advocate a hasty marriage, since he had flippantly dismissed Miss Lydia's indiscretion several months ago. But he had sent her to stay with Mr and Mrs Collins – and Darcy could not help scowling at the notion of Elizabeth being likewise banished, much as that would distance her from Lady Catherine's spite, should Whittaker babble. And theirs had *not* been a mindless indiscretion, he thought, his fists clenching at his sides. She must not imagine that. Neither should her father.

Good heavens, he must find a way to get through to her and regain her trust! The matter was sufficiently fraught already. He could not afford to have another obstacle in Mr Bennet, Darcy decided, altering his course at the top of the staircase. Instead of heading along the opposite corridor towards his chambers, he took to the stairs, his pace brisk and firm.

⁕

Mr Bennet was in the library, as expected, in his customary place at the farthest end of the large and pretentiously ornamented room. By strategically placing two small tables on either side of his armchair, he had fashioned himself a rather comfortable corner there. He had a glass and the port decanter within easy reach at his right elbow, several haphazardly stacked books at his left, and a book in hand – naturally. He lowered the latter, but did not close it when Darcy walked in and saw the older gentleman glancing up towards the door, a brow slightly raised at the interruption.

Darcy bowed his head in lieu of any other greeting, then instead of joining Mr Bennet in his corner, he turned to feign some interest in the nearest bookcase. He had not lost his courage – not as such. The firmness of purpose with which he had embarked upon the mortifying and potentially hazardous endeavour was still with him. However, the ability to choose his words was not.

Darcy struggled to regain it as he stared through narrowed eyes at the shelves before him, seeing nothing but a countenance aflame with the deepest blush and a pair of fine eyes alight with indignation.

'*… this morning brought one disgrace too many, and you should not be here. If neither I nor your own conscience can make you see that my quarters are out of bounds, then you shall have to hear it from my father.*'

Disgrace, she had called it, her lips curling in distaste.

"Imbecile," Darcy hissed under his breath.

Yet apparently he was not sufficiently quiet, for his companion looked up from his book again.

"Sir?" Mr Bennet queried. "Did you say something?"

"No, nothing," Darcy dissembled, then felt compelled to add, "I beg your pardon, I was…"

He let his voice trail off, reluctant to finish his sentence and acknowledge that he was talking to himself. He walked along the book-lined wall, retraced his steps when he reached the corner of the room, and before long what had begun as an aimless amble turned into steadily pacing back and forth. The fact that his current employment had gained him Mr Bennet's full attention escaped Darcy's notice. He did not mutter as he paced but, lips pursed, he proceeded from hissed invectives to a silent and grim analysis of his performance.

Naught but blunder after blunder, and idiotic ones at that. Ambushing her in her quarters. Pressing his suit when she was clearly uncomfortable and most unwilling to have that conversation – and thus compounding the dreadful blunders of the morning. His proposal, seasoned with talk of their disparities – her connections – Lady Catherine. The unhinged mutterings that followed.

He could not fully remember what he said during the otherworldly encounter that still mystified him, but it was little wonder she thought him suffering from sunstroke or the like. And despite his ill-judged remarks on her station in life, she had stayed to watch over him – had shown him concern and kindness. Why the devil could he not respond in kind? He might have helped her to her feet – might have reworded his proposal in a gentlemanlike manner, instead of—

Yet even then, for all the self-reproaches, his breath caught as he revisited those glorious moments in the grove. Her warm weight in his arms. Her enticing form draped over him, pressed against him. Soft flesh under his fingertips, under a thin layer of muslin. Soft lips under his. Her startled gasp when she had held her breath, only to release it in a rush and let it wash over his face, sweet, fragrant and warm, driving him to distraction. Compelling him to kiss her again.

And she had kissed him back. She had! Surely, he had not lost his senses to the point of imagining that. She had closed her eyes and kissed him back.

"Spoilt for choice, Mr Darcy?" Mr Bennet suddenly asked, making him start.

"I beg your pardon?"

"You seem to have some difficulty in selecting a book. Were you looking for something in particular?"

"Yes. No, I mean…" Inwardly cursing his newly-acquired propensity to babble, Darcy squared his shoulders. "May I join you?" he brought himself to say.

"By all means, feel free. Find yourself a good book and a glass, if you are so inclined. The port is here, but look in the customary place if you favour brandy over port, or anything in between," Mr Bennet said, gesturing towards the decanter at his right, and then in the vague direction of the marble-topped dresser where the drinks were kept.

Darcy nodded his thanks and ambled towards the older gentleman's end of the room, stopping along the way to pour himself a brandy. He chose a chair, moved it a little closer to Mr Bennet and angled it in his direction, then sat, glass in hand. He did not drink, and he likewise disdained the subterfuge of opening a book and feigning interest in it as he chose his words. He shifted in his seat and crossed his legs. He tugged at his neckcloth – tied too damnably tight when he had attempted to make himself presentable upon his return to the house – then crossed his legs the other way.

Across the small distance between them, Mr Bennet looked up to cast him a half-amused, half-exasperated glance.

"Is there anything troubling you, sir?"

"I— Yes," Darcy acknowledged. "I came to speak to you, if you can spare the time. There is something I must say."

"Is there? Very well. My time is yours, Mr Darcy, and seemingly in limitless supply," Mr Bennet evenly replied, closing his book and setting it aside. Then he refilled his glass, raised it amicably towards the other, took a sip and motioned him to begin.

Darcy raised his own glass and drained it. Mr Bennet chortled.

"That bad?" he mildly remarked. "By all means, pour yourself another, if you find yourself in need of a few more drops of Dutch courage."

"I thank you, no. I had better get on with it."

"Pray do. So, what did you come to speak of?"

Wishing he had made due offerings to all the gods that endowed one with eloquence, Darcy straightened in his seat.

"I came to ask— No, that is— Hm! Mr Bennet, I… er… I feel you should hear it from me that this morning I kissed your daughter," he said at last, only to mentally kick himself for the abysmally blunt delivery.

He braced himself for the repercussions. But Mr Bennet folded his hands around his glass of port and airily asked:

"Oh. Did you? Which one? I have five – well, six, but I imagine you are not speaking of Mrs Collins."

"No. Of Elizabeth," came Darcy's crisp reply, as he fought to suppress a scowl at the untimely levity.

"Elizabeth, eh?" the other echoed, a quirk in his brow. "Am I to understand you are here to ask for my consent?"

"No, sir."

"No? You puzzle me, Mr Darcy. Precisely why *are* you here, then? I daresay you are not concerned that I might call you out to settle the matter. But," he added, all lightness of tone freezing under a layer of smooth menace, "if you imagine I shall sit idly by and allow you to trifle with my Lizzy's affections—"

"Of course not!" Darcy forcefully cut him off. "I would not."

"Then pray enlighten me as to your intentions. In my day, they were clearly stated before one progressed to taking liberties."

Darcy's eyes narrowed. The interview would be as difficult as he had anticipated. Submitting to authority did not come easily when that habit was long lost. It was all the more difficult now, when he knew himself in the wrong – a distinctly unfamiliar experience – and when faced with one whose manner differed so drastically from his own. In every dealing and every circumstance, especially one as momentous as this, he would have chosen plain-speaking and serious-minded discourse. Predictably, Mr Bennet seemed to favour irony and archness.

Darcy did not pause to consider that the very same traits he unquestionably adored in Elizabeth must have had their origins in the older gentleman's manner; that she must have learned levity and archness at his knee.

It was too vexing an experience to find himself so flippantly questioned – and worse still, to know that, however aggravating the approach, the inquisitor must be courteously indulged, for he was the one with the power of veto. So he fought the urge to bristle at the reference to liberties, and opted for a placating tone.

"I would have stated them already, sir. But I thought it only proper to do your daughter the courtesy of applying for her consent before seeking yours."

The other tilted his head sideways, by way of concurrence.

"I take it then that you have not proposed," he observed.

Darcy frowned.

"I began to. But matters got out of hand."

"How?" Mr Bennet asked, and took another sip of his port, skewering Darcy with a steady glance that joined forces with his current conundrum to make him squirm.

He could not possibly tell Mr Bennet about the voice that had interrupted his proposal. The man would see merit in sending an express to Bedlam. Darcy made a nervous gesture.

"This morning I sought your daughter out with the intention of offering for her. But before I could finish," he summarised, in an endeavour to omit that perplexing incident, "I am sorry to say that—" He stopped short, recognising the falsehood for what it was, even before the forbidden recollections flashed through his overwrought senses. Not sorry, not that! He was all manner of things – mortified beyond endurance to find himself in the wrong, positively terrified of what she might have made of it – but certainly not sorry. "I am compelled to own," he amended, "that halfway through my garbled proposal, I kissed her."

"I see. Must I conclude that she was not best-pleased?"

Darcy looked away.

It was the wrong time and place to dwell on the aforementioned forbidden recollections – here and now, in the middle of a conversation with her father. Yet therein lay the answer to Mr Bennet's question, and to his own tormenting doubt. Did she take exception? Her gasp – it had not signified shock or outrage, had it? Just surprise, surely. She had kissed him back – tangled her fingers in his hair. The outrage came later. Much later. Yet still too soon by far.

"I do not know," he truthfully replied at last. "Before the matter was decided, we were interrupted. The curate—"

Mr Bennet straightened in his chair, and his gaze took undertones of steel.

"Are you telling me that her reputation is at stake and she would be expected to marry you regardless of her wishes? That will not come to pass, sir," he declared with unprecedented sternness.

Darcy's response was just as fierce.

"You may be assured I will not force her hand."

"A wise choice," Mr Bennet remarked, the sternness barely mellowed by a fraction. Then he added, "I will have a word with Mr Whittaker. He is a sensible man, or at least more sensible than Mr Collins. He will heed me if I ask him to keep his mouth shut."

Darcy gave a quick gesture of impatience.

"He has already agreed to hold his peace for now. That is not the reason I came to see you."

"Is it not? Then I am compelled to ask again: why exactly are you here?"

Before he could even begin to examine what force might have propelled him to his feet, Darcy found himself striding towards the bookcase behind him. He raised both hands to run his fingers through his hair and spoke without turning.

"Because I love her! I love your daughter with all my heart and soul, yet I seem to do nothing but antagonise her."

"Ah," was all that Mr Bennet said, and by necessity rather than choice Darcy saw fit to turn around and face him. He saw the older gentleman easing himself forward in his seat to reach for both glasses. He diligently filled them, then set the port decanter down and motioned towards the drinks. Darcy shook his head. With a little shrug, Mr Bennet retrieved his and took a measured sip.

"Am I to understand that you wish me to teach you how to court my daughter?" he asked with a mild and not unfriendly smile, as he gestured towards Darcy to resume his seat.

Reluctant as he might have been to sit still and calmly discuss the matter, Darcy did as bid, then thought better of rejecting the liquid offering. He drained a sizeable proportion of the port Mr Bennet had poured for him, and tentatively returned his companion's smile.

"Your advice will not go amiss, sir, if you are willing to supply it. My last attempt to speak to her was a disaster. She bade me leave, on pain of incurring your displeasure. As if hers was not bad enough."

"So you came to find me and give me your version of events before she did," the other remarked, with a shake of his head. "You may imagine that Elizabeth will regard your haste with a jaundiced eye. I daresay she might label it as slyness."

Darcy glanced up with a start. He had not considered that. He sighed, and did not ask Mr Bennet if he was of a mind to censure the said haste as well. Elizabeth's likely response concerned him a vast deal more. Yet there was no censure, but a diverted twinkle in Mr Bennet's eyes when he resumed:

"Just out of interest, have you ever courted anyone, or do damsels tend to drift into your path and do all the courting?"

Darcy suppressed a snort. He should have known that the words of wisdom – such as Mr Bennet might be prepared to impart – would come seasoned with a substantial amount of raillery. He shrugged and drained the rest of his port. It remained to be seen if it was worth enduring Mr Bennet's manner for the doubtful benefit of his advice, but for now he chose to be truthful.

"With the risk of sounding insufferably conceited, you are not wrong there. No, I have never courted anyone before. And the devil of it is that my hands are tied. I cannot even court your daughter openly – here, at Rosings. You must be aware of my aunt's expectations."

"What expectations might those be?"

"That I marry Anne. Neither I nor my cousin have any wish to become united," he hastily added, "but Lady Catherine is not in the habit of brooking disappointment. She will make Elizabeth's life a misery if I so much as pay her any marked attentions. There is nothing that I would like better than to put hundreds of miles between her and Lady Catherine's wrath. But until she allows me to remove her to Pemberley, the only way to protect her from my aunt's ill-will is to keep my distance – which does nothing to help me gain her trust and her consent. So you may imagine that I am… utterly at sea," he concluded, spreading his hands out in an abrupt gesture of frustration.

Mr Bennet nodded and drained his glass as well.

"Quite a dilemma, I grant you," he casually agreed. "Well, at least you have not described yourself as being caught between the devil and the deep blue sea, for then I would have been legally and morally obliged to protest."

Darcy endeavoured not to glower, but he doubted his success. It was beyond galling that he should have come to bare his soul in the hope of understanding and assistance, only to be regaled with witticisms as the only answer to his plight.

"Yes, well," he said tersely, torn between storming away in a fit of pique and remaining there to take the rough with the smooth until Mr Bennet might supply anything remotely helpful.

Yet a moment later, the older gentleman seemed inclined to do just that.

"Have you considered a courtship by correspondence?"

Darcy raised an inquisitive brow.

"Would you sanction it?"

"I am not discounting the possibility."

Darcy shook his head.

"No, I have not."

"You might wish to. From what I gathered, some have greater ease in putting thoughts to paper than in expressing them in conversation."

It was plain to see that Mr Bennet rather astutely judged the statement to apply to him, and while quick to see the merits of the scheme, Darcy was not backward in recognising its disadvantages.

"At this point in time, I expect your daughter would consign my letters to the flames unopened. Besides, if you are suggesting I write from anywhere but here, all I can say is I would rather not leave."

"I see. Well, then, I imagine—"

Much to his disappointment, Darcy was not to learn what the older gentleman was about to impart. All he could ascertain was that, quite understandably, Elizabeth's father was far better equipped than he to predict what she might make of any given circumstance – for the door was opened without warning and she came in, only to freeze in her tracks and glare at finding him in conference with Mr Bennet.

Darcy sighed and stood to greet her with a bow that was barely acknowledged, then turned towards his elderly companion.

"I thank you for your time, sir. I should leave you now."

He could see no other option.

"I daresay you should," the other evenly agreed.

Lips pursed, Elizabeth advanced into the room. It was the greatest hardship to merely step aside and offer her another bow when their paths crossed, and then continue on his way. He could not tell if the tension prickling up his spine was a sign that her eyes were boring into him, but when he reached the door, a glance over his shoulder put paid to speculations. She was already at her father's side, her hand in his – and she would not look back.

Chapter 24

Rosings, 16 April 1812

Had Darcy been able to overcome his scruples about eavesdropping and remain in the library unseen – two equally challenging tasks – he would have gained little insight into Elizabeth's thoughts, and even less reassurance from what she was prepared to share with her father. It was Mr Bennet who began, with a light chuckle.

"I am not likely to finish my book today, am I? It seems my company is assiduously sought. First your intriguing suitor, and now you."

"My intriguing suitor!" Elizabeth scoffed, a rosy tint creeping into her cheeks.

"Pray sit, my dear," Mr Bennet said, indicating the chair that Darcy had vacated, "and tell me, are you objecting to my describing him as intriguing, or as your suitor?"

"Both," Elizabeth replied with forced nonchalance as she did as bid and sat.

"I see. Well, let it be said, I do find him intriguing. And he is certainly determined to be regarded as your suitor."

Elizabeth pursed her lips.

"And have you disabused him of that notion?"

"Whyever would I do that? After all, if we discount Mr Collins' half-hearted inclination before he was encouraged to look elsewhere, this is the most eligible offer you have received since Hugh Goulding declared, aged nine, that he would ask for your hand in marriage when he turned one-and-twenty."

"If memory serves, that would be in August, so perhaps we should defer this conversation till the summer," Elizabeth replied, matching raillery like for like.

"So you are not in the least curious to hear what Darcy had to say? Very well. I shall encourage him to decamp to Pemberley and return in a few months' time, although you may imagine his disappointment, should he rejoin us and find young Goulding here. By the bye, I gave him leave to write to you – Darcy, that is to say, not Goulding."

"You have?" she spluttered.

Mr Bennet shrugged.

"I saw little reason not to. He may prove me wrong, but he strikes me as one who would be more communicative on paper than in person. Would you not agree?"

"That is immaterial, and I hope you are not in earnest. He has no business to write to me."

"Are you quite certain?"

"Naturally," Elizabeth declared with energy. "Can you not imagine Lady Catherine's displeasure if he does?"

"I will own, your stepmother's displeasure featured heavily in our conversation. Well, I expect Darcy is too honourable to use his sister as a guise, so I might have to advise him to write to you through me. Although that is bound to put a damper on his tender eloquence," he added with a wicked snicker, making Elizabeth laugh despite herself and shake her head in mock despair.

"I should have known you spoke in jest."

"Oh, rest assured, I did not. At least not about advising Darcy to consider a courtship by correspondence."

"Papa!" Elizabeth gasped, her shock apparent, and then her disappointment, when she admonished him, "I would have thought you were the last man in the world who would turn matchmaker."

"Too true," her father gleefully agreed. "Your dear Mamma, God rest her soul, would have said the same. She would never have thought I had it in me."

"Goodness, must you always make sport of everything?" Elizabeth asked, exasperated.

With an affectionate and unrepentant smile, Mr Bennet reached for her hand, and held it fast when she made a nervous motion to withdraw it.

"What else is there to live for, child?" he asked, stroking her fingers, then gently patting them. "What I would dearly like to know, my Lizzy, is what has happened to your sense of humour? And what is it about a certain gentleman that riles you so?"

Since her right hand was still clasped in her father's, Elizabeth raised her left to cover her averted cheek as she stammered, "Papa! If you must know, this morning, he—"

She could not continue. It was Mr Bennet who mildly remarked: "Ah. That."

Elizabeth flashed him a wide-eyed glance.

"He told you?"

"He did. With rather less contrition than the circumstance required, I might add."

"Contrition!" Elizabeth scoffed, her blush deepening. "What good would that do now?"

"Very little," Mr Bennet conceded. "I would be forced to think him either doltish or deceitful, if he should kiss *you* and then claim to be sorry."

"Really, Papa," Elizabeth remonstrated. "This is hardly the time for levity."

Faced with her obvious distress, Mr Bennet could not fail to own that the current circumstances certainly required contrition, and was prompt in showing it.

"Darling girl," he said, pressing her hand, "pray forgive an old man's teasing. I am rather unaccustomed to this side of parenthood, and not altogether comfortable with it either. I fear I shall mishandle it, by and by. Your dear Mamma would have made a better job of it, I imagine. Or mortified you more, who is to say? What I would ask is this: what do you suggest we do about your young man now?"

"He is not *my* young man, Papa," Elizabeth protested.

"Oh, I think he is. Or rather, he would dearly like to be."

She gave a quiet little snort.

"Mr Darcy would dearly like to have his way in everything, by virtue of his being the owner of the largest estate in Derbyshire."

"That, he is not," Mr Bennet countered. "To the best of my knowledge, he owns Pemberley, not Chatsworth. That aside, Lizzy, if you think I would go no further than weighing a man's purse to assess his merits as a suitor, then you would do well to leave me to mull over my failings as a father, and on how I fooled myself for above fifteen years that we understood each other."

Elizabeth cast him an apologetic glance.

"Forgive me. I know you would not be swayed by wealth. But you were swayed regardless," she noted with suspicion.

"I might have been," her father acknowledged.

"Why?"

Mr Bennet smiled.

"Shall we say because, the good Lord be praised, I am not a spirited young woman, too fiery and wilful to pause and examine every facet of the matter?"

The apologetic glance promptly soured yet again into reproach.

"So you have crossed over to his camp? As easily as that? You, Papa?"

"Ah. Here comes the '*Et tu, Brute?*'*³" Mr Bennet remarked with a mild laugh. "Very well, I will confess I rather like him, and not merely because he promises me great opportunity for sport over many years to come. That in itself is a vastly attractive prospect, but I might easily enjoy the benefits if he remains my nephew. He does not need to become my son-in-law to afford me ample sources of amusement. But before we settle the matter of my crossing over to his camp, pray enlighten me, which camp might that be?"

Elizabeth waved her free hand in a gesture of impatience.

"The tight little confederacy that tirelessly sings his praises at every turn – Anne, Georgiana, even the colonel on occasion. To my shame, it was a fair while until I came to notice those schemes for what they were, but with hindsight they could not be plainer."

"And if that be the case, should you not be pleased they are going to so much trouble to advance his case with you? Their seal of approval, and all that?"

"What is so extraordinary about his sister and cousins approving of him?" she retorted with a shrug. "Besides, they might very well be following instructions."

"You can be uncommonly obtuse when you set your mind to it," Mr Bennet affectionately chided. "I meant that the schemes, as you call them, show they approve of *you*. And since all three of them seem to be pleasant and right-minded people, that must count for something, must it not? As for following instructions, pray remind me to ask the colonel when I see him at dinner if Darcy supplies them with a new list of recommended praises every day, or if they are encouraged to improvise on given themes."

---

*³ *You too, Brutus? (Lat.) – William Shakespeare, 'Julius Caesar', Act III Scene I*

His quip was met with a dark look of censure, but – still unrepentant – Mr Bennet finally released her hand, leaned back in his chair and casually advised:

"Do not scowl so, Lizzy. There is naught amiss with laugh lines. I will even go as far as to say they should be encouraged. But frown lines are hideously unbecoming."

"And yet you are determined to provoke me into scowling. Perhaps you could tell me when I might safely speak to my father, rather than to one of Mr Darcy's champions."

Her father tittered.

"Now, now. You are too old to be bent over my knee and justly chastised for your sauciness. I have never made use of that parental privilege, but I am sorely tempted to do so today," he said, his arch tone belying the comment. "I am not his champion, Lizzy," he resumed after a while, the twinkle in his eye giving way to a steady, almost solemn look. "But this conversation is patently overdue. I should have spoken to you long before Darcy came to give me fresh proof that, for all his large estate in Derbyshire and whatever other qualities, he is remarkably unable to court the object of his affection."

"His affection!" Elizabeth muttered.

"You doubt his attachment?"

"Infatuation, I would call it. Or self-deceit and downright wilfulness."

"Would you? They seem to be the fashion. Nevertheless, I think you should have your papa's opinion, for what it may be worth. I think he is attached – has been for some time – and that novel emotion could not fail to baffle him. I imagine he is not the first, nor will he be the last, to be taken unawares by the sentiment."

"Since you can grasp Mr Darcy's thoughts and sentiments in such fine detail, 'tis unfortunate indeed that you are not a spirited young woman. Then he might have been inspired to lavish *you* with his affection."

Mr Bennet chortled as he shook his head.

"I see I shall have to bend you over my knee after all. But I think I shall defer it. Just now, I might ask Darcy and the colonel to join me for a game of cards."

"Cards, is it? Or have you other games in mind?"

"None whatsoever," Mr Bennet said, his mien a picture of angelic innocence. "Feel free to sit and watch, if you wish. It might prove diverting."

Elizabeth tossed her head back with manifest exasperation.

"I thank you, but I have already had all the amusement I could stomach in one day. And I need not tell you that at this point in time I wish Mr Darcy on the way to Timbuktu."

"And me, no doubt," Mr Bennet said, nodding in cheerful acceptance of that fact. "What about the colonel?"

"What of him?" Elizabeth grumbled.

"He seems an agreeable young man. Do you wish him on the way to Timbuktu as well?"

"Not yet," she replied crisply. "But I might, if he should also begin to regale me with speculations on Mr Darcy's sentiments."

"Am I to understand you would rather the valiant colonel was courting you himself?"

"Oh, no," she retorted without hesitation. "Our tempers are too similar."

Mr Bennet arched a brow.

"Is that not commonly regarded as an advantage?"

"Not in this case. Besides—"

"Yes?" her father drawled, then smoothly prompted, "Pray continue. Were you about to comment on the old adage that opposites attract?"

"Not at all," she firmly assured him. "I was about to say that, agreeable as the colonel may be, he is but a lively relation to me. And I to him, I'd wager. Firstly, he must marry money, and a vast deal more than three thousand pounds."

"And secondly?"

"Secondly, there may be plenty of banter, but there is no sparkle."

"Sparkle or sparks?" Mr Bennet differentiated.

Elizabeth shrugged.

"Neither."

"Whereas sparks fly with conspicuous regularity in another quarter," Mr Bennet remarked, only to provoke his daughter into a terse rejoinder:

"That is a matter of opinion."

"Is it? You know, methinks thou dost protest too much," he said with a mild smile, then resumed softly, "I have been of that opinion for quite some time, if you must know, which is why I was prepared to give your young man the time of day in the first place. But never mind that now. You are too fired up to consider that old eyes might be keener than young ones, with or without the benefit of spectacles. If you wish to leave me to my entertainment, then by all means, pray go. I daresay the gentlemen will amuse me for a while. Or you could join us for the delights of conversation, or sit and read in that alcove there. Better still, you might wish to lighten the poor footmen's burden and sort through a bookcase or two. I declare those tomes were grouped by nothing but their size and colour. The content never came into it at all. Now, my grand plan is to reorganise this library alphabetically by subject matter. Tall order, that, but it will be worth the effort. Such a blessing that Sir Lewis had amassed a wonderful collection, and how fortunate that your stepmother takes no interest in it. But those poor lads, the footmen, will need months if not years to make sense of the entire business. I imagine a little of your time would be appreciated. And you might appreciate the occupation. Idle hands and agitated spirits make for an explosive combination."

"My spirits are not agitated in the least!" Elizabeth declared and stood.

Yet the impetuous movement and the tone of her voice lent little weight to that firm statement, so it was no wonder that her father chuckled mildly as he retorted, "So I see."

He stood as well, came to put an arm around her shoulders and leaned to drop a light kiss on her temple. Then he cupped her cheek to make her look at him.

"You know you are the apple of my eye, and there is nothing I want more than your happiness, do you not?"

Elizabeth sighed and her back lost some of its stiffness as she cast him a rueful smile.

"I know, Papa. But sometimes you have the strangest ways of showing it."

"Never predictable, that is my motto. Your stepmother might wish to incorporate it in her coat of arms. Speaking of which, my child," he tenderly added, "will you forgive your old papa for thinking I would rather have you cherished at Pemberley than tolerated in Lady Catherine's house, when I relinquish my earthly shell? Admittedly, Rosings has its advantages over leaving you in Mr Collins' care," he added when Elizabeth drew breath to speak, "and the addition to your portion, and your sisters', is not to be sneered at either. But even if such considerations and one fine library could persuade me to become prince consort, I would much rather not entrust your stepmamma with the task of disposing of the four of you in marriage. Least of all you, Lizzy. And say what you will, but you cannot dispute that there is no better match for your wits than Darcy in the entire breadth of our acquaintance. I daresay it speaks in his favour that he came to recognise it too."

Still ensconced in his embrace, Elizabeth released another sigh – and could not bring herself to be as forthright with him as she had been with her eldest sister about merits that had remained unrecognised until his second marriage had raised her consequence, and about men who married for sheer infatuation, only to tire of their wives. But she could not withhold a flippant comment of her own:

"You deny championing him, but you keep finding arguments in his favour. What of that fine speech some years back, about the twelve labours of Hercules and watching my suitors like a hawk?"

If she imagined the mild reproach would disconcert her father, she was proven wrong. Mr Bennet tightened the hold of his arm around her and shook his head, the old mischievous glint as bright as ever in his eyes.

"Foolish child," he softly chided. "What do you think I have been doing ever since he stood up with you in Meryton?"

Chapter 25

Rosings, 16 April 1812

'*What next?*' Darcy dispiritedly wondered, as he noiselessly closed the heavy door behind him. Pacing outside the library like some wretched lost pup was definitely not an option. Pacing in his chambers was far from palatable too, but it would be preferable to exposing himself to his relations' scrutiny, especially Lady Catherine's, when he was in no fit state to govern either his mien or his temper. At a loss for a better choice, he bent his steps towards the staircase nonetheless – yet a cheerfully affectionate voice stopped him in his tracks.

"Oh, here you are. Richard and I were about to go for a ride. Would you like to join us?"

Pasting a faint smile upon his countenance, Darcy turned around.

"Leave him be, Georgy," Fitzwilliam advised, grinning at him over Georgiana's shoulder. "He might be otherwise engaged. Are you, Coz?"

No, he was *not*, as cursed luck would have it, Darcy bristled, but made no audible answer, distinctly unwilling to acquaint either his cousin or his sister with his dismal lack of progress in his attempts at courtship. Not that the entrance hall was an adequate setting for it anyway. Lady Catherine's voice, imperiously ringing from the drawing room, came to prove that point, even if no more proof was needed.

"Is that my wayward nephew?" she called. "Where has he been all morning? Let him come in and explain himself."

Darcy rolled his eyes.

"On second thought, meet us in the stables," Fitzwilliam delivered *sotto voce* with a droll glance towards the side door and a tilt of his head meant to half-humorously, half-earnestly indicate that Darcy should make a prompt escape while he still could.

The latter shrugged. A ride might have served, but only if he were to tear over the countryside alone. He was ill-disposed towards canter and conversation, not even with his nearest and dearest. And he would be damned if he would scurry out of the side door like a child.

Even if he would have been of a mind to do so, he would have lacked the time. Lady Catherine sallied out of the public rooms, the ends of her shawl fluttering behind her.

"Where on earth have you been?" she repeated, her tone leaving them in no misapprehension of her displeasure. "I expected you would drive Anne in her phaeton again this morning, yet you took yourself away for upwards of two hours. You had better make haste while the day is still warm. I will not have her catch a chill on a late outing."

Either because she did not trust her voice to carry, or too well-bred to call out from another room, Anne saw fit to join them in the great hall before she made her opinion known.

"Our outing is best left for another day, Mamma. I was about to call on Dr Beaumont with the letter for his son, and I would prefer to go alone. Or with you, if you would like to accompany me. It would be good of you, a gracious gesture. Pray let me send word for the carriage."

Lady Catherine scowled.

"That letter? 'Tis not even written yet."

"Oh, it is, Mamma. You only need to sign it."

Much as Anne's persistence and newly-acquired confidence raised his admiration – and grateful as he was to her for saving him the trouble of finding an excuse for cancelling the proposed outing – Darcy still felt his irritation mounting at finding himself detained in the great hall and surrounded by something that had begun to ludicrously resemble a Greek chorus.

Albeit for different reasons, Lady Catherine's countenance betrayed a very similar emotion.

"I see no need for haste," she enunciated.

"Whereas I see no need for procrastination," Darcy disagreed, driven in equal measure by the noble wish to assist his cousin and the far less noble urge to rile his meddlesome aunt as much as she riled him. "Now that the matter is decided, the sooner it is formalised, the better."

"Goodness, Darcy," Lady Catherine exclaimed, incensed. "Frankly, your eagerness to command at Rosings is unseemly. Since you are such a proponent of formalising matters, I daresay you should hold your horses until you and Anne are wed."

"I am in no haste to command at Rosings, ma'am," Darcy retorted rather harshly. "Merely to encourage Anne to do so."

Lady Catherine pursed her lips.

"She seems in no need of encouragement," she resentfully shot back, her baleful glance travelling from her nephew to her daughter. "Nor is there any reason why she should insist on delivering letters herself, like a common post-boy," her ladyship sniffed.

"Speaking of post-boys, Brother," Georgiana placatingly intervened, "a messenger arrived this morning with a note for you. Judging by the rather unmistakable hand, it was from Mr Bingley."

"Oh?"

Darcy's brow furrowed upon hearing his friend's name mentioned yet again, and his thoughts could not fail to turn towards the other references, less than an hour earlier, during that awful exchange in Elizabeth's sitting room. Her scathing remarks on gratitude and disappointment. Her puzzling comments about Bingley aiming to come into Kent, and awaiting his express permission. Her sharp suggestion that he take his mind off other matters and attend to his correspondence instead.

Georgiana's next words added new urgency to that injunction.

"The boy was told to await your reply, but you were not to be found, so he had to leave without it. I asked our aunt's butler to let him know you would see to it upon your return. I sent the note up to your chambers. Ask Weston if you cannot find it."

Darcy nodded. Chances were that he need not ask his valet. The man must have placed it with the rest of his neglected correspondence.

"I thank you, dearest. I appreciate it. I should see to it now," he decided. Seemingly, it had to be done, and it would give him a good excuse to absent himself from Lady Catherine's presence.

But, as was often the case, her ladyship had different thoughts on the matter.

"Your letter can wait, and so can your cousin's. You had much better drive out in the phaeton together as planned. Fresh air will do you good, Anne."

"True, Mamma. Then I shall be sure to call upon Dr Beaumont in an open carriage," Anne said with her best impression of dutiful obedience, which Darcy might have found highly diverting under more auspicious circumstances.

He might have found similar amusement in Lady Catherine's question – especially as, strangely, it did not seem to be rhetorical:

"Whoever taught you to be so irksomely headstrong?" she remonstrated with her daughter. "You used to be a model of compliance."

"The advantages and disadvantages of growing up, Mamma," Anne smiled, undaunted.

Lady Catherine snorted.

"Hm! What of you, Darcy? What have you to say for yourself?"

"Nothing other than I must attend to my friend's letter. It was brought to my attention that I have neglected him for long enough."

"What of it?" Lady Catherine scoffed. "Who is he, that he must not be neglected? A mere tradesman."

"Mr Bingley is a gentleman," Darcy was prompt in stating his view on the matter.

"Is he! With the whiff of northern mills still clinging to his coat. How far removed is he from the mill floor, pray tell?" she disdainfully asked.

"Two generations, if not more. That should be enough for anyone. If you will excuse me," came Darcy's crisp reply, before he gave his aunt a scant nod and made his way towards the staircase.

He paid no heed to his aunt's icy, "Not enough for me, nor any self-respecting gentlefolk." But he stopped on the half-landing to bow to Jane, as she glided past him to gain the lower floor.

※ ❦ ❦ ❧ ※

Just as Darcy had expected, the stack of correspondence was left in a prominent place on the escritoire. He gathered up the letters, quick to discover that the uppermost was indeed in Bingley's hand. But that was the full extent of what he was allowed to ascertain for now. A loud and imperious knock on the door of his bedchamber drew him from his employment. He dropped the envelopes on the escritoire with an oath, and strode back into the adjoining room.

"Come," he called, just as the door was impatiently opened and his aunt marched in, without waiting to be asked.

"I am not accustomed to insolence from you or anyone, Nephew, and I assure you, I will not tolerate it," she declared.

Darcy stared grimly back, sorely tempted to retort that he was not accustomed to insolence either, nor to overbearing aunts or indeed anyone else barging uninvited into his quarters. The time when he could return to Pemberley could not come soon enough.

"I fail to see how I have offended you," he coldly said instead.

"You offend me every day, and Anne too, by failing in your duty to her," Lady Catherine relentlessly gave vent to her old grievance. "You have kept the pair of us waiting for long enough. You ought to announce the betrothal and make arrangements for your nuptials, instead of encouraging her in foolish schemes. And then the appalling discourtesy of walking away in the middle of our conversation, so that you can pander to inconsequential tradesmen. This is not to be borne, Nephew, and it shall not be!"

A heated response burned on the tip of Darcy's tongue, and it was devilishly hard to swallow it. The urge to tell his aunt once and for all precisely what both he and Anne thought of her matchmaking schemes was overpowering, and could only be conquered with a superhuman effort, in the full knowledge that he could not afford to have the doors of Rosings barred against him. Not now. So he sealed his lips and fought to hold his peace.

"Well?" Lady Catherine snapped.

Another knock on the door mercifully saved him from having to supply an answer, for it *would* have been a harsh one. Keeping silent was difficult enough. He would be damned before he obliged his aunt with an apology.

"Come," he called again, and was moderately relieved to see Anne making her way in.

"Mamma!" she softly remonstrated. "Pray do leave my cousin be. Come to my sitting room and sign the letter to Mr Beaumont. I wish to be gone as soon as possible."

"I am sick of all this talk of Mr Beaumont," cried her ladyship.

"I am sorry to hear that," Anne replied calmly. "You should have said so sooner. Then I would have made all the arrangements without troubling you for your assistance."

"Nonsense. You cannot arrange anything without me. And let me tell you here and now, I will not accede to this foolish whim about his preferment until your betrothal to Darcy is announced."

Darcy snorted. Anne released a weary sigh.

"Really, Mamma! There is no need to slide into open conflict and blackmail is beneath you, particularly as it has no substance. You know as well as I do that on the day I turned one-and-twenty I gained the right to please myself in all things. The fact that I delayed making use of that prerogative is neither here nor there."

A third knock made Darcy roll his eyes in acute exasperation. What had his chambers turned into, a busy hostelry?

"Come," he barked, and this time the door was opened with patent hesitation and a footman crept in, the angry tone of voice doubtlessly making him wary of his reception. Darcy sought to regulate his temper when he asked, "Yes? What is it?"

"Mr Bennet would like you to join him in the library, sir, if it is convenient," the man said.

Darcy's back stiffened. However inconvenient, this was a summons he had no wish to ignore.

"Mr Bennet can wait," his lady declared.

"I see no reason why he should," Anne smoothly countered. "You should go, Cousin."

Darcy cast her an uncertain glance. Leaving Anne to face her irate parent without assistance sat ill with him, but he was not of a mind to refuse Mr Bennet's invitation either.

"Are you quite certain you can spare me?" he felt obliged to ask his cousin, who promptly reassured him, with a good-natured little shrug.

"Of course. I have a letter to deliver. I shall see you upon my return," Anne blithely said and left his chambers with her mother on her heels.

"Anne! Whatever is the matter with you, child?" her ladyship called out. "Why on earth can you not see reason and have a care for your health? You look wan and pale again. You should take your tonic and go for a restful drive. I will not have you tax yourself with pointless morning calls and— Anne, I insist you heed me," she demanded, her voice still reaching Darcy through the open door.

He shook his head. Sadly, one could not choose one's relations. Although Lady Catherine was right in one regard: Anne did look wan and pale, more so than she had of late. Tangled affairs of the heart must be putting a severe strain on her as well.

Hopefully, the letter she was so determined to deliver would help settle the matter for her, Darcy told himself and, squaring his shoulders, he left his quarters to mind his own tangled affairs.

⊙⊙ ⊙⊙

Mr Bennet was not alone. Just as Darcy had both hoped and feared, Elizabeth was still there, at the furthest end of the room. The small party gathered in the library now included her sister Jane and also, unexpectedly, Fitzwilliam and Georgiana. Darcy took a deep breath, vainly endeavouring to resign himself to another difficult interlude with a large audience. But there was nothing for it, so he advanced into the room and bowed.

"I thought you were about to go for a ride," he observed as he approached the spot where Georgiana stood busying herself with aligning some books upon a shelf.

Her sole response was an affectionate little smile. She scrupled to openly avow she had remained indoors to assist him in any way she could, but her warm glance conveyed as much nevertheless. So did Fitzwilliam's, although his eyes had a roguish glint as they briefly met Darcy's, then returned to the chessboard that stood on a small table between his chair and Mr Bennet's. The latter was the only one who offered a verbal greeting:

"Ah, Mr Darcy. Do join us. Find yourself a chair. I was thinking of suggesting a game of cards, but as you can see, the young ladies were more inclined to assist me in my grand project of reorganising your late uncle's library. For my part, I could not resist your cousin's offer of a game of chess. Pray sit with us, if you have nothing better to do," Mr Bennet said with a casual gesture towards the nearby empty chairs, then reached to make his move on the chessboard.

Guardedly, Darcy did as bid, although his glance in Elizabeth's direction might have betrayed that, to his way of thinking, he did have something far better to do than witnessing a game of chess.

She had barely acknowledged him, but at least she had not left the library upon his arrival, but continued with her employment in rearranging the books on the furthermost shelves.

He suppressed a sigh at the thought of such pitifully meagre consolation as he repositioned his chair so that he could catch the odd glimpse of her, beyond the chess-players, only to find that she would often wander off to assist Jane or Georgiana.

All he could do then was push the chair back, aiming for a wider angle, sit still and bide his time.

"That was a bold move, Colonel," Mr Bennet observed when he lost a rook to the other's bishop. "Were you as impetuous on the battlefield?"

"I found it was mandatory on occasion, sir," Fitzwilliam replied.

"The same can be said of foresight, I imagine," Mr Bennet retorted smoothly, quick to spot and make use of the ensuing flaw in his opponent's defence. "So, Mr Darcy, have you any fascinating tales to distract me with, so that your cousin may have a sporting chance against me?" he amiably quipped.

Fitzwilliam chortled.

"No such luck, I fear. For all his many talents, Darcy is not a storyteller."

"A pity."

"Aye," the colonel laughingly agreed as he took his queen out of Mr Bennet's line of fire. "By the looks of it, I need all the help I can get."

And so did he, Darcy thought and shifted uncomfortably in his seat under the gaze the older gentleman settled upon him over the spectacles, before he redirected his attention to his other companion.

"I see. Well, then, if the gift of the gab is not among your cousin's talents, I imagine it would be pointless to ask him about those he does possess."

"It would, sir," Fitzwilliam concurred. "He is too modest to elaborate on them."

Darcy suppressed a huff of exasperation. It was bad enough to feel like some curious insect impaled on a board and displayed for Mr Bennet's scrutiny, as he sat listening to them speaking of him as though he were not there. Catching Elizabeth's incredulous glance and her quiet snort when she heard him described as modest was a vast deal worse.

He bit his lip and shifted in his seat again. It was positively maddening, this constant lack of privacy; this feverish quest for a few stolen moments, that had only served to put him on edge to the point of rushing into it, babbling heedlessly and making her think so wretchedly ill of him.

He ran his fingers through his hair. However dubious a talent, the gift of the gab had its distinct advantages. But he was not likely to be endowed with it all of a sudden, so Darcy tore his thoughts from painful musings and fruitless wishes and sought to heed Mr Bennet when the older gentleman turned towards him with a crooked smile.

"My apologies, sir, if my talk of your talents made you uneasy. Unless you are fidgeting because you have spotted the flaws in your cousin's game and are anxious to advise him. If that be the case, feel free. I flatter myself I can face your combined skills. In fact, I am of a mind to test that theory once I win this game, else the pair of you might accuse me of pride and excessive vanity."

"I think I can safely speak for both of us when I assure you we would not dare accuse you of either," the colonel smilingly replied. "Besides, one can be justly proud without being vain. Take my cousin, for instance," he added, making Darcy cringe in expectation of another one of Fitzwilliam's attempts to misguidedly assist him. "I daresay he is proud of his achievements without being vain."

"There we are, Mr Darcy," their companion observed. "We seem to have circled back to your talents and achievements."

"I wish you would not," Darcy said with a quelling stare at his cousin.

But Fitzwilliam would not be swayed.

"Whyever not? It was no mean feat, following in my uncle's footsteps at an age when most men are still keen to be boys, and taking charge of that dear old bundle of conundrums that is Pemberley and all the souls who make a living there."

Darcy gave an impatient shrug.

"No reason to make a virtue of it. It was a necessity."

"So it was," Fitzwilliam conceded, as he carelessly sacrificed one of his knights. "And you might have followed in the footsteps of all the fools who lost their fortunes in the pursuit of pleasure or gambled their inheritance away. Come, Darcy, do not seek to make me believe you are not proud of keeping Pemberley as prosperous as in my uncle's time, or I shall begin to accuse you of false humility."

"Ah, the fine line between genuine modesty and false humility," Mr Bennet remarked. "Hard to distinguish, whether or not Mr Darcy openly admits that he is proud of his estate."

More than a little tired of whatever game the pair of them were playing – apart from chess, that is – Darcy bristled.

"Proud? Aye, I daresay I am. It is the dearest place in the world. If I am proud of anything, it is of being a link between its past and its future."

"So how is it that you have not secured its future yet?" Mr Bennet asked.

"I beg your pardon?"

"How is it that you have not married?" the older gentleman clarified, only to release a disbelieving "Eh?" when he found that his opponent was more cunning than he had originally thought, and the sacrificed knight had merely been a ploy to lure him into exposing his queen to danger.

For his part, much as he disliked being put on the spot, Darcy lost his willingness to dissemble and valiantly spoke up:

"Simply because for years I have not come across anyone I wished to marry."

Mr Bennet arched a brow.

"Are you so fastidious, sir? With a plethora of eligible misses on the marriage mart, you could not find a single one to suit your exacting standards?"

Darcy could not keep himself from glowering at his older companion. Was Mr Bennet in a temper over his lost queen and mischievously choosing to play him like a fish on a hook – setting him up for a worse fall? Or was he devising the opportunity for him to have his say? If that be the case, it was the strangest opportunity of all, but come hell or high water, Darcy took it.

"I might have called it fastidiousness at one time," he evenly replied. "These days I call it blind obstinacy. You see, I am determined that nothing but ardent love will ever induce me into matrimony."

"Is that so?" Mr Bennet muttered, his gaze fixed on the chessboard.

As for Darcy's, it was fixed beyond the players, on a slender form that kept her back turned. It was the longest time until he was rewarded with a glimpse of her profile, when she took a few steps towards the adjoining shelves balancing a large and heavy-looking book atop the ones she was already holding.

Mr Bennet nudged his remaining rook and made it slide three squares to the left.

"Check," he announced. "Are we boring you, Mr Darcy? For my part, I find the game has just become interesting. But by all means, feel free to leave us and go for a ride, if that takes your fancy. Unless you might be willing to help my daughter with that pile of books she seems about to drop?" he added, without looking up. "Really, Lizzy, you should be more careful. Your toes would not appreciate that tome landing on them any more than the tome would."

Darcy did not wait to be asked again, despite the fact that, unlike her father, he caught the brief scowl Elizabeth cast in their direction. He left his seat and hastened towards her.

"Allow me," he said, and took the heavy tome away. "Where do you wish it put?"

"Anywhere," she curtly replied and turned away under the pretext of setting the other three books down, then standing on tiptoe to make room for them on one of the shelves above.

"May I be of assistance?" he offered.

"I thank you, no. I can reach well enough."

Her visible lack of welcome could not deter him. He did not withdraw, but remained precisely where he was. It was Elizabeth's eldest sister who chose to step further away from them, thus earning Darcy's silent gratitude for her kindness in allowing them more privacy, however illusory.

"Is there nothing else I could do?" he insisted.

"Nothing whatsoever," Elizabeth said, quietly but firmly. "You might as well go for a ride, as my father had suggested."

Darcy's countenance grew sombre.

"Would you like me to?"

It was only then that she cast him a quick glance.

"Would you not rather be anywhere but here just now?"

"A few moments ago – yes. Now – quite the contrary," Darcy said, surprising himself, and very likely her as well, with a bold reply.

Elizabeth sighed and set down the book she was holding to one-handedly rub at her temples.

"Forgive me," Darcy retracted. "I do not wish to make you uncomfortable."

She gave a bitter little laugh.

"It seems to me that you, your cousin and my father are in league to achieve precisely that."

Darcy sighed.

"I am distraught you feel this way," he said quietly. "If you wish me to leave—"

"Of course not," she firmly cut him off, raising his hopes for a few fleeting seconds, before dashing them again when she continued, "I will not have you curtail your visit in Kent on my account."

"I meant leave now. Leave the library," Darcy wistfully clarified.

"I cannot leave Rosings."

"I should imagine not," she blandly concurred. "Lady Catherine would not be best pleased."

"This has nothing to do with Lady Catherine," Darcy shot back. "I cannot leave *you*."

His earnest avowal was ill rewarded. There was censure in her eyes, and in her voice as well, when she replied:

"Sir, one of these days you must learn to brook not having your way in everything."

"Will you cease regarding me as an overbearing ogre or an overindulged child?" Darcy whispered in no little exasperation. "I cannot leave you because in eight-and-twenty years no one has made me feel as you do. And because— Because this morning I dared hope you were not indifferent. At least... until we were interrupted."

Elizabeth drew a sharp breath, her flaming cheeks a picture of shock and mortification.

"That is the most ungentlemanly... ungenerous... nay, self-deluding and self-gratulatory—"

"Good God, desist, I beg you!" Darcy rasped, clasping her hand in his, pain plainly written in his countenance, and the dark fire in his eyes showing just as clearly that he was struggling to remember they were not alone; that, were it not for their relations, she would have been in his arms by now, and hungry kisses would have silenced her as effectively as his broken plea, and would have sought to demonstrate his point a vast deal better. That was not an option, so he could only tighten his hold when she attempted to tug her hand free. "Forgive me," he entreated in low and very earnest tones. "That was... beyond the pale, and ungentlemanly too. I deserve any name you may wish to call me, but I beg you would not say this morning was self-delusion!"

"Yet it was," she shot back in a harsh whisper, and freed her hand at last. "Excuse me."

And with that she was gone, the heels of her slippers hitting the floor in a rapid clatter on her way to the door. Instinctively, Darcy moved to follow. It was Mr Bennet's solemn voice that stopped him in his tracks.

"Mr Darcy, I believe you should go for a morning ride after all," he said, raising his eyes from the chessboard, and however smooth the tone, it left Darcy in no doubt that it was a request, not a suggestion.

⁊ℇ ℈⁊

Nevertheless, Darcy did not go for a morning ride. Violent exercise might have quelled some of his tormenting devils, but he knew the respite would not last. Besides, he could not bear to take himself away from the house as yet. Thus, when Fitzwilliam left the library, hard on Darcy's heels, his countenance clouded with affectionate concern, he found his cousin halfway up the staircase.

"What can I do?" the colonel called, just loud enough to carry.

"Nothing," the other retorted as he continued his fast climb up the stairs. "There is nothing you can do. Just... take Georgiana for her ride."

It was only later, when his agitated pacing in his apartments took him into his sitting room, that Darcy remembered the reason that had brought him to his quarters nigh on an hour earlier. With a long sigh of vexation, he picked up the envelope addressed in Bingley's unmistakable hand from the top of the pile of perhaps a dozen other letters, only to learn that it never rains but it pours. The note was dated from the Pulteney at seven in the morning, and it was brief and uncommonly hostile:

Darcy, his friend had written,

I will be at Rosings on the morrow. If you will not be of assistance, I trust you will at least have the decency to stay out of my way and refrain from deliberately hindering me in my purpose.

Underneath, Bingley had appended his signature with no salutation and no flourish, just a forcefully dotted '*i*'. Darcy frowned. The matter seemed to be of grave concern – more so than he had anticipated. He rifled through the other letters, only to discover two more in his friend's hand: one in the middle of the pile, the other at the very bottom. The oldest was noticeably the thickest, so with a reasonable expectation of garnering more information from the longest missive, Darcy chose to begin with that. It was likewise dated from the Pulteney, several days ago – a se'nnight? – no, eight days prior – but the tone was markedly different.

Dear Darcy,

I am at my wits' end. I received some shocking intelligence today – nay, positively staggering. God willing, you might be able to assist me. I beg your help, my friend. You are my only hope.

This morning I called at Longbourn and discovered that I failed her in the worst possible manner! I was wrong – we all were. She would not have felt compelled to marry without affection. She loves me, Darcy! Or at least she did. She was attached to me as far back as last autumn, and I left her! All those months of misery since I took myself away – she suffered too! Suffered from my abandonment. I have it all from her sister, Mrs Collins, who now resides at Longbourn in the Bennets' stead. Once I gave her my best wishes on the occasion of her marriage, I drummed up the courage to ask if any of her sisters had formed an attachment – if her eldest sister had – and she said—

Two illegible lines followed, heavily crossed out, then:

Darcy, she cast me the severest look and said it was none of my concern if her eldest sister should form an attachment – that she offers daily prayers for Jane to encounter a more deserving member of the opposite sex. She lectured me on the brittleness and beauty of a young lady's reputation, and on the unconscionable cruelty of exposing one to the pity and derision of her neighbours for her disappointed hopes.

I beseeched Mrs Collins to explain her meaning, only to be told in the coldest tone that I should not add insult to injury by feigning ignorance. But she was too incensed to hold her peace, and at long last the truth came out: that her sister was deeply attached to me – expected an offer – and was ignominiously discarded without a word – without so much as a civil adieu.

You cannot possibly imagine how I felt – how I feel. My deepest wish is to rush to her, beg her forgiveness, beg her to have me. But why on earth should she, when I injured her so? And now that she is so far above me in the world?

She always was above me. Her father is a gentleman. So was her grandfather – great-grandfather. Mine were not. But now she is Lady Catherine's daughter. Earls and viscounts are her kin. She may very well suspect me of courting her with an eye to her connections, not for the marvel that she is. And yet I must conquer my abject fear and throw myself at her mercy. I cannot make a life without her, Darcy. I tried, but I cannot!

I see no other way forward but to beg your assistance. Will you speak well of me, to the best of your abilities? I hear you are fixed at Rosings for the foreseeable future – I learned as much in Berkeley Square, when I called. I left Hertfordshire as soon as I took my leave of Mrs Collins, and rushed to town, looking for you. It was a heavy disappointment that I could not find you, I dearly wished I could speak to you, yet I take some comfort from knowing you are there. You can see her, speak to her, and all the more freely now that you are her cousin. Will you find a way of mentioning me, and giving her some indication of my sentiments and wishes – of what they have always been?

I cannot and will not ask you to assure her I would not have left, had I not been persuaded of the wisdom of it. I and I alone should carry the blame for that abysmal failing. I should not have allowed myself to be persuaded. But if you could give her some indication of my sincerity and longstanding affection, I would be forever in your debt.

I will come into Kent as soon as I have your reply. If you could send it express, I would vastly appreciate it. I will take lodgings in the nearest village – Hunsford, is it? I would not impose upon you and your aunt with any hopes that I might be asked to stay at Rosings, and besides Miss Bennet might be uncomfortable with that. I have never been to Hunsford – is it a big place? Or at least big enough to boast a coaching inn? If not, I would be glad of your advice as to the nearest hostelry that might accommodate me. Pray write soon, Darcy! I will count the hours until I hear from you.

Yours in anticipation,
C. Bingley

Darcy folded back the letter and raised a hand to rub his furrowed brow. No wonder that his friend had sent such a terse third note, once this heartfelt plea had remained unanswered.

He almost did not dare open Bingley's second letter, fully expecting a dose of recriminations. He did open it though, there was nothing for it, and found that his expectations were confirmed.

Darcy,

I am yet to receive your reply. I had imagined that was because my first found you en route to Pemberley or goodness knows where else, but I called in Berkeley Square again this morning and learned that your people had received neither tidings nor instructions that would suggest you might remove from Kent.

I hope your silence is not an indication of your reluctance to assist me. Just as I wrote four days ago, I know the full extent of my own failings, but must I remind you I was about to return to Hertfordshire and offer for her, when you argued in the most convincing terms that the affection was one-sided? I also know that, unlike Caroline and Louisa, you had my interests at heart rather than your own, and advised me in the best of faiths. But best intentions sometimes go awry, and this is one of the occasions.

It would do no good to ask you to demean yourself and tell her it was your firm belief in her indifference that carried the day. She would scarcely see me in a better light if I sought to lay the blame on you. But I rely on our longstanding friendship and your sense of justice when I ask again if you would impress upon her that, for all my faults, I am not false-hearted. I need her to believe I come to her with the humble wish that my mistakes might be forgiven, and not in order to secure admittance into the upper echelons.

Pray write soon. I cannot bear the wait much longer.
Yours,
C. Bingley

With a muted oath, Darcy set the letter down and rifled once more through the remaining correspondence to ensure he had not missed another note from Bingley. He had not, but it made little difference. Having disregarded three so far was bad enough.

Most of the senders were easy to identify, even at a cursory glance. His housekeeper in town. His steward. His business agent had sent two letters, and one was from Fitzwilliam's mother – his cousin was hardly a timely correspondent, so Lady Malvern must have grown impatient for tidings about Lady Catherine's second marriage, and had written to him as well.

The last three were directed in unfamiliar hands – from indifferent acquaintances, no doubt – and Darcy dropped the handful of envelopes on the escritoire without bothering to open them. If they had waited for above a se'nnight, they could be left for a few days longer. It was Bingley's letters that must be urgently attended to. His beleaguered friend deserved much better than to be abandoned in his hour of need.

Darcy countenance darkened. Guilt was a damnable feeling. Their wretchedness – his friend's, and seemingly Miss Bennet's too – lay squarely at his door. It had been his interference that had carried the day. His convincing arguments, as Bingley had put it in his second letter. The recollection of its contents made him wince. *He* held the greatest share of the blame, however firmly his ever-loyal and right-minded friend had declared otherwise, even when cross. He had always known that Bingley was naturally modest, far more modest than was good for him. He had been given ample proof over the years that his friend had a stronger dependence on *his* judgement than his own; that Bingley lacked the strength of his convictions, and he had never been encouraged to develop it.

As for himself, he should have never undertaken the weighty responsibility of directing his younger friend's life. Not even in small matters. Least of all in momentous ones. What right had he to determine how Bingley was to be happy? What on earth had given him the right to voice opinions, even in those cases when his opinions had been impartial? And in this instance, they had been nothing of the sort. Far from it.

Darcy frowned, forced to acknowledge that, even in his reproachful letter, his friend had given him more credit than he deserved. His advice might have been given in good faith, but it had been far from unbiased. He *had* followed his own interest, just as Bingley's sisters had. He, too, had pondered on his own consequence, rather than the feelings of others. He, too, had urged his friend to distance himself from Miss Bennet in fear of closer ties with her relations. He had dreaded having Elizabeth constantly thrown into his path.

And now he stood to pay for it. Now, when his belated suit was so wretchedly fraught already, untimely revelations about his interference would blast his every hope of persuading Elizabeth to give him another chance to win her heart.

Darcy pressed his lips together into a tight line. This could not be. It must not come to pass! There must be a way of delaying the damaging disclosures, while still assisting Bingley in his plight.

The obvious solution was not late in coming for, regardless of his other failings, Darcy was neither slow-witted nor faint-hearted. The preparations took mere minutes, once his mind was made up. He stored away Bingley's second letter, under lock and key in a compartment of his strongbox. He carefully examined the first one that his friend had sent, to assure himself that he had a full grasp of its contents, especially the revealing paragraphs, then folded it and wrapped it in a blank sheet along with the most recent one, and placed them both securely in his pocket. With a careless gesture, he pushed the unopened envelopes out of the way and hastily penned two notes, then rang for his valet to entrust him with delivering one to his sister upon her return from riding with the colonel, and the other to the lady of the house, but in an hour's time and not a moment sooner.

A change of apparel might have been in order, but Darcy would not trouble himself with trifling matters. He merely urged Weston to diligently follow his instructions – as though the loyal and most efficient man needed to be told – then left his chambers, grimly steeling himself for the last mandatory task.

Chapter 26

Rosings, 16 April 1812

When Elizabeth had made her escape from the library, she had rushed into the garden, anxious for the freedom to roam out of doors, just as she always did when troubled or upset. She could not bear to be within. Moreover, she did not trust Mr Darcy to refrain from seeking her in her sitting room again, and she would *not* confine herself in her bedchamber to avoid him!

She narrowed her eyes into slits and released a semblance of a growl. There was no avoiding him at Rosings, and his wilful obtuseness – nay, his selfish disdain for her wishes – was nothing short of galling. Was it so thoroughly beyond his comprehension that she needed at least a modicum of quiet reflection to sort out her feelings from her fears? That far too much had happened in one day, in mere hours, and she needed time, not this relentless pursuit? That she would not be browbeaten into making a grievous mistake, one way or the other, by either mindlessly accepting or mindlessly refusing him? That ambushing her thus at every turn – alone and worse still, in company – was not the answer, and it would only provoke her into instinctively protecting herself with foolish falsehoods?

For it had been a foolish, gross and likely damaging falsehood to claim that the morning had been self-delusion. Her cheeks grew hot as she inwardly acknowledged that while it had been ungenerous and ungentlemanly of him to mortify her by pointing out she had given him enough reasons to believe she was not indifferent, the remark was neither self-deluding nor self-gratulatory. She *had* been carried away – *had* responded to his kisses. Freely. Shamelessly. Fervently, too. Until they had been interrupted.

She cast her eyes down and sought to calm the storm of mixed emotions roiling inside her. Her father was in the right. She did protest too much. Seemingly, Mr Darcy knew it too. And would relentlessly harry her into admitting it.

Jane found her on the way to the Rotunda a short while later – affectionately anxious, the dear soul must have left the library within minutes of her own exit, to come in search of her – and as always, the reassuring company of her dearest sibling served her well. With the benefit of sisterly conversation and Jane's quiet wisdom, Elizabeth's agitated spirits were soothed a little – enough for her to acknowledge that since the other was all that was kind and good, but not a great walker, they would do well to bend their steps back towards the house. She would not go in, but was persuaded to sit with Jane in the cosy alcove they both favoured, under the flimsy pretext of watching Lydia and Kitty as they amused themselves with a game of quoits.

Her younger sisters' skill in making the rings fly and neatly land over the embedded spike was of little interest to Elizabeth, however, as she availed herself of the continued opportunity to share her thoughts in hurried and hushed whispers. If her gaze drifted towards Lydia and Kitty, it was only a blank stare as she chose her words. Yet the blank stare turned into a startled glance when, beyond Kitty's lithe form, leaning forward and poised for another throw, Elizabeth espied the very object of her troubled confidences, approaching at a steady pace along the gravelled path.

She frowned, provoked by his stubborn persistence, and indeed the insensitivity of it. Goodness, was she to be granted no respite from trying encounters and awkward conversations? Not now – nor later, at dinner – nor over breakfast on the morrow, and for however long it would please him to remain at Rosings? Must she hide in her chambers to be assured of a moment to herself, or should she go as far as to seek sanctuary away from Kent, with her uncle and aunt Gardiner?

She would not train her gaze upon him to follow his progress, but merely looked up when he reached their secluded alcove and bowed.

"Pray forgive me for disrupting your privacy," he said, thus betraying, to her further vexation, that he knew full well his arrival was an imposition, yet that had not deterred him. "I will only detain you for a moment," he added, producing some folded papers from his pocket, which only made Elizabeth flash a disbelieving glance at him.

He did not let grass grow under his feet, did he? He had taken her father at his word when her papa had so ill-advisedly suggested he might sanction some form of correspondence. Well, since neither of them had taken the trouble to secure her agreement to the scheme, they should amuse themselves by writing to each other, Elizabeth resentfully thought and, lips pursed, she pointedly clasped her hands together in her lap.

She did not fail to note that a shadow crossed his countenance at her telling gesture and a knot formed at the corner of his jaw. A fraction of a second later, her own facial muscles did not fare much better. Yet they did not tighten – they went slack, and her mouth fell slightly open when, to her surprise, the folded sheets were held out towards her sister, and it was Jane he quietly spoke to:

"This is… hm… unorthodox to say the least, but I hope the circumstances will excuse the impropriety. Will you do me the honour of reading these letters? They are best read in order, and kept private. They ought not go beyond the present party," he concluded, encompassing both sisters in a solemn look.

Unlike Elizabeth, Jane did not clasp her hands together in a sign of marked refusal. Yet she did not reach for the papers either, but cast an uncertain glance from one of her companions to the other.

"If you have concerns as to propriety and privacy, might you not relate their content in a few words instead?"

Hand still outstretched, along with the offering, Darcy shook his head.

"A summary would not have the same ring of truth. I daresay similar tidings will reach you eventually from Mrs Collins, but they might come too late. If I could have devised other means of apprising you of the facts and assuring you of their veracity, pray believe I would have done so. As it stands, I can only entreat you to read these by the morrow, in the hope they might make the happiness of many."

Elizabeth's lips shaped themselves into a tight line of suspicion and displeasure. Many times over, he had shown himself fully aware of his power over her unruly senses and had not scrupled to use it to his advantage. By the sound of it, he knew Jane too, and could work upon her in different ways, but with no less cunning.

There was no better way of persuading dear Jane to do his bidding than by appealing to her generous nature with a hint at making others happy. And what had Mary to do with the entire business anyway?

"Lizzy, did you see that?" Lydia called out, vastly pleased with what must have been a successful throw, and Elizabeth saw merit in supplying a necessary falsehood.

"I did. You are growing very skilled at this," she encouragingly offered.

"I always was. Better than you, I'd wager," Lydia carelessly replied, far more adept in a game of quoits than in showing good manners and graciously acknowledging a compliment.

Elizabeth did not see fit to censure such failings at that point in time and in the present company. Her gaze travelled back to Jane, and it came as no surprise to her that, urged to work towards other people's happiness, Jane took the folded papers.

"I thank you," Mr Darcy said.

Elizabeth squared her shoulders and held her peace, loath to interfere and make a scene before Lydia and Kitty. But if Mr Darcy thought he would sway Jane – that her dearest sister would become his ally – he clearly did not know either of them as well as he imagined, and would soon discover his error of judgement.

Her chin came up at the reassuring thought. Jane had always seen eye to eye with her, listened to what she had to say, supported her, given her comfort. Jane always would. Nothing could change that. But his determination to press his point and bend everyone around her to his will was insulting, infuriating and exhausting. And it only served to emphasise his most objectionable trait of all: the inability to countenance not having his own way.

She raised her eyes to settle a censorious look upon him, and found no hint of apology in his solemn glance.

"Excuse me. I should leave you now," he merely said and bowed.

She nodded, in what could be taken as acknowledgement of the parting words or agreement that indeed he should make his adieus and leave them, and she did not much care which one of the two meanings was conveyed. He seemed inclined to speak – say something further – but must have grasped the futility of it at last, for instead he gave another restrained bow and walked away.

Her shoulders slumped, and it was only when they lost their tension as she released a shaky breath that she could tell just how much his presence had unnerved her. She grimaced and sought to dismiss the thought – the only sensible approach to everything that she could not control. Another grimace came when the rustling of papers told her, without the need to look, that curiosity had got the better of her eldest sister. It got the better of her too, Elizabeth discovered, when she caught herself stealing a glance at the handful of sheets covered in an uneven script. Uneven, virtually illegible and exceedingly untidy – not the sort of penmanship she might have expected from one so fastidiously neat as Mr Darcy.

The brief glance was not enough for her to decipher anything, and she was not of a mind to try harder. With the papers that much closer, Jane seemed to have better success, but whatever she found therein must have been hardly to her liking, for she gave an audible gasp, followed by a shocked and patently grieved whisper of "Oh, the troublesome thing! *Why* did she have to say that?"

Jane stood and walked away from their bench in the greatest agitation, and Elizabeth might have followed her, had she not seen her sister make an about-turn, head back and resume her seat as she whipped the top page aside, to read the next.

"What is the matter? Who said what?" Elizabeth asked, concerned in no small measure by Jane's troubled countenance and her pallor, but the other made no answer, too engrossed by her reading matter.

The second page was read, and then the third, which bore but a few lines upon it, and then the papers were allowed to resume their folded shape when, still clutching them, Jane let her hand drop into her lap.

"Oh, Lizzy," she said in a pained whisper, and Elizabeth could see tears welling in her sister's eyes when Jane turned towards her.

She wrapped an arm around Jane's shoulders, bringing her close, and still unwilling to make Lydia and Kitty party to the sorry business, Elizabeth sought to keep her voice down when she gave vent to her frustration.

"And now he has distressed you too. Odious man! Oh, dearest, I knew you should not have indulged him. He had no right to involve you in his—"

"You do not understand," Jane firmly cut her off. "This has naught to do with you or Mr Darcy's suit. The letters are from Mr Bingley."

ⱷℯ ℯⱷ

She had never felt more foolish in her entire life, Elizabeth decided, as she walked along the path that skirted the shrubbery, her arm linked with Jane's.

They had abandoned their alcove, for it was not sufficiently secluded to fit the purpose. Lydia and Kitty were still at their game, and more privacy was needful after Jane's first agitated confidences: that those were Mr Bingley's letters to his friend; that he had learned everything about her sentiments from Mary, who was perhaps not quite so troublesome after all; that he was deeply attached – had always been – had always loved her; and that he was coming into Kent, fearful of his reception. He was coming on the morrow!

The staggering tidings were dwelt upon as they walked, paying no heed to their direction and indeed their surroundings, and seeking only to distance themselves from the house to be assured of continued privacy. At long last, Jane fell silent. So did Elizabeth, at a loss for something else to say, once she had asked every question she could think of, in an endeavour to clarify the perplexing matter, and once she had given every comfort and encouragement that was in her power to give.

In the ensuing silence, Elizabeth was left to vainly seek comfort for her own growing unease. How foolish, how self-absorbed she must have seemed, making such a show of refusing to accept those letters that were not meant for her, and had nothing to do with her after all. A blush crept into her cheeks at the thought of facing Mr Darcy later on, at dinner, when both of them would know that she had acted like a child. A wilful child who thought everything revolved around her. How utterly humiliating, to know oneself in the wrong! It was so much easier when she could hold the higher moral ground and think ill of him for his initial desertion, and then for the obstinacy of pressing his suit without giving her the chance to draw breath. And now, how mortifying it would be to show – and show she must – that she had misapprehended his reasons for joining them in the garden, and he deserved not censure but appreciation for his efforts to help set Jane and Mr Bingley's troubles to rights.

"I should have listened to Charlotte," Jane suddenly remarked, breaking Elizabeth's uncomfortable train of thought.

"Pardon?" she said, slow to focus on anything but her agitated musings.

Jane gave a wan smile.

"Do you not remember? You told me many months ago, at Longbourn, that Charlotte said a young woman had better show even more affection than she felt. She was right. Sometimes it *is* a disadvantage to be so very guarded, and 'tis but poor consolation to know that our former neighbours were left in the dark as to my feelings, if I hid them with as much success from Mr Bingley too."

"Oh, Jane," Elizabeth exclaimed, clasping her arm tighter. "You should not reproach yourself. You have acted with the utmost propriety. He should have known. He should have stayed in Hertfordshire for long enough to ascertain your sentiments."

Jane shrugged.

"Perhaps. If he were not so unaffectedly modest, and had I not persuaded everyone of our acquaintance – his own circle included, seemingly – that my heart was not touched. All those months of misery might have been so easily avoided…"

"Pray do not torture yourself so," Elizabeth entreated, but Jane was not swayed.

"You will tell me next that I should think of the past only inasmuch as the remembrances give me pleasure," she softly chided with another rueful smile. "I might, but not before this sorrow is removed from us. Poor Mr Bingley! What he must have suffered. And I dread to think how he might have suffered still – how coldly I might have received him, were it not for his friend's intervention. I trust you can see that, Lizzy," she solemnly added. "Mr Darcy has been exceedingly kind, and I must thank him, regardless of… everything else."

With a sigh, Elizabeth fixed her stare ahead and nodded.

"Yes. I know," she blandly said. "And so must I."

The bedchamber was very quiet, once Elizabeth had dismissed Sarah, the Bennets' maid from Longbourn, who had followed them to their new home in Kent, in equal measure driven by loyalty to the family and drawn by the attractive prospect of being elevated to the loftier position of ladies' maid to Elizabeth and Jane.

Elizabeth had been the first to enlist Sarah's help that evening, for she had retired earlier than was her wont, leaving the others to amuse themselves with conversation and a game of cards. For her part, she could not abide a lengthy stay in the drawing room, nor was she equal to sitting still and chatting or playing at cards. Confusion ruled supreme, jumbling her thoughts and rendering her incapable of even feigning an interest in her companions and their pursuits. All was confusion, troubled confusion, ever since Jane had tentatively asked as they were going in to dinner, if they should not wait for Mr Darcy to join them as well, only to receive Lady Catherine's terse reply:

"My nephew is no longer at Rosings. He took himself away this afternoon, with nothing but a curt note to apprise me of the fact. Come along now. I will not dally here to discuss him, and keep dinner waiting. He has caused enough disruption in this house," her ladyship had resentfully concluded.

The intelligence had stunned Elizabeth speechless, which was just as well, for otherwise she might have incautiously exclaimed something along the lines of *"He left?* Without a word of warning? Without any explanation?"

And then the recollection of the manner of their parting had crept upon her, to trouble her anew. He might have explained his reasons then. He had appeared about to. But that attempt she had rebuffed. She had given every indication that she was not prepared to listen.

"Oh, bother," Elizabeth muttered, shuffling forward on her stool, before her dressing table.

Her tresses were inordinately tangled or she had grown uncommonly inept at taming them. Nevertheless, she impatiently sought to force the brush through the aggravating obstacle, but with little success. The handle slipped from her careless grasp, leaving the implement almost comically suspended halfway down her chestnut locks, until gravity claimed its due and the brush fell on the dressing table with a clatter.

Pursing her lips, Elizabeth retrieved it and resumed her efforts with as little skill but renewed vigour, tugging mercilessly, her eyes fixed on her reflection in the glass. She saw her mouth twist into a wince, yet persisted with staunch determination, refusing to acknowledge that the pained grimace had less to do with punishing her scalp than with aching thoughts that would not be silenced.

"Nonsense," she said aloud, seeking to silence them nevertheless.

She might have saved her breath. Thoughts clamoured still, insistently demanding her attention, and their onslaught made her wince again. Had she been cruel too, not just self-absorbed and foolish, during that last, ill-fated interview? Had her unremitting coldness driven him from Kent? Or had he simply left because Mr Bingley had requested he keep out of the way?

She gave a loud huff of exasperation that ended in a sigh. There was no way of knowing. She frowned and worked the brush through her tresses with renewed force. It was positively perverse that she should sit there now, regretting his departure. Her papa had suggested as much in the drawing room, after dinner, when he had come to press her hand and quietly remark that she seemed to have settled on being perversely disappointed by the developments, when by all accounts she had her wish, and she should be pleased.

"Unless of course you are peeved to hear he has only gone to town instead of making tracks towards Timbuktu," her father had teased, then soberly added, "Must I remind you of the old adage that claims you should be careful what you wish for?"

"Thank you, Papa, that is vastly helpful," she had ill-humouredly replied, only to see her father shake his head, a rueful twist to his lips.

But then, rather than purposely provoking her, he had opted for kindness and, doubtlessly for her benefit, had asked Georgiana if she knew what urgent business might have called her brother away, and when he was expected to return.

The young girl's reply had afforded but little information.

"He did not explain much in the note he left for me. He merely said he must go to town on account of Mr Bingley, and that he would write again to apprise me of his progress and his plans, but did not mention how long he would be away. I daresay he knew not, otherwise he might have told me."

"On account of Mr Bingley, was it?" Mr Bennet had remarked, his tone of voice deceptively bland.

"Yes," Georgiana had confirmed. "But I imagine he will return soon. He has every reason," she had added with a warm smile towards Elizabeth, which the latter found she could not mirror. To her profound discomfort, she felt compelled to privately acknowledge she had given him no reason to return.

This was preposterous, Elizabeth thought, tossing her head back. She had always prided herself on her good sense, yet there she was now, as senseless as any. For it was beyond senseless to be vexed with him in the morning for pressing his suit with untoward insistence, and by nightfall be severely disappointed that he had been too quick to give it up.

Was she perversely disappointed, as her papa said? She sighed. There was truth in that. Blaming him for leaving her last autumn was easily done. Blaming herself for driving him away now was not as easily endured. And spending days upon dreary days at Rosings without a glimpse of him, without any indication of his thoughts, was a dark prospect indeed.

She gave a mirthless little laugh. What a triumph it must be for him, were he to become aware of her foolish musings – were he to learn that his company, so proudly spurned but a few hours earlier, was now seen as something she might grow to pine for. He was generous, she doubted not; too generous to gloat. But he was human, so there *must* be a triumph.

She let her hand drop, still clutching at the smooth brush-handle. Aye, it was highly unreasonable of him, and conceited as well, to assume that after vanishing from her sight and keeping his distance for months on end, all he had to do now was beckon, and she would come running. But was it not unreasonable and equally conceited of *her* to resent his delay in paying his addresses?

However tactless and ill-timed his comments on her station in life, their truth could not be disputed. She *had* been but the daughter of a modest country squire until her father's second marriage had brought her into higher spheres. She knew so little of the fashionable world, yet even so, its immutable laws were not, and should not be, beyond her grasp. Only a self-deluded and unpardonably romantic simpleton would expect decisions of great import to be guided by nothing more than partiality.

She might have been flattered, had he allowed his sentiments to rule him, unalloyed by either reason or reflection – but should blind partiality be trusted more, respected more, than a decision made with his eyes wide open? Did it not speak better of him and his attachment, and not worse, that he had not acted on impulse, and instead had chosen to carefully consider how their union would affect not only them, but everyone around them?

The light tap on the door that separated her bedchamber from the sitting room was barely audible, but she was so highly strung that it made her jump. Her eyes darted towards the muted sound, only to remain fixed on the panelled surface as recollections forcibly intruded – deeply affecting recollections of a charged and all too brief encounter. Dark eyes boring into hers, weakening her knees and luring her into ungovernable temptation. Her hand clasped in his – raised to his lips. His deep voice, by turns avowing, protesting, pleading. Her inexcusable wish that she were held and kissed breathless, even as she had stormed at him.

With a frown, Elizabeth shook her head and struggled to dismiss the treacherous thoughts. She had only moderately succeeded when she squared her shoulders and quietly asked her eldest sister to come in.

It *was* Jane, of course – who else? With a soft and sympathetic smile, she did as bid and closed the door behind her.

"How are you, Lizzy? Forgive me for dallying below-stairs. I came up as soon as I could free myself from Lady Catherine's whist table."

"Thank you, dearest. But you need not have," Elizabeth replied as she resumed brushing her hair and sought to rally her spirits, for her sister's sake if nothing else.

Yet the warm glance she met in the glass when Jane came to stand behind her served to show her sister was not so easily deceived.

"Let me do that," Jane softly whispered, as she took the brush from her and began to run it through Elizabeth's tangled locks with all the gentle patience that the latter was lacking.

The snarls were tenderly coaxed and tamed with quick, light touches rather than forceful tugs, until the brush could glide smoothly and ever so soothingly down the full length of Elizabeth's tresses, over and over. Gentle, caressing strokes that seemed to brush away some of her tension too.

"There. That is much better," Jane smilingly observed, raising her eyes from her handiwork to meet Elizabeth's in the looking-glass again, before she leant forward to drop a kiss on the top of her sister's head and wrap her arms around her. "How are you, Lizzy?" she repeated, searching the reflection of her sister's countenance as they stood thus, cheek to cheek.

Elizabeth patted her arm.

"Well enough. Truly," she insisted, in response to Jane's arched brow at the valiant but not very credible claim, then sought to change the subject: "But *you* are the epitome of sweetness and goodness. There you are, on the brink of a most unnerving day, and you still find it in you to fret over other people's troubles."

"Not other people's. Yours," Jane corrected her in a whisper, before she turned to press a soft kiss on Elizabeth's cheek. She then straightened up and resumed the slow and gentle brushing, quick to see its uses in soothing agitated spirits. Jane let it work its magic for a while, and at long last she brought herself to ask without looking up, "Were you distressed by his sudden departure?"

"I was – am – all manner of things," Elizabeth owned with a sigh. "Distressed too, aye. Perversely so, as Papa so aptly put it," she said, in an endeavour to strike a lighter note.

"Did he? When?"

"Tonight. After dinner."

"I see," Jane said, still guiding the brush through Elizabeth's tresses in long, leisurely strokes. "Is it too much to imagine Mr Darcy left because he wished to see Mr Bingley?"

Elizabeth grimaced and gave a little shrug.

"I know not. Only time will tell. But speaking of Mr Bingley," she added with feigned cheerfulness as she turned around to face the other way, clasp her sister's hands and glance up towards her, "it will not do for him to find you looking wan and tired on the morrow. He might suppose you lost sleep over him and think rather too much of himself," she affectionately quipped.

Jane smiled as she crouched down.

"I should not mind, if it gives him comfort. I did lose sleep over him often enough. Just as you did over Mr Darcy. I wish you would not lose much sleep tonight. I think he will return for you, Lizzy," she fervently declared, and her eyes grew troubled and almost severe as she just as fervently added, "If he does not, then he does not deserve you."

"That is hardly fair. I gave him no encouragement," Elizabeth felt compelled to say in his defence.

"I made the same mistake with Mr Bingley. Yet he is coming back."

"You cannot possibly compare our manner," Elizabeth protested. "You were reserved. I was downright hostile."

"You were unnerved by the fast pace and by everything coming to a head in just one day. If he loves you, he will understand. If his attachment is not strong enough to withstand this, then the loss is his. You said last December that if he was disinclined to claim your affections and your hand, you would soon cease to regret him. You did once. You will do so again."

The corners of Elizabeth's lips briefly curled up into a forced smile – the only sign of gratitude she could offer Jane for the supreme confidence in her abilities. She suppressed a sigh as she inwardly acknowledged that she did not share it. It had been wretchedly difficult to forget him at Longbourn. It would be a thousand times worse here, in this house, where there was so much to remind her of him, and where he would be frequently mentioned.

"What will be will be," she said at last and reached to clasp her sister in a warm embrace. "Enough now. 'Tis time we took ourselves to bed."

Chapter 27

Rosings, 17 April 1812

"So, what have we here? A treatise on brewing… next to one on rearing sheep. Hm. Then, what? Angling. Ah, very well. Do set Mr Walton's compendium aside, Lizzy. I think I shall peruse it later. And pray have a care up that ladder. If you should fall and sprain an ankle, I fear we shall both go distracted. Speaking of which, how are you holding up, my dear, on this fine morning?"

"I am well, Papa. Do not concern yourself," Elizabeth replied with a gesture of feigned indifference as she did as bid on both counts and cautiously leaned sideways to place Mr Izaak Walton's tome upon a lower shelf that could be reached without the aid of the finely carved ladder – one of the many conveniently placed along the book-lined walls.

It was a falsehood, naturally. She was far from well. Her musings had kept her awake far into the night, long after Jane had left her, and the same troubled thoughts had driven her out of her bedchamber shortly after dawn.

Thus, her morning had begun much earlier than her father's. A fine morning it was indeed – at least as far as the weather was concerned – and she had bent her steps towards the ornamental gardens to wander along the paths with a heavy heart, while all around her the early mist slowly dispersed into hazy wisps, as the sun rose higher and the air grew warmer.

Her troubling thoughts were not as easily dispersed, and after a while Elizabeth gave up trying to make her peace with them, cross with herself at noting that instead of behaving like the rational creature she had always been, she had of late veered towards playing the inglorious part of the moping jilted damsel.

She had returned to the house in time for an early breakfast, soon to be joined by Georgiana and Colonel Fitzwilliam, and then Jane, which was out of character, for her eldest sister was not in the habit of rising with the lark. Still, today of all days, it did not surprise her that Jane had neither the ability nor the inclination to linger in bed.

Likewise, it came as no surprise that Jane had as little interest as her in the plentiful fare, and as little patience for the needlework to which they eventually applied themselves, when Lady Catherine found them in the morning room and decreed they should seek some employment for their hands, rather than wander to and fro and stare blankly out of windows.

Her ladyship then left them and went to break her fast, but that did not afford them a very long respite from her overbearing company for, as ever, she was very frugal with the first meal of the day. She returned in less than half an hour, shepherding Elizabeth and Jane's most unwilling younger sisters, and sat them all at their embroidery, while she amused herself with determining what sort of weather they would have over the coming days, and then with scheduling their music lessons, along with those meant to improve their drawing skills and their proficiency in French, so that they would not be completely overwhelmed when resident masters would be engaged.

"Elizabeth, you may join Anne in her French studies. I am given to understand you have caught up with her quite nicely and so has Jane, to some extent. But the younger girls are utterly hopeless," she enunciated, indifferent to the fact that Lydia and Kitty were sitting right beside her. "Either of you may wish to tutor them in your spare time, and goodness, I dread to think how you will all fare with studying the Italian language. I will not have the expense of masters go to waste. If you aim to go no further than parroting some arias with no understanding of what it is that you are saying, you might as well own as much from the beginning. I have undertaken to give you a proper education, but I shall not persist in trying to turn sows' ears into silk purses unless you keep your side of the bargain and apply yourselves. Patience, that is what I always say, and a great deal of practice. You can never expect to excel at anything without patience and practice."

Elizabeth had winced and bit her lip as the sharp point of her needle had unerringly found her fingertip yet again. Patience was in short supply that morning. She had precious little to spare for Lady Catherine and her exhortations, and even less for the frustrating needlework. Yet she silently kept tangling the silken threads with the odd huff and frequent glances towards Jane, which her eldest sister ruefully returned, until their father mercifully joined them and put an end to the tiresome drudgery. To Elizabeth's relief, she and Jane were asked to come and assist him in the library. As for Lydia and Kitty, they were told that Anne had awakened and broken her fast, and would like them to join her in the music room.

Lips pursed, Lady Catherine had declined to comment, presumably unwilling to acknowledge that, proficient as Anne might have been in French and Italian, her musical abilities were far behind Georgiana's and even Elizabeth's, and in that regard the two youngest Bennets were the most fitting counterparts for her skill.

If Lydia and Kitty had hoped that, by eagerly setting their needlework aside, they would also be free of their stepmother, her ladyship was quick to disabuse them of that happy notion. She stood and regally declared she would come and oversee their practice to ensure they would not slide into nonsense and inane chatter, and that Anne's willingness to devote her energies to music would be justly rewarded.

Elizabeth could only stroke Kitty's arm in passing and cast Lydia an encouraging and sympathetic glance, unable to tell them in so many words that they should take heart for, knowing Anne, she would not allow her mother to take full control and ruin their amusement. Then, once the three of them were gone, she followed Jane and their father into the library, glad of the excuse to evade Lady Catherine's society by assisting Mr Bennet in his grand project, little patience as she might have had for that as well.

Jane was asked to sit at the escritoire and make use of her fine penmanship in compiling a list, as Mr Bennet selected volumes one by one and read out the author and the title, while Elizabeth – the more naturally active of the two – was encouraged to climb up the ladder and neatly arrange them on the shelves.

Georgiana found them thus engaged a fair while later, when she returned from whatever employment had kept her amused since breakfast, and cheerfully said:

"Ah, there you are. I have been looking for you, Jane. Is this not a glorious morning? I do hope I can persuade you to join me on my ride. There are some fine prospects I should like to share with you."

Puzzled, Elizabeth glanced her way. Georgiana had never suggested anything of the sort before, presumably quick to gather that Jane did not share her fondness for long rides and impromptu gallops. It was a pity that the overtures should have come today, when Jane must be unwilling to leave the house for the joys of the countryside.

"Why, I…" Jane floundered, but before Elizabeth could think of a way to assist her sister in graciously declining the surprising and ill-timed invitation, Jane found her words at last. "I do think I should remain indoors today," she said, only to have Georgiana settling a long and meaningful glance upon her.

"Pray believe me, you most assuredly should not," the younger girl declared with energy. "Do come. I promise you will not be disappointed."

Elizabeth found Jane's eyes darting towards her as her eldest sister released a startled "Oh?" An unspoken query passed between them. Was the kindly girl seeking to orchestrate a propitious encounter, away from Lady Catherine's prying eyes and her disdain for young gentlemen with the whiff of northern mills clinging to their coats? On the previous day, during their rambles, Jane had mentioned her ladyship's diatribe against Mr Bingley and the origins of his fortune, so there was every reason to think that the reunion – deeply unnerving in itself – should be as far away as possible from Lady Catherine's drawing room.

Whether their suspicions as to Georgiana's intentions were founded or not, Elizabeth could not tell, but there was one way to find out, she determined, and set aside the armful of books she was in the process of arranging, before climbing down the ladder with all the speed and agility of an excitable marmoset.

"If Georgiana thinks so, then you must go," she firmly said. "In fact, under the circumstances, I am of a mind to come along. You might need me on your ride."

The well-meaning but ill-judged words had barely left her lips, when three pairs of eyes settled upon her with overt surprise.

"You, Lizzy? But you never choose to ride," Georgiana exclaimed.

"This time I think I shall," Elizabeth insisted, and belatedly grasped her error only when she heard Mr Bennet drawl:

"Is that so? How extraordinary. Those prospects that Miss Darcy mentioned must be very fine indeed, if they can entice you to venture out on horseback. Do you know, I think I should like to see them too. I say we all go. Let me send word to the stables."

Elizabeth flashed a panicked glance towards her father, and her eyes grew apologetic when they alighted upon Jane.

"Perhaps I was too hasty," she stammered, ineptly seeking to retract the offer of sisterly assistance, since it had backfired so disastrously. "Nay, Papa, I think we should stay behind and continue with our project. We are making good progress."

"Suit yourself," Mr Bennet shrugged. "Feel free to stay, my dear, and carry on without us. I shall escort your sister and Miss Darcy. After all, they should not ride out unaccompanied. We shall regale you with tales of our exploits on our return."

"But, Papa—" Elizabeth protested, quickly seconded by the others, who spoke at the same time to dissuade him from pursuing that scheme.

"You need not concern yourself, Papa," Jane said. "A groom can escort us—"

"My cousin will ride with us, sir. Rest assured, we shall not be unprotected," Georgiana spoke up too, thus reinforcing Elizabeth's suspicions about the propitious encounter the dear girl might have hoped to orchestrate.

Unfortunately, Georgiana also seemed to unwittingly divert Mr Bennet, who did not hesitate to amuse himself further and drolly observed:

"Anne will protect you? I thought she was practising her music. Now, I do not doubt she is a force to be reckoned with, but still, I would much rather be at hand as well."

"No, I was speaking of my cousin Richard," Georgiana hastened to say, but to no avail.

Clearly, Mr Bennet had caught the scent of mischief, and he gleefully pursued it with all the enthusiasm of a terrier.

"Ah, the valiant colonel. Capital. Capital. He is excellent company, and will keep me entertained with his stimulating conversation while you ladies admire the fine prospects and whatnot. Let us be gone. So, what say you, Lizzy? Will you stay behind, or are you still brave enough to join us?"

With another brief exchange of telling glances, his daughters and their friend could do nothing but bow to the inevitable. There was nothing for it – he would not be dissuaded. So, with a sigh, Elizabeth resigned herself to doing penance for her folly that had precipitated the entire business, in the hope that she might at least atone for it by finding ways to assist Jane and provide moral support, as she had originally intended.

"I will come along, Papa. But pray promise you will lag behind with me if the others choose to break into a gallop," she said, in an endeavour to prepare the ground, so that Jane might eventually evade unwanted scrutiny by tearing ahead of their inquisitive father.

The bell was duly rung, and the footman who came to attend them was asked to send word to the stables and fetch pelisses, bonnets and Mr Bennet's hat. Once the requested apparel was brought and donned, they made their way out of the side entrance, and Elizabeth could only rejoice in the modest satisfaction that they had not attracted Lady Catherine's notice. She followed the others along the winding path and finally rounded the corner into the stable-yard, berating herself for her folly and praying she would not pay for it with a twisted ankle or, God forbid, a broken neck – when suddenly she could not spare another thought for sprained limbs and intractable horses. Her lips parted to release a gasp, then curled up into a smile. Across the crowded courtyard teeming with grooms and saddled horses stood Mr Darcy.

৵৹৹

Their eyes met, and her surprised delight was a response he clearly had not anticipated. His wary glance warmed, and he returned her smile. He advanced to greet them – greet her – and then he mirrored Georgiana's rueful grin when she said:

"We have all decided to go riding after all."

"Yes, I gathered as much from Mr Bennet's message," he replied in a matching tone, and made no other comment.

He likewise kept his peace when Colonel Fitzwilliam furrowed his brow and cast him a look of mock confusion:

"So, are you coming with us after all, Coz? I thought you said you would repair to the house and charge me with escorting Georgiana. Honestly, man, can you not make up your mind and stick to it? You will have me giddy."

Darcy's sole response was a heavenward roll of his eyes. Nor did he attempt to assist Elizabeth in negotiating the saddle, but left that task to her father and an obliging groom and instead went to hold the bridle of Georgiana's horse, when she mounted with a practised ease which Elizabeth could not hope to equal. Nevertheless, the deed was eventually done, and seeking to muster her courage and any riding skills she still possessed – or at least a good semblance of them – Elizabeth nudged her thankfully compliant mare into joining the other riders as they made their way out of the stable-yard.

The lane was wide enough for three to ride abreast, and the gentlemen courteously allowed the ladies to precede them. Hesitantly, Elizabeth pressed on. She was not at ease. Her back felt stiff as a board. But seeing as her mare's gait was slow and measured, she was forced to inwardly acknowledge that her nervousness sprang less from the activity she could not count among her favourites, and a vast deal more from Mr Darcy's presence somewhere behind her. How close behind, she could not tell. She did not dare turn to look, and not just because she felt her balance in the saddle was bordering on the precarious. Not far though, judging by the sound of his voice. She could hear it, deep and resonant, its timbre delectably appealing, even if he was merely exchanging civil nothings with the colonel and her father.

"I hope you will not think us meddlesome," Georgiana tentatively whispered to Jane when they were sufficiently far ahead of the gentlemen for an explanation to be offered with impunity, "but I ought to tell you now that my brother and I were hoping to bring about a certain meeting, away from Rosings."

A charming blush overspread Jane's countenance when she replied:

"I think I can understand your meaning. I should thank you and Mr Darcy for the kindness. He was doubtlessly correct in thinking that Lady Catherine might dampen his friend's spirits," she added with a smile, not backward in showing she had fully grasped the essence of the scheme, and that she was a willing and grateful participant in it.

"This is as good a time as any for me to apologise," Elizabeth softly intervened. "I was unpardonably late in seeing I would have assisted Jane far better had I not made a point in joining you on your ride. Papa was bound to be intrigued by it. But I was in earnest earlier," she assured both her companions. "Do go ahead. At a gallop, preferably. I will encourage Papa to stay behind and ride at my pace. He cannot very well race after you and leave me to my own devices," she concluded with a little laugh, which Jane was quick to echo. But Jane's mirth had a wry ring to it.

"I would not put it past him, especially as he might rest in the knowledge that he can safely leave you with the others."

As if on cue, Mr Bennet nudged his mount forward and broke ranks with the gentlemen to ride on the grass verge, at Elizabeth's left.

"How are you faring, Lizzy?" he cheerfully asked. "Regretting your intrepidity yet?"

"Not at all, Papa," she replied, daring to remove one hand from the reins for long enough to gesture towards Jane and Georgiana to ride ahead and make room for her father on the lane.

They both complied with alacrity, and Elizabeth resumed her firm clasp on the narrow strips of leather. She did not turn her head, and thus missed Mr Bennet's smile, but she could hear it in his voice when he remarked:

"I am glad to hear it. You are much too tense, if you ask me. But I daresay it cannot be helped," he teased and winked, which rather suggested he was speaking of her frame of mind, not just her posture. "Still, 'tis good to see you are undaunted. Loosen up, and I imagine all will be well," he advised, affecting not to notice that by then Colonel Fitzwilliam seemed intent upon outstripping them and was stealthily advancing at Elizabeth's right.

"Are you enjoying the ride, Mr Bennet?" he asked after a while, when the manoeuvre was well-nigh completed and his mount was half a length ahead, and Elizabeth could not doubt that her astute father was merely toying with them all as he allowed the colonel to draw him forward under the pretext of conversation, so that Mr Darcy could supplant him at her side.

That her papa was indeed toying with them all became apparent soon enough, when the colonel tentatively suggested:

"Perhaps I might persuade you to leave the ladies in my cousin's capable hands and join me for a brisk ride towards the home farm? You might appreciate the exercise, and the tenants' labours form a pleasing prospect."

"Oh, I will not dispute that exercise is highly beneficial and the results of industry are to be greatly appreciated," Mr Bennet drawled, and then was quick to demonstrate the futility of any endeavour to hoodwink him, as he cheerfully added, "Now, sir, you strike me as a straightforward young man who favours plain speaking, so I shall speak plainly. The only pleasing prospect I am of a mind to see right now is the one that had enticed my daughters to go for a morning ride. Once I have seen that fine, nay, fascinating prospect, you may show me anything you wish."

A few steps behind, on her tame mare, Elizabeth rolled her eyes and her lips curled into an exasperated little smile. She glanced towards her current companion, and thus found a matching grin altering his habitually solemn countenance into the wholly unexpected but winsome look of a mischievous schoolboy. But Mr Darcy was too well-bred to comment on her father's refusal to be side-tracked. Instead, he casually remarked:

"I thought you seldom chose to ride."

Elizabeth flashed another quick glance at him.

"True," she acknowledged.

"Yet you never told me why."

"Did you ever ask?" she parried; then, just as he began to answer, she remembered.

"I did. On the first day of our acquaintance."

"Oh, I think you will find it was the second day, if memory serves," she replied with a twinkle in her eye, the beginnings of the first light conversation they had shared in ages easing her discomfort enough to encourage her towards mild teasing. But she regretted it as soon as she noticed a shadow clouding his countenance, so she amended, "Although one might argue that the length of the acquaintance should be measured from the day when we were properly introduced. But let us not quibble over the details. In answer to your question, I seldom choose to ride because I took rather too many tumbles to develop a true fondness for the sport. Still, I could hardly own as much at an assembly, where one would generally hope to pass oneself off with some degree of credit and put on a good show of dignity and grace."

His lips twitched, giving her to suspect he was reminded of his own antics, when he had collided with his friend at the end of the dance. And then he spoke and showed that was precisely what he was thinking.

"A feat I failed to achieve on that particular occasion," he said, with a self-deprecating grin.

Elizabeth gave a mild chuckle in her turn, and amiably offered:

"I imagine Mr Bingley was swift to forgive you for temporarily incapacitating him."

His answering smile seemed more than a little tense.

"Aye. And for worse transgressions too. To my good fortune, he is an uncommonly forgiving sort."

"An ideal friend, then," Elizabeth guardedly observed, not entirely convinced this was the best of times to ask of what worse transgressions he was speaking. Instead, she chose to pursue a different topic; one that should not be avoided any longer. "My sister did not have the opportunity to thank you for – what did you call it? – your unorthodox approach yesterday, but I cannot imagine she would mind my being the first to tell you she greatly appreciated it. And so did I. You were in the right, it might make the happiness of many."

"I do hope so," Mr Darcy replied with energy, then tentatively added, "If Georgiana did not have the chance to explain, there was a purpose to this ride…"

"Your sister could not explain, nay, but we gathered as much. So here we all are," she said with a little rueful laugh, "a larger greeting party than one might wish for, but it could not be helped."

Mr Darcy gave a wry chuckle of his own.

"Seemingly not. Courtships with an audience are all the rage at Rosings these days."

She blushed.

"That they are. So I hope Mr Bingley has a good sense of humour as well as a forgiving nature, for surely it would be easier if one were to find amusement in sidestepping obstacles, rather than be vexed by them."

The glance he cast her reflected mild surprise, but also cautious pleasure.

"I am very glad to hear you think so."

She smiled, and decided it was high time she offered some encouragement.

"And I am very glad you returned so soon. I did not expect it."

This time his surprise was great, and clearly apparent.

"Did you not?"

She shook her head and blushed again as his countenance warmed with something that bordered on awed delight.

"Did you—?"

He did not finish his sentence, leaving her to wonder whether he had been about to ask if she had missed him. To her relief, he thought better of it and decided against such bluntness. She was not ready for it yet, much as his sudden absence had taught her to be honest with herself and acknowledge that the last thing she wished was for him to be gone. Encouraging him was one thing. Openly admitting she had lost sleep over him was quite another.

Whether or not Mr Bingley had a sense of humour remained to be seen, but Elizabeth was thrilled to be reminded that Mr Darcy did. For what he said instead was:

"I imagine this is not the best of times to point out that wild horses could not have kept me away."

She laughed.

"No, pray do not mention wild horses at the moment. Although thankfully this mare is anything but wild."

"Her name is Persephone," Mr Darcy told her. "Your father sent word to request she be readied for you. A wise choice. She is the mildest-tempered creature in Lady Catherine's stables," he assured her, then dazzled her with the warmest smile as he continued, "Very well. No talk of wild horses. Even so, you must know that I could not stay away a moment longer than strictly necessary. Indeed, I would not have left. Elizabeth, I—"

The earnest avowal was cut short, and Mr Darcy tightened his lips into a grimace, and tightened his grip on the reins as well, in order to avoid Mr Bennet when the older gentleman slowed his mount's gait and turned around in the saddle with a tilt of his head towards the solitary rider Elizabeth could by then espy ahead of them, his shape outlined against the sky next to that of a tall and slender garden folly.

"I do believe we are to have some company on our ride," Mr Bennet dryly observed. "I wonder who it might be. A neighbour, I imagine. Or perhaps a trespasser with an interest in garden temples? I have but a scant knowledge of the follies adorning my wife's garden, so I shall have to rely on your better information, Mr Darcy. Which one is that, the temple of Aphrodite or is it perchance Cupid's? A pity it was never fashionable to build garden follies for Master Shakespeare's characters. Puck certainly deserves that honour," he drolly remarked, only to continue in a very puckish manner, "If I did not know better, I would say this is beginning to look like an assignation. What say you, gentlemen? Is it by design, or just a strangely fortunate coincidence, this encounter?" He did not wait for an answer from those thus questioned and resumed: "I have the oddest notion that we are about to run into a young man we have not seen in months. How inconvenient that my eyesight should begin to fail me precisely when I need it most. You have no such encumbrance, Mr Darcy, have you? So pray tell me, do you not think that gentleman looks suspiciously like your friend, Mr Bingley?"

"Papa!" Jane and Elizabeth chorused, gentle reproof mingled with consciousness in their tones.

"Yes? What is it? I trust the pair of you are not about to reproach me for amusing myself as I see fit. It would be grossly unfair if you did, and impolitic too, for as yet I have not upbraided you for your slyness."

There was but mild and diverted censure in his voice rather than genuine sternness, but Mr Darcy felt obliged to intervene:

"The fault is mine, sir," he firmly said. "But pray allow me to assure you that there are mitigating circumstances for the slyness."

Mr Bennet's eyes came to be fixed on him.

"Are there? Would you be so kind as to elaborate?"

"Of course. Your eyesight is not failing you. The gentleman is indeed Mr Bingley. He accompanied me from town to pay his respects to you and your family, but he was… hm… uncertain of the welcome he might receive at the house."

"Is that so?" Mr Bennet drawled. "Was it my lack of welcome he was fearing, or Lady Catherine's?"

"Both, I imagine," was all that Mr Darcy said.

"I see," replied Mr Bennet. "Well, if the young man is so anxious to pay his respects, then by all means, let us not keep him waiting. I, for one, am eager to stroll with him and have him entertain me with tales of his pursuits over the intervening months," he delivered as a parting shot and nudged his mount towards the unsuspecting source of further entertainment.

·ঌ૭ ૭ঌ·

Finding unholy merriment in the plight of beleaguered suitors was doubtlessly beneath him, and uncharitable too, Mr Bennet was willing to privately own. But dash it, mild facetiousness was one of the last remaining joys when a man had to prepare himself for the unpalatable prospect of no longer having the first claim on the affections of his most deserving daughters and, worse still, for relinquishing them into other men's keeping. So facetiousness would have to do, it seemed.

Thus, he allowed himself to be quietly diverted by Mr Bingley's acute discomfort when they joined him, and likewise by his and Darcy's disappointment when the father, rather than the suitors, was the one to assist his daughters to dismount.

If he had been highly diverted by the subtle manoeuvres destined to bring Darcy to ride alongside Elizabeth on the way there, the subsequent schemes amused him no less. Why, the stealthy moves aimed at rearranging the pairings on their walk resembled a nimble and well-choreographed ballet with conspicuous changes of partners. That was beneath him too, but the older gentleman could not resist the devilish impulse to subvert the schemes, get in the way and monopolise the conversation.

Yet when his daughters' doleful glances told him that enough was enough, the mischievous but loving father saw fit to take pity on them all and abandon his game. He fell behind alongside the colonel and Georgiana, allowing the others to outstrip them.

Bingley and Jane led the way, several yards ahead. Kind and right-minded, Darcy and Elizabeth chose to lag at least a dozen steps behind to allow them their privacy. Much as he knew he was in the wrong and despite his companions' efforts to slow his progress, Mr Bennet could not quite bring himself to oblige his second daughter and her suitor in like manner. Thus, he was close enough to notice Darcy stroking Elizabeth's hand when he offered her the small bouquet of bluebells and primroses he had gathered on their walk, during the stealthy movement of troops aimed at rearranging the couples. That had amused Mr Bennet too – seeing Mr Darcy bending down now and then to pluck them, and doubtlessly flattering himself that he was inconspicuous about it.

A pity that it was impossible to hear what Bingley said to Jane to put such a warm glow in her countenance when she turned her head to gaze at him, but the unconventional chaperone could easily conjecture, seeing as he was not deficient in understanding and knew his eldest daughter's affectionate disposition well enough.

As to the other suitor, fortunately for Mr Bennet, there was no need for him to tax either his imagination or his hearing. Thanks to his determination to cling to his second daughter's hem like goosegrass and to the fact that, however quiet, Darcy's resonant voice carried, Mr Bennet had the questionable satisfaction of catching almost every word.

"Pray allow me to apologise for yesterday – for virtually all of it. You were right to censure me and think me unpardonably self-absorbed and overbearing. It was Bingley who opened my eyes to it last night, with something he said. He spoke of how he failed your sister when he took himself away for months on end, and of his sole recourse and purpose, which is to devote himself now to gaining her trust and good opinion, however long it takes. I am ashamed to say I was too caught in my own feelings to see that this applies to me in equal measure. I have done little, if anything, to gain your trust and good opinion, and I should do my best to alter that. Yesterday you spoke of self-delusion— Nay, pray allow me to continue, for it must be said. I hope it was not self-delusion. But how are we to know if I cannot court you? I wish to court you openly – shout from the rooftops that you have no equal. That I have found in you every trait I wished for in myself – liveliness, wit, an open and engaging manner. But I cannot court you under Lady Catherine's eagle eye, or she will make your life a misery if I so much as speak to you more than Anne, or ask you to walk with me, or turn your pages at the pianoforte. Her wish that I attach myself to Anne has long been a nuisance to both my cousin and myself, but I never expected it would hamper my every endeavour at pleasing the one most worthy of being pleased. I am profoundly grateful to your father for his goodwill," he said noticeably louder after a brief pause, leaving

Mr Bennet in no doubt that this communication was largely for his benefit, and then Darcy dropped his voice again when he continued – little as that affected Mr Bennet's enjoyment of the young man's speech. "But I fear it will not be enough. Would you consent to come to Pemberley, if Mr Bennet could be persuaded to escort you? Would you allow me and Georgiana to show you the dear place? Even if Lady Catherine insists on being of the party, my people are well-accustomed to outmanoeuvring any number of overbearing relations, and so am I, on my own ground. Will you come, Elizabeth?" he entreated softly. "Will you spend some time in Derbyshire and get to know me better – give me a chance to show you the overbearing ogre at his most besotted? You need not fear I would rush you as I did," he added swiftly. "I promise – no demands, no expectations. I can only hope to make you see I would be the happiest man in the world if one day you were to come and stay, make my house a home and my life complete."

Mr Bennet's lips shaped themselves into a wryly appreciative smirk as he affected great interest in the shape of a tall lime tree, his right and better ear adroitly angled towards the couple in an endeavour to catch Lizzy's reply. Her voice would not carry quite so clearly, and his efforts were bound to be hampered by the fact that, at that precise point in time, she chose to close the distance that separated her from Darcy by the simple expedient of taking his arm. But sometimes determined efforts are rewarded, and Mr Bennet could just about hear a very softly spoken, "I shall ask Papa."

He grinned. Good, good, a trip into Derbyshire would be welcome in so many ways. And then he chortled, allowing himself the wicked entertainment of picturing Darcy's countenance and manner, were he to toy with the lad and feign reluctance for it. Still, perhaps he should resist that particular temptation. The young man had yet to learn to be laughed at, and it might be rather too early to make a beginning. Not to mention that Lizzy would enjoy teaching him that skill herself. Well, at least it was highly reassuring to discover Darcy was quick to learn that fiercely independent creatures should be tenderly coaxed and not abruptly cornered – and he needed no instruction in courting Lizzy after all.

Chapter 28

Rosings, 17 April 1812

Before too long – minutes, to be precise – Mr Bennet also discovered that he had underrated Mr Bingley's eloquence, and likewise that the young man in question had grossly overestimated the amount of time he would require in order to persuade Jane to entrust him with her heart and her hand.

Mr Bennet was still indulging in pleasing reflections on Darcy's courtship skills and the appeal of a trip into Derbyshire, when Jane and Mr Bingley chose to abandon the lead and remained waiting for the rest of the party to catch up. Seeing as the young man's countenance was split into the widest grin and his demeanour showed all the tranquil collectedness of a racehorse chafing at the bit, Mr Bennet was quick to grasp that some great excitement was in store. He was not mistaken, and he was to learn the reason when Jane left her euphoric companion to walk with Georgiana and the colonel, and came to clasp his arm and ask him to lag behind with her, for she had something most particular to say.

Mr Bennet justly prided himself on being a *connoisseur* of human weakness and had great tolerance for it. Yet he was shocked to learn that any daughter of his, even sweet-natured Jane, should be so forgiving and so lacking in prudence and discernment as to be swayed by a few fine words on a morning walk into promptly accepting the offer of a fickle suitor. To his way of thinking, Mr Bingley had a vast deal of explaining to do and some sins to atone for, and there was no reason why his path towards proving himself should be any less rocky than Mr Darcy's. He was of a mind to either withhold his consent or request an exceedingly long engagement, and he did not scruple to make his views plain to his eldest daughter. But Jane merely smiled and squeezed his arm.

"I feared you would say that," she evenly remarked, "which was why I told Mr Bingley I should speak to you first. Papa, there is more that I have not imparted yet," she began, then proceeded to relate a long tale of shared letters and misapprehended sentiments, which in the end succeeded in appeasing her father's discontentment and his fears, and persuaded him that Mr Bingley had no greater sins than a faulty lack of confidence in his abilities and judgement. Thus, when the young man was permitted to approach him, Mr Bingley had a better reception than he would have had half an hour earlier, and his petition for Jane's hand a far more favourable answer.

The party that eventually returned to Rosings included Mr Bingley, for Mr Bennet saw fit to invite Jane's betrothed to join them for dinner, and when the introductions were performed, he calmly asked Lady Catherine to welcome that gentleman as a future son-in-law and an upcoming addition to the family.

Her ladyship's sentiments could be easily guessed, and she had no qualms in expressing them with all her customary frankness.

"So I am not only expected to tolerate a tradesman's offspring at my table, but accept him as a son-in-law? Mr Bennet, I am astonished and severely disappointed in you. Is Anne to have such a man for a brother? Is this your daughter's gratitude for my attentions to her and all her sisters – throwing herself away in this disgraceful manner? I had the best scheme in place for Jane. She was to marry Captain Hayes. He is Lady Metcalfe's naval brother and an excellent match for your eldest. Not of exalted stock, naturally, but suitable and above all, eminently respectable—"

"Lady Catherine, so is—" Mr Darcy sternly cut her off, clearly intent upon defending his friend, whose sentiments her ladyship made no effort at sparing as she vented her frustration in Bingley's presence, as though he were of no more consequence to her than a coal scuttle.

But Mr Bennet raised a hand to indicate he should hold his peace. He made to speak in Darcy's stead, only to find that Lydia was quick to take advantage of the very brief silence.

"A naval captain," she gushed, clapping her hands together. "If Jane is to have Mr Bingley, pray let Captain Hayes have me! Do, Mamma, and I vow to obey you in everything and not put another foot wrong, ever," she pleaded.

But upon noticing the baleful glare Kitty cast her way, doubtlessly cross that she had not had the presence of mind to petition for the captain first, Lydia swiftly added, "And if there could be such a one for Kitty, a fellow officer or another captain or some such, oh, Mamma, that would be positively marvellous!"

Lady Catherine scowled, although not so much at the overly familiar appellation – she was the girls' stepmother, after all.

"Will you cease apportioning captains as though they were the last sweetmeats on a plate?" she snapped, too incensed at her husband's betrayal and the youngest Bennet's unseemly exhibition to find any satisfaction in finally being given the means of breaking the two troublesome fillies to harness. "There you have it, Mr Bennet," she fulminated. "This is the result of a permissive upbringing: hoydenish ways and unsuitable matches."

"As to the latter, my dear, pray oblige me and allow me the free use of my judgement in the matter, and likewise the paternal right to dispose of my daughters in marriage as I see fit."

"Sir, I am most seriously displeased. Why, the very essence of our arrangement – the main advantage to your family, as agreed – was that I would introduce them to adequate suitors."

"Indeed, and as you could gather from Lydia's much too vocal outburst – by the bye, my girl, you do need to grasp the merits of holding your tongue – my two youngest would be exceedingly grateful for that honour. But let us not turn our affairs into such a public concern. We may examine the terms in detail if you wish, but I daresay you will find I retained the right of veto. I aim to make full use of it, especially when proposed matches are at odds with prior attachments. By the sound of it, Captain Hayes is a worthy fellow, but his claim to Jane's hand, such as it is, cannot take precedence over Mr Bingley's."

Lady Catherine drew herself up to her full height.

"Mr Bennet, I was under the impression that you were a sensible man who could be reasoned with, and that Jane was a most tractable creature. If the pair of you refuse to defer to me in this, there will be consequences, I assure you. My generous nature and family obligations will compel me to continue to receive Jane, but I will never be prevailed upon to extend that privilege to her husband and her new relations. Liberties will not be tolerated, and any attempts on their part to secure my aid in gaining them admittance to the best circles will be uncompromisingly rebuffed. I hope I am making myself clearly understood."

"Perfectly so, my dear," Mr Bennet replied with amiable unconcern. "From what I gathered, Mr Bingley has already reconciled himself to such hardships, and I daresay Jane will eventually follow his example. Now, since we seem to have reached a suitable compromise and settled the matter to everyone's satisfaction, do you imagine we might have some tea?"

No one could doubt that Lady Catherine was far from satisfied. She remained in high dudgeon, harried and harangued the servants, finding fault with the refreshments, and when Elizabeth excused herself to place her small bouquet of wildflowers in water, her ladyship ill-temperedly remarked:

"If you choose to take an interest in such things, you may assume the housekeeper's duties in arranging the floral displays in the house, but look into the orangery as the first choice and take instruction from the head-gardener. He could have told you that primroses and bluebells are a poor choice in that regard, and are better left to grow where you found them. They never last, so gathering them up for ornament is utterly pointless."

Elizabeth wisely received the grumbling advice with nary a comment, retired to her bedchamber to carefully arrange the fresh-scented token in a small vase on her nightstand, and promptly returned to the drawing room to find that her ladyship had not quite finished taking everyone to task. Georgiana was the only one who somehow escaped her ire. The colonel was soon reprimanded for talking too loudly, Lydia for laughing too much, Kitty for slurping her tea, Elizabeth for tardiness, Jane for conversing solely with Mr Bingley, Mr Bingley for fidgeting and nearly spilling Mrs Jenkinson's tea, Mrs Jenkinson for piling sugared almonds upon Anne's plate when she knew full well that Anne did not favour them, Anne for not complaining of it herself, Mr Bennet for bringing books into the drawing room when no one wished to find them there, and Mr Darcy for sitting in a distant corner, busily engaged with pencil and paper.

"What are you scribbling there, Darcy?" Lady Catherine called out.

"Just jotting down something of significance, ma'am," he replied, unperturbed, raising his eyes from his employment only for as long as civility required.

"What can be so significant that it cannot wait? You had much better come and explain why you left for town yesterday with nothing but the curtest note to me."

"There is nothing to explain further to what I had already written in my note: that an urgent matter required my presence."

"And is that urgent matter likely to claim you again?" her ladyship irritably asked.

Her nephew, on the other hand, was calm personified when he replied, "I should imagine not."

"Hm," Lady Catherine sniffed. "Pray quit your scribbling. Your tea is getting cold."

"No matter. But I thank you for your concern. I shall conclude shortly."

True to his word, he soon folded the paper and put it in his pocket along with the pencil, then came to take a seat next to Anne and Elizabeth. Merely dull nothings could be exchanged as they drank their tea, but that was to be expected. What Elizabeth did not expect was to find him approaching her a while later, when the ladies were the first to leave their seats to withdraw and dress for dinner, and handing her a slim volume with a bland expression and an equally bland "Yours, I believe."

A look at the spine told her it was a compilation of Mr Hazlitt's essays, and although she had never read any of them, Elizabeth knew better than to dispute his statement. Which was just as well. As soon as she opened the book in the privacy of her bedchamber, she found a folded piece of paper tucked behind the title page. She unfolded it, only to see it was covered almost in its entirety by a pencil sketch of a large bouquet of bluebells, primroses, narcissi, tulips and daffodils, which barely left room for the words written underneath in a neat script that bore no resemblance whatsoever to Mr Bingley's scrawls:

'Until I can gather them at Pemberley.'

❧❦❧

Dinner was reasonably uneventful, although it could not be said that Lady Catherine's temper had improved. Predictably, she monopolised the conversation and was the only one who did not hesitate to address herself to whomever she wished, regardless of their place at the table.

This behaviour Darcy was not about to emulate, and not merely because it was unmannerly. Elizabeth was seated on the other side, several seats away, and the light-hearted, innocuous but nonetheless private exchanges he would have hoped to have with her were not the sort that could be bandied about across the distance between them. So he sought to content himself with the odd glance towards her as he made small talk with Anne and Jane, his closest dinner companions, and listened with a fair amount of hopeful anticipation to Mr Bennet, who was making plans for an outing on the morrow.

"What say you of a spot of fishing, gentlemen? The ladies may accompany us, if they undertake to keep sufficiently quiet so as not to scare off *all* the fish, and weather permitting, we might finish with a picnic."

The suggestion was warmly welcomed by virtually everybody, not least Bingley and Darcy, who had a vested interest in any scheme that might afford some privacy and the freedom of the outdoors. It was only Lady Catherine who turned her nose up at such plans.

"The girls had much better stay at home. They have no business to be traipsing along muddy banks. As for a picnic…" she said with a grimace, allowing her voice to disdainfully trail off in a clear indication of her disapproval.

"I think it a splendid notion," Anne quietly disagreed. "I would dearly like to go on a picnic. 'Tis a very long time since I had that pleasure."

Lady Catherine sniffed.

"If you are of a mind to eat *al fresco*, although goodness knows why anyone would, you can picnic on the lawn. I see no reason why you should go to such lengths as joining a fishing party."

"Pray rest easy, Mamma, I do not aim to fish," Anne reassured her with a mild laugh.

"Whyever not? Darcy could teach you," Fitzwilliam slyly intervened, quick to exploit the well-known chink in her ladyship's armour and play on her wish to throw Darcy and Anne together at every opportunity.

This time, however, he had misjudged the situation.

"I will not hear of it," Lady Catherine decreed. "What if she should fall in?"

"My cousin is teasing me, Mamma," Anne said, with something of a moue. "He knows full well I will have no truck with the ghastly business, live baits and whatnot. No, I wish to spend the day in the fresh air with Georgiana and my sisters, and I daresay you would be pleased to have the house for yourself for a while, and enjoy a peaceful morning. You need not give yourself the trouble to join us. I know you share my views on fishing, and cannot abide picnics."

"Oh, I had no intention to join you," Lady Catherine declared, to everyone's relief, then shrugged. "I daresay you are not wrong there. A peaceful morning would not go amiss. They are in short supply at Rosings of late," she spat, glaring at Mr Bingley; and since he did not even give her the satisfaction of noticing, for he was gazing adoringly at Jane, Lady Catherine redirected her glare towards her husband.

"Is that a hint that my cousins and I have overstayed our welcome?" the colonel quipped. "What say you, Darcy? Should we take our leave after the fishing expedition on the morrow?" he asked with a commendably straight face, and his mien remained a picture of cheerful innocence even when both Darcy and his aunt turned matching scowls upon him.

From his seat at the end of the table, Mr Bennet took in the scene with ill-concealed amusement, and promptly revised some of his views on his second daughter's suitor. Seemingly, the young man did have some experience in being laughed at. What he had yet to learn was that he might come to enjoy it.

⚬◗◖ ◗◖⚬

The remainder of the evening, with all its limitations, afforded precious little enjoyment to Darcy. As he sat surrounded by a bevy of relations, chagrined by the lack of opportunity to say more than a few meaningless words to Elizabeth, he felt obliged to forcefully remind himself that he should be grateful for the improvement in his fortunes and dwell on that instead. No further than last night, he was miles away from her, grimly reflecting on the disasters of the day, on her severe countenance and her reproaches, with nothing to sustain him but brandy and the tormenting recollection of a few perfect moments in the grove. True enough, now they could barely talk, but there was neither bland reserve nor censure in her eyes when their glances met – and they met often – and the impish smile that had bewitched him months ago had reappeared, to tug at the corner of her lips. Their time together on their walk and her response to his apology had kindled hope and brought more joy than he had dared anticipate, so Darcy sat back with his tea, determined to be wise and count his blessings.

The reward for that sensible choice came soon enough, when Elizabeth left her seat and withdrew towards the table where the tea things were arrayed, to refill her cup. Darcy drained his and followed, to be met with the old adorable archness that made his hopes soar.

"I must thank you for the delightful sketch. Had I not seen you so diligently at work, I might have thought it was your sister who had drawn it," Elizabeth teased as she poured his tea.

Darcy's lips twitched as he daringly replied in kind:

"It pains me that you should think I cannot master something as simple as spring blooms. Admittedly, I would not try my hand at a likeness with any expectations of success."

Her eyes crinkled at the corners as she returned his smile.

"I cannot boast of any particular skill in that regard either. By way of example, I fear my rendition of the Fitzwilliam profile still leaves a great deal to be desired. Sugar?"

"I thank you, no," was all he said, choosing to err on the side of caution and not voice the hope that she would have abundant opportunity to practise. No demands, no expectations. He had vowed as much that very day and, by Jove, he would keep his promise.

But his eyes widened in surprised delight when she observed:

"I daresay I shall have to devote myself to extensive practice."

"Pardon?"

Elizabeth gave a little shrug as she set his full cup before him.

"Your aunt's exhortations. Only this morning, she sought to impress upon me and my sisters that the key to mastering any skill is patience and a great deal of practice. I imagine she will kindly sit for me until my efforts do justice to the subject matter."

Darcy allowed himself a wide smile and an intrepid retort.

"If my aunt is too busy to indulge you, pray feel free to apply to other members of the family."

"Even if the result should be pert?" she asked, her eyes dancing, as she glanced at him over the rim of her cup.

"Especially then. You may remember I have long thought there is everything to be said for pertness."

His second intrepid remark was rewarded with a warm gaze that went a long way towards showing she had a very good recollection of what was said in the glade carpeted with forget-me-nots, but mischief still rang clearly in her voice when she replied:

"I thank you. I will be sure to bear that in mind next time I take Lady Catherine's likeness."

A bark of laughter escaped him at the mental picture of his aunt's likeness sporting a pert nose, and moreover her reaction to such handiwork. Unfortunately, it was so loud and so out of character that it did not fail to attract her ladyship's notice.

"What amuses you so, Darcy? What are you and Elizabeth talking of? Let me hear what it is."

Cursing his regrettable slip – and his aunt too, for good measure – Darcy smoothed his countenance and fought the urge to roll his eyes.

"We are speaking of drawing, ma'am," he said, when a reply could no longer be avoided.

"Of drawing? What is so entertaining about drawing?" her ladyship wished to know.

"Nothing, as such. But talk of sketches reminded me of Mr Gillray's caricatures. Pray forgive my distraction," he said to Elizabeth with a restrained bow, hoping she would understand he was speaking of the lapse in concentration that had drawn his aunt's attention to their *tête-à-tête*, and that, in her turn, her ladyship would lose interest in it if she thought him dwelling on Mr Gillray's etched satires, rather than his companion.

The twitch of Elizabeth's lips gave him to hope she had grasped his meaning in more ways than one, and she could guess that the caricature he had in mind was not one of Mr Gillray's.

"Think nothing of it," she replied and turned away to rejoin the others, leaving him to scald his mouth with fresh tea and hope for better chances on the morrow.

Chapter 29

Rosings, 18 April 1812

It was a great relief for Darcy to finally see Elizabeth making an appearance at breakfast – much later than was her wont, to his disappointment, but thankfully earlier than Lady Catherine – and an even greater pleasure to find her choosing the seat next to his. She cheerfully greeted the assembled party – her father, her younger sisters, Georgiana and him – then placed the slim volume she was holding in the empty space between their plates.

"Yours, I believe," she said with a hint of a smile.

Darcy's was substantially wider, as he pocketed the book.

"Fitzwilliam's, in fact. I thank you. He will be glad to have it back."

"You are very late this morning, Lizzy," Lydia piped up. "You always come down long before me. Or did you go traipsing in the gardens like you did yesterday? You were up at the crack of dawn."

"Save your breath to cool your porridge, child," Mr Bennet admonished her. "What were you doing up at the crack of dawn anyway?"

"The room was awfully cold. We left the windows open. I got up to close them and saw Lizzy walking around in circles like a mad thing."

"It was hardly the crack of dawn, Lydia," Elizabeth protested, her cheeks flushed a bright shade of crimson.

"It was at least six in the morning," Lydia insisted, always one for holding her ground.

"Well, I am pleased to see your sister had a better rest this time. Now pray oblige me and attend to your breakfast," Mr Bennet spoke up to end the matter, but to his second daughter's way of thinking, his remark was not helpful in the least.

For his part, Darcy was of a vastly different mind, as he made every conceivable effort to keep his elation from showing plainly in his countenance. He had awoken as early as he could, in the hope that Elizabeth would indulge in her habitual fondness for a morning walk and he might encounter her in the gardens, but the brief exchange and her utterly charming blush easily did away with the regret that it did not come to pass. Any such disappointment would pale before the encouraging intelligence that yesterday her sleep had been disturbed, and this morning it had not.

He stole a glance towards her out of the corner of his eye, to find her buttering her toasted muffin with quick motions and uncommon energy, her cheek still a delightful shade of pink. Since this was not the time to reach for her hand and tell her precisely how he was faring yesterday at six hours in the morning, he reached instead for the preserves he knew she favoured – raspberry jam and Scotch orange marmalade – and moved them a little closer to her plate. She still would not look up when she quietly thanked him.

∘୧୧ ୨୧∘

"We are in luck. Excellent weather for our outing," Colonel Fitzwilliam gleefully observed a short while later, when he joined them in the breakfast room along with Lady Catherine.

"Yes, yes," her ladyship intervened with an impatient wave of her hand, and went to occupy the chair that the colonel had obligingly pulled out for her. "I ordered the phaeton," she informed her other nephew. "I trust you will be able to drive Anne on this outing she is so keen on."

"It would have been my pleasure, ma'am," he evenly replied, "but from what I gathered yesterday, Anne would like to travel in the landau with the other ladies."

Lady Catherine pursed her lips.

"I cannot imagine why. She would be much more comfortable in the phaeton than crowded in the landau."

"I expect she would. Yet if it pleases her to go with the others, surely she must have her choice," Darcy countered. "In fact, I was about to ride ahead to ensure everything is in readiness for their arrival," he added, and forbore to disclose that he was also meant to meet up with Bingley by the same garden folly as on the previous day, and show him the way to the spot chosen for their fishing expedition and their picnic. It served no purpose to provoke his volatile relation by mentioning a future son-in-law she could not abide.

"Your thoughtfulness does you credit, Coz," Fitzwilliam smirked, knowing too much as always – and, as always, too quick to have his say.

Silence fell, disrupted only by the clink of china and silverware, and a few moments later by the entrance of a footman, who came to inform his mistress:

"Mr Beaumont is here, ma'am. He wishes to see Miss Anne, but she is not down yet. Shall I ask him to wait?"

Lady Catherine grimaced.

"Miss de Bourgh is preparing to go out. Let Mr Beaumont state his business to the butler," she said, and with a careless gesture dismissed the footman from her presence and the caller from her notice.

Darcy made to speak and insist that Anne should be given a choice in that too, knowing all too well how distraught she would be, were Mr Beaumont to receive such treatment. But a new thought occurred to him, so he changed tack.

"Mr Beaumont can state his business to me," he said instead, then dabbed his lips with the napkin and stood.

ఴఴ

As the door of the breakfast room closed behind him with a muted click, Darcy could see the air of sombre expectation in the visitor's countenance instantly freezing into a grim mask of displeasure. Mr Beaumont's stare hardened and he pushed his shoulders back.

"I thank you. You may leave us now," Darcy said to the footman, then gestured towards the side entrance. "Would you kindly walk with me towards the stables, sir? We might speak on the way."

The frozen mask unyielding, Mr Beaumont barely moved his lips when he made his reply:

"I was hoping to see Miss de Bourgh," he tersely delivered, and the cold tone of voice grew abrasive when he added, "I beg your pardon. I had not considered I should address myself to the prospective master of Rosings instead."

A sympathetic grin tugged at Darcy's lips, but he kept it in check with some determination. It would be misconstrued as gloating, and that would never do. It was the easiest thing in the world for him to recognise the emotion that had prompted the barely civil tone and the baleful glare. He had been spared the bite of the venomous green serpent, praise be, but with the pangs of yearning he was all too well acquainted. Knowing that it was in his power to relieve them in another was highly gratifying.

"Do walk with me, sir. I shall endeavour to make it worth your while," he insisted, since the conversation he had in mind could not be carried out in Lady Catherine's hallway and in her servants' hearing.

"You are all kindness, but I would rather not," came the clipped retort.

Darcy fought the urge to roll his eyes, as his sympathy for Beaumont was swiftly giving way to exasperation. Anne was in the right about the man: he was as headstrong as they come. She would have her hands full. He frowned. Manhandling the other out of the house or blurting out in Lady Catherine's hall that he would *not* marry her daughter were equally unappealing notions. A different approach seemed to be in order.

"Mr Beaumont, I have something to say, which may be of some interest to you. I prefer to say it in private. So, will you walk with me or not?"

An arched brow and a reluctant nod were Beaumont's only answers. Without another word, they made their way towards the side door. No sooner had it closed behind them than Beaumont gave a curt and impatient, "Well?"

"Not here," Darcy said, just as curtly, and gestured towards the winding path.

They had not taken many strides along it when Beaumont predictably bristled, "Sir, I have no interest in Lady Catherine's topiary. 'Tis Miss de Bourgh I came to see.

"My cousin cannot receive you now. We are to—"

"I see," the other cut him off, pain warring with profound hostility in his voice and manner. "Then perhaps you will oblige me by informing Miss de Bourgh that I am most grateful for the offer of the living at Hunsford, but I cannot accept it. Mr Whittaker or a new incumbent will have to officiate at your nuptials."

"That will not be necessary—"

"Pardon? What is your meaning, sir?"

"If you had the goodness to let me finish, you would not have to ask," Darcy retorted, his patience running thin even as his gratitude for Fitzwilliam's forbearance was steadily increasing, now that he had a better understanding of just how taxing it was to play Cupid to the obdurate. "Anne and I are not betrothed, nor are we to wed. Of the entire family party at Rosings, 'tis only Lady Catherine who still labours under that misconception, and for the sake of harmony we have not disabused her of that notion yet. Hence the need for keeping this conversation private," he observed, finally allowing the warm and understanding smile to show, as a kaleidoscope of very different but just as easily recognisable emotions played upon his companion's countenance. "Now, what I also began to say," he resumed after a brief pause, "was that my cousin cannot receive you just now because we are to go on an outing. You are welcome to join us and discuss the Hunsford living with her, or whatever else you might see fit. So, on that note," he said, the warm smile turning almost brotherly, "pray tell me, Mr Beaumont, do you fish?"

༄ ☙ ❧ ༄

"You should have had your aunt's people set the picnic rugs half a mile from the water's edge," Mr Bennet affably said to Darcy as he leaned back into his canvas chair and sipped his burgundy. "We shan't have any sport now, unless there are deaf fish in that pond yonder. Have you ever heard such a racket? Just look at them!"

Darcy had no need to be thus encouraged. He would have been hard-pressed to take his eyes off Elizabeth anyway. She and most of their companions were boisterously amusing themselves with a game of sticks-and-quoits, also known to the ladies as the game of graces. An apt name it was, too. Nothing could be more graceful than Elizabeth poised to catch the beribboned circle with her pair of sticks, only to send it flying in the air, and in short order bound after it again – a rosy picture of perfection, eyes sparkling, cheeks aglow. A nymph clad in primrose-coloured muslin, revelling in the freedom of movement, away from the tedious constraints of the drawing room. Never before had he been privileged to see her thus, everything about her enticing countenance and form

304

exuding her unparalleled *joie-de-vivre* and her enjoyment of the day. The most ravishing creature on God's green earth, she was – and he yearned for her like never before. Yet he had never felt so happy.

"Are you not inclined to join the fray?" Mr Bennet asked, a faint smile on his lips.

"I think not, sir," Darcy replied. The rewards of observation were much greater. So he remained precisely where he was, lounging lazily on the picnic rug, his head propped on one hand, a glass of claret in the other. He flattered himself that he was still adept at keeping his mien expressionless. He could only hope that Elizabeth's father was not skilled in the art of reading minds.

Given his previous interaction with that gentleman, he should have known better than to overrate his own abilities and nurture such utterly foolish hopes.

ᴑᴥᴑ ᴥ

Far from the jolly group and their game of graces, Anne was silently strolling with Mr Beaumont, her hand in the crook of his arm. She would not have called it a companionable silence and it had lasted long enough, she decided, then broke it.

"So, did you have a pleasant journey?"

"Journey?" Mr Beaumont echoed, a clear sign that his thoughts were otherwise engaged.

"Your visit to your uncle and aunt in Buckinghamshire. When my mother and I called the other day, your father told me you had gone to spend a se'nnight with them."

Truth be told, finding that he was from home had been a severe disappointment, but in some ways a relief as well. She could be nothing but glad he had not been present at that interview. It was a relief he had not heard Lady Catherine dismissing his father's warm thanks for the honour of her visit, so rarely bestowed, and offhandedly remarking she had merely called at Anne's insistence, but to her way of thinking, it should have been the prospective master of Rosings who accompanied her daughter on that errand, and not she.

Anne's lips tightened. With any luck, neither Dr Beaumont nor his middle-aged maid who had been at hand to serve their tea had related that specious nonsense to him.

"I was away, aye. Otherwise I would have come to see you that very evening, as soon as I read your letter," Mr Beaumont replied swiftly, although that was not what she had asked him. It was, however, what she wished to know, so Anne did not redirect the conversation towards his journey to his relations' home in Buckinghamshire.

"Oh?" she said instead by way of encouragement, but upon reflection, she should have thought of something more cogent to offer as, far from encouraged, Mr Beaumont kept struggling for words.

"I am overwhelmed by your generous offer. Most generous indeed... Nevertheless, Anne, I— Miss de Bourgh—" he floundered.

She pressed his arm.

"Pray do not revert to formality," she urged him. "Anne will do, particularly when we are alone. We have known each other for too long. Nearly all our lives."

"Aye. We have," Mr Beaumont said, his voice as solemn as his manner, and fell silent yet again.

Anne frowned. It was just as she had told her cousin Darcy a few days ago: the headstrong object of her affections perversely persisted in not assisting her at all. Must she truly take a leaf out of her mother's book and be the one to propose marriage? She stole a glance at her companion. He was intently staring at the ground ahead, as though he were picking his way through a treacherous marsh, rather than strolling in a meadow. She made to speak, yet nothing came to mind but words born from the proverbial assertiveness of the Fitzwilliams, and something told her this was not the time to assume control and remind Mr Beaumont which one of them held greater power – in theory at least.

When at last he spoke, it was only to tentatively ask:

"Would you care to sit?"

Anne cast a glance towards the large log he had indicated, sun-bleached and stripped of bark. Probably damp too, but it mattered not. Aye, she did need to sit. This conversation, coupled with her longstanding and very vexing frailty, was weakening her knees and making her heart pound. She felt dizzy and her ears were ringing. Perhaps her mother was in the right, and she should fortify herself with Dr Beaumont's tonic, for all its foul taste.

"I would," she averred, only to find he had also considered the possibility that the log might be damp, and sought to remove his coat, for her to sit on.

She smiled. Appealing as it might have been so see him in his shirt-sleeves, there was no need to have his coat marked with mould.

"I thank you, but I can easily use my shawl," she said.

"Will you not be cold?" he solicitously asked.

"No, not at all. 'Tis a warm day." And heat seemed to radiate from her chest in rapid bursts, as erratic as her heartbeats, and spread through her apace. But she kept that to herself.

Mr Beaumont took the shawl from her, folded it ever so neatly, laid it on the impromptu seat and took her hand to assist her in perching herself upon the log. A new wave of heat flushed her cheeks and her heartbeats grew even more erratic when he kept her hand in his as he sat, and took to running his thumb over it in an almost imperceptible caress. She raised her eyes to his, and found them troubled, intense and very dark.

There was intensity and a new sort of tension in his voice when he finally brought himself to speak:

"Your offer is more generous than I deserve—"

"Not so!" Anne was compelled to forcefully disagree, little as she might have wished to interrupt him. But she could not allow him to either utter or give a single thought to such absurdity.

"Pray let me continue," he entreated in a whisper. "I must say… I must confess I am… very torn. I should not wish to seem ungrateful, to you of all people, but I cannot see myself as the new vicar of Hunsford."

Anne's brow furrowed.

"And why not?"

His gaze dropped away from hers, and Mr Beaumont fixed it upon her hand instead, as he cradled it in both of his.

"I had an… illuminating conversation with Mr Darcy earlier," he hesitantly disclosed.

Anne's eyes widened.

"Did you? Illuminating – in what sense?"

A faint self-deprecating smile fluttered on Mr Beaumont's lips when he glanced up at her once more.

"Your cousin kindly gave me to understand that of late I have been giving far too much credence to Lady Catherine's claim that you would marry him."

Anne gave a little huff of exasperation.

"I told you as much last summer. Why should you credit Darcy, and not me?"

"You did tell me, aye. But this time his stay in Kent was longer than ever. I thought... No matter—"

"Oh, I think it matters a great deal," Anne promptly disagreed.

"Yes. And at the same time, it does not. If it is not Mr Darcy, it will be someone else. Last summer you did say you would not marry, but one day you must. And when you do, I cannot hold the Hunsford living and be expected to officiate. If nothing else, I hope you can see that. Pray do not ask it of me," he entreated with sudden and unmistakable fervour.

There was a matching fervour in Anne's retort when she shot back:

"I never did and never shall." And then she raised her chin. The proverbial Fitzwilliam forthrightness – Lady Catherine's manner, direct and uncompromising – was threatening to break through, and there was very little she could do to stop it. She drew a sharp intake of breath, and resolved to cease fighting it. For better or worse, she *was* Lady Catherine's daughter. And sometimes forthrightness was the last resort, Anne decided, her heart beating faster than ever when she firmly spoke: "I confess I simply wished you to have the Hunsford living so that you would remain in Kent. But admittedly I had not given proper consideration to the matter. My understanding of the rites and customs of the Church of England is limited, of course, yet even I knew that a vicar cannot officiate at his own wedding."

The reaction she had hoped to elicit was as immediate and forceful as in her brightest dreams. Mr Beaumont's troubled gaze – Henry's gaze – grew incandescent with wild hope as he clasped her hand to the point of pain.

"Anne," he whispered hoarsely, "you are much too kind to toy with me. Tell me, then, have I any chance of ever succeeding?"

Relief flooded her heart, as the boundless love that had ruled it for years – for nearly all her life – was finally to find fulfilment.

"Dearest Henry," she whispered back, her eyes misting as she drew her hand from his clasp and raised it to his cheek. "You succeeded long ago. There never was anyone but you."

⊰⊱

The game of graces was abandoned when the merry party decided that the animated disport had rendered them in great need of refreshment, and they all gathered on the rugs to partake of lemonade, orgeat and cinnamon-water, along with delicacies left over from their picnic.

Just as Mr Bennet had expected, it was not long until Mr Bingley intrepidly asked Jane to walk with him, and they excused themselves to wander off in a quest for a modicum of privacy. It was equally unsurprising that Mr Darcy was eager to follow his example, although not his footsteps. When Elizabeth agreed to join him on a stroll, he chose to amble in the opposite direction from his friend – which doubtlessly pleased Mr Bingley – and did not head towards the distant spot where Anne was sitting with Mr Beaumont either.

Mr Bennet reached for the burgundy, refilled his glass and reassumed a comfortable position in his chair as he surveyed his surroundings and his charges. Lydia was vastly entertained nearby, partnered by the colonel in a game of battledore, while Kitty and Georgiana chose to start another game of graces. Anne and Mr Beaumont were rather too far away for him to either hear what they were saying or read their countenances, but given that they were sitting quite close together on their log, holding hands, there was every reason to suspect that something of interest would soon arise from that quarter. Good. Lizzy would be safe from Lady Catherine's wrath, should Anne come to openly declare that her matrimonial intentions had nothing to do with Darcy.

Mr Bennet cast a glance towards his second daughter and her suitor, strolling away towards the coppice, only to be distracted by a peal of laughter coming from the other way. He sipped his wine, contentedly reflecting upon the changes the betrothal had wrought in his eldest offspring. All her life, Jane had been given to mild smiles. Now she laughed.

Mr Bennet snorted. That young man of hers was to be commended for making her so happy, but he would do well to develop a backbone too, or he would face an irate father-in-law if he were to dither meekly and distress her again. Mistakes ought to be forgiven. Recurrent folly should not be, and would not.

Thankfully, they would be settled within very easy distance from Rosings. Netherfield was but fifty miles away – little more than half a day's journey. It would please Jane to return to live near Meryton, so very close to her old home, and it would please *him* to be able to visit her often, once she was married.

If only Derbyshire were not so distant, Mr Bennet inwardly grumbled, and made a mental note to speak to Whittaker of the betrothal announcement the reverend was expecting, when he would see the man about the banns for Jane and Bingley's wedding.

It would come, that other betrothal. Likely not within the curate's prescribed fortnight, the doting father reassured himself and privately rejoiced – he was woefully unprepared to part with his dearest girl as yet. Still, Lizzy's betrothal would eventually come. Mr Bennet had no doubts on that score. So he should tell Whittaker to hold his horses, brook the delay and make no more fuss about it.

Mr Bennet sighed. It was deeply reassuring for a father to see his daughters settled not only comfortably, but happily too. Still, it did not follow that he should dance a jig in glee. Seeing them fly the nest was no gleeful matter. It would only bring bittersweet contentment.

"Maudlin old fool," Mr Bennet chastised himself, then drained his glass of wine and motioned towards the small troupe of servants gathered together at some distance to come and clear away the remnants of the picnic. "Set the wine aside, and the refreshing beverages too, but otherwise help yourselves to whatever takes your fancy," he instructed, and sent them forth to disport themselves as they saw fit, while the family enjoyed the day and the temporary freedom of their own amusements.

৯৩৫ ৩৯৬

The temporary freedom from Lady Catherine's scrutiny, and even her father's, put a spring in Elizabeth's step as she and Darcy wandered together into the coppice carpeted with bluebells. She could not forbear a warm smile when she saw him bending down to gather another small bouquet.

Yet when he offered it, the warmth was predictably seasoned with a touch of archness:

"I thank you. Although we do have it on the very best authority that they will not last."

He shrugged.

"Then I shall have to present you with others."

"Real or sketched?" she asked, a twinkle in her eye.

He mirrored it as he replied, "Just as the circumstance requires."

"You are most attentive."

"'Tis kind of you to say so. I will make it my business to continue in that vein."

She raised the small offering to inhale its faint but refreshing scent, and could not quite resist the impulse to tease him:

"You will forgive me if I am still unaccustomed to open gallantry from you."

"Of course," Mr Darcy said in a matching tone. "In fact, it has recently occurred to me that you might find it helpful if I were to devise a schedule."

A chuckle escaped her lips.

"A schedule, sir?"

"Indeed – for a gradual progression from feigning complete disinterest in your person and employment, to straying no further than ten steps away and hanging on your every word. I have already grasped that leaping directly to the latter might be disconcerting, so I have undertaken to apply myself with some diligence of purpose to mapping out the stages."

"Have you?" she said, surprised but no less delighted by his jocular manner. "And what is your success?"

"I thought I might begin by arranging such little compliments as might be adapted to ordinary occasions, along the lines of Mr Collins' attempts at flattering with delicacy."

This time she laughed wholeheartedly.

"Mercy, no, not Mr Collins' brand of courtship. I daresay you can do a little better."

"My thanks for your vote of confidence," he replied, laughter in his eyes and a twitch in his lips.

Elizabeth's glance effortlessly took the same playful gleam when she prompted, "And then, what would the next stage be?"

"I might offer my company on a walk to gather wildflowers if the opportunity arises to do so with impunity, however long they are expected to last in a vase. I might even show some skill at making daisy-chains. I had a fair amount of practice when Georgiana was younger. Although I would probably draw the line at wearing them for your amusement."

"That is very reassuring, Mr Darcy. It would be far too great a shock to see you turning into love's fool."

"Would it?" he replied, a new timbre to his voice that sent a strange quiver rippling through her senses. She dismissed it as unaccountable and foolish, and ascribed it solely to the feel of his fingertips brushing over the back of her hand, before he captured it in his and brought it to his lips. The quiver returned, not to be dismissed this time, when he whispered, his breath a warm caress over her skin, "I was rather hoping you might grow accustomed to that notion, as you are likely to see repeated evidence of it as time goes by."

Her colour deepening by a shade or two, she withdrew her hand. Mr Darcy made no protest, but raised his to the ringlets at her temple. He twirled one around his finger, which might have accounted for the third and equally foolish quiver when he added softly, "As I was hoping you might grow accustomed to calling me Fitzwilliam."

She drew away from the barely perceptible but deeply affecting caress, and gave a little shaky laugh as she resorted yet again to archness.

"Oh, goodness, no, that will not do. What if I were to become careless and address you thus in your aunt's presence?"

He gave a faint shrug, clearly unperturbed by her defensive teasing.

"No matter. We could easily persuade her you were speaking to my cousin."

"And if he were not there?"

"Of him, then," he said, once more reaching for her hand.

This time she did not withdraw it. But neither did she stray from the comfortable realm of playfulness.

"I must confess this has puzzled me for some time – his name and yours."

"I imagine it would be a most improper show of vanity if I were to declare myself gratified that you should puzzle over my name," he remarked, his eyes dancing, "so I will only say it was my parents' wish that I should bear my mother's maiden name."

"A family tradition?"

"No. Just their wish."

"That is a relief. I would have found it very strange indeed if our firstborn were to be christened Bennet," she spoke without thinking, only to see the new and rather pleasing hint of mischief vanishing from her companion's eyes, to be replaced with the warmest look of unadulterated tenderness. She blinked, shocked at how much it changed him, and no less at the sudden thrill that coursed through her without warning at finding herself enveloped into a gaze such as that. "What is it?" she asked, still unthinkingly, and inwardly chided herself for how ludicrously breathless she sounded.

His first response was a little smile. His second was to raise her hand again, but this time the kiss was not a light brush of his lips over the back of her fingers, but a soft and lingering caress on the skin of her palm. Soft lips, eliciting the strangest of sensations that made her fingertips twitch against his cheek. He sighed – nay, drew a deep breath – and whispered, "You think of such things? Thank you."

"For?"

"Not dismissing the matter out of hand. Not dismissing *me*."

Elizabeth chuckled ruefully.

"You are making it very difficult indeed for me to dismiss you."

"How so?"

She shrugged as she gave a little conscious laugh and a flourish of her other hand.

"You have an uncanny ability to fluster me, as you well know."

Still warmed by tenderness, his eyes widened with such stark surprise that she could not but regard it as genuine.

"Oh? I assure you, this is news to me," he said, unmistakable delight in his low and pleasantly rumbling tones. "Exceedingly welcome news, I would call it if I dared say something quite so ungentlemanly, but news nevertheless."

He did not press his lips into her palm again, but brought their hands down, hers still ensconced in his.

His gaze did not veer from hers either, not for a long time, until at last he smilingly remarked, "In that case, I expect it would be unfair to use that information to my advantage and ask if I might kiss you."

Another rueful chuckle left her lips.

"What amuses you?" Mr Darcy wished to know.

"Only that you would give yourself the trouble to ask, this time round."

"Ah, but I try to learn from my mistakes, you see."

"Do you?" was all she could say, only to inwardly censure herself yet again, on this occasion for finding no better a rejoinder than an inane question.

He did not answer it. Instead, he turned towards her and raised his hand to run his fingertips over her flushed cheek, trail a line to her chin and tentatively tilt it up as he drew nearer, only to remain poised inches away, his dark eyes delving searchingly into hers. A spellbinding gaze, intense, compelling and oddly vulnerable, that would have just as easily held her in thrall in a crowded ballroom as in a deserted coppice. Somehow, nothing mattered in the world but the unspoken question in his eyes.

Her eyelids fluttered, and she let them drop. He must have taken that for the abandon and the silent consent that it was, for a fraction of a second later she felt his warm breath over her mouth and chin, and the lightest touch of his lips on hers. Lighter than a feather. The softest caress. She released the breath she had been holding, and her shoulders lost their tension, which surely must have been the only reason why she leaned towards him. Eyes closed, she registered a second kiss, still brief, still light – a third, a trifle longer – a fourth – a fifth that sought to part her lips. After the seventh she lost count, along with any interest in counting. Or perhaps the kisses blended into one, long, hungry and insistent, until she found herself clutching at his shoulders, breathless, a little dizzy and more than a little disappointed when his lips left hers. Yet he remained close – there was no doubt about it, she could still sense the warmth of his breath on her face. She opened her eyes then, to find his. They were dark and bright, and crinkled at the corners.

"It was not self-delusion, was it?" he whispered, and there was no smugness in his words, but deep earnestness, so she did not turn away in renewed mortification.

Instead, she flashed him an impish grin and answered his question with another:

"Must you always go a step too far?"

"Indeed," a low drawl rang quite close beside them, making them jump apart, dreadfully conscious.

Mr Darcy cleared his voice, but made no reply.

It was Mr Bennet who resumed in a calm and measured tone.

"I consider myself a reasonable and forbearing man, Mr Darcy. But I suggest you do not try my patience. It would be unwise."

Looking some twelve years younger and very much like a reprimanded schoolboy – endearingly so, Elizabeth discovered – Mr Darcy ran his fingers through his hair and, visibly against his every inclination, he acknowledged the justness of the reproof with a nod and a crisp, "Yes, sir."

"Good. Do bear that in mind. Now, I would very much like to take the measure of you as an angler. I trust you will oblige me at your earliest convenience."

"Of course," Mr Darcy resignedly complied.

"This way, then. You can sit with us and keep count if you wish, Lizzy, but pray do not feel obliged to do so. As I recall, you have no patience for that sport. Tedious, you used to call it. So rejoin the others at your leisure, we shall not impose upon you," Mr Bennet blandly said, but Darcy could distinguish the by now familiar glint of mischief in his eyes.

So could the gentleman's daughter, apparently, for she replied in kind:

"That was when I was far too young to appreciate its finer points, Papa. I daresay the art of fishing has its merits, and I might come to watch the pair of you demonstrate your skill. Besides, I can always bring a book to entertain me if it becomes too tedious," she added, and ran gaily off.

⁂

She did not join them straight away. In fact, to Darcy's way of thinking, she took her time in coming. But she did come to sit on a folded rug, lean against a tree trunk at the water's edge – and thoroughly distract him with the play of dappled sunlight over her exquisite countenance and figure.

She had brought a book, but paid it no heed. The volume remained abandoned in her lap as she sat gazing over the glistening waters, seemingly oblivious to her companions, and his stare. It was beyond him to look away from the bewitching picture, and his gaze lingered, taking in every detail of the ever so alluring form that he had held clasped to his chest not long ago. Reflected sunlight now caressed the skin he had caressed – flawless and as translucent as the finest porcelain. Warm skin, bathed in warm light. Perfectly shaped lips, rosy and full, that had been so soft and pliant under his, their remembered fragrance all of a sudden invading his senses and making his grip tighten on the rod, and his Adam's apple bob under the restraining neckcloth quite as violently as the forgotten cork.

When dark eyes flashed towards him, the jolt was no less violent. Breath caught in his already too-tight chest when she did not look away, nor did she arch a brow in censure at his unremitting stare, but rewarded him with the beginning of a smile.

Darcy drew a deep breath, the need for air registering at last. Little else did. Still, he could not miss Mr Bennet's admonition:

"They are biting, Mr Darcy, and eagerly too. Would you kindly spare *some* attention for the fish?"

❦

Since Darcy found it well-nigh impossible to comply with that particular request – much as he sought to, in deference to Elizabeth's father – and as the other gentlemen joined them only briefly, nothing but a token gesture, likewise in deference to Mr Bennet and his fishing expedition, it was only the latter who made any notable contribution to the basket that was eventually delivered into the Rosings kitchens.

However modest the catch, the party returned home in excellent spirits – excessively high spirits, in Lady Catherine's opinion, and that also applied to her own daughter. Why, Anne could barely sit still at dinner and afterwards in the drawing room, although her general air spoke of fatigue that bordered on exhaustion. Thus, the great lady severely upbraided her second husband, the stepsisters and Darcy for thoughtlessly exposing her daughter to such damaging exertions, and escorted Anne above-stairs herself when the latter was finally persuaded to retire.

"Never tax yourself thus again," her ladyship exhorted. "Take your tonic and rest. You are to let her sleep late in the morning," she sternly instructed the lady's maid, then rearranged the covers around Anne's lithe form and nodded in some satisfaction when her daughter dutifully took a good dose of Dr Beaumont's tonic.

⁘

Anne smiled as she nestled under the bedcovers. Her mother had left her, and so had the lady's maid. Drowsiness enveloped her, and she tucked the corner of the counterpane under her chin and closed her eyes to gratefully explore her happiness. Betrothed to Henry, at long last. The beatific smile that curled her lips grew a little rueful at the thought that, on the morrow, her mother would have to be apprised of it.

"Poor Mamma," she whispered. "She will not be happy…"

Nevertheless, Anne held great hopes that all would be well – eventually, after the first fierce gales had passed. In truth, she had always known that her mother's aim was to ensure her comfort and safety, which was the main reason for advocating her union with Darcy, whom Lady Catherine thought well of and instinctively trusted.

In time, she would learn to trust Henry, too.

"In a very long time," she mused aloud again, not relishing the intervening period, when she would have to devote herself to persuading her mother that Henry was no fortune-hunter and loved her for herself.

Well, she would have to muster all her energies and achieve that feat, even if she had to swallow gallons of Dr Beaumont's tonic. It seemed to be working, the wretched thing. It did taste like pond-water – or at least like what she imagined the taste of pond-water would be, never having experienced it for herself, she thought with a wry smile – and the spoonful she had taken had a nauseatingly acrid smell, but it seemed to be working. At least it had calmed her nervous excitement to a degree. So she took another dose and settled once more under her bedcovers.

Chapter 30

Rosings, 19 April 1812

The house was very quiet when Elizabeth made her way down the great staircase on the following morning. This time, it was not remorseful restlessness nor unanswerable conundrums that had driven her from her bed, but a mild suspicion that her presence in the gardens was, if not expected, then at the very least hoped for.

The pleasing suspicion was confirmed when she left the house and found Darcy sitting with a small volume on the bench that commanded an unrestricted view of the side entrance, and she saw no reason why she should not mirror the warm smile she received in greeting along with a quietly cheerful, "Good morning," as he stood and bowed.

She replied in kind, just as brightly, and followed it with an impish, "Are you always such an early riser?"

"Yes," he said simply, and pocketed his volume without specifying whether or not it was also in his habit to while away the very early morning hours in the garden, with a book.

She did not ask for such clarifications, rather persuaded she already knew the answer. It was Darcy who asked if he could join her on her walk, and once more, Elizabeth saw no reason why she should dissemble.

"Of course," she said without hesitation.

"Where would you wish to go?" he casually asked as they fell into step together and, given their location, must have seen little wisdom in the intimacy of offering his arm.

"Nowhere in particular," she replied. "Have you any suggestions?"

His lips twitched as the quick glance he cast her clearly showed he would readily advocate for a very long walk that would take them as far away from the house as possible, and in the end, he did not scruple to put his reflections into words.

"Oh, plenty. 'Tis a very large park, after all. Sadly, any suggestions I might have are bound to try your father's patience," he added, sending her cheeks aflame with a fierce blush at the recollection of the instance that had prompted Mr Bennet's admonitions.

"Not to be encouraged, then," she remarked, and Darcy smiled wryly in response.

"Probably not, seeing as he is also an early riser."

"And so is Lady Catherine, on occasion," Elizabeth saw fit to remind him.

But Darcy shrugged.

"Not often, in my experience. Besides, something tells me that as of today, my aunt will grow vastly preoccupied with other matters."

"Oh?"

"Anne found a moment to share a confidence with me before she retired for the night. She and Mr Beaumont are engaged," Darcy elaborated, to Elizabeth's complete lack of surprise. She had long suspected the attachment, and on the previous day, as and when she could spare a thought for other people's concerns rather than her own, she had easily detected enough signs that indicated a happy resolution was in sight. "My aunt will be told later today," he finished by disclosing, and Elizabeth could not suppress a rueful chuckle.

"Poor Lady Catherine," she remarked. "Or should I say, poor Anne?"

"Poor Mr Beaumont, certainly," Darcy countered with a smile. "Still, he is a man of the cloth, so I imagine he will endure the upcoming weeks with Christian patience and composure. Which is more than—"

It was his tone of voice, rather than the truncated sentence, that made Elizabeth glance up towards him.

"Yes?" she softly prompted, only to see her companion tighten his lips and look away.

"Nothing," Darcy said quietly, and a sudden wave of tenderness welled in her at the strong suspicion that what he had refrained from saying was *'Which is more than I can say for myself.'*

A misty little smile tugged at the corner of her lips as Elizabeth inwardly disputed that opinion. He should give himself more credit. He had grown admirably patient of late – and just as admirably set on keeping his word and not rushing her with demands and expectations.

Many might have regarded the gesture as brazen and unmaidenly, but Elizabeth did not pause for very long to reflect upon such matters. A creature of impulse, she obeyed the one that urged her to reach out, seek his hand and clasp it, her fingers interlaced with his.

It was only a fraction of a second later, when his gaze was burning into hers, that it belatedly occurred to her she might have found a better setting for the reassuring overtures – the bluebell coppice, by way of example, rather than the Rosings shrubbery. She had no need to be told in so many words that, given enough privacy, he would not have kept his distance; nor that he was exceedingly hard-pressed to do so now.

She blinked under the overwhelming gaze that tampered with her senses as it easily evoked the gamut of emotions his kisses had already sparked in her. She grew light-headed – ludicrously so – at the mere recollection of the dizzying whirlwind of sensations, and she blinked again, at pains to decide if she was cowardly relieved or severely disappointed that, for now, the need for distance would keep it at bay.

'Disappointed. Oh, definitely disappointed,' she felt compelled to own, her cheeks blazing scarlet, when at last he dropped his gaze and they resumed walking hand in hand, his thumb tracing delectably disconcerting little circles on her palm.

ঌৰ৹ ৹ৰ৹

The house was still quiet when they eventually made their way within, which was more than a little fortunate, seeing as they would have been wise to return a little sooner. Nevertheless, the great hall was deserted, so Elizabeth had no reason to find fault with Mr Darcy for stroking her wrist when he escorted her to the bottom of the stairs and took his leave with a quiet, "I shall see you at breakfast," before she hastened up, the glow in her countenance a fairly good reflection of the glow in her heart.

The sound of footsteps rushing the other way was a trifle disquieting, yet when she reached the half-landing Elizabeth could see it was only Anne's lady's maid, rather than a more ominous presence. Still, the woman's mien was ominous enough, so Elizabeth was moved to ask, "Is there aught amiss? You seem troubled."

The woman gave a solemn nod.

"'Tis Miss Anne, ma'am. She is poorly. I have a mind to send for Dr Beaumont."

"Oh?" Elizabeth said, and before she could ask what ailed her stepsister, Darcy did so from below – he must have heard their quick exchange, however quiet.

"She is nauseous and feverish, and complains of great thirst and a severe headache," the lady's maid just as quietly told them. "Dr Beaumont should see her. And I had better rouse her ladyship."

"You think so?" Elizabeth doubtfully countered. "Lady Catherine will awaken soon enough. I can sit with Anne till then. But there is no harm in sending for Dr Beaumont."

"Indeed," Darcy agreed. "I will see to it myself."

"Do go back up to her, Mrs Evans," Elizabeth instructed the older woman. "I shall join you directly. There is something I should do first," she said and retraced her steps to the floor below without elaborating. "Mr Darcy?" she called softly, making him turn back from his avowed purpose of finding a footman and sending him to fetch the doctor.

He paused in the doorway with an expectant look, and Elizabeth approached him to clarify her meaning – or rather, judging by his countenance, to puzzle him exceedingly with an odd question:

"You would not know your way to the kitchens, would you? The stillroom, preferably."

A hint of a smile fluttered on his lips, and it went a long way towards suggesting he would be hard-pressed to locate the stillroom in his own home without assistance.

"I fear not. Why should you wish to know?"

"Our old housekeeper, Mrs Hill, had an excellent remedy for nausea. A fair quantity was brewed at Longbourn over the years for our benefit, mine and my sisters'. It was quite effective. With any luck and the right ingredients, I hope I can prepare some for Anne."

"You?" he asked in disbelief.

Elizabeth raised her brows at the stark proof that, to his way of thinking, ladies of good breeding had no business in the kitchens. She briefly pursed her lips, before delivering rather crisply:

"Unladylike as you might find it, I assure you I know my way around the stillroom and the pantry. I have prepared home remedies, pomatums and scented soaps, made preserves and baked more than a few sweet concoctions. I trust in due course you will recover from the shock of such disclosures, and bear them with tolerable equanimity."

Swift to note that he stood on quicksand, Mr Darcy had the good sense to act accordingly.

"Forgive me, I had no wish to imply—" He made to take her hand, but caught himself at the last moment. "Elizabeth, that was not my meaning. I am—" he faltered, visibly caught between the wish to voice some heartfelt entreaty, and the need to refrain from such revealing displays.

The rather endearing struggle could not fail to soften Elizabeth's displeasure as well as her manner.

"Come, sir. Let us find a footman. He should be able to assist us both," she mildly said with a wry grimace while Anne's lady's maid left them to go about their business and, as bid, hastened back to her mistress's bedchamber.

ᴄᴏᴇ ᴐᴀ

A footman was easily found. His training was impeccable, else he would not have lasted longer than a se'nnight in Lady Catherine's employ, so he did not bat an eyelid when instructed to escort Elizabeth into the hidden quarters of the house. He undertook to show her to the housekeeper's room, and then send someone to fetch Dr Beaumont.

When Elizabeth's intentions were made known to her, the housekeeper betrayed as much astonishment as Mr Darcy. She followed it, however, with little to no contrition, for after all the unexpected and – frankly – unwelcome visitor neither ruled her heart, nor was she the formidable lady of the manor.

Still, the fact that Elizabeth aimed to exert herself for Miss de Bourgh's benefit gained her admittance into the stillroom, as well as the housekeeper's assistance in locating the necessary ingredients. One of them could not be found. The soothing effects of dried lime tree flowers were unknown in the Rosings household, so the fragrant offerings were never gathered. Thus, Elizabeth was forced to make do. She pondered over a suitable replacement and she measured, brewed and stirred, hoping that a variant of dear old Mrs Hill's trusted remedy would be as effective as the original.

Once the herbs were infused to her satisfaction, Elizabeth filled a large teapot and placed it on a tray, along with a smaller pot of tea, cups and a few slices of sparsely buttered toast, and carefully took the tray up herself to Anne's bedchamber.

"I thank you, Evans," Elizabeth heard Anne say in a hoarse whisper as she came in. "Enough of that for now. I would rather have more water."

She cast Elizabeth a wan and half-apologetic smile while, obligingly, the lady's maid set aside the bowl and the cloth with which she had been dampening her mistress's flushed cheeks and brow, and stood to fill the glass on the nightstand. She brought it to Anne, who propped herself up and drank deeply, draining it.

"I have never seen such thirst," Anne whispered. "I would have another, but I fear I would not keep them down."

"Perhaps you would like to try some of this in a while," Elizabeth suggested, as she poured out a cup of the soothing beverage she had brewed.

"What is it?" Anne asked.

"An infusion of peppermint, lavender and camomile sweetened with honey. Our old housekeeper swears by it. She always claimed it works wonders for nausea, and in my experience, she was right. I tried to replicate it as best I could. I hope it brings you some relief."

Anne reached out and lightly stroked her sleeve.

"That is so kind, Lizzy. You need not have. I thank you. I shall try some, if only to please you. At the moment, my throat tells me to drink an entire barrel and my stomach warns it would not take another spoonful," she sought to jest, but her smile was weak, and her rasping voice barely audible. Nevertheless, she spoke again. "What wretched luck," she sighed. "This was not the time to come down with a fever. I had so much to do today."

"There is always the morrow," Elizabeth encouragingly said, but when she brushed Anne's hair off her brow and felt the burning heat of her skin, she could not help fearing that the illness might last a great deal longer than one day.

She took her stepsister's hand in hers and gently stroked it, as she urged Anne to rest. Yet Anne would not. She tossed and fretted, wishing her ailment away, but only making herself worse with the constant agitation. She asked for another glass of water, then drained a cup of Elizabeth's infusion. But, just as she had predicted, she could not hold quite so much liquid down and was violently sick in the bowl the efficient lady's maid promptly fetched for her.

Mrs Evans took the bowl away, and Elizabeth brought a fresh cloth for Anne to wipe her mouth, then she helped her suffering stepsister settle back as comfortably as possible against the pillows.

"And now I lost another dose of the medicine," Anne sighed. "There is not much left, the last bottle is all but empty. I want to take another spoonful and rid myself of this wretched cold, but I dare not, lest *that* happens again," she said with a vague gesture in the direction of the vanished bowl.

"Rest a little, then take it. All well and good if you can keep it down, but do not fret if not. Dr Beaumont is sure to bring another bottle, or he could send some later," Elizabeth sought to reassure her.

Anne cast her another pallid smile, and in due course followed her advice. For all the tormenting thirst, she did not dare drink a full glass of water, but sipped some of it, then ventured to take another dose of medicine.

To her moderate relief, she kept it down this time, although nausea still threatened. She took long, deep breaths, in an endeavour to subdue it, and also still the wild beatings of her heart.

It made little difference. She sighed and closed her eyes, her lips curling upwards of their own volition when her betrothed's image was easily conjured up – a source of joy, and her greatest comfort. If Henry came to call with his father, perhaps she could still see him that day. Evans and Elizabeth would help her dress. All she had to do was summon the strength to stand and walk into the sitting room. And also the strength to prevail over her mother's protestations, which were bound to come.

Surely, the strength could be summoned. It must be. Perhaps she would be able to summon it that much sooner if she could rest a little, Anne told herself, but it was easier said than done.

Her unquiet mind refused to lapse into the torpor that steadily claimed her fatigued body, and disjointed thoughts and images kept chasing each other in her head. Yet, with firm determination, Anne willed her breathing to slow down, and was somewhat reassured when it obeyed her. With any luck, her racing heart and restless mind would obey too.

⚬ৎ৩ ৩ৎ⚬

"What is it, Jenny?" Mrs Evans whispered when a young maid tentatively came into her mistress's bedchamber. The lady's maid stood from her place by the bed to meet the girl at the door. "Keep your voice down," she instructed, and Elizabeth could not fail to inwardly agree.

They should not wake her, she determined, filled with compassion at the sight of the frail form tossing under the bedcovers.

"I am come to give you this," the maid said, producing a small, dark-coloured bottle from the pocket of her apron. "The doctor's maid's just brought it. Said she were told to fetch the old 'un back."

"When is he coming?" Elizabeth asked from the bedside, in just as quiet whispers.

"Who, ma'am?"

"Dr Beaumont."

The girl shrugged.

"Dunno. His maid didn't say. She just asked me to take this one up an' bring back the old 'un."

"Which old one?" Mrs Evans impatiently asked.

"The medicine Dr Beaumont mixed for Miss de Bourgh yesterday. She said it won't do all it's meant to, for he'd left out some root or another. Black hellebore, it sounded like, whatever that might be."

Mrs Evans gave a little wave signalling vexation.

"Well, you can tell her that Miss de Bourgh has emptied that bottle now, useless or not. I hope Dr Beaumont had taken better care with this one, and that it does its office. Ask her to hasten her master along, will you?"

"I'll be sure to, right away," the girl said, bobbing a swift curtsy, and left to do as bid.

The lady's maid closed the door behind her and allowed herself the liberty of exchanging a look of exasperation with Elizabeth as she returned to the bedside.

"What should we do now, ma'am? Wake her for a dose of the proper stuff?"

Pursing her lips, Elizabeth pondered, concerned in no small measure by Anne's exceedingly heightened colour and the incoherent murmurs escaping her parched lips. She dearly hoped that, forgetful as he might be, Dr Beaumont would be of some assistance, and that he was not long in coming.

"Pray hand me the wet cloth," she asked the other, once she had come to a decision. "If I run it over her face to cool her, perhaps it will also serve to rouse her. That is, if she is ready to awaken. If not, we might let her doze for a little longer." And she would do well to rouse Lady Catherine too, and let her know that her daughter was unwell, Elizabeth told herself as she took the dampened cloth from the older woman and applied herself to the appointed task.

The gentle ministrations had no effect in waking Anne; but when the door swung open under a decisive hand, Elizabeth discovered she need not concern herself with waking Lady Catherine.

"Why was I not told that Anne was poorly? Must I hear it from a footman?" her ladyship rasped as she came in.

Elizabeth stood and forbore to instruct her overbearing stepmother to keep her voice down. Instead, she said:

"I thought I should sit with her till you awakened, ma'am, and that you might need your rest."

"When I need rest, I shall be sure to tell you," Lady Catherine retorted, lowering her voice of her own accord when she saw that her daughter was asleep. "But I suppose I should thank you for looking after her," she grudgingly added.

"Not at all. Think nothing of it," Elizabeth replied, and moved aside to make room for Lady Catherine, who came to take her seat on the edge of Anne's bed.

"When was Beaumont summoned?"

"The best part of an hour ago, your ladyship," Mrs Evans spoke up. "Mr Darcy undertook to send for him when he returned from his early morning walk with Miss Elizabeth."

Elizabeth's shoulders stiffened. She sought to smooth her countenance into an even mien when, as expected, Lady Catherine's baleful glare was settled on her.

"Is that so? What business had you to go for an early morning walk with my nephew?"

"No business as such, ma'am. He must have also found it a fine morning for a walk," Elizabeth replied blandly, adding a shrug to the show of nonchalance.

It was Anne who unwittingly saved her from Lady Catherine's further probing. She stirred and thrashed, then seemed to awaken, her countenance twisting into signs that Mrs Evans easily recognised.

The lady's maid barely had the time to fetch the necessary bowl before Anne voided her stomach.

"Why is that wretched fool not here yet?" Lady Catherine fulminated *sotto voce*. "Go and keep watch for him and send him in the moment he arrives," she ordered Elizabeth, perforce compelled to leave remonstrations about morning walks for later.

Too concerned over Anne's ill-health to rejoice in the escape, Elizabeth left the room and made her way towards the staircase, only to find Kitty coming out of the bedchamber that she shared with Lydia, her mien inordinately gleeful.

"Oh, Lizzy," Kitty burst out in quiet whispers. "What a grand scene you have missed. And Lydia too. She was so cross that she dallied above-stairs and deprived herself of such sterling entertainment."

"What grand scene?" Elizabeth asked.

Kitty came to clasp her arm and draw her to a spot where she might share her tale at leisure.

"Come into our chamber and I will tell you all about it."

"I cannot, dearest," Elizabeth replied, shaking her head. "I must rush down and—"

"It will only take a moment. But I imagine I can tell you here," Kitty said with a careless gesture that encompassed the empty corridor. "No one should mind. Lady Catherine was positively marvellous in her fit of fury. You *must* hear this, Lizzy! You will never believe it: at long last, Miss Bingley was upbraided just as she deserves," Kitty chortled.

Despite herself, Elizabeth's eyes widened.

"How?" she could not help asking, and Kitty was all too glad to enlighten her.

"She came to call with her brother and the Hursts this morning, and finished by being unceremoniously driven out. Lady Catherine told her butler that never again is he to admit any of them into her house. But let me start from the beginning. Our stepmamma was not best-pleased to have her breakfast interrupted, especially when she learned that the offending callers were the very trade-tainted folk she had raved against two days ago. She sternly reprimanded Mr Bingley for not heeding her request to keep his relations from her doorstep, and by the bye, I felt for him. He looked beet-red and exceedingly uneasy. I am prepared to wager he did try to keep them away, but would they listen? And then—"

Immoderate yet necessarily quiet laughter cut the flow of her disclosures, threatening to choke her, but Kitty valiantly conquered it at last, so that she could continue.

"Oh, you should have seen Miss Bingley's face when she found herself pilloried as an impertinent *nouveau riche* barging in where she was not wanted. And then she made the capital error of asking Mr Darcy to champion her. She verily clung to his arm and asked him to defend the sincerity of her intentions to his aunt, in the name of their longstanding connection. That might have been innocent enough, but you know that she is constitutionally unable to speak to him – glance at him, even – without pouting and flirting and batting her eyelashes like some besotted damsel. Red flag to the bull, I tell you," Kitty choked out, in another silent fit of giggles. "Lady Catherine turned an interesting shade of puce and demanded that Miss Bingley cease importuning her daughter's betrothed in such a shameless manner. *'Betrothed?'* Miss Bingley could not fail to cry – well, screech, rather – and then Mr Darcy was—"

Much as Elizabeth sympathised with that gentleman in what must have been severe discomfort, and much as she would have liked to know how he had fared at that mortifying time, she was suddenly reminded of the far more serious matter that should claim all her attention when she heard quick footsteps and turned around to find Mrs Evans hastening along the corridor, her countenance betraying distress bordering on fear. The same sentiments beset her too, and Elizabeth gasped, "Is she worse?"

"Yes," the lady's maid confirmed, censure in her eyes at finding Elizabeth chatting to her sister rather than continuing on her errand, as if by keeping watch for the good doctor Elizabeth could have summoned him by dint of will.

"Who is worse?" Kitty wished to know.

"Anne," came Elizabeth's brief reply.

"So this is why Lady Catherine rushed above-stairs when Thomas came to speak to her?"

"Most likely," Elizabeth said just as tersely, and this time with an impatient grimace, before glancing back towards Mrs Evans.

"Worse, how?"

"What ails her?" Kitty asked, at almost the same time.

"She is raving now – speaks of seeing things that are not there."

"Raving?" Kitty cried.

"Hush," Elizabeth admonished her. "What can we do?" she asked the older woman.

"Pray that Dr Beaumont comes soon. And we should try to cool her with crushed ice or some such. Another messenger should be sent to the physician. Lady Catherine wishes it, in case the first one is dawdling with a sprained ankle and I know not what."

"I will go down to tell them," Elizabeth offered. "And let them know about the ice as well."

With hurried thanks, Mrs Evans was swift to retrace her steps, and Elizabeth hastened below-stairs with Kitty on her heels wishing to know more about Anne's condition.

There was little that Elizabeth could tell her. Likewise, there was little she could tell Mr Darcy and her father, when the sound of her breathless voice relaying Lady Catherine's instructions to a waiting footman brought them out of the drawing room.

This was not the time to warn Mr Darcy about Mrs Evans accidentally mentioning their morning walk to Lady Catherine, and besides Anne's severe ill-health was a far more serious concern.

Jane seemed to share those views and was ready to set her own concerns aside when she returned to the house a few moments later and learned the reason for their troubled countenances.

"Is Bingley well?" Mr Darcy asked her as soon as Elizabeth had finished imparting everything she knew about Anne's illness.

Jane cast him the shadow of a smile.

"Reasonably so, I thank you. He has just left, muttering about procuring a special licence and confining his sisters to the dungeons."

"Did he, now? How singularly bold of him," Mr Bennet said. "I assume you heard about the little fracas we had earlier, Lizzy."

"Yes, Papa, I told her," Kitty piped up.

"The special licence might not be such a bad notion," Mr Darcy observed, and most civilly refrained to comment on dungeons.

"Indeed," Jane agreed. "But never mind that now. What of Anne?"

Elizabeth frowned.

"We are waiting for Dr Beaumont. And for ice. I had better go and see if it was brought up. Lady Catherine and Mrs Evans might need some assistance."

The others nodded, and Elizabeth was not surprised when they chose to come up as well. Mr Bennet bade Kitty return to Lydia, lest his youngest might grow impatient for company, and when she most reluctantly obeyed and left them, Mr Darcy led the way into Anne's sitting room.

Elizabeth went to tap lightly on the door that gave onto Anne's bedchamber, and Mrs Evans came to let her in, along with Jane.

Little had changed in the sickroom in her absence. Her stepsister was still in a fitful sleep, and Lady Catherine was still looking like thunder.

"No sign of Beaumont yet?" her ladyship hissed.

"No, ma'am," Elizabeth told her.

Lady Catherine threw her arms up in the air, then clasped her hands before her and resumed pacing at the foot of the bed.

"How dare he absent himself when he is needed? And Mrs Jenkinson too. She had no business to leave Kent!"

None of those present saw any wisdom whatsoever in pointing out to her irate ladyship that it was she who had granted Mrs Jenkinson permission to quit her post for a few days. In defence of a long-suffering comrade, Mrs Evans only said, "Her sister is severely ill, ma'am," but upon reflection even that mild reminder should have remained unuttered, for Lady Catherine scowled.

"Yes, well, so is my daughter. 'Tis Anne she is paid to look after, not some sister," she unfairly and uncharitably spat. "And where is that ice? Pray tell me the bungling dunces have not gone all the way to the icehouse to fetch it!"

"They must be still at work crushing it," Jane opined, and Mrs Evans nodded.

"That might be so. Let me go hurry them along."

At Lady Catherine's impatient nod, the lady's maid left the room by the servants' door. But she must have promptly come across the very ones she was seeking, for Mrs Evans did not tarry long in the labyrinth of concealed passages devised so that countless souls could scurry unseen hither and thither, and tend to the whims and needs of their betters.

When Mrs Evans stepped back into her mistress's bedchamber, there were two young maids on her heels, each carrying a large bowl of crushed ice.

The goggle-eyed girls were swiftly sent away and, quietly efficient, Mrs Evans, Elizabeth and Jane took to wrapping handfuls of ice fragments in clean cloths, then placing the cooling bundles on Anne's brow, on her parched and still incoherently murmuring lips, and running them along her limbs, carefully wiping off the excess of water as the ice gradually melted from the profuse heat of the patient's skin.

Dr Beaumont found them thus employed some time later, when he came in to be greeted by the lady of the house with a fierce, "At last! Where on *earth* have you been?"

"My deepest apologies, your ladyship," Dr Beaumont gasped, panting from the exertion, his florid countenance more flushed than ever. "I was from home. What has befallen Miss de Bourgh?"

"She came in much fatigued after an overlong outing yesterday," Lady Catherine informed him, glaring at Elizabeth and Jane as a sign that they were amongst those whom she held responsible for the outing and the length of it. "The morning found her nauseous and exceedingly feverish. And now, as you can see, the fever has rendered her insensible and delirious. What can you do to set her to rights?"

"That remains to be seen, ma'am," Dr Beaumont cautiously said as he set his leather bag on a chair by the bedside and reached for the patient's wrist to feel her pulse.

Anne's three attendants moved away to make room for the physician and, along with Lady Catherine, stood watching him, only to see Dr Beaumont's mien clouding with concern as he shook his head. This could neither please nor encourage Lady Catherine.

"Be sure to settle what is to be done and get to it as soon as may be," she demanded.

Dr Beaumont nodded.

"Of course, ma'am. Once I have ascertained what ails her."

He placed the back of his hand upon Anne's brow, opened her mouth to peer at her tongue, examined the whites of her eyes, tapped and prodded, then straightened up at last.

"She must be bled, of course, to reduce the heat of the body and relieve the strain on her heart. Then she must take plenty of diluting fluids—"

"But she cannot keep anything down, sir," Mrs Evans intervened. "She was violently sick a couple of times already."

"We must persist, there is nothing for it. We must persist with the greatest diligence. And I shall prepare a cooling draught. Her fever is a great deal too high for my liking," the physician said as he bent over his patient to explore the heat of her brow again.

His deep voice, in such close proximity, somehow reached Anne in her stupor with an inflexion she must have found familiar, for suddenly her eyes opened wide into a fixed stare, and her chapped lips curled into the semblance of a smile. She stirred, reached blindly and finding Dr Beaumont's hand, she clasped it into a tight grip.

"You are here at last... Thank goodness... Were you in our meadow? That dear place... I wish to go there today... See Mamma first... Where is Mamma? I wish to see her... then our meadow..."

"Here, Anne. I am here," Lady Catherine said swiftly, her voice strangely hoarse, but Anne did not seem to hear her as she stared at Dr Beaumont.

For his part, Dr Beaumont stared back.

"Soon, dear girl. Aye, soon," he soothingly said to his patient, but his tones had a very different ring when he spoke again. "Pray step aside, your ladyship," he requested, and, supremely indifferent to Lady Catherine's indignant splutter, he continued, just as firmly. "I must have more light. Those curtains – pull them back," he told Mrs Evans, "and let the sunlight in. Let me see..." he muttered, as he disentangled Anne's fingers from around his wrist despite her incoherent protests, and went to rummage in his leather bag.

He produced a small mirror and returned to his patient.

"Raise her head," he asked the lady's maid, and when Mrs Evans promptly did as bid, Dr Beaumont reached to gently push back Anne's right eyelid and, deftly catching a ray of sunlight in his mirror, he sent it shining back into her fixed pupil. The uneven patch of light flickered to and fro and Anne sought to blink, but the physician persisted, before moving the mirror into his other hand and examining her left eye in the same manner.

"You can let her lie down now," he instructed Mrs Evans, and recommended to inspect Anne's countenance, her mouth, her pulse, her skin.

"It fits," he muttered to himself after a while. "Aye, it fits, by Jove."

"What fits? Speak, man!" Lady Catherine commanded, and at that Dr Beaumont released Anne's hand, let it rest upon the covers and looked up at her ladyship.

"Aye. We must speak. But firstly, would you trust Mrs Evans with your daughter's life?" he ominously asked.

Lady Catherine's brow furrowed.

"What sort of a question is that?"

"A plain one, ma'am. Is Mrs Evans to be trusted?" he asked again, taking no notice of the lady's maid injured and silently outraged look, as if she were not party to that conversation.

Lady Catherine pursed her lips.

"She has tended to Anne for the best part of ten years. If Evans cannot be trusted to ensure my daughter's welfare, then I do not know who can," she said crisply, only to receive a warm "I thank you, ma'am," from the woman in question.

"Very well," Dr Beaumont said, bowing to her opinion, then turned to the lady's maid: "Pray forgive me, Mrs Evans, but foul times require foul questions. I have every reason to believe Miss Anne was poisoned. With the juice of the deadly nightshade, to be precise."

Chapter 31

Rosings, 19 April 1812

Dr Beaumont's pronouncement was met with a chorus of shocked gasps. Lady Catherine found her voice sooner than all the others. Formidable in her horror and fury, she still kept her voice low when she echoed in a ferocious hiss:

"*Poisoned*, you say? By whom?"

"This is what we must ascertain, and promptly."

"Aye!" Lady Catherine agreed with fierce determination. "But what of Anne? Will she be well?" she asked, with no effort at concealing her acute anxiety.

Dr Beaumont's stern countenance mellowed into compassion.

"I fear 'tis much too soon to tell, ma'am. Many forces are at play. The amount of poison she has ingested, the amount that was eliminated, her physical strength…"

His voice trailed off and Lady Catherine winced. They both knew that physical strength was not something Anne could boast of.

"The first day – indeed, the first hours are crucial. We will see the ground we stand upon in a few hours' time. The poison must be eliminated with strong emetics, or clysters if need be. I shall not waste time in returning home to mix a preparation. The apothecary in Hunsford village can send the ingredients, and I will blend them in your stillroom, if I may."

"Naturally," Lady Catherine granted permission with an impatient wave of her hand.

"Very well. And in the interim, Mrs Evans, pray procure a long feather."

The lady's maid's eyes widened.

"A long feather, sir?"

"Aye. To coax your mistress into emptying her stomach. Tickling the back of the throat is a crude method, I grant you, but effective until an emetic can be had," Dr Beaumont said, then reached for the half-full carafe, sniffed, poured a few drops into his hollowed palm, drank, and added, "If she should complain of a severe thirst, and well she might, let her have nothing but this. Small sips, mind. Now, let me write to the apothecary at once. Where might I find pen and paper?"

"Over here, sir," Elizabeth found her voice at last, and indicated the door into Anne's sitting room.

With a curt nod, Dr Beaumont strode out of the bedchamber.

ஒ௦ ௦ஒ

"Poisoned?" Mr Bennet and Mr Darcy chorused, as shocked as the others, when Dr Beaumont's diagnosis was made known to them as well.

"Aye. With nightshade," the physician darkly confirmed as he appended his signature at the bottom of the note to the apothecary and proceeded to fold and seal it. "All the signs are there. The skin, dry and hot, giving the appearance of a severe fever. Very dry mouth. Fast and erratic heartbeats. Slow breathing, delirium, severe nausea. And above all, the vastly enlarged pupils that fail to shrink when exposed to bright light. What of that feather, Mrs Evans?" he called towards the open door leading into Anne's bedchamber.

"I sent word to the kitchens, sir," came the quiet reply.

"Very well. Pray have this conveyed to the apothecary at once, ma'am," he asked Lady Catherine, when the note was duly sealed.

"Allow me," Jane said, and Lady Catherine gave her a nod of appreciation.

"Come to think of it," Dr Beaumont suddenly reconsidered, "I should go hand this to a footman myself. There is another message I should send."

"What message, sir, and to whom? I could send that one also," Jane offered.

Given Dr Beaumont's gentle response to Anne's ravings about her dear meadow, Elizabeth felt she could consider him fairly well informed about her stepsister's secret affairs of the heart, and readily surmised that the physician's other message was meant for his son.

Her supposition received some confirmation when Dr Beaumont grew evasive in response to Jane's offer:

"'Tis a verbal message, and I had better supply proper directions. Pray excuse me," he said, and was gone.

Predictably, spirits ran high in the small room that he had just quitted. His countenance set in harsh lines, Darcy declared:

"This cannot go unpunished. Evil must be rooted out, lest it strikes again."

"Aye," the others chorused in agreement, Lady Catherine louder than them all.

"This is a matter for our wits," she enunciated through tight lips. "You should involve Fitzwilliam. His military head must count for something. And the parish constable, for what he is worth. Lord Metcalfe is Justice of the Peace for these parts, and he will support me in everything. The full force of the law must be brought into play. I want the culprits found, and I want them to hang," she said with quiet ferocity.

"You are not the only one," her nephew assured her, bringing a grim ghost of a smile to Lady Catherine's lips. "We must ascertain what Anne has taken, and when. It could not have been at dinner. No one else was affected. The poison could have only been in whatever Anne had consumed overnight and this morning. Can anyone tell exactly what it was?"

Elizabeth frowned, seeking to remember.

"Just water, to the best of my knowledge. But Dr Beaumont has just declared that the water in her carafe was safe. And the same must be said of his tonic and—"

She was not suffered to finish. From the doorway into Anne's bedchamber, Mrs Evans fixed her with a steady glare and her voice came in a rough whisper:

"What of *your* much-lauded remedy?"

Elizabeth stared back.

"What of it? Surely you are not suggesting I brewed the juice of the deadly nightshade into it?" she said, with a disbelieving laugh.

"Will you have us think that Dr Beaumont mixed it into his preparations?" the other sneered, her voice low and hard. "I will tell you this, and swear to it at the Assizes: my sweet lady has had naught but water, the doctor's tonic and your *'tea'* – and she was violently sick once she had drunk it."

"Nonsense, woman," Mr Bennet spluttered, speaking over Darcy, who snapped, "That is preposterous!"

Her eyes narrowed into slits, Lady Catherine rounded on Elizabeth.

"*You? You* are responsible for poisoning *my* daughter? Oh, I see your game at last," she hissed in a cold rage, undeterred by the protestations coming from all the other people in the room except Mrs Evans. "I see it now, so very clearly. Your morning walk with Darcy, your missish simpering and all those glances, I see their meaning now. You aim to usurp Anne's place!" she cried, her voice raising to the acutest pitch as she shaped her long fingers into claws.

"Madam, pray see sense. You cannot possibly imagine that my daughter would seek to poison yours," Mr Bennet sternly intervened, gesturing towards Jane and Darcy to indicate that they should hold their peace.

Their features tightened into grim masks, they struggled to obey. Darcy also seemed to struggle with subduing the impulse to come and stand beside Elizabeth, just as Jane had, and wrap a protective arm around her shoulders. Provoking his elderly relation in like manner, at that point in time, would scarcely help matters. Yet he still came forth to stand between them.

"Lady Catherine, this is unsound," he firmly said.

"And you would know," his aunt sneered.

"I would."

"How? Did you see that potion brewed?"

"No. But it makes no difference."

With a soft glance towards him, which only served to send Lady Catherine's nostrils flaring, Elizabeth sensibly argued:

"It was brewed in your own stillroom, ma'am, in your housekeeper's presence, from ingredients she supplied. 'Tis Mrs Hill's remedy, Papa," she explained.

Mr Bennet snorted.

"A harmless tisane, madam."

"Is it?" Lady Catherine shot back. "Evans, that tray, if you please," she commanded with nary a glance towards her daughter's lady's maid, who hastened to obey.

The tray was duly brought and placed on the table. Without another word, Lady Catherine stepped forth, took an empty cup and filled it to the brim.

"If it is harmless, sir, then drink it," she hissed at her second husband, encompassing both him and Elizabeth in her glare.

Mr Bennet's eyes crinkled with rueful amusement.

"Appointed as the queen's cupbearer, am I? So be it. Lizzy, my child, has this brew left your sight at any time?"

"Only when I came down to ask for ice, Papa. But Lady Catherine and Mrs Evans remained in Anne's bedchamber."

"Hm. One might safely assume they had no wish to poison her either," Mr Bennet said, and reached for the concoction poured out for him.

"A moment, sir," Darcy intervened, and with a firm hand raised the teapot and filled another cup.

Mr Bennet smiled. Lady Catherine glowered.

"What the blazes are you doing, Darcy? I will not have you knowingly expose yourself to danger. Set that cup down this instant," her ladyship commanded when she saw him lifting it.

"Yet you are not concerned for my safety, madam?" Mr Bennet asked. "I will own, that cuts me to the quick."

"Oh, I should have never married *you*," his lady viciously spat. "Anne is now paying for my folly, and I can only pray she will not pay with her life. But you, Nephew? What has come upon you? My daughter lies there struggling, and you are prepared to do *this* in defence of a brazen hussy? Lord above, she has truly sunk her talons into you! But pray do not tell me you have completely lost your reason."

"Not my reason, no," Darcy evenly replied, and the glance he settled on Elizabeth told her once more that he would not say the same about his heart.

The warmth meant for her gave way to a companionable glint when his eyes flicked towards Mr Bennet. The older gentleman mirrored it as he raised his own teacup.

"Wassail, m'boy," Mr Bennet toasted the health of his favourite daughter's suitor in Old Norse fashion, and they both drained their full cups in one draught.

Elizabeth's eyes shone with unshed tears when her gaze drew Darcy's yet again.

"That was the noblest and most foolish thing you could have done," she whispered. "You had no certainties."

"Oh, I beg to differ," he quietly replied.

"I will not tolerate this abomination," Lady Catherine burst out with renewed fury in response to their exchange, but Elizabeth paid her no heed, and could only tear her gaze from Darcy's when her father chortled softly:

"What, no such thanks for me, Lizzy? So much for filial gratitude and devotion."

"Oh, Papa," Elizabeth said, excusing herself with a little smile from her sister's supportive half-embrace and advancing to clasp her father's arm.

Mr Bennet patted her hand, then glanced at his wife.

"So, madam, will you have me empty that teapot to demonstrate that the tisane is perfectly safe and Elizabeth is owed a profuse apology?"

"'Tis too soon to tell," her ladyship hissed, tossing her head back.

"I see. Pray feel free to wait and examine my pupils whenever it suits you. I assure you, I am hale and hearty and not in the least nauseous. What of you, Darcy?"

"Likewise, sir," the other said.

"There you go, madam. You need not have harboured any fears for your nephew's safety. He is not about to void his stomach either."

"I should not care if he does," Lady Catherine sneered. "If this is all the regard he has for Anne and her suffering, he should experience it too."

"Speaking of which, should you not tend to your daughter, instead of harassing mine?" Mr Bennet suggested. "What news on that long feather, Mrs Evans? Perchance Darcy here might also wish to use one. What say you, young man? Are you in need of a very long feather?"

"Come, Papa. Leave be. This is not the time," Elizabeth entreated softly, with a vague gesture towards the adjoining chamber to indicate that she would like him to bring resentful sarcasm to an end not in deference to Lady Catherine, but to Anne.

Mr Bennet patted her hand once more.

"Of course. You are in the right, my dear. So I shall, for now. But your stepmother and Mrs Evans should bear in mind you *are* owed a proper apology."

Mrs Evans was the only one who had the grace to look slightly abashed. Yet she insisted:

"Nevertheless, Miss Anne has had nothing but that brew, clear water, and Dr Beaumont's draughts. What should we blame this on, if not the tisane?"

Her question hung in the air as all her companions but one stared at each other, at a loss for a plausible answer. Lady Catherine scowled.

"I maintain 'tis too soon to say that the tisane is safe."

Mr Bennet grimaced in acute vexation.

"Then you had better ask Dr Beaumont how long we need to wait. But when you do, make sure to ask if he has not been careless with his ingredients."

"Nonsense," Lady Catherine scoffed. "He has been tending to Anne's health for as long as I can remember."

But Mrs Evans' countenance grew troubled, and when Elizabeth darted a pensive glance towards her, the lady's maid held it for a few long moments, rather than looking away with hostile disdain, before she felt compelled to contradict the formidable lady of the house.

"Oh, madam," she gasped, "but it turns out he has been careless afore. I – Miss Elizabeth and I – have it from his maid."

"What do you mean, careless?" Lady Catherine snapped.

"His maid said this morning that he had forgotten to add some root or another—"

"Black hellebore," Elizabeth supplied.

"Aye, that," Mrs Evans corroborated, the pair of them finally in some sort of agreement. "The woman sent word up with one of our girls, to say that the medicine he had prepared yesterday might not work all that well, and he supplied a different batch."

Lady Catherine frowned.

"Forgetting a root is not the same as adding poison," she argued.

"Aye, ma'am. But what if it was added in error? Given his age and everything?"

"He has no business to store the deadly nightshade with his medicinal ingredients," Lady Catherine declared.

"Pray tell me, madam, have you perchance learned the apothecaries' skill? Or the physicians'?" Mr Bennet pierced her with his own poisoned dart.

"Spare me your witticisms, sir. Anyone knows that physicians and apothecaries do not dispense poisons."

"Anyone with a grain of sense knows that they *do*," Mr Bennet countered, "and what is cure to some is poison to others. Pray go in search of Dr Beaumont, Lizzy. To my way of thinking, he has tarried too long below-stairs, and 'tis high time we had another word with him."

⚬ღ ღ⚬

Elizabeth's errand was easily completed. When she went in search of Dr Beaumont, she found him coming up the stairs. She did not ask him any questions on the way, and sensibly chose to leave that office to her father. Yet when Dr Beaumont was readmitted into Anne's sitting room, it was Lady Catherine who hastened to address him.

"I hope you can assist us with our experiment, sir."

Dr Beaumont's countenance took an air of impatient surprise.

"Now, ma'am? I should see to Miss Anne. How is she?"

"No change," Lady Catherine said grimly.

"Was a feather procured?"

"Evans has gone to the kitchens to see what is keeping them. Now, our little experiment, sir: my husband and my nephew have just sampled this tisane," she said, a curl in her lip, "to see if that was where the poison was concealed—"

"That was very foolish," the physician interjected, casting a severe glance from one gentleman to the other. "And an unnecessary risk, moreover. You only had to ask me."

"How can you tell?"

Dr Beaumont sighed in some exasperation.

"The juice of the nightshade berry has a distinctive bitter-sweetness and an equally distinctive acrid and rather nauseating smell. If it is added to food or to a beverage in enough quantity to harm, either the taste or the smell or both can be detected by one trained in such matters. I flatter myself I could have easily told you if the tisane was safe or not."

"Pray tell us now," Lady Catherine requested.

"Very well. Although I imagine that by now the gentlemen might also be able to enlighten you. Any dryness of the mouth? Dizziness? Blurred vision?" he asked, his glance darting back and forth between the two possible patients. "I see," Dr Beaumont said when those questioned shook their heads. He turned to examine the smell and taste of the brew in the teapot in the same manner in which he had investigated the water in Anne's carafe. Then he shrugged. "No wonder you have none of the symptoms. This is perfectly harmless. Peppermint and lavender."

"And camomile," Elizabeth quietly supplied.

Whether or not Mr Bennet might have been moved to gloat and his wife to scowl was destined to remain undecided. Sounds coming from the sickroom told them that Mrs Evans had procured the feather and had rather successfully made use of it.

"Excuse me. I should be with Miss Anne," Dr Beaumont said.

For the first time that morning, Lady Catherine showed herself in perfect concord with her second husband when Mr Bennet halted the physician's progress with a hand on his arm and a stern, "Nay, sir. I think you had better wait."

⁂

"I *beg* your pardon?" Dr Beaumont spluttered, vastly affronted, when Mr Bennet smoothly put it to him that once the water in the carafe and the herbal infusion were deemed safe, it was the medicinal draughts that remained under consideration, for Anne had taken nothing else over the last twelve hours. "There is naught amiss with my draughts!" he forcefully declared, his indignant breaths rushing in and out as loudly as the air in a smithy's bellows. With what seemed to be a considerable effort, he sought to subdue both his breathing and his temper, before finally resuming in a semblance of restraint, "We are but superficially acquainted, sir, so I shall let that pass. As I said to Mrs Evans earlier, foul times require foul questions. I will concede that you would wish to leave no stone unturned. Very well. There is an easy way to settle this. Pray show me the potion Miss Anne has taken."

But his eyes grew flinty when he could not fail to note their looks of doubt. His voice was also as hard as flint when he spoke again.

"Should you see no merit in appointing me judge and jury in my own case," he enunciated, "I give you my word as a Christian and a gentleman that I value Miss Anne's welfare above my own, and you will hear nothing but the truth from me."

Lady Catherine exchanged quick glances with her husband and her nephew. The earlier acrimony notwithstanding, in this new conundrum theirs were the sharpest wits at hand. The wordless exchange served its purpose. She straightened her shoulders and made her way into the adjoining room.

"How is she, Evans?" the others could hear her asking.

With equal ease, they heard the sorrowful reply:

"Still feverish and insensible, ma'am. But she has voided her stomach and drank half a glass of water."

"That is as it should be," Dr Beaumont muttered to himself, obliged to be content with treating from a distance, since he was currently kept from his patient's room.

"Are these the draughts she took?" Lady Catherine asked.

"Aye, ma'am. That near-empty bottle."

Six pairs of eyes settled upon Dr Beaumont when Lady Catherine returned to the sitting room and handed him the dark-coloured receptacle. Even the lady's maid had come to watch from the doorway. They saw him remove the stopper. They saw him sniff and taste what was left of the contents. And then they saw him blanch.

No clamour of outraged voices rose around him, but their mien spoke volumes, just as Dr Beaumont's did.

"Did *you* taint it?" Lady Catherine hissed.

"As God is my witness, I did not!" the other fervently shot back.

"Neither on purpose, nor in error?" she insisted, her eyes burning into his as if they were endeavouring to blaze their way into his soul.

"The oath I took forbids the first. My conscience, the latter. I would never imperil a patient through either malice or negligence. Least of all Miss Anne," Dr Beaumont said with some sternness.

Lady Catherine's tone readily conveyed the same emotion.

"So you say," she retorted crisply. "Your draughts should be above suspicion after all these years, but I hear you are not always as free of error as you claim."

Dr Beaumont's back stiffened.

"What did you hear, your ladyship?"

"Tell him, Evans," Lady Catherine ordered.

For her part, Elizabeth was rather glad of her stepmother's enduring ill-will, if it meant she was not the one asked to heap accusations upon the very man who had declared her potion harmless and had absolved her of all blame. But just as she was seeking to set aside such considerations, which must pale before Anne's safety, Dr Beaumont snapped:

"What is this, servants' gossip?"

"If it is, Miss Elizabeth can corroborate it. She heard the report as well," Mrs Evans stubbornly said, not laggard now in enlisting Elizabeth's assistance.

"What report?" the physician asked, spinning around to face Elizabeth instead.

Gratifyingly quick to grasp her reluctance to point an accusing finger at another, Mr Darcy intervened:

"We have dealt in hearsay all morning. I suggest we apply to the source."

"What do you recommend?" Mr Bennet asked. "Or rather, whom?"

"Dr Beaumont's maid who came this morning, if she is still in the servants' hall. If she is not, we should begin with the girl who came up with her message."

"Let them be summoned," Mr Bennet agreed.

"My maid? Which one?" Dr Beaumont asked.

"I confess myself unacquainted with your domestic arrangements and the names of your servants," Mr Bennet replied, as Darcy went to tug the cord.

"What is her tale, then?" the physician insisted. "I would prefer to hear the gist of it sooner rather than later."

"Very well," Mr Bennet said, as astute as Darcy in perceiving Elizabeth's unease and willingly stepping into the breach. "From what I gathered, your maid claimed you forgot to add black hellebore root to the draught. 'Tis not wholly unreasonable to think that something else might have gone into the admixture in its stead."

"What nonsense is this? I did not forget to add anything," the incensed physician protested. "And what fool would confuse black hellebore root with nightshade berries?" he scoffed.

"True," Mr Bennet conceded, an edge to his voice. "But a root might look much the same as another. And country folk claim that every part of the nightshade plant is deadly: berries, leaves *and* roots."

"Is that an accusation, sir?" the physician asked, his tone gravelly and his mien dark.

Mr Bennet met his grim stare squarely.

"The accusing voice is your maid's, not mine."

"Let us fetch her, then," Dr Beaumont said, a challenging glint in his eyes, "and have her repeat her absurd claims to my face."

"She will be fetched," Lady Catherine said, very tersely. "But in the interim, you had better tell me why you saw fit to supply a different batch this morning. You send a new bottle every week, not every day."

"I did *not* send a bottle this morning," the physician declared with great emphasis.

"But I have it here," Mrs Evans argued, darting into her mistress's bedchamber only for long enough to retrieve the other bottle and return with it, held high.

"Let me see that," Dr Beaumont ordered, and was not gainsaid.

He examined the contents with as much care, and in the end pronounced, "This contains nothing untoward. By all accounts, 'tis Miss Anne's habitual medicine."

"Did you prepare it?" Lady Catherine asked.

"It has all the properties of my own draught. But I only prepared one bottle, and sent it yesterday."

"Yet this one came this morning. And I was told to send the old one back. Which I could not do, for by then my lady had taken all the poison," Mrs Evans said with profound bitterness, and despite her station in life, she did not disguise the heavy tinge of accusation in her voice and manner as she fixed her stare on one of her betters.

Dr Beaumont drew himself up to his full height, and addressed himself not to the accusing servant, but the stony-faced lady of the house.

"You have my word, ma'am, that I prepared one bottle, and one bottle only. I did not ask for it back. And I most assuredly did not taint it with nightshade."

"Do you use nightshade in your preparations?" Lady Catherine demanded to know.

"Aye," the other said simply. "On occasion, I do, and with the utmost care. I would never make such a ghastly mistake as to confuse it for any of the ingredients in Miss Anne's medicine," he attested, his tone almost severe. But that accent was consumed by ardent earnestness when he added, "On my immortal soul and my son's, madam, your daughter's life as is precious to me as Henry's. I do not err when their safety is at stake."

Lady Catherine's fierce countenance crumpled into the weary wince of a very old woman, before she smoothed it back into reflecting her real age and her customary manner.

"Go to Anne," she said. "The rest of us will root out the culprit."

Dr Beaumont solemnly nodded his thanks for the few words that demonstrated he had been reinstated in her confidence, and sought to do as bid.

"Just one more question, sir," Darcy spoke up, once he had pressed his aunt's arm in a brief gesture of support, yet did not follow it with the lingering clasp of forgiveness. "Who else in your household could have handled the other bottle except you?"

Dr Beaumont's eyes regained a wary look, mingled with revived fervour.

"I prepared the draught and my son brought it when he called at Rosings yesterday. I thought no one else had laid a finger on it until it was delivered into your cousin's hands. No one in my household had any business to. But someone must have, for my son and I would rather die than see Miss Anne harmed."

"I can believe that," Darcy said quietly, then pushed his shoulders back. "My aunt is in the right, sir. Pray tend to Anne. The rest of us will find the culprit."

"I, for one, would dearly like a word with this maid who fetches potions when no one bids her, and asks for old bottles back," Mr Bennet said, his tones deceptively bland.

There was no blandness in Darcy's voice when he rasped, "Indeed."

Chapter 32

Rosings, 19 April 1812

No sooner had the room grown quiet than someone gave a light tap on the door, as if they had been biding their time in the hallway until the end of the exchange that sounded like a disagreement.

"Come," Lady Catherine called.

It was a housemaid answering the earlier summons, and she was promptly sent to learn if Dr Beaumont's menial who had called earlier could still be found in the servants' hall. If she had already left, the girl was to ask around and discover exactly which one of the physician's maids had shown her face at Rosings that morning.

As they waited for one sort of information or the other, Lady Catherine had to face a difficult choice. She wanted to keep watch over her daughter, but she just as fervently wished to go about, ask questions, harry and harass, until she laid hands on whomever had sought to take Anne's life.

She was not the only one torn by the desire to be in several places at once. For his part, Darcy was as driven as his aunt to go forth, investigate and root out the evil that had touched his cousin, yet he was unwilling to leave Elizabeth exposed to Lady Catherine's venomous resentment, now that her ladyship had grasped it was Elizabeth, not Anne, who was firmly lodged into his heart.

The fact that she had been indisputably acquitted of Lady Catherine's wild and wrathful charges had done little to soften that resentment. Her ladyship's manner had already made it plain enough. Yet she did not hesitate to give further confirmation once the maid had left them, when she pointedly told her nephew, an ugly twist to her thin lips:

"I trust you will bestir yourself and protect Anne from further harm, rather than loitering here at *her* beck and call," she sneered, with a dark glare and a nod towards Elizabeth.

Darcy stared grimly back.

"I know where my duty lies, ma'am. You need not remind me."

"Is that so?" Lady Catherine scoffed. "Then you had better prove it. Deeds, Nephew, not fine words. Rest assured, when Anne is recovered I shall have a great deal more to say to you on the matter. And no less to *you*," she glared at Elizabeth again through narrowed eyes glinting with malevolence. "Believe you me, you have not heard the last of it either. My prime concern now is Anne's safety, not your insolent ambitions, but depend upon it, your shameless conduct will not go unchecked. To ingrates, I give no quarter."

"What shameless conduct?" Darcy snarled. "Lady Catherine, you will desist—"

Mr Bennet's hand came to rest on his sleeve as soon as he had drawn a sharp breath to speak, but the light touch had to turn into a tight grip before the ferocious outburst was cut short and Darcy's head whipped around, his glower transferred from his aunt to the one who was so keen to interrupt him.

The glower was met with a steady look.

"My place, I think," Mr Bennet smoothly remarked, and since he was in no position to dispute that, Darcy clamped his lips together and lapsed into sullen silence.

The older gentleman gave a curt nod of satisfaction and, having tamed one refractory will, however briefly, he applied himself to grappling with the other.

"Now, then, madam, pray curb your temper and save your energy for your daughter rather than expending it on plaguing mine. Come, Lizzy. And you too, Jane. We had better repair below-stairs."

"I thank you, Papa, but I would rather help Mrs Evans tend to Anne," Elizabeth said, only to have her father and her suitor chorusing in disbelief.

"You would?"

"After all this?" Darcy added.

A rueful little smile fluttered on Elizabeth's lips as she shrugged.

"Of course. Anne is my sister and my friend. This has naught to do with her."

Incorrigible, Lady Catherine snorted. Darcy's gaze warmed as he returned Elizabeth's faint smile. Mr Bennet shook his head, astonished to discover his error in thinking he had just one daughter whose angelic forbearance bordered on the ludicrous.

It was only Jane who showed no surprise, but cast her younger sister a serene glance of approval. Mr Bennet shook his head again and grimaced.

"Very well. I daresay it makes no difference if I wait here or elsewhere until the doctor's maid is found, eh, Darcy? Just have my man fetch me a book, if you would be so kind."

"Certainly, sir," replied the other, all of a sudden looking rather less troubled by the prospect of leaving the room, and possibly the house.

Seemingly, the young man knew a Cerberus when he saw one, Mr Bennet mused with a wry twist of his lips, and pulled himself a chair.

⁕⁕⁕

The doctor's maid could not be found in the servants' hall – she was long gone from Rosings – but the girl who had spoken to her and carried her message up to Mrs Evans could at least reveal who she was. One Martha Gibbs, apparently, known to have been in Dr Beaumont's employ for a decade, if not longer. When applied to, her master could describe her as a mild-looking woman in her middle age, who kept herself to herself and diligently carried out her duties. Not one's notion of a poisoner by any stretch of the imagination, but an honest and hard-working servant whose loyalty he had never had cause to question. Gibbs had been a long-standing fixture in his house – she and his housekeeper had practically raised his son, after Mrs Beaumont's premature demise – and however economical with words, she was not one to spare herself when there was hard work to be done.

"What of her duties? Has she ever assisted you in mixing draughts?" Mr Bennet asked.

"Of course not," the physician blustered. "I would never assign such a delicate task to anyone, much less a maid of all work. She only comes into my study and my preparations room to clean."

Mr Bennet exchanged puzzled glances with his nephew by marriage and his wife. The woman in question had just been represented as a long-trusted paragon of virtue, rather than some dubious new addition to Dr Beaumont's household, lurking in the shadows and hatching evil schemes.

"I want her fetched, nevertheless," Lady Catherine declared, and Mr Bennet could only tilt his head sideways with a faint grimace of agreement.

If this Gibbs of few words was honest and hardworking, it did not necessarily follow she was also bright. Someone might have put her up to it, and she was too much of a simpleton to see the implications. Besides, he had nothing better to suggest. For now, questioning this woman was the only avenue they had.

His wife and her nephew had eventually left him – the latter with a silent adieu to Elizabeth, and the first with very firm instructions to Mrs Evans to notify her at once, should there be any change in Anne's condition. True to his word, Darcy had conveyed Mr Bennet's request to his man, for the trusted fellow soon came to bring the book that could be found on the nightstand, in the older gentleman's bedchamber. Yet at that point in time, Mr Bennet found he had little patience for Signor Machiavelli's *'Art of War.'* His man was sent to the library to fetch him another book instead: a rather large tome, very finely bound, its spine adorned with golden swirls around the lettering that proclaimed it a herbal.

There was, of course, an entry for the deadly nightshade, and at the very top of the page bearing an engraving of the plant and several detailed sketches of its leaves, flowers, fruit and roots, Mr Bennet could find the name the learned knew it by: *Atropa Belladonna.*

He pursed his lips. Of botany he had studied very little, yet he was sufficiently well-schooled to know that in the myths of Ancient Greece, of the three Fates that held each mortal's destiny in their immortal hands, Atropos was the one who cut the thread of life with her sharp shears.

His glance rose off the page, to drift towards the door into the adjoining chamber, left slightly ajar, and he sighed. He could only pray that the dear, innocent girl who lay there would not be so cruelly cut down in the prime of her life.

☙❧

Once she had ordered her butler to send for Martha Gibbs, Lady Catherine took herself to the drawing room to pace in expectation. For his part, Darcy went in search of his sister and Colonel Fitzwilliam to acquaint them with the harrowing events.

Horrified and tearful, Georgiana promptly excused herself and went up to help care for Anne. As for the gentlemen, all they could do for now was join Lady Catherine in the drawing room.

Little was said between the three of them as they waited. The young men knew full well that their formidable aunt would disdain trite words of consolation. It was not the Fitzwilliam way to exchange commiserating platitudes in the face of adversity. Their nature and upbringing had taught them otherwise: adversity should be met not with weak-spirited prattle, but with resolve, unity, self-possession and sharp wits.

⁓⧫⧫⁓

The footman sent in the steward's gig to the physician's house to fetch his maid returned without her. Martha Gibbs was nowhere to be found. All he could learn from the housekeeper was that the woman had not been seen since the servants' habitually early breakfast, and that her scrupulously tidy room in the attics was now in a shocking state of disarray.

Colonel Fitzwilliam arched a brow at the intelligence.

"An abrupt departure and a sign of guilt?" he speculated.

"Obviously," Lady Catherine retorted, quick to condemn without a hearing. "Find her," she commanded, her imperious glance settling upon one of her nephews, then the other.

The colonel's brow furrowed.

"Any kin we might apply to?"

The footman shook his head.

"I asked, sir. She knows of none, the housekeeper said. No one called upon Gibbs and she never asked for leave to go visiting. She hardly ever left the house, in fact. Not even on her half-days off."

"I see," the colonel muttered, then he decisively spoke to the footman. "Send word to the stables for my horse and my cousin's, will you? And have them set up a search party."

"Aye," Lady Catherine nodded fiercely. "I want every man who can ride or walk—"

"I doubt it will come to that." Darcy intervened, prepared to have his say at last.

His aunt frowned.

"Why not?"

"Darcy is in the right," Fitzwilliam confirmed. "It was pursuit I had in mind, rather than combing through every bush and looking into every crumbling barn."

"How do you know where she went?" Lady Catherine asked with no little surprise.

The colonel shrugged.

"I do not know, as such. But where can a maid with no known kin hope to conceal herself better than in London?"

⊱⊰

"What meadow does she keep speaking of? Where does she want to go?" Mrs Evans mournfully asked as she dampened her mistress's brow, distraught to see her restlessly moving her head from side to side, barely intelligible whispers escaping her parched lips.

Elizabeth knew better than to enlighten Anne's lady's maid, and predictably Dr Beaumont shared that view, for he spread out his hands into a gesture of defeat.

"She is delirious. It is to be expected in cases such as hers, and the same can be said of hallucinations. You cannot set store by anything Miss Anne says while she is raving thus," the physician attested with great insistence.

Indeed, with most particular insistence, to Elizabeth's way of thinking, as if he sought to prepare the ground for dismissing other disjointed whispers in like manner, should they arise – such as a certain name, or news of an engagement which should reach Lady Catherine from Anne's own lips, if and when she recovered, rather than be conveyed by a startled lady's maid.

Thoughts of Mr Beaumont stayed with Elizabeth as she raised her stepsister's head and endeavoured to coax Anne into taking a few sips of water and a spoonful of the draught the physician had prepared from the ingredients sent by the apothecary. What must poor Mr Beaumont feel when he learned of this terrible misfortune, right after the day when happiness seemed so close!

It was beyond her to set aside the deep concern and pity she felt for the man Anne loved, so when Dr Beaumont eventually retired towards the edge of the room to stare out of the window, Elizabeth was compelled to follow him and ask in a quiet whisper:

"You did send him word, sir, did you not?"

Dr Beaumont turned towards her with a start.

"Send word? To whom?"

Elizabeth reached to discreetly press his arm in a telling gesture, and accompanied it with a mild glance and few soft words:

"Anne's joyful tidings are no secret to me, although I can see why for now they must remain so to others."

Dr Beaumont kept his assessing eyes on her for a long moment, and then he sighed and looked away.

"Aye. They must." He fell silent for a while, before he acknowledged, "I did send him word. Although goodness knows how soon my man can reach him. He has gone into Surrey, right after sharing the happy news with me at breakfast," the old physician said with another deep sigh, doubtlessly aggrieved by the stark contrast between that joyful time and the harrowing present. "He went to speak to a good friend of his, in the hope of having that gentleman stepping in to minister to the people of his parish, so that he could be free to take the Hunsford living and—"

Dr Beaumont countenance twisted into a wince and he broke off, visibly unable to continue speaking of exuberant hopes and arrangements that belonged in the auspicious hours of the morning. Her compassion easily extending to Mr Beaumont's father, Elizabeth pressed the physician's arm once more.

"He had to be told," the old gentleman quietly resumed, his stare fixed grimly ahead upon the rolling landscape that showed no sign of an approaching rider. "Though I know not what good it will do. He cannot be allowed in here, and it will be the worst torture for him to keep away."

"Yes," Elizabeth whispered.

She barely knew Mr Beaumont, but she was no stranger to love. With every fibre of her being she knew it *would* be the severest torment if she were forced to stay away when the one she loved was in mortal danger.

She shivered at the horrifying notion, but this was not the time for quiet reflection, so she had no opportunity to dwell on the strange workings of her mind and heart.

It was a fair while until Elizabeth found herself at leisure to consider just how odd it was, and how perplexing and contrary, that she had mistrusted her sentiments and his – had mistaken them for mindless attraction – when he had held her close and ardently kissed her, yet the simple and primeval fear of losing him was enough to make her see beyond the shadow of a doubt that she was in love with Fitzwilliam Darcy.

It was also a fair while until she could reflect on his leap of faith with a brimming heart and tears in her eyes, and find no reason why she should not trust him with her love and her hand, if he loved her enough to trust her with his life.

But for now, in her stepsister's bedchamber, it was her fear for Anne's safety and her concern for Mr Beaumont that brought tears to her eyes. Elizabeth sighed as she glanced up at that gentleman's father. Her countenance overshadowed with compassion, she quietly but firmly put the sentiment into words:

"Then those of us who understand his torment should seek to give him as much comfort as we can."

The old physician made no answer. He only raised his free hand to cover hers, where it still lay on his sleeve, and clasped it in silent gratitude, his gaze fixed upon the deserted drive.

৩৫ ৩৯৬

At that point in time, Mr Beaumont had barely left Hunsford. Darcy, the colonel and Lady Catherine's grooms, who had joined them on their quest, came upon him and the physician's coachman on the outskirts of the village.

That Beaumont was nothing short of frantic was plain to see from the first glance, and Colonel Fitzwilliam did not fail to notice.

"Ah. What have we here?" he muttered. "Heavens. Poor wretch, he is in a frightful state."

"He would be," Darcy said tersely, reeling in shock at the sudden thought of how he would have felt, had Elizabeth been the one who, even then, was fighting for her life. He wanted to lay hands on whomever had sought to harm his cousin Anne and tear that vile creature limb from limb, that had never been in question. But every wisp of coherent thought was instantly combusted into an explosive blaze of terror and fury – an all-consuming flare that overwhelmed him – at the very notion of Elizabeth's life being thus threatened.

"Steady, now," Fitzwilliam said, his ability to read his mind and mien as uncanny as ever. "You had better ride back with Beaumont and keep him out of mischief, for I doubt he will have a care for himself," the colonel advised.

"Perhaps I should," Darcy conceded, reining in as they approached the man in question and his companion. "But what of our mission?"

Fitzwilliam shrugged.

"Beaumont's man can take your place, and besides the parish constable is due to meet us in the village. But I imagine these fine fellows and I can get by without assistance," he added with a nod towards their aunt's grooms. "After all, who needs an army to apprehend a middle-aged woman?"

"You are after Gibbs?" Mr Beaumont exclaimed a short while later, when they drew up alongside and their purpose was explained to him, along with the suggested change of plans. "That is utter nonsense. Martha Gibbs would not hurt a fly. You must look elsewhere."

"That is as may be," Darcy grudgingly allowed, "but for now she is all we have. And you must own, the message she brought to Rosings and her sudden disappearance are highly suspicious."

But Beaumont had no time for speculations. He cast an uncertain glance over his shoulder, seeming to ponder for a moment on whether he ought to tarry in Hunsford and assist in shedding light upon the matter, but he shook his head and tightened the reins, his mind clearly made up.

"Go with them, Hiram," he told his man, then glanced at the colonel. "He will know her, if you do not."

"Nay, I do not know her, but I have with me some who do. No harm in having another," Fitzwilliam replied and, with a parting nod, he turned away and urged his mount and his men forth, leaving Darcy and Beaumont to their purpose.

The latter would not waste another moment.

"Thank you," was all he said to Darcy – for the moral support, the other assumed, and for turning back with him to gain him admittance into Lady Catherine's house – before digging his heels into his horse's flanks and making the obliging beast leap into a full gallop.

Darcy tightened his grip on the reins and followed without a word. As they rode together at breakneck speed towards Rosings, he had no need to be told that Beaumont was beyond the reach of any words of comfort, even if his companion could have heard him over the thundering hoofbeats and the inner clamour of harrowing thoughts.

An intimate knowledge of Rosings Park, with its intricacies and less-travelled passages and stairs, stood Darcy in good stead when he sought to lead Beaumont to the right part of the house without attracting undue notice. They made it into Anne's sitting room unchallenged, and it was only then that the young reverend's presence was unavoidably brought into question.

"Why have you summoned him, sir?" Mrs Evans could be heard asking the physician, an accent of desperation in her voice, when she learned of Mr Beaumont's arrival. "Pray tell me 'tis not for the last rites! Oh, my sweet lady," she tearfully lamented, only to hold her peace with a gasp when the doctor replied swiftly:

"Hush, Mrs Evans. You will frighten and distress her if she can hear you. Your mistress needs all our help and all our prayers. She also needs fresh ice. Would you be so kind as to go down to the kitchens and have them fetch some more?" he urged the distraught woman, who promptly stood and, wiping her tears with the backs of her work-worn hands, hastened to obey and vanished into the servants' passage.

Elizabeth left her place on the other side of the large bed and stood aside when Dr Beaumont went to fully open the door that led into the sitting room, and motioned his son within.

The younger man's countenance, frozen in pain and ashen, filled her with compassion, and his ragged voice tore at her heart when Mr Beaumont came to clasp Anne's hand and brokenly whispered, "I am here, my love. Stay with me. Try to fight this, and stay with me. Good God, Anne, don't leave me!"

Elizabeth found it impossible to tell if he could reach Anne in her stupor. There was no sign of it in her stepsister's flushed features. But when Mr Beaumont's heartrending plea ended in a muted sob, she knew she had no business to remain there and witness his grief in this very private moment. She had already turned towards the door when Jane's gentle hand came to press her shoulder and nudge her in that direction. They left the room, as did Georgiana, and without hesitation Elizabeth made her way to Darcy, to seek his hand and link her fingers with his.

This time, he did not trace discreet little circles in her palm, but wrapped his other arm around her and brought her very close.

Nary a sound of protest came from Mr Bennet. Instead, he opened the door into the hallway and quietly stepped out, no doubt to act as Cerberus for Anne's benefit now, and Mr Beaumont's, keep watch and delay his wife, should Lady Catherine be suddenly driven to return above-stairs. Presumably of the same mind, Georgiana followed.

Nary a sound of protest came from Jane either – not even a conscious or cautioning glance – when Darcy released Elizabeth's hand to clasp her to his chest in a tight embrace, full and unabashed, press his lips on her brow, then rest his cheek atop her head and remain thus, still holding her tightly, as though he would never let her go.

⁂

It was at Jane's suggestion that a while later, when the physician had to urge his son to leave Anne's apartments, Darcy took Mr Beaumont across the hall, into the sitting room Elizabeth shared with her eldest sister.

Despite his wishes, the gentleman had eventually complied, so now there they were, Beaumont staring fixedly out of the window, and Darcy casting uncertain glances at his companion's profile as he racked his brain for some adequate words of encouragement and comfort. He frowned, finding none, and deemed it a pity that he could not even offer the other the doubtful palliation a glass of brandy might afford, as nothing of the sort would be found in the sitting room belonging to a couple of young ladies. His own quarters were at some considerable distance, at the end of the opposite corridor, and Beaumont would most likely be unwilling to accept a sanctuary so far removed from where Anne was. Well, he could go and fetch the decanter, if it came to that, Darcy decided, and some minutes later he was compelled to make that offer.

"I thank you, no," Beaumont said, and then lapsed once more into silence, his head bowed.

Darcy could only assume the other man was in prayer. He sighed. It was an example he should follow. Beaumont's father was in the right: Anne needed all their help and all their prayers. He bowed his head as well and struggled with the words, although not with the sentiment.

Catching a glimpse of Beaumont out of the corner of his eye and seeing him leave his place by the window was a distraction, but Darcy refused to let it take hold. Head still bowed, he prayed for Anne's safety, not with the prescribed words perhaps, but from the depths of his heart.

Darcy turned around at last, to see that Beaumont was now sitting motionless in one of the armchairs, eyes closed and chin resting on his folded hands. Still in prayer? Or in heartrending reflection? For the other man's sake, Darcy hoped it was the former rather than the latter, and that prayer might bring him the sort of hope and solace that no amount of brandy could provide.

Yet when Beaumont stirred so suddenly that it made him start, Darcy found not hope but abject horror in his eyes, and there was nothing but abject horror in Beaumont's voice as well when he groaned, "Good Lord in Heaven, *I* brought this upon her!"

Darcy's jaw tightened. He had no need to ask the other of what he was speaking. He already knew full well, from the physician's answers to his own inquiries about the tainted bottle.

Seemingly, Beaumont's time of quiet reflection had merely served to order his thoughts and cast light into a corner that had mercifully escaped his notice until then.

It no longer did. Beaumont's voice broke, then found its strength again, to culminate into an anguished outburst:

"*I* gave her the poison – with my very own hand!"

Chapter 33

Rosings, 19 April 1812

The Rosings library had gained the appearance of a courtroom, ever since a great number of the interested parties had congregated there soon after Colonel Fitzwilliam's return with the parish constable, the pair of them escorting the elusive Martha Gibbs. She had been apprehended at *The Bell* in Bromley, the second stage on the journey from Hunsford into town.

Lady Catherine was in attendance, naturally, yet despite her exalted position and direct interest in the proceedings, it was not she who presided over the affair, but Lord Metcalfe, who had obligingly responded to her request for his involvement and assistance. Mr Bennet was also of the party, along with Darcy, Colonel Fitzwilliam, Dr Beaumont and the parish constable. Yet their concerted efforts to get to the bottom of the harrowing business were frustrated by the woman's tearful insistence that she had done naught wrong.

Darcy shifted uncomfortably in his seat. It was a sorry sight, this: a collection of local worthies, a colonel in His Majesty's army and himself, all gathered there to badger that wretched woman. He would have taken pity on her and spoken up to spare her from further distress, but there were no two ways about it: Anne must be protected. And the servant's claim was not supported by known deeds.

The others clearly shared his views. Not least Lord Metcalfe, who continued to press her.

"So you say. Yet you came here this morning with a bottle of potion and sought to retrieve the tainted one that was delivered yesterday."

"How was I to know it were tainted?" the woman pleaded. "I juss did what I were told."

Lord Metcalfe gave a gesture of vexation.

"Doubtlessly you heard Dr Beaumont as well as I did. He said he told you nothing of the sort."

"His word against mine, m'ludd," the woman sobbed. "But you'll believe him, and not me."

Lord Metcalfe raised a hand to silence the incensed physician who stood, about to protest.

"Who would disbelieve a trusted member of the medical profession and instead give credence to a maid of all work?" his lordship scoffed.

"Aye. Too true," Martha Gibbs bitterly retorted. "But who has the learning to prepare potions? The good doctor here, or a maid of all work?"

"Have you no shame, woman?" Dr Beaumont cried, wide-eyed and flushed with outrage.

The woman shrugged.

"I speak as I see."

"Do you?" Mr Bennet was moved to intervene. "No great learning is required when it comes to the deadly nightshade. Any shepherd knows he would do well to keep his flock away from it."

Martha Gibbs shrugged again.

"I'm no shepherd. And I put no nightshade into the bottle I brought."

"No," Lady Catherine hissed. "You added it to the other."

The maid's eyes glinted darkly, then filled once more with tears.

"How can you say that, ma'am? I never touched it!"

Mr Bennet laid a restraining hand on his wife's arm and nodded sagely towards the other woman.

"I will give you that. You were most careful there, and the only bottle you are known to have handled is the untainted one. But pray tell us, if you did nothing wrong but merely carried out Dr Beaumont's instructions, why did you flee?"

"Aye," Lord Metcalfe spoke up in manifest agreement. "You had better tell us that. Have you a good answer?"

Lips pursed, the woman raised her chin.

"The best answer lies before you, sirs. I feared I'd be blamed. And I wasn't wrong there, was I?"

"That is preposterous!" Dr Beaumont fumed. "Why should you fear that, when you have naught to do with my draughts?"

"I've naught to do with them, and never had," the maid replied. "But here I am, quizzed about draughts *you* mixed, sir."

"Of all the—!" the physician blustered, then with visible effort he sought to regulate his temper. "Why are you doing this, Martha?" he resumed, his voice a great deal more subdued and tinged with a solemnly entreating accent. "You received naught but kindness in my house. Why would you repay me thus?"

The woman looked down, shuffling from foot to foot.

"I did, sir, aye," she muttered, yet her voice gathered strength when she added, "But it ain't kind to pin this on me."

Lady Catherine gasped.

"What if the doltish creature speaks the truth and we have gone the wrong way about this?" she cried. "After all, 'tis not she who brought the tainted bottle." She spun around to face Dr Beaumont. "Your son did. And for all your protestations above-stairs, that he would rather die than see Anne harmed, from what I hear he, too, had left Kent in uncommon haste."

Darcy's glance darted from the physician to Mr Bennet as he struggled to decide if it would be to the young reverend's advantage or the reverse, were Lady Catherine to learn that Henry Beaumont had returned just as hastily to Kent, and was even then concealed in his own quarters, once the distraught man could not be trusted to remain in Jane and Elizabeth's sitting room. After his most unfortunate epiphany, Beaumont had to be forcibly restrained from bursting into the sick-chamber, and his father had necessarily been summoned. The old physician did come, and impressed upon him in no uncertain terms that unless he wished to attract undue notice and find himself removed from Rosings, he had better keep his voice down and his temper under regulation.

"Now I have Anne to care for," Dr Beaumont had declared with unprecedented sternness. "Mr Darcy has kindly offered to take you to his quarters. Go with him and wait for tidings. Go, I say, and stay there or, by Jove, you will leave me no option but to sedate you with laudanum," the father had forcefully ordered and, distraught but not rendered altogether witless, young Beaumont had thankfully complied.

Upon reflection, some laudanum might have served him. Yet he would not take it, and for all the commanding manner, his father did not go as far as to force a sizeable dose down his throat.

With any luck, he would have enough sense to remain there and not seek to bodily prevail over Weston, who was left to keep him company – or rather keep an eye on him – when Mr Bennet came to let Darcy know they were wanted in the library.

This time Mr Bennet chose to remain silent, and Darcy followed his example. As for Dr Beaumont, he responded to Lady Catherine's speculations with no details, just a forceful protest.

The firmest exhortation came from his maid:

"The poor lad has suffered enough. Leave him be, ma'am," she demanded, in a manner utterly unsuited to addressing one's betters and certainly not fit for speaking to an incensed Lady Catherine.

It came as no surprise to anyone that the great lady rounded upon her like a fury.

"Hold your tongue, woman! How dare you use that tone with me?"

But the maid of all work would not be daunted.

"I shan't sit by and see ruin visited upon that dear boy. I reared him, and I should know there's no kinder soul than he in the whole of England."

Lady Catherine snorted.

"The kindest soul in the whole of England brought the poisoned bottle to my daughter," she snarled.

"He wasn't meant to!" the other forcefully shot back. "His father was. The dear boy didn't know. He shan't be blamed for this! Leave him be, I tell you. He'll be in too much pain as it is. Poor boy. Poor, foolish boy, to give his heart to your accursed seed," she spat, glaring at Lady Catherine, her bloodshot eyes burning with nothing short of hatred.

"Hush, woman," Dr Beaumont sternly spoke.

For her part, Lady Catherine stalked towards the physician's maid, giving every impression that she was about to strike her for her appalling insolence. She did not. Instead, she glowered at her from close quarters and hissed, "*What* did you say?"

Martha Gibbs twisted her lips into a grim sneer.

"Henry Beaumont wouldn't poison your daughter any more than you would. He loves her. He is to marry her."

If there were gasps of surprise or dismay from their companions, Lady Catherine did not hear them, or did not deign to acknowledge that she did. Her gaze remained fixed upon the servant woman.

"You are insane. Or in your cups," her ladyship jeered.

"Am I?" the other retorted sharply. "They are engaged, I tell you. I heard Master Henry say so to his father at breakfast this very morning. The dear boy. Foolish boy," she muttered, and her voice rose in pitch until the quiet lament turned into a wail. "I didn't think he'd be so foolish. I didn't know. I didn't know!"

"But when you found out, you sought to abort the vile scheme you started," Dr Beaumont exclaimed in sudden comprehension. "You brought the proper medicine and asked for the poison back."

Lady Catherine's glare turned nothing short of murderous.

"So it *was* you!" she said, each word frightfully distinct. "You shall pay for this. A pity I cannot have you drawn and quartered!"

Martha Gibbs did not cower. She pursed her lips and her mutinous scowl seemed to teeter between denial and defiance. It was not long until defiance won. Martha Gibbs bridled.

"Oh, rest assured, I was tormented enough! Every moment of the last three decades," she spat as she drew herself up to her full height, the deferential air that came with submissively hunched shoulders suddenly discarded like a borrowed cloak. The commoner's speech was gone too, along with the country accent, and her vitriolic outburst came in the cultured voice of education. "You say I shall pay. Perhaps I shall. But if there is any justice in the world, you should pay too. Why should *your* daughter be blessed with riches and good fortune, when my babe moulders in a lonely grave? My Ada should have been the mistress of Rosings, and she *would* have been, were it not for you and your sainted mother-in-law, who could work so easily upon her milksop son."

Her fierce monologue was unstoppable now, but then no one was of a mind to interrupt it. Even Lady Catherine seemed to have acquired the good sense to keep her fury in check and let the festering disclosures pour out. And pour out they did. Spittle gathering at the corner of her pale lips, Martha Gibbs growled:

"He was *my* husband first. We went on a jaunt to Gretna Green together, did he tell you that? I imagine not," she promptly answered her own question and tossed her head back as she released a bitter laugh. "Sir Lewis never had the stomach for uncomfortable conversations, had he? And no backbone, either. Everything was taken from me, respectability, rank, love – such as it was – yet he would not lift a finger to defend our union. He gave me up!

At his mother's persuasion, he gave me up! Because of *you*, with your airs and graces, and all for the sake of the precious de Bourgh name. The old baronet went berserk when he learned of our marriage. Burst a vein and died. And Sir Lewis's witch of a mother played on his sorrow and guilt and persuaded him that he owed it to his father's memory to fulfil his last wish and make a *suitable* connection. My marriage was annulled to make room for you in his bed, and for your dowry in the de Bourgh coffers," she venomously spat. "An apothecary's daughter was no match for an earl's. Oh, this comes as a surprise, does it?" she scoffed when she noted a violent twitch in Lady Catherine's frozen countenance at the mention of her parentage. "Aye, I am an apothecary's daughter. And my father taught me well. I am a quick learner, I assure you. It was child's play to adulterate your daughter's draughts. I have done so for years. A drop of this, a dash of that, added without notice. Enough to sap away the strength day by day, just as the constant drip of water wears down into the stone." Her glance flitted searchingly over Lady Catherine's countenance and a harsh cackle escaped her taut lips. "It angers you, I see. Good. That was what I have always wanted, to anger and distress you as you see your precious child waste away. Why should I have any mercy for your daughter if no one took pity on mine? I had to watch my dearest Ada sicken, away from her father's love and deprived of his protection. The meagre allowance I was granted could not afford her the care she deserved, and when I sent word to Sir Lewis to beg his financial assistance for our daughter's sake, I received naught but twenty pounds and a scathing letter from his mother, questioning Ada's parentage and forbidding me from making unsubstantiated claims on her son's estate. When it comes to medical men, twenty pounds won't go a very long way. But I need not tell *you* that, do I, Dr Beaumont?" she sneered towards the physician. "You would know all about a medical man's fees, would you not?"

Dr Beaumont made no answer, and only fixed her with a stare of disbelief and unmistakable abhorrence. Supremely unaffected by it, Martha Gibbs did not wait for a reply. Her narrowed eyes took a derisive glint as she continued:

"You appealed to my better sentiments, and to a servant's loyalty. You and your repulsive breed deserve nothing from me. None of your upright and merciful brethren, the so-called disciples of Hippocrates, would lift a finger to save my Ada's life when it emerged I lacked the means to pay them. I begged and pleaded, but to no avail. So I will tell you this: I loathe the very name of your vile and grasping brotherhood. Believe you me, these many years I was sorely tempted to taint *your* tea and coffee. I would have just as easily got away with it. Do not flatter yourself into thinking you could have caught me out. I have sufficient learning – well-nigh as much as you, I'd wager. Aye," she vigorously nodded, "I could have found some stealthily acting poisons that would have served you nicely. But I was no fool to cut off my nose to spite my face. To your good fortune, my need of you was greater than my loathing. What better connection to this place was there to hope for?"

She gave a snort and her lips curled into a grimace of unholy glee as she contemptuously added:

"Oh, you had your uses. It was ever so diverting to see you hastening to Rosings whenever you were summoned – for of course Miss Anne should have the best care and your full attention. The de Bourgh fortune entitled her to nothing less. Oh, how right it felt, and just, to see you scurrying away with the draughts I had adulterated, and to know that she would profit none from her ability to buy your services and lay claim on your time. So rewarding it was, that poetic justice!" she cackled towards Lady Catherine who, to everyone's vast surprise, still remained as motionless as a stone, and equally as silent. "An eye for an eye, your ladyship, and your anguish for mine," Martha Gibbs spat. "I would have happily seen you fret over your daughter's steady decay for years. But *he* came," she viciously hissed, turning her glare upon Darcy. "He came into Kent again, and this time he stayed, and there was talk of an imminent marriage. He would have taken her to the north, out of my reach. I had to change tack – opt for something different, that would act a great deal faster. And I would have had my revenge at last."

"Your revenge!" Lady Catherine cried, no longer willing or able to keep herself in check. "On an innocent soul who has done you no harm in her life!"

"The only innocent souls for whom my heart bleeds are my Ada and dear Henry," Martha Gibbs shot back. "Ada is gone, my poor darling. But Henry is the only one who has lived to repay my affection with joy instead of heartache or ill-treatment."

"And how did *you* repay him?" Dr Beaumont fulminated in his turn, and it was only then that the savage and unrelenting spite in the woman's eyes gave way to a shadow of remorse.

"I did not know," she said in a rough whisper. "Just tell him this: I did not know. I do not expect him to forgive me—"

"He shan't," Dr Beaumont confidently spoke for his son. "Even his Christian charity must have its limits."

"Never mind the limits of Mr Beaumont's charity," Lady Catherine cut him off. "We shall have to address the matter of his presumption ere long. But firstly, this... creature," she glowered at Martha Gibbs with an angry gesture and an ugly twist to her lips.

"You can safely leave her to me," Lord Metcalfe spoke up, prompt in taking up his judicial duties.

Lady Catherine's gave a grimace of impatience, her countenance plainly showing she was about to insist upon having a substantial involvement in that particular affair. There was precious little that could distract her from the desire to draw blood. Of the very few things that would have done the trick, the one most likely to succeed was the very one that happened: Georgiana came into the room, her face aglow.

"Anne has regained consciousness," she joyfully announced. "Aunt, she would like to speak to you."

Chapter 34

Rosings, 19 April 1812

By the time Lady Catherine had returned from her daughter's chamber, Lord Metcalfe and the parish constable had long gone, taking Martha Gibbs with them. Rosings had grown quiet and lay half-asleep, enveloped in the shadows of the night. Yet to all its occupants' vast relief and humble gratitude, the darkest shadow that had loomed over it – unseen, but ominous and horribly oppressive – was now lifted. Anne would live. The physician confidently vouched for that. She was still dreadfully weak, and could not say a great deal to her mother. The fact that Anne could recognise her, that she was conscious and could speak at all, albeit in a very faint voice, was a source of great joy to Lady Catherine. What her daughter had to say pleased her a vast deal less, for Anne asked to see Mr Beaumont, her betrothed. Rendered wise by the long hours of fear and grief, her ladyship knew better than to launch into a controversy with her beloved child, who had only just returned from the valley of the shadow of death. She merely urged Anne to rest, and undertook to send for Mr Beaumont in the morning.

Lady Catherine was thwarted in her purpose, naturally. Anne and Mr Beaumont had many more allies in the sick-chamber than she. This time they did not even need to manoeuvre around Mrs Evans. Anne came an unquestionable first in that worthy woman's loyalty, and Lady Catherine – a very poor second. Thus, when her ladyship finally left the sickroom and Mrs Evans was given to understand that her sweet lady would not have a peaceful rest until her request was granted and, moreover, that granting it would be the easiest thing in the world, she was easily persuaded to collude with Anne's other allies and bring about the briefest interview.

On this occasion, severe restrictions were imposed on the young man's visit, as in Mrs Evans' book a brush with death was an insufficient excuse for wholly dispensing with every notion of propriety. Under the lady's maid watchful eye and firm guidance, Mr Beaumont was allowed no further than the doorway. All he could see of Anne was her face, through the narrow aperture between the gathered bed-curtains and the edge of the screen strategically placed by Mrs Evans. The lady's maid also insisted upon regulating how far the door between the bedchamber and the sitting room could be opened, and took the trouble to stand by and monitor the width herself. The good doctor rolled his eyes at that, and Anne's stepsisters and younger cousin did likewise, but Mr Beaumont was far too happy to protest. Seeing Anne's face was enough, if she was smiling – however pale the cheeks and wan the smile. It was a glorious improvement on the harrowing sight earlier that day. He could not speak to her in private, he could neither hold her hand nor kiss it, but he could wait and he could hope. So Mr Beaumont took himself away with no more substantial a memento than Anne's smiling countenance and the kiss she blew him. It was enough. It was enough for now.

To Mrs Evans' satisfaction, her dear mistress then agreed to rest. As for Mr Beaumont, he returned to his appointed sanctuary at the far end of the opposite corridor, to finally partake of the cold repast that Weston, Mr Darcy's valet, had kindly procured for him.

Unbeknownst to him, similar arrangements were soon made for the others, at Lady Catherine's particular request. Not unreasonably, she claimed that the household had been severely disrupted, so the habitual family dinner could not be contrived in time. Trays in their apartments would have to suffice.

That she might have had other reasons for keeping them from congregating around the dinner table became apparent to Darcy soon enough – namely, when Lady Catherine came to find him in the library, where he sat with Mr Bennet and the colonel around the much-needed and warmly appreciated port decanter, and asked him to join her in her private parlour across the hall.

"You may bring your port, if you wish," Lady Catherine graciously allowed him, and Darcy refilled his glass, his lips twitching at the air with which she had vouchsafed him that privilege, as though he were a youth fresh out of Cambridge, and not a grown man of nearly nine-and-twenty. But such was her way, and however tiresome it was to be still treated like a youngster, he was too relieved by the stark improvement in Anne's condition to take exception to trifling details, and had no wish to squabble with his aunt.

That set of noble sentiments remained with him for about a quarter of an hour, as he sat in Lady Catherine's private parlour and received a detailed report on Anne's current state of health.

"She is very feeble, but the physician assured me that with good rest and light nourishment she would be able to leave her bed in a fortnight. Maybe sooner."

"Thank goodness," Darcy replied with genuine fervour. "That is excellent news."

"Aye. Excellent news, indeed. So I am prepared to let bygones be bygones, and look to the future rather than revisit the past."

"A sensible choice," Darcy remarked, once he had taken a sip of his drink.

"Why, thank you," his aunt replied with a thin smile which, along with her tone, suggested she found it a backhanded compliment. "I have always been sensible. I trust you will follow my example."

Darcy took another sip and asked, "Your meaning?"

Lady Catherine gave a fleeting grimace.

"Come, Darcy, you must know I am speaking of your marriage to Anne. It must take place as soon as possible," she declared, and thus put paid to her nephew's good intentions about preserving the family harmony.

Darcy set his glass down and straightened in his seat, the earlier noble sentiments vanished and his mien stern.

"I thought this charade was set aside, and that facts could not be plainer to you and everybody else. Anne does not wish to marry me, nor I her. This chimerical scheme of yours will never come to pass. 'Tis high time you let it rest."

Lady Catherine skewered him with a formidable stare.

"I most certainly shall not! I can barely forgive myself for allowing you to leave it in abeyance for so long. Had you married her five, six years ago, as you were meant to, and taken her away to safety, this— this abomination might have been avoided. And she would not have been exposed for so long to that vile woman's debilitating potions."

"So much for not revisiting the past," Darcy said grimly. "As to the debilitating potions, you may have the satisfaction of knowing that Anne only took them when you hovered over her and badgered her into it," he remorselessly drove in a hit he might have otherwise refrained from and considered it beneath him. As it was, he continued, "I have that from Anne's own lips: she loathed the taste of the revolting things, and when you left her to her own devices, she and her lady's maid disposed of spoonful after spoonful in her washbowl and a small crack in the floor."

Lady Catherine gasped.

"She never said a word to me."

Darcy shrugged.

"Why should she? Instead of warm encouragement and attention to her wishes, she received edicts and dictates. Who should blame her for choosing the path of least resistance? But she has struggled under your domineering rule for long enough. She deserves to have her wishes heeded. She wishes to marry Henry Beaumont, not me. And as you well know by now, it is Elizabeth I wish to marry."

"Hush, child," Lady Catherine snapped. "This nonsense must come to an end. I will not hear another word about Anne's ridiculous infatuation, nor yours. She cannot marry a mere vicar, and you certainly shall not marry some penniless chit I was foolish enough to admit into my home. Anne needs you. Of course the pair of you must wed – and you shall, as soon as she can stand. The week after Trinity Sunday will do nicely. She will be recovered by then, and there is just enough time for the banns to be read."

His countenance darkened into a scowl of anger and exasperation, Darcy stood, fists tightened at his sides.

"The date of my marriage is not of your choosing, nor is my bride. I will marry Elizabeth, not Anne."

"Enough!" Lady Catherine enunciated. "Hear me in silence. You will do your duty to Anne. You owe it to her, to me and to your mother. You will take Anne to Pemberley and keep her safe there, away from this pernicious influence. Heavens above! Beaumont! Do you imagine I would allow her to marry into that family, who cannot even keep their servants in good order?"

"It is her choice. I fail to see how you aim to prevent it. She is of age, and her fortune is her own. You cannot even threaten her with disinheritance."

Lady Catherine's lips twisted into a malevolent half-smile.

"I can ensure that Lord Metcalfe does not get distracted, and remembers to prosecute old Beaumont for criminal negligence," she hissed. "That cursed maid of his admitted in our hearing that she had been suffered to adulterate Anne's draughts for years, and he had noticed nothing."

"Good God! You would stoop to *that?* " Darcy exclaimed, wide-eyed with outrage.

"It will serve the purpose," his aunt sneered. "Not to mention the attempted murder, with deadly poison added to the draughts under his very nose."

"*Attempted* is the material word," Darcy shot back, only to send her ladyship into a loud paroxysm of horror.

"What? Did you want Gibbs to succeed? Are you so enslaved by that hussy's base charms as to wish for your own cousin's demise?"

Darcy glared back.

"You will not speak thus of Elizabeth. And pray cease with this utter nonsense. Of course I do not wish Anne harmed. All I said was that there was no crime."

"No crime? *No crime?* " Lady Catherine spluttered. "That vile creature sought to take Anne's life, fed her noxious draughts for years and for all I know caused untold damage to her health – yet you call this no crime? Others were sent to Botany Bay for stealing a kerchief, a loaf of bread or a card of lace. This is the attempted murder of a baronet's daughter – an earl's niece," she pointed out, raising her chin with an air of supreme self-consequence. "Do you imagine that I – or good old English law, for that matter – will allow any of those responsible to remain unpunished? And that I will sit by and let Anne trade her ancient name for one tainted by scandal?"

"I have no doubt that Anne will tell you precisely what she thinks of your interference in her affairs as soon as she can speak at length," Darcy retorted sharply. "As to what *I* think, you can hear it here and now: you have no business and no right to interfere in mine."

"I have *every* right! I am your mother's sister. One of the few remaining links to her that you have in the world. And I am entitled – nay, duty-bound – to have a say in all your nearest concerns."

"Is that so?" Darcy scoffed. "How frightfully convenient, your ability to unite duty with pleasure."

Had there been any witnesses to that scene, they would have found uncanny similarities between the two protagonists that continued to glower at each other. The famed Fitzwilliam profile stood out as the most notable, of course – but several other ones could be identified upon closer inspection. Dark eyes, the same colour and shape, narrowed into flinty stares. Nostrils flaring with deep intakes of breath. Taut lips, thinned into matching grimaces of displeasure. And above all, the same resolute air of strong-willed characters for whom submission was unthinkable. It was the great similarity in their disposition that made them hold each other in mutual respect and rarely-displayed affection. Yet that very similarity was sure to bring almighty claps of thunder whenever their wills and their tempers clashed.

The witness, when he came – unerringly drawn by the raised voices – had little opportunity to reflect upon the advantages and disadvantages of equally unyielding natures. Mr Bennet was only regaled with the rather diverting sight of identical glares, turned towards the door at the interruption. Much as he expected it would rile them further, he could not suppress a chuckle at that *tableau vivant*. He came in and closed the door behind him before approaching them, a glass in each hand.

"Oh, dear. I thought we have had enough excitement for one day," he good-naturedly remarked, and offered one of the glasses to his wife. "Sherry, my dear? My apologies, Darcy. If you require a refill, I fear you may have to procure it yourself."

"No need, I thank you," Darcy muttered, and reached for his abandoned glass, still almost full, and had the good manners to refrain from sullenly draining it in one draught.

Across from him, on the other side of the now quiet arena, Lady Catherine had a word of thanks for her attentive husband and took a sip of her own drink.

"I have just persuaded the colonel to retire," Mr Bennet casually informed them, "and I hope to have as much success with the two of you. What say you, ma'am? Shall I escort you above-stairs? Rest will do you a world of good after all your exertions. And I imagine a few drops of laudanum will not go amiss."

"Your concern does you credit, sir, but pray let me assure you, I am none the worse for my exertions, as you call them. And laudanum is for weaklings."

Mr Bennet chortled.

"Surely not. I hear the Prince of Wales breakfasts, dines and sups on it."

"Bah. My point entirely," Lady Catherine scoffed.

"Regardless," shrugged Mr Bennet, "I think we should seek our beds and leave further debates for the morrow. Matters tend to have a sunnier aspect in the morning."

For all their earlier differences, Darcy and Lady Catherine were instantly united in their visible inclination to dispute that statement, as the glances they cast him clearly showed. It was her ladyship who hastened to give voice to her sentiments, without equivocation:

"I disagree. I have long come to see it is your way to avoid unpleasantness and conflict, Mr Bennet, but I am cut from a different cloth. Conflict shall not deter me from my purpose, nor make me shy away from speaking plainly. My character has always been celebrated for its frankness, and in so momentous a circumstance as this, I shall certainly not depart from it. Matters must be addressed. They have been set aside for long enough, and look at the resulting mischief: that awful woman's deeds and the unsavoury complications with your second daughter. Rest assured, I will acknowledge my own error," she declared, and the unprecedented statement gave Darcy pause in his obvious intention to object to the reference to Elizabeth and *'unsavoury complications.'* Yet he could not fail to snort when Lady Catherine continued, "No one can claim that I am prejudiced or unjust. If ever I find myself in the wrong, I address the matter fairly and promptly. So, everything considered, I owe you an apology for my unfounded allegations regarding Elizabeth's tisane—"

Mr Bennet's reply came with a tight smile and the habitual dose of sarcasm:

"I thank you, but I think it is Elizabeth who is owed this apology. Seeing as one cannot apologise to a tisane."

Once more, Darcy found himself in agreement with his aunt. Judging by her turn of countenance, she resented Mr Bennet's comment as much as he. Likely for very different reasons. He found the older gentleman's levity misplaced. She, no doubt, took umbrage at the notion of apologising to Elizabeth.

Her ladyship pursed her lips and resumed, pique now obvious in both her mien and her terse tone of voice:

"Yes, well. That is as may be. Nevertheless, it must be said that I brought you and your daughters into my home to please Anne and give her a new zest for life, yet your Elizabeth has caused me naught but trouble. And I will be frank in this as well: I shall brook no opposition, from you or anyone else. My daughter, and not yours, will be installed at Pemberley as Mrs Darcy."

"Over my dead body," Darcy spluttered.

Lady Catherine darted a fierce glance towards him.

"It can be arranged."

"I imagine so. But it rather defies the purpose, does it not?" Darcy retaliated, as apt as his aunt to resort to harsh and bitter sarcasm.

And that was when he saw Mr Bennet truly lose his temper.

"Heaven help us! *Will* you be quiet, sir? You may bluster at Pemberley at your leisure, if that is your wish, but as yet you do not command at Rosings. I hope I make myself clear. The library, sir! Be off with you and seek some brandy. It will work wonders for your temper."

However ominous the sight of Mr Bennet in the heat of anger, Darcy could not suppress his instinct for rebellion.

"I highly doubt it," he shot back. "It is not my way to drown my troubles, but tackle them head-on."

"And it is not my way to have my kin exposed to violent and unrelenting conflict. Is that understood?"

"Is this your last word?" Darcy asked through gritted teeth, his eyes shooting daggers. "Then let me tell you, there is always Gretna."

Mr Bennet squared his shoulders and fixed him with a dark stare.

"You have not heard my last word yet, but by God, you shall if you cannot curb your temper. There will be no more talk of Gretna, or anything of the sort. The library, Mr Darcy!" he indicated with a formidable gesture, thus leaving the younger man with few options beyond scowling back in impotent fury and stalking out of the room.

Lady Catherine sighed and sipped her sherry, then glanced at her partner in life.

"You have my thanks, sir," she wearily said. "I thought my second husband was as weak-willed as my first, but I am rather pleased to see I was mistaken."

Mr Bennet smoothed his lapels and flicked a little white speck off his sleeve.

"Glad to be of service, my dear. Now, pray do retire. I will join you directly, as soon as I have smoothed your nephew's ruffled feathers," he finished with a chuckle.

"I appreciate it," Lady Catherine said, then sighed. "Sadly, Darcy is his father's son, and as headstrong as they come. But fortunately he is also his mother's. His will is no match for mine – just as my sister's never was, God rest her soul – and I do not doubt I shall prevail upon him to do his duty by his mother and her final wishes. Still, it is a comfort to have your support. I must confess I did not expect it. Never predictable, you said," Lady Catherine concluded, and cast him one of her rare smiles as she set down her empty glass.

Mr Bennet bowed. On her way to the door, Lady Catherine paused beside him to press his arm in silent gratitude.

A comfort, aye, and a pleasant surprise to finally have an arm to lean on, after all those years, she mused. Two-score and sixteen years of fighting her battles without assistance. Sir Lewis's supporting arm had been as weak as a twig, and long before his passing she had had nothing but her own inner strength to draw upon. Ruling by dint of will was doubtlessly exhilarating, but it was exhausting too. Now more than ever. Lady Catherine shrugged. No, she was by no means ready to acknowledge that she was getting old. Nevertheless, it was an unexpected comfort to have a man about the house at last.

✦✦✦

The man of the house made his way into the library to be met, just as he had expected, by Darcy's angry glower from the fireside where he stood, brandy in hand.

Good, at least the lad had followed that piece of sensible advice, Mr Bennet thought, and this time did suppress the untimely chuckle. Still scowling, Darcy tossed down the contents of the glass, slammed it upon the mantelpiece and turned to eye him squarely with an unfriendly stare.

"Perhaps you will be so kind as to explain what *that* was about," Darcy asked, the tone just as unfriendly. "Am I to understand I am the last one to care for your daughter's happiness and interests?"

Mr Bennet shook his head and his lips twitched as he poured himself a generous measure of the selfsame amber liquid. Then, taking the decanter with him, he leisurely strolled towards the fireplace to join his grim-faced inquisitor.

"You might very well wonder why I tolerate your appalling insolence with such equanimity," he said with a benign smile as he refilled Darcy's glass. "The truth, my boy, is that it warms my heart. Ah, to be young, impetuous and head over heels in love!"

His eyes twinkled in renewed amusement when he heard the other's wrathful snort, and he set down the decanter to affectionately clasp Darcy's shoulder.

"You have a vast deal to learn about the married state, and the sooner you apply yourself to the task, the better. To begin with, has no one ever told you, Son, that flies are caught with honey and not vinegar?"

Chapter 35

Rosings, 20 April 1812

The first two hours of the new day had already ticked away, and Lady Catherine still could not fall asleep. She tossed and turned, and pondered on getting out of bed to nibble on something from the supper tray she had barely touched, or coax sleep with another glass of sherry. She stared at the mantelpiece clock, illuminated by the rays of the full moon as she pondered on a rather more fantastical notion – namely, returning to her husband's chamber. Well, not fantastical as such. She had not gone through the vast trouble of consulting with her attorneys for weeks on end and regulating the de Bourgh affairs for the sole purpose of pleasing Anne and spending the remainder of her days in a celibate marriage. Her second husband had not disappointed her in that regard, which was just as well. Her first marriage had brought more than its fair share of disappointments.

And lately it had emerged she had not known the half of it, Lady Catherine thought and snorted. An elopement. An annulled marriage. Sir Lewis de Bourgh had been a dark horse indeed.

It was inevitable that her thoughts should drift towards the woman who had crawled out from Sir Lewis's past and sought to obliterate Anne's future. Had distilled poison, to cut her down in the prime of her life. Had ruined years upon years of her girlhood, making her weak and sickly. And after the protracted torment she had inflicted upon an innocent child, no similar penance would be visited upon her – nay, just an all too brief encounter with a very tight noose. Violent fury stirred in Lady Catherine's breast and rose to her throat. Justice had lost its way. If only she could travel back in time two hundred years, and take Martha Gibbs with her! They meted out the right punishment then. That woman richly deserved to be drawn and quartered.

Yet it was her own chest that suddenly felt the stabbing pain, and then another, and another. Not knives, but venomous snakes, burying their fangs into her breastbone and her neck, then slithering along her arm, still biting as they went.

Lady Catherine clutched at her throat, but the snakes would not be prised away. Instead, they bit deeper and with renewed fury. A choked gasp broke free from her lips as she wished she had spent the night in her husband's bed – then he would have been at hand to give her assistance. Her left arm was still tormented by the fierce snakes but, clutching at her throat, Lady Catherine reached out towards her nightstand, fumbling, groping, too overcome by pain to know what she was seeking.

The bell-pull was elsewhere, near the headboard. She did not seek it, did not pull it. No maid was woken, to come and find her struggling, and then rush in panic to rouse Mr Bennet and summon Dr Beaumont.

The first was snoring softly two doors down, in his bedchamber that lay just beyond Lady Catherine's sitting room. The latter was slumbering in a wingchair as he sought to keep watch over Miss de Bourgh, having ceded his bed to his son, and Henry Beaumont had finally succumbed to sleep as well, exhausted in both mind and body.

Apart from three careworn maids shuffling up the backstairs towards their garrets and two young people who still lay awake in their beds at opposite ends of the great house, yearning for each other and for the sweet madness of a secret assignation, everyone else sheltered under the roof of Rosings Park slept the sleep of the just, while Lady Catherine struggled. And then her struggle mercifully came to an end at last.

⚜

The light of dawn crept into the eastern skies, and on this backdrop, the outlines of the lime trees atop the hillock opposite steadily grew easier to distinguish, as the still-hidden sun inched its way along its daily journey. For want of better employment, George Darcy was amusing himself with watching rosy tints slowly prevailing over dark-grey and purplish hues, when a voice he had not heard in above nine years and had never missed suddenly put an end to the tranquillity.

"Good morning. It must be, for some. I wish to see my sister."

George Darcy spun around on his insubstantial heel.

"Catherine! You are... dead?"

"Of course I am dead," his sister-in-law snapped. "How else would I be walking through the walls of your long gallery?"

"Ah. I am distraught to hear that, for everyone concerned." Himself included, George Darcy thought with a wry grimace. "What has befallen you?"

"That is irrelevant," Lady Catherine impatiently replied. "I must see Anne. She is somewhere around here, I gather."

"She is. Anne?" George Darcy called, and his wife promptly joined him from wherever she was seeking ways to entertain herself, blissfully unaware of the unexpected distraction in the gallery.

"Heavens! Catherine!" Lady Anne gasped.

"Pray do not ask if I am dead," Lady Catherine tersely forestalled her. "Your husband just did. But then he always was one for overstating the obvious."

"Now, now," Lady Anne mildly checked her sister's outburst with a quiet chuckle. "I will not have spirited disagreements. I have had my fill of them while we were alive."

"Spirited—" Lady Catherine spluttered. "I am ashamed of you, Anne. Stooping to puns, and such a poor one, too."

"I thought it was inspired," George Darcy intervened, sharing a smile with his wife. What a pity they had not experienced this camaraderie and the gratifying sentiment of presenting a united front against his confounded sister-in-law while they were still among the living. He gave a rueful chortle and could only console himself with the same old adage he had repeatedly resorted to, ever since he had entered this new plane of existence: better late than never.

Lady Catherine fixed him with a withering stare, then turned towards her sister.

"This is no time for levity. We have grave matters to address. I called for you – insistently and repeatedly, I might add – but since you would not come and assist your elder sister, I was forced to hie off all the way up here to fetch you myself. Make haste, Anne, there is no time to lose."

"Make haste? Where to?" her sister asked.

"Rosings. We must go there at once."

"Why? And more to the point, *how*? How is it that you are here, if you passed away at Rosings? I could never leave Pemberley, much as I wished."

Lady Catherine pursed her lips.

"You wished it lamely. Something in the vein of *'Oh, if only I could leave,'* I do not doubt. You must will it with the firmest determination—"

"Oh, I did!" Lady Anne cut her off. "With the firmest determination I wished I could go to Georgiana when she—"

"When she – what?" Lady Catherine prompted her younger sister into finishing her truncated sentence.

Understandably, Lady Anne would not share the grievous tale.

"No matter," she said crisply. "But I assure you, it was not a lame wish. Nevertheless, it led to nothing."

Lady Catherine gave a dismissive shrug.

"Then it must have been your lack of confidence in yourself and your abilities. That had always been your greatest failing. Not enough drive, you see, and easily settling for what you were given. Accepting the first offer of marriage you received was a case in point."

"That was uncalled for, Catherine," Lady Anne admonished her.

George Darcy snorted.

"Of course, marrying a scatterbrained baronet with a fondness for the gaming tables was *so* much better."

"At least Sir Lewis had the decency to pass away in his prime and leave me to my own devices, rather than putting me through the pain and peril of childbirth time and again for the sake of his lineage," his sister-in-law viciously retaliated.

Lady Anne gasped in shock, even before she caught the look of profound injury in her husband's countenance.

"Catherine! How *dare* you tax him with that? You will apologise at once, or you will leave my house," she declared, a fierce blaze in her eyes, which mellowed beyond recognition into persuasive softness when she turned towards the father of her children. "You know it was not so. I wanted a son as much as you did. I wanted a houseful of children."

George Darcy winced.

"She is in the right. We... I should have left you be once Fitzwilliam was born. Then perhaps—"

"Then perhaps we would not have had the little closeness that there was," Lady Anne said with energy. "We were never good at talking to each other and sharing our thoughts, more was the pity. But there was closeness then, and I relished it."

"You did?" George Darcy's eyes warmed, yet somehow they were still full of sorrow. "Foolish girl… You never said. I thought you barely tolerated my attentions—"

"Heavens above! I have not come all the way to Pemberley to listen to this kind of talk. Pray save the mortifying details of your unrewarding marriage for when you are alone," Lady Catherine cut in rolling her eyes, thus goading her brother-in-law beyond endurance.

George Darcy turned on her with a dark sneer.

"Pray tell me, *why* have you come all this way in your nightclothes, Sister? And why will you not discuss the manner of your passing?"

Under George Darcy's steady glare, his sister-in-law's eyes widened in outrage, and her visage instantly dulled into opaque grey. He had invariably noticed a similar transformation whenever he had made Lady Anne's ghost blush, but judging by the colour in Lady Catherine's cheeks, if she were alive her complexion would have burned bright crimson. He tossed his head back and laughed.

"What is it?" Lady Anne asked.

Her sister spluttered, "If you say another word, George Darcy, I shall—!"

"What? Kill me? Swear eternal enmity? I hate to point out the obvious, as I am apparently apt to do, but I am already dead and we heartily detest each other."

Lapsing into ribaldry was improper even by the standards of his more permissive and bawdier generation, and doubtlessly beneath him, George Darcy inwardly acknowledged, but Catherine was insupportable. And after all, when one was dead, one should be allowed at least *some* meagre share of entertainment. So he gave in to the temptation to provoke her:

"My, my," he drawled. "My compliments to Mr Bennet. Not too shabby for a man his age. He must be no spring chicken if he has five grown daughters. What a pity you have not remarried sooner, Sister. Then you might have had a more measured response to marital delights, and would not have ended with your claws up in the sawdust like an old bird fallen off its perch."

Her cheeks still a dull grey, Lady Catherine scowled disgustedly.

"You always were horribly uncouth, but this is despicable, even for you. It was nothing of the sort, I will have you know, and you can keep your shameless fantasies to yourself."

"Do you imagine I have lost my senses to fantasise about your intimate exploits, much as they proved themselves to be something to die for?" George Darcy shot back.

"What sparkling wit," Lady Catherine jeered. "As I just said, you are wholly off the mark. My demise was all that was proper and decorous, while I was trying to fall asleep. Not that this is any concern of yours."

"And you found yourself in a deeper sleep than you had bargained for. And permanent, to my misfortune."

Her ladyship glowered.

"Of course, I passed away simply to disoblige you," Lady Catherine scoffed, then shrugged. "I expected nothing better than self-centredness and crude remarks from you. After all, you always were but an obscenely rich sheep farmer," she venomously spat.

"If my sheep farm is not good enough for your exalted lineage, why are you still badgering my son to marry your daughter?"

"Because the boy has the best of both: your wealth and the Fitzwilliam backbone. He will take care of her."

"What if they do not wish to become united?"

"Nonsense. This union was agreed upon ever since they were in their cradles."

"Not with me, it was not. And not with my wife, either. You did what you always do: hear only what you wish to hear and seek to browbeat everyone into submission. It will not serve you this time. Fitzwilliam will not marry Anne. Not while I have any breath left in my body."

"You have neither breath nor body," came Lady Catherine's mordant jibe. "You are dead, have you forgotten? Your word is no longer law at Pemberley. My sister's son is master here, while you rot under the lime trees. And the betrothal was agreed upon. Anne, tell him."

But the incensed demand received no answer, and at last the fierce opponents tore their eyes from each other to cast a glance around them and find they were alone. Lady Anne had literally vanished into thin air.

"See, you have distressed her, just as you always do," George Darcy bitterly reproached his sister by marriage, then called, "Anne? Where are you, my dear? Your sister is leaving, I can promise you that."

"Yes, well, you always were one for making promises you were powerless to keep."

"Catherine, I am warning you—"

"Oh, save your empty threats. You can have your wish. I *am* leaving."

"Anne? Have you heard? She is leaving."

But to his increased vexation, Lady Catherine snorted.

"Not without my sister, I am not. Anne will come with me."

"Where is she now?"

Lady Catherine's thin lips curled into a smug grimace.

"Why should I tell you? I think it speaks volumes that you cannot sense her."

"And you can," George Darcy scoffed.

"Of course," his nemesis sneered. "She is my sister. Family ties will not be broken, and they are always stronger than the paltry attachment the pair of you might have. I can sense her from hundreds of miles. How did you think I knew she was at Pemberley, and not in town or goodness knows where else? But never mind that now. She must accompany me to Rosings."

"How?" George Darcy asked, cold hatred still glinting in his eyes.

But his glare had no effect on Lady Catherine. It merely served to fuel her glee.

"Oh, would you not like to know?" she taunted him with an evil little chuckle – and vanished from his sight.

"Anne, where are you?" George Darcy called in the now empty gallery. "Catherine? Has she left Pemberley? How can I follow her? So help me, Catherine, don't you dare leave without telling me!"

But all he could hear was a faint but clearly vengeful cackle that almost drove him wild with rage. Seeking vainly to subdue it, George Darcy sifted through the exchanges of the last half-hour. Yet they did not serve him. His reviled sister-in-law had revealed nothing about how she could travel from one part of the country to the other. She had merely spoken of firm determination and supreme confidence in one's abilities.

"Brazen confidence, rather," he growled, "and selfish disdain for everything but her own wishes." Moreover, the wretched woman was wrong. He *could* sense his wife's presence. Not from hundreds of miles perhaps, that had never been tested, but he could sense her in her old parlour. The dispute must have distressed her – conflict always did. And the same could be said about her sister.

"Catherine, I would dearly wish to wring your neck," he muttered as he willed himself above-stairs, into his wife's private sitting room.

To his relief, she was still there. Sadly, so was Lady Catherine.

"How should I know why you could not travel from one place to another?" his sister-in-law unfeelingly blustered. "You should exert yourself more. But this is not the time to dally and experiment. Let me do the work now. Give me your hand, and I will take you with me."

"Can you?" Lady Anne asked, her voice full of doubt.

There was not a shade of it in Lady Catherine's when she replied:

"Of course. Nothing had ever stopped me from doing as I pleased when I was alive, and I see no reason why this should change now. Come, let us be on our way."

"And my husband?" Lady Anne asked, before she had even noticed his presence. "I will not leave without him," she declared, warming his heart.

Lady Catherine cast him a grim scowl.

George Darcy had no scruples about returning it.

"Oh, very well," she grumbled. "I will tolerate him for a short while, if I must. I need you with me."

Lady Anne gave a small nod of satisfaction and followed her sister's sullen gaze, only to discover her husband. She cast him a smile and stretched out her hand. It was only once it was firmly linked with his that she would place sufficient trust in Lady Catherine so as to establish the other connection.

"Should the pair of you not hold hands too?" she asked the two arch enemies, but Lady Catherine bridled at the very notion.

"I am *not* holding his hand! Let him fall behind, for all I care."

Lady Anne pursed her lips, and George Darcy could sense her focus on their joined hands growing more intense than ever.

"Are you ready?" Lady Catherine asked, but her sister would not answer. Her eyes were on her husband, and thither also went her thoughts.

"Don't let go," was the last message George Darcy registered, before something akin to a fiercely whistling wind assaulted his hearing.

⋇

At first, he could barely take note of the altered surroundings as he fought the dizziness and willed it to pass. It did, and a vast deal sooner than he would have expected, whereupon he could see that they were no longer in his wife's parlour at Pemberley, but in a large and heavily-gilded drawing room he had not seen in above a decade. Anne was there too, her hand still linked with his.

Relief washed over him, at the same time as surprise at how incredibly easy it had been to get there. Instantly too, or at least it felt like it. Goodness, if he had only known how to achieve that feat. If only Anne had known. Then the poor darling would not have been marooned at Pemberley for so many years. With any luck, the other would eventually have the heart to share the secret, whatever that might be, and teach Anne how it was done – if not out of sisterly affection, then at least so that she could rid herself of him. But how galling indeed to owe that knowledge to Catherine!

He still could not tell if the vile woman could hear his every thought, just as Anne did, or only those he meant for others to hear. Either way, she stood some six yards away, eyeing him with profound displeasure.

"So you made it. A pity," she scornfully intoned with a tilt of her head that sent the feathers of her turban fluttering.

Somehow, she had already changed from her immodest attire into some sort of an evening dress, but George Darcy could not care less for his sister-in-law's fashion choices or for her lack of welcome. His gaze returned to his wife to ascertain how she was faring against what must have been a similar attack of dizziness. He did not even notice the new presence in the room – but Lady Catherine did, and spluttered:

"Who *are* you, madam?"

At that, George Darcy finally glanced up.

The newcomer paused in her tracks and curtsied.

"Good morning, ma'am," she cheerfully said. "Delighted to make your acquaintance at long last. I am Mrs Bennet."

Chapter 36

Rosings, 20 April 1812

The loudest gasp left Lady Catherine's ghostly lips.

"You have no business here, madam. This is *my* house."

The new apparition shrugged.

"I have every business to follow my daughters. And my husband, for that matter."

"Your husband! He is my husband now. What have you to say to that?"

"Only this: now that you and I are both dead as doornails, your claim on him is pitiful in comparison. You were married for – what? A fortnight or so? I was his wife for nineteen years and bore him five daughters. If any of us has the right to follow him, 'tis I. Not to mention a mother's right and duty to watch over her daughters."

"This is not to be borne," her unwilling host exclaimed.

"I fear you must learn to bear it with equanimity, your ladyship," the first wife said. "While they are still here, so am I."

Lady Catherine's eyes became awfully wide.

"No! Pray tell me you have not been here the entire time."

The other shrugged again.

"I fear I cannot oblige you. I came into Kent when Lydia did, the sweet child. My youngest, you know. She has always been the apple of my eye. I stayed at the parsonage first, with my daughter Mary. When my other girls moved here, I followed. What was one to do?"

"Heaven knows. Find a crypt or haunt some ruin, but begone from my house and keep away from my husband."

Mrs Bennet tittered.

"Why, your ladyship, I do believe you are jealous."

"Jealous? Of you? A tradesman's daughter who has been dead for years? Do not flatter yourself. If anyone exhibits that unworthy emotion, 'tis you."

The sudden jerk of Mrs Bennet's head sent her locks bouncing. She must have been justly proud of her wavy tresses, for she did not hide them under a matron's cap, but wore her hair adorned with beads and ribbons, and ringlets framed her still youthful countenance. She seemed to have passed away in her late thirties, just like his dear Anne had, George Darcy speculated. Perhaps at an even younger age than Anne, judging by her barely lined features. And very handsome features they were too, hinting at great beauty in the full bloom of youth.

If she had bestowed those good looks upon her daughters, no wonder Fitzwilliam was thoroughly besotted with one of them. What a pity she had lost her life and left them all when they badly needed her, just as Fitzwilliam and dear Georgy needed their mother. Poor Anne. And this poor woman, too.

But the turn of Mrs Bennet's countenance did not seem to invite pity. The look she cast Lady Catherine was mildly condescending and supremely unconcerned.

"Oh, not at all, I assure you. He married me for the deepest love when I was barely out of the schoolroom. Why would I be jealous, when I know full well he only married you for the girls' sake? If anything, I was rather pleased with him about it. I never thought he would give himself the trouble."

"Trouble!" Lady Catherine snorted. "Are you implying he regarded it as trouble to wed the daughter of an earl? Or that he married me for my fortune?"

"Clearly not for your looks," Mrs Bennet giggled, endearing herself immensely to the former master of Pemberley, who roared with laughter.

His sister-in-law's far from feminine visage developed an uncanny resemblance to a toad as her cheeks puffed up in profound outrage.

"I have never heard such—"

"For goodness' sake, *enough*," Lady Anne called out, the force of her passion making the windows rattle. "No, Catherine," she forestalled her sister with a firm voice and a promptly raised hand. "No more of this. I came to see my son. Where is Fitzwilliam?"

"Are you speaking of the charming colonel, or his exceedingly handsome cousin, ma'am?" Mrs Bennet chimed in.

"The latter," Lady Anne smiled, understandably gratified by the compliment to her son.

"By the bye, how do you tell them apart in conversation? At first, I found it most confusing. It was very hard indeed to determine if your lovely daughter was speaking of her cousin or her brother."

"You would have had to face no such difficulties if you were not eavesdropping on the conversations of your betters," Lady Catherine resentfully retorted.

"Sister, calm yourself," Lady Anne urged, then turned back to Mrs Bennet. "Madam, my son?"

"Yes, of course. Pray follow me. I think I know where we might find him at this hour in the morning."

"And now you presume to play hostess in my house?" Lady Catherine fumed.

"That is because she knows where I can find Fitzwilliam," Lady Anne replied with a tired sigh. "Do *you?* "

"Why, in his bedchamber of course, at this early hour. Or perhaps the library. Where else?"

"Pray follow me, your ladyship," Mrs Bennet spoke up again with a smug little smile that told them she set no store by Lady Catherine's statement. "But might I ask, why did you choose to bless the young man with such a mouthful of a Christian name?"

From her place beside George Darcy, a proximity that was displeasing to both, Lady Catherine snorted yet again.

"A mouthful indeed. Do not presume to pass judgement on matters beyond your grasp. You have no understanding of the ways of the highest circles. This mouthful you speak of is the exalted name of my forefathers, bestowed upon my sister's son to honour an ancient lineage."

The first wife chose to ignore the second, and continued to address herself to Lady Anne instead:

"Goodness. And your husband went along with it, ma'am? For his firstborn, moreover? I doubt Mr Bennet would have, if we ever had a son," she mused, then resumed, "The name of Darcy puts me in mind of the French, so to my way of thinking his lineage is as long as yours. Longer even, if it went all the way to the Norman Conquest."

"A valid point, do you not think?" George Darcy taunted Lady Catherine, only to receive a grim scowl for his efforts, along with a mild shake of his wife's head at his determination to nettle her sister.

Then Lady Anne civilly spoke to Mrs Bennet:

"Pray pardon my lapse, madam. I have neglected to introduce my husband."

George Darcy bowed as the lady curtsied, then beamed.

"Oh. I was wondering who the gentleman might be, but I did not wish to pry. Ah, I see it now, the family resemblance," she added, settling a long look upon him. "In the line of your jaw, sir. And also the firm cheekbones and wide brow. Not the eyes," she decided, upon further inspection. "Your son has your wife's eyes. A most successful combination of very handsome features, if I may say so," the lady concluded with a flirtatious little smile, then turned away and indicated, "This way, if you please. We might as well look into the library, seeing as we are here. Lady Catherine is in the right as to your son's fondness for it, I will give her that," she nonchalantly added. "But since he favours his privacy more, and my husband would not budge from any library for hours on end, given half a chance, young Mr Darcy can but seldom have the run of it. But, might I ask, why are you seeking him? And how do you propose to communicate with him once you have found him? I have never been able to get my point across to my relations, and believe you me, I tried and tried."

"We must find a way," Lady Catherine intervened before Lady Anne could answer.

"Why is that?" Mrs Bennet inquisitively queried.

"Not that it is any business of yours, but he must be persuaded to marry Anne forthwith. I will not have her unprotected, now that I am gone."

"Not this foolishness again—!" George Darcy began, but Mrs Bennet was there before him.

"Oh, do cease fretting," she admonished Lady Catherine. "Miss de Bourgh is in no need of protection. Mr Bennet will deal fairly with her. He would never cheat her out of her inheritance even if he could, the foolish man. And had he wished to, you have already ensured he could not. I saw the marriage settlement when you signed it."

"You sneaky creature!" Lady Catherine cried.

"I had the right to know what was being done for my girls," Mrs Bennet said with a shrug. "And give me leave to say you could have been more generous, given your vast fortune. Still, better than nothing. Not too bad, ten thousand pounds split between my daughters when my husband joins us. Oh-ho, it should be vastly entertaining when the three of us make it to Heaven, if and when we do. Eternity with two wives, of which you are one," she chortled and winked at Lady Catherine. "True and fitting punishment for ignoring me for the latter part of our union. Oh, my dear Mr Bennet, long may you linger above ground, for afterlife will be a far cry from what you have envisaged."

She was still chortling when she glided into the library ahead of the party, only to make an about-turn when she discovered it was empty.

"Where next?" Lady Anne asked.

Mrs Bennet's rather fine eyes twinkled.

"The garden. I'd wager you will find him strolling within sight of the side entrance, waiting for my Lizzy. I am pleased to say he makes a habit of it."

"He does no such thing," Lady Catherine protested.

But Mrs Bennet gave a gleeful snort.

"How would you know? Did you not hear from Evans that they went for an early morning walk together yesterday? Pray do not flatter yourself into thinking it was the only time he sought my Lizzy out. So there you have it: even if you can communicate with young Mr Darcy, he will never be browbeaten into marrying your daughter for the simple reason that he is very much in love with mine. There, madam, and pray feast upon it."

"Who is Evans?" George Darcy asked.

Predictably, Lady Catherine ignored him.

"A preposterous infatuation," she hissed. "He has more sense than to succumb to it."

Another smug little smile tugged at the corner of Mrs Bennet's lips.

"You may think so, if it gives you comfort. But mark my words, you are headed for a disappointment. I know of what I speak and, moreover, I have evidence to support it."

"What evidence?"

"That of my own eyes."

"Pah!" Lady Catherine scornfully dismissed her, but Mrs Bennet would be neither cowed, nor silenced.

"Listen first and you can snort at leisure later. He watches her when she is not looking."

"He most certainly *does not*," Lady Catherine declared with the firmest conviction. "I have not seen anything of the sort in all the time he has been here."

"As if he would be foolish enough to let you of all people see it," Mrs Bennet scoffed. "But you can take it from me, and you can put it in your pipe and smoke it: he does watch her, whenever he thinks he can do so with impunity. He always has, from the very first days of their acquaintance. All the time, you hear me? *All-the-time.* Hair-raising, I found it at first. Positively disturbing. But that was before I caught his meaning. I still find it hair-raising, I grant you, but in a good way. The sort of smouldering stare that melts the heart and gives you goosepimples. That young man's eyes could melt a rock, if I might be so bold as to say so to his parents."

"Bold? I call it brazen and immodest. Especially in one your age," Lady Catherine spat, eyeing Mrs Bennet up and down with profound contempt, while the parents at the receiving end of the questionable compliment chose to keep silent.

"And why is that?" Mrs Bennet argued back, undaunted. "If I am dead and buried, do you think I am blind to other people's passion? I can easily imagine why you would be. I'd wager no one had ever glanced upon you thus, so no wonder you cannot tell a look of passion from a halibut. Well, never you mind. Once the funeral is over, he can get on with the courtship without having to conceal it from you."

"My nephew would never injure my daughter's feelings in such a callous manner," Lady Catherine enunciated. "Courtship, indeed! He would never be so lost to every notion of decency as to court another under my bereaved daughter's eyes, when he has been promised to her from his cradle."

Mrs Bennet glanced from Lady Anne to Mr Darcy, doubt mingling with censure in her eyes.

"Truly? Now, I am all for finding spouses for one's offspring as much as anybody, but I must say, this was a vast weight dropped upon a tiny cradle."

George Darcy regaled her with a wide grin that made Mrs Bennet's lashes flutter.

For her part, Lady Anne gave a flourish of her hand towards both of Mr Bennet's late wives, as if to say "Pray leave me out of this."

"Any which way," Mrs Bennet resumed, "your bereaved daughter shan't object. You may not have noticed that she has given young Mr Darcy every assistance in courting my Lizzy – bless the pair of them, they sought to hide that from you as best they could – but you know as well as I do that your daughter would not have your nephew if he came on a silver platter. You only need to accept it," she firmly said, and at that declaration both of the gentleman's parents arched a brow.

They both knew full well that Anne had no romantic inclination for their son, but there was a world of difference between that and deeming him not good enough for her. *'Fitzwilliam not good enough for Anne? Preposterous!'* their looks said when they glanced briefly at each other.

Animated by very different sentiments, Lady Catherine nevertheless chose the same word to express them.

"Preposterous!" she spat. "Of course she will have him."

"I tell you she shall not. She will marry Mr Beaumont, and now there is nothing you can do to stop her," Mrs Bennet triumphantly pointed out, and at that Lady Catherine instinctively brought her hand to her chest as if she still had a racing heart there.

"But I *must* stop her," Lady Catherine rasped. "The heiress of Rosings wed to the penniless son of a country physician! No fortune. No connections. This is not to be borne!"

"Pray tell me, how will you go about it? Might I remind you that she cannot hear you, much as you rant and rave?"

"Oh, she will hear me! I must find a way."

"Leave the poor child be. You should know better than to seek to torment her from the grave. She will suffer enough when she learns you are gone. She seems to love you, for some reason that I cannot fathom."

Lady Catherine harrumphed.

"I am her mother. What better reason is there?"

Mrs Bennet made no answer, but moved towards the nearest window and raised a translucent arm, the sleeve richly adorned with lace.

"There is your son," she said to Lady Anne. "What did I tell you? Up with the lark, same as yesterday, waiting for my Lizzy."

Her companions approached and glanced out.

It was only Lady Catherine who scowled when she saw her nephew there. Her scowl grew even darker when he took out his pocket watch, checked the time, then placed it back and cast a glance towards the house, heaved a deep breath and took to pacing up and down along the gravelled walk.

"An assignation," she muttered. "That shameless little hussy has consented to a secret assignation."

The insult to Mrs Bennet's daughter was met not with that lady's anger, but with her diverted chuckle.

"Not that I know of, more's the pity. The young gentleman is hopeful, that is all. With any luck, the silly goose will awaken and glance out of her window. She had better bestir herself and not keep the poor man waiting long."

"She had better not," Lady Catherine retorted grimly. "In point of fact, I shall see to that myself," she declared and, intent upon her purpose, she swept towards the staircase out of habit, rather than simply willing herself above-stairs.

Mrs Bennet's derisive taunt rang cheerfully behind her.

"Will you, madam? How?"

Lady Anne and George Darcy exchanged quick glances and knew better than to enlighten the other ladies as to the ways in which departed souls might make their wishes known to those left behind. Instead, they moved closer to each other, and closer to the window. They made no effort to either follow their son into the garden or reach him with the joint power of their minds, but stood there, content to behold him yet again.

It came as no surprise that Mrs Bennet soon lost interest in them and their pursuit and glided away after Lady Catherine.

"Shall we go and see what your sister and her predecessor are up to?" George Darcy half-heartedly asked.

"I expect it might be diverting," Lady Anne said with a wisp of a smile, but did not stir.

Neither did he. Standing there with two of his nearest and dearest was more appealing than watching Lady Catherine grappling with the limitations of her current state. Besides, if he stood still and listened carefully, he might catch enough from where he was. Catherine had never been a quiet sort. Alive or dead, she would never be quiet.

❧ ❦ ❧

George Darcy's expectations were confirmed. Although his sister by marriage had long vanished up the grand staircase, he could clearly hear her remonstrating with Mrs Bennet:

"Is there any part of this house where I am free of you and your impertinence? Begone! You have no business to follow me. You shall not restrain me, I assure you."

Apparently, Mrs Bennet was not a quiet sort either, for her reply was no less audible:

"A fine spectacle that would be, us brawling like a pair of fishwives. What would Mr Bennet make of it, I wonder? Nay, rest easy, I did not come to restrain you. There is nothing you can do anyway. You cannot tie my Lizzy to a bedpost, nor lock her in her chamber. You cannot stop her in her tracks. But it shall be highly entertaining to see you try."

Lady Catherine growled.

"Goodness, your ladyship, you do have a frightful temper," Mrs Bennet snickered.

A few moments later, George Darcy could hear her gleeful chortle. There was no telling what might have amused her, but in the end the good lady seemed to have lost her patience.

"Madam, I am sorry to say that you are as dense as you are obstinate. Feel free to exert yourself further if you are so inclined, but I daresay you should accept the sad truth of our condition: they cannot hear us, and they will do just as they please, regardless of our wishes. Speaking of which, I think there is something you should see. I thought I should spare you that particular experience, seeing as this is the day of your demise and we should show you some gentleness and compassion, but by the looks of it, they are wasted on you. Come. Come and see why you should leave my Lizzy be, for the future is ordained and you shall not change it. Come along, now."

"Where? And of what are you speaking?" Lady Catherine snarled.

Mrs Bennet did not choose to explain herself. At least not in words. A silence followed, and it was very brief. A piercing shriek broke it:

"What is *he* doing here?" cried Lady Catherine.

"Would you like to go up now?" George Darcy asked his wife but, eyes still fixed upon their son's expectant countenance, Lady Anne shook her head.

"No need," she whispered. "Doubtlessly my sister will share the cause of her vexation soon enough."

⚬⚬ ⚬⚬

Lady Catherine's sentiments went unimaginably beyond vexation as she reluctantly followed Mrs Bennet into Anne's bedchamber and found Mr Beaumont sitting on the edge of her daughter's bed, her hand in his.

"How *dare* he?" Lady Catherine thundered. "In her rooms! Seeking to ruin her good name – take advantage of her weakness—"

"Oh, do be quiet," Mrs Bennet said. "Your daughter sent for him herself. She asked the good doctor to summon him when she awoke. You did tell her she could see Mr Beaumont in the morning, after all," she added with a sly grin, revealing to Lady Catherine that she was privy to all manner of conversations her ladyship might have once thought private.

While Lady Catherine's chest heaved with impotent fury, her daughter and the doctor's son continued their quiet conversation, which was not as private as they imagined, either.

"You should go now, my love," Anne said softly. "Go home and have some decent rest, and come to call in the afternoon. We shall have none of Evans' screens then, I promise you," she added with a smile. "I shall prevail upon your father to allow me to dress and await you in my sitting room."

Mr Beaumont stroked her hand and took it to his lips.

"How are we to prevail upon your mother, though?" he asked. "I expect her ladyship will bolt and bar the doors against me."

Anne gave a mild little laugh.

"She will surely try. But we shall prevail upon her, too."

"Never!" Lady Catherine growled.

At this new evidence that her ladyship still seemed to forget her present condition, Mrs Bennet shook her head, her mien half-sympathetic and half-exasperated.

"She loves me, Henry," Anne continued with a very tender smile. "I grant you, she often shows it in the most overbearing and highly aggravating manner, but she does love me. Dearest Mamma!

395

She thunders and blusters, but deep in her heart she wants me to be happy. All I need is to make her see there is no happiness for me without you."

"There you have it," Mrs Bennet said, her arm outstretched towards the couple. "She thinks the world of you, the poor lamb. The question is, has she judged you rightly?"

There were no tears in the afterlife, Mrs Bennet knew full well. Nor did Lady Catherine strike her as one who would allow herself the weakness and indulgence of tears. Yet her ladyship's eyes held a strange glint – a very strange glint indeed, as if they were brimming – when she blustered:

"How on earth did he live with you for nineteen years? Madam, do you *ever* hold your tongue?"

⋰⊙ ⊙⋱

When Lady Catherine made her way to the top of the grand staircase to return to her younger sister and seek the comfort of her presence, she could easily espy the slender figure that was scampering down the stairs. Yet, true to form, Mrs Bennet simply could not hold her tongue.

"Here goes my Lizzy," she needlessly pointed out.

"Eh," Lady Catherine muttered with a desultory wave of her hand.

Her despondent air of apathy remained unchanged even when she came to stand beside Lady Anne and looked out of the window at the young couple who were now holding hands, both of hers clasped in both of his and gathered to his chest, tender smiles brightening their faces.

"Thank you," said Darcy. "I scarce dared hope you would come."

"Yet here you are," she whispered back. "I hope I have not kept you waiting long."

He shook his head.

"No matter. You are worth the wait."

No snort came from Lady Catherine at her nephew's statement. Her chin taut and the corners of her lips still dragging down into a grimace of *blasé* indifference, she made no further comments about shameless little hussies when Elizabeth withdrew a hand from Darcy's to reach up and stroke his face, then slowly weaved her fingers through the unruly tangle at the back of his head to draw him closer as she stood on tiptoe to press her lips to his.

Mrs Bennet made no comment either, but smiled smugly and nodded in approval when he responded to her second daughter's overtures as warmly as a man violently in love could be expected.

It was only George Darcy who spoke:

"We should give them their privacy."

"Of course. In a moment," Lady Anne replied, then pondered, "She does love him, do you not think?"

"I believe she does," her husband said. "She certainly makes him happy."

Staggeringly, Lady Catherine did not remark upon that either, although the pair remained just as they were for some considerable time – right there, in full view of most if not all of Rosings' eastern windows – until they eventually came up for air, their faces but inches apart as they gazed at each other. Neither one drew back any further, even as Elizabeth said, "We will be seen."

"Should we still care?" he asked. "I must own, I do not. Do you?"

She chuckled.

"Not as such. But you are in the right: everything should be a vast deal easier at Pemberley."

His eyes took a hopeful glint.

"You will come? Has your father agreed?"

"Not yet. But he will."

The hopefulness dimmed.

"You think so? He gave me a different impression yesterday."

Elizabeth laughed mildly.

"Yes. He told me." And then her tone and countenance grew earnest when she added, "All will be well. I have had opportunities aplenty to learn that my father can be utterly infuriating at times, the dear man, but I trust him, Fitzwilliam. So should you."

"Say it again," he urged.

"Pray, do trust my father."

"Not that. My name."

"Fitzwilliam," she willingly obliged, her lips curled up into the softest smile.

Apparently, it was beyond his powers to resist its allure, and Darcy did not even seem inclined to try. His arm went about her waist and he brought her close for another long kiss – in truth, for several. He only drew back to ask, "How soon do you imagine we might leave?"

"I cannot say. But with any luck, as soon as Anne is recovered."

Darcy nodded, and his free hand came up to brush a stray lock off her face.

"I hope you can be persuaded to stay for as long as possible."

Her eyes twinkled at that.

"I confess I find myself in a quandary now. I am not altogether certain what response I should make."

"How so?"

Her gaze grew warmer, as did her smile.

"Well, strictly speaking, you have not asked me a particular question, so I fear it might be presumptuous and unladylike to say I was rather hoping I could stay indefinitely."

It came as no surprise to their relations – and presumably not to the directly interested parties either – that a fraction of a second later she was gathered to his chest, gloriously close.

"I love you," Darcy whispered raggedly between hungry kisses. "Good God, Elizabeth—" he groaned, tightening his hold. "I will brook no delay. A special licence – we shall procure a special licence and marry by the months' end. And my aunt can go hang."

"Charming," Lady Catherine muttered.

"Now, now, dear, you know he is not in earnest. He has always been so very fond of you, and will be distraught to hear of your passing," her sister said placatingly, only to receive a scowling "Hmph. He had better be. Our final exchange was a monstrous row."

George Darcy rolled his eyes. The woman was insufferable. He suppressed a gasp at the frightful notion that Anne might take pity on her and ask her to come and stay at Pemberley.

Good Lord, surely not!

And then he sighed with a measure of relief. The dear girl might, she was so tender-hearted, but with any luck Catherine would not wish to leave her daughter for long, if at all.

The question was, would Mrs Bennet seek to follow *her* daughter? It would be an imposition. Still, better than having Catherine to stay. Or, heaven forfend, the pair of them, an even more frightful thought suddenly occurred, and George Darcy shuddered.

Unwittingly proving his point, Mrs Bennet ill-advisedly prodded Lady Catherine.

"See, ma'am? Just as it should be, for your daughter and mine. Say what you will, but it warms the cockles of my heart to see them and their young men so full of joy and hope, and so in love."

"Yes, yes," Lady Catherine irritably cut her off. "And they shall all live happily ever after. But this house will go to wrack and ruin with me gone. I was distracted for one day, and 'tis in decline already. Look at the time. That good-for-nothing gal, my maid, is late with my morning tea. Heavens! Several hours have gone by, yet still no one knows nor cares that I'm dead!"

As if on cue, a wail and a loud clatter came from the direction of her former chamber.

"At last," Lady Catherine sniffed, rolling her eyes.

Epilogue

Pemberley, Summer 1820

Gleeful voices reached her through the open windows, and Elizabeth Darcy set aside her pen and her letter to her youngest sister and went to cast a glance outside. The warmest smile graced her countenance at the enchanting scene. The five people dearest to her heart had taken themselves into the gardens to enjoy the morning sun and their morning frolics. They were cheerfully lining up for a race, it seemed. A horse-race of sorts. Richard, her eldest, was in the middle, astride his hobbyhorse. Her beloved husband, whose playful side no longer surprised her after all these years, but never ceased to delight her, willingly served as darling Anne's mount. Their daughter – christened Anne Catherine five years ago – was squirming on his shoulders in a fit of giggles, her frilly cap askew, and her vast amusement unerringly fuelled Frederick's, her two-year-old sibling, who was perched on his grandfather's shoulders, chubby legs held fast as his little hands wreaked merry havoc in his own mount's silver hair, yet gave rise to no protest from the latter.

Elizabeth's smile grew wider.

Her darling Richard, with his fascination for the outdoors, was the first known person ever to succeed in drawing his grandpapa away from bookish pursuits. Then Anne had come to add fresh incentive for strolls and spirited gambols, and now Frederick was continuing the pattern. The exercise was doing her father a world of good. He looked younger than his years, suntanned and happy. They all looked happy, bless them. May they always be so.

Richard's cry gave the signal for the race to begin, and they set off across the lawn apace. Elizabeth unrestrainedly giggled at the sight of Anne and Frederick urging their mounts onward with squeals and none-too-gentle tugs at the dark wavy locks of one and the thinning white hair of the other.

Predictably, Richard won, either through skill and chance, or more likely thanks to his father's and grandfather's affectionate indulgence. Elizabeth laughed. Doubtlessly, before too long her son would see through their schemes and insist they raced him in earnest, rather than letting him win. Or he might go one step further and ask to ride a real horse. Fitzwilliam would enjoy teaching him that skill – he had had little success with her in that regard. Not that they had diligently applied themselves to that endeavour, once they had discovered a far more rewarding way of exploring the delights of Derbyshire on horseback. Riding in front of her husband's saddle, with his arm wrapped around her waist and his lips now and again teasing the sensitive skin on the back of her neck was too pleasurable for both to leave them with much incentive to hone her skills in managing her own mount.

The merry party made their way into the shrubbery, and before long fresh squeals of laughter and lower-pitched but just as cheerful voices came to show they were all enjoying their game of hide-and-seek. With a soft smile, Elizabeth returned to her escritoire to flick her inkwell closed and store away her unfinished letter. There was no rush. She would continue later. At the moment, a game of hide-and-seek held vastly more appeal.

꧁ ꧂

For quite some time now, Mr Bennet was the sole grandparent to keep watch and delight in the gambols of the Darcy brood.

It was not so when he, Lydia and Kitty first came to live at Pemberley after the triple wedding whereby Jane, Elizabeth and Anne were joined in matrimony with the men they loved. Following that happy event, Pemberley had become a very busy place for a while. To George Darcy's and Lady Anne's moderate discomfort, Mrs Bennet had predictably followed her daughters, but to everyone's manifest advantage, she did not stay long.

She was vastly proud of her second daughter's achievement in making such a fortunate alliance – and said so as often as she could – but it was her eldest and her youngest who had the greatest claim on her affection.

Unbeknownst to Mr and Mrs Bingley, she often went to stay with them at Netherfield, and later at the Staffordshire estate Mr Bingley had purchased, not thirty miles from Pemberley.

But, as she had once declared, it was her youngest who was the apple of her eye, so to Lady Catherine's dismay, she visited at Rosings whenever Lydia did. And Lydia visited often, for she had set her heart upon Captain Hayes before she had even met him, and even more enthusiastically once she had.

Many times during their courtship Lady Catherine fervently wished she were still alive and able to use all her influence over Lady Metcalfe and her brother in order to expedite the marriage and thus rid herself of her unwanted guest. When it finally came to pass, her ladyship heaved a long sigh of relief to see the last of Mrs Bennet. That lady joyfully followed her youngest daughter, never to be seen again at Rosings and but rarely at Pemberley, at the Bingleys' Staffordshire estate or at the parsonage in Kympton, where Kitty eventually went to live after her own marriage.

To her immense good fortune, Mrs Bennet discovered that the afterlife was wholly free from the inconvenience of seasickness, and nothing could dampen her delight at travelling the world with Captain and Mrs Hayes.

Mrs Bennet had never prided herself on her intellect, either in her lifetime or beyond, and could never claim she had a real understanding of the mysteries of the afterlife.

She could only assume that, as must have been the case with that harridan, Lady Catherine, and Mr Darcy's parents, she had been tethered to this world by love for her offspring and the fervent wish to stand by them and protect them in their time of need.

No doubt, Lady Anne must have been keen to watch over her sweet babe, Miss Georgiana, just as she herself was fiercely determined to protect and succour dearest Lydia. And the others too, naturally. But they were older, and did not need her quite so much. If anything, it was *she* who needed to stay with them for long enough to be assured that all the girls would be married and settled.

The notion that she and Mr Darcy the elder had so much in common was a source of great amusement for Mrs Bennet. To her way of thinking, that gentleman had stubbornly clung to this world with the same purpose as she: to see that his children – well, his son, more specifically – made a proper match and continued his lineage.

For her part, Mrs Bennet did not care a straw for such things as lineage, but she could see why the elder Mr Darcy would. Well, now he could rest easy in that regard, the lady thought, ever so smugly.

Lizzy had done so much better than poor, sickly Miss Anne de Bourgh – that is to say, Mrs Beaumont. That long-suffering girl had recovered from her ills in sufficient measure as to give her husband a daughter – but Lizzy had already provided Pemberley with an heir and a spare, and had many years ahead of her to prove herself as fruitful as her mother. In a crucial point, Lizzy had in fact surpassed her, Mrs Bennet felt compelled to own, and sighed. If only she and Mr Bennet had a son…

There was no knowing when her husband would depart this world, and for that matter, when would she. One might have thought she would go forth, now that the object of her life had been accomplished and all her daughters were provided for. Still, she would not quibble. Travelling the world with dear Lydia and living vicariously through her was, if not a good substitute, then at least some compensation for her own curtailed existence.

What compensations Lady Catherine's spirit was seeking, Mrs Bennet did not know and did not care. She had long ceased thinking of her husband's second wife – around the time when she had ceased calling at Rosings with Lydia, to be precise.

If Lady Catherine would not go forth either, but cling to her daughter and her former home, that was entirely her business. A pity that Sir Lewis had never cared for anything or anyone enough to linger in this world as well. He might have kept Lady Catherine company. Or driven the old bat distracted, who could say?

With any luck, her ladyship would continue to hold fast to her earthly existence, and not go forth to stick her much-too-manly nose into whatever sort of connection she might establish with her husband, Mrs Bennet thought, if and when the pair of them would meet again in Heaven. Although he might continue to ignore her, even then. It was indeed a pity that one knew not what to expect, and could only discover the mysteries beyond the veil step by step, as they were gradually revealed. For instance, it would be of some use to know if there were any such things as vast libraries in Heaven. If so, there was no hope of ever finding Mr Bennet's spirit out of them.

Although their powers of perception surpassed Mrs Bennet's by a substantial margin, Lady Anne and George Darcy could not claim they understood the whys and wherefores of the afterlife any better than she.

Still, they did not quibble either, but were profoundly grateful that the birth of their first three grandchildren and Georgiana's marriage had found them still at Pemberley.

Had George Darcy been aware of Mrs Bennet's speculations as to what kept him tethered to this world, he would have disagreed. Of course he was not merely concerned for his lineage, but for his son and daughter's happiness as well. It was a great relief to see his darling Georgiana finding her true match in one of their neighbours, Lord Vernon's eldest son. Likewise, it was immensely reassuring to see Pemberley brightened by the joys of companionship and love; to hear the ancient halls ringing with cheerful young voices and a great deal of laughter.

Thus, with light hearts, they eventually felt ready to go forth, assured of their son and daughter's happiness and the continuation of their line. Their duty and best wishes were fulfilled, and it was time to relinquish earthly ties and leave Pemberley to their descendants.

There was great charm in the thought of lingering on to see their grandchildren grow up – see *them* settled and happy. Yet some ill-defined sense told them it was time to go, and there was truth in that. The torch should be passed to Fitzwilliam and Elizabeth. They would safeguard their children's future, and thus Pemberley's.

The precise reason why they had been allowed to remain together until they were ready to bid adieu to their earthly existence and travel hand in hand beyond the veil remained unknown to them for the longest time. It was finally revealed one quiet winter morning, when Elizabeth came to find their son in his study, bringing with her a very old parchment and a freshly-written piece of paper.

"Am I disturbing you?" she asked from the doorway, only to be answered with a smile and a softly-spoken, "Foolish girl. You never do, and my time is yours. Should you not know that by now?"

Elizabeth smiled back.

"I daresay I should," she said, and came to nestle in his arms with all the ease of longstanding habit.

"Any particular reason for your visit?" Darcy asked, running his fingers through her hair.

"Mmm, let me see. Firstly, there is this, if I remember rightly," she playfully replied with a delightful pout, and shifted slightly in his lap so that she could kiss him.

It was a fair while until he asked, "And secondly?"

"How very disappointing that my first reason was not good enough," she teased, and before he could either respond in kind or protest, she set the parchment and the piece of hot-pressed paper before them on the desk, side by side.

"This is my second: a peace offering from my father. By the bye, he still wishes you to know he might never forgive you for resisting his grand scheme for restructuring the library – he never got over the unfinished business at Rosings, I am sad to say – but he sends you this and his assurances that he will let the matter rest for now, for the sake of family harmony."

Darcy chortled.

"How very generous of him. And that is?"

"A very old parchment he found last night in a book he thinks might have remained untouched since the Restoration. Seeing as it is so old and frayed and the ink so faded with the passage of time, he had amused himself with copying it and making some guesses as to the missing fragments. He had dispensed with the *thinketh* and *dost* and *shalt* to make it easier reading for Richard when he is old enough, and for his sons and grandsons, as it has some bearing on them too."

Darcy's brows arched with an admixture of interest and concern.

"How so?"

"You should read it," she said simply and a little solemnly, then the arch smile was on her lips again. "Oh, and Papa said he trusts Richard might endure the *thou*, *thee* and *thine* without too much discomfort, for he had chosen to preserve them."

"Why?"

"I was intrigued by that, too. And you might as well have his answer verbatim: "*Whimsy, child, what else? You should know better than to ask.*""

"I see," he chuckled, and reached for the old parchment.

It was dated a very long time ago. A very long time indeed: one hundred and seventy-one years in the past, almost to the day. It was signed by another Richard Darcy, and addressed to his son Edward.

"The Grim Knight?" Darcy mused aloud.

"Pardon?"

"I suspect this was addressed to the armoured gentleman in the long gallery. He of the forbidding countenance, which is what had apparently earned him this sobriquet in the household."

"Did you know of this?" Lady Anne asked her husband.

As a rule, the pair of them never intruded upon their son's private moments with his wife, but the reference to an age-old letter that had a bearing on the Darcy line had brought them to the master's study in a trice.

The intelligence was at the very least intriguing, if not an indistinct cause for concern. Particularly as George Darcy had never heard of it before, and he promptly said so.

He leaned over his son's shoulder for a better look at the spidery penmanship. Deciphering the exceedingly faded message written in the quaint script of days of yore was no easy work for the parents. Seemingly, not for the son either, for after examining the old parchment for a while, he turned his attention to his father-in-law's handiwork. Mr Bennet's penmanship was far easier to read:

My Dearest Boy, the letter began

I expect these are the last lines thou shall receive from me, but pray do not distress thyself over my passing. Mourn me not, my son, and think not that I left thee. Think of me joyously beholding thy dear mother.

For it shall be thus. I know it. Ever since the dark day of her passing, I have always felt her enduring love washing over me, over the pair of us, and her spirit standing guard beside us. I have always known I had not lost her – I merely could not see her. And as I pined for the sight of her sweet countenance, my comforts these many years were but two: thine own good self, and the belief that thy mother and I could not be parted.

Whence came this belief, thou might very well ask, and 'tis time I told thee, just as my sire told me, when he was preparing to depart this vale of tears. 'Tis an old tale, from the time when the Old Faith was still firmly rooted in this realm, and saintly men still walked the earth amongst us.

The story goes that in the distant mists of our lineage there was a righteous and deeply devoted couple, whose dearest wish was to remain at each other's side forever. Much like the ancient tale of Philemon and his beloved Baucis, if you will. And their good deeds and their devotion to each other so endeared them to our Lord, that their wish was granted.

Moreover, *it was ordained that for as long as their line endured upon this earth, the selfsame blessing would be bestowed upon their scions if they be virtuous, and their hearts be true, and their devotion to their spouses all-abiding.*

Thy grandfather firmly believed the tale was true, as did his sire before him. As do I. If thou should be preserved from mortal peril, return home and marry wisely, I trust thou shall come to believe it likewise, and pass this belief onto thy children, and thy children's children. If thou should perish, I shall find comfort in our early reunion, and in the knowledge that you laid down your life for our martyred King and our noble cause.

I shall close now, with my love and my fatherly blessing. May the Good Lord keep thee safe, preserve thy life and the strength of thine arm, and grant thee all the joys thou have bestowed upon me. Farewell, my son, until we meet again.

Thy loving father,
Richard Darcy

⋅ঙ৹ 9৹ৰ⋅

Lady Anne's brimming eyes left the letter and drifted upwards to meet her husband's, and find them also brimming.

"You… loved me? All this time?" she faltered, prey to the greatest wonder.

"It would appear so," he tentatively smiled, barely less shaken by the discovery.

"But… what of your Constance?"

George Darcy gave a weary little shrug.

"There should be naught but the truth beyond the grave," he said softly. "I loved her, aye, and I dearly wish I could have spared you the pain of learning it. But it does not follow that one love should detract from the other. And I also wish I learned long before now that you loved me too."

His wife's lips curled into a smile that was just as rueful as his, yet equally as warm.

"'Tis not so very late. We do have eternity before us, after all."

⋅ঙ৹ 9৹ৰ⋅

407

Vastly more fortunate and a great deal wiser, their son and his wife had not waited quite so long to discover and declare their feelings for each other. Thus, when Darcy also finished reading the copy of the old letter and sought his wife's glance, a very different sort of wonder was mirrored in their eyes.

Elizabeth's sparkled with unshed tears as she reached to interlace her fingers with his, even though the message was already known to her from the minute her father had placed the transcription into her hands.

"If this is to be believed," she tenderly whispered, "all you need to do is love me, and we shall never be parted. A great comfort, I must say, and immensely reassuring."

"Aye. So it is," Darcy whispered, his gaze warm, yet his hold tightened around her as if even that reassurance was still poor comfort, should he ever lose her.

Elizabeth's smile grew misty as she leaned closer to offer more tangible comforts, her lips soft and eager under his. She drew back after a while, but remained nestling in his arms with her head on his shoulder, stroking the hands crossed over her waist and still holding her very close.

"Would you say," she tentatively whispered after a long and thought-filled silence, "that this goes some way towards explaining what you once told me about the day of your halted proposal, when I thought you were suffering from sunstroke?"

"I would," he owned, ever so quietly.

Her voice was also very low and almost reverent when she asked:

"And do you think they are still with us?"

It could not be said that George Darcy and Lady Anne held their breath – it was another physical impossibility. But they froze in their tracks, and instead of gliding out of the room as they had intended, they paused to listen. They had to wait a while; their son's reply was long in coming.

"I know not," Darcy said at last. "I have never heard him since." There was wistfulness in that admission, and a great deal of emotion in his voice when he added, "A part of me hopes they went forth and found their peace." However, when he shared the rest, the deep emotion gave way to a rueful chuckle: "Whereas the other part thinks that, should I come up with something quite as dreadful as that bungled proposal, I will hear him again."

Although deeply moved, his parents knew better than to strive to send forth a comment or any other indication of their presence. As for Elizabeth, she turned around to cup her husband's face into her hands.

"'Tis hard to imagine how you could possibly make such a ghastly error twice," she teased, then sought his lips. When she drew back, it was only by the smallest fraction, so that she could whisper, "Well, there we have it: I can no longer claim I did not marry you for your heritage. Somehow, I have long sensed that the Darcy legacy was love."

The End

ABOUT THE AUTHOR

Joana Starnes lives in the south of England with her family.
A medical graduate, over the years she has developed
an unrelated but enduring fascination
with Georgian Britain in general
and the works of Jane Austen in particular.

You can find Joana Starnes
on Facebook at www.facebook.com/joana.a.starnes
on Twitter at www.twitter.com/Joana_Starnes
or on her website at www.joanastarnes.co.uk

Or visit her Facebook page
www.facebook.com/AllRoadsLeadToPemberley.JoanaStarnes
for places and details that have inspired her novels.

CPSIA information can be obtained
at www.ICGtesting.com
Printed in the USA
FSHW011307051118
53562FS